T0196611

For the Love of a SEAL

The Hearts of Valor Series by Dixie Lee Brown

Heart of a SEAL
Honor Among SEALs
For the Love of a SEAL

For the Love of a SEAL

Dixie Lee Brown

LYRICAL PRESS
Kensington Publishing Corp.
www.kensingtonbooks.com

LYRICAL LIAISON BOOKS are published by

Kensington Publishing Corp.
119 West 40th Street
New York, NY 10018

Copyright © 2019 by Dixie Lee Brown

All Kensington titles, imprints, and distributed lines are available at special quantity discounts for bulk purchases for sales promotion, premiums, fundraising, educational, or institutional use.

Special book excerpts or customized printings can also be created to fit specific needs. For details, write or phone the office of the Kensington Sales Manager: Kensington Publishing Corp., 119 West 40th Street, New York, NY 10018. Attn. Sales Department. Phone: 1-800-221-2647.

Lyrical Liaison and Lyrical Liaison logo Reg. U.S. Pat. & TM Off.

First Electronic Edition: April 2019
eISBN-13: 978-1-5161-0650-9
eISBN-10: 1-5161-0650-4

First Print Edition: April 2019
ISBN-13: 978-1-5161-0653-0
ISBN-10: 1-5161-0653-9

Printed in the United States of America

Chapter 1

"Hey, Sorenson! You've got a visitor!"

Blake's focus automatically swept to the gravel parking area. He spotted the green Kia partly concealed on the downhill side of the office. How had he missed someone arriving? He scowled before returning his attention to the map pinned with magnets to the open door of the hangar. His friend and sometimes-boss, James Cooper, leaned over the second-floor banister in the newly constructed office of Sorenson Aviation and yelled toward the hilltop hangar loudly enough for everyone on Skyline Ridge to hear.

What bug has crawled up Coop's ass now? It made no difference. Blake didn't have the time or desire for a conversation with *anyone* right now.

"Gotta go, Coop. You're the one who keeps sayin' we're behind schedule." Blake removed his sunglasses from the neck of his T-shirt, settled them on his nose and could just make out the broad shoulders and muscled pecs of the former Navy SEAL as he braced both arms on the railing.

"True that." A sly grin appeared on Coop's mug as a figure stepped from the doorway behind him and sashayed toward the stairs. "Still... might be worth your while." He licked his index finger, touched it to an imaginary target in front of him and let out a long, slow sizzling sound.

The three-man delivery crew, who'd been loading supplies into Blake's Bell 206 helicopter on the pad to the right of the open hangar door, abruptly fell silent and craned their necks to catch a glimpse of Blake's visitor. Harv Farrington, performing a preflight check on the chopper, let out a wolf whistle just about the time Blake's gaze landed on the smoking-hot brunette descending the stairs, her light blues fixed on him.

The flight maps he'd been poring over momentarily forgotten, he swiveled to get a better look. Long legs, tanned and toned, started from red damn stilettos and went up…and up…and up, until his scrutiny was blocked by the hem of her hip-hugging blue denim skirt. Her flat stomach and slim waist were accentuated by the silky white, button-up shirt meticulously tucked into the waistband. Sleeves rolled to just below her elbows gave her the illusion of being just one of the guys, which he wasn't buying for a second.

Two buttons left undone at the neckline of her shirt teased him with more tanned skin, disappearing between glorious mounds of what were surely pure heaven. Fine hips dipped and swayed with every step she took.

Blake shifted uncomfortably, aware every man within range was equally as mesmerized by the show. He didn't have a friggin' clue who the woman was, but, by damn, she was here to see him, and that automatically made her off-limits to this collection of womanizing fools. He cleared his throat, and when they glanced his way, gave them his best don't-you-have-something-to-do frown.

The loading crew grumbled but resumed stacking the last few boxes into the cargo hold. Harv replied with an unconcerned grin. He crossed his feet at the ankles, calling attention to his screwy tiger-striped cowboy boots with gold stars on the toes, and leaned one shoulder against the side of the chopper.

Asshat!

Blake's attention flicked back to the vision in red, white and blue. *Hmm… gotta love a patriotic woman.* The graceful column of her throat peeked from behind locks of dark-brown hair, so silky looking he could almost feel his fingers sliding through—fisting. *Damn.* Again, he shifted. This time because his wayward thoughts were intercepting his blood supply and sending it to regions south of the belt.

As she reached the ground floor and started up the well-worn path toward the hangar, he scrutinized her unsmiling features and, for the first time, noticed the rosy tint of her cheeks. The attention of the men, watching and drooling over her every move, appeared to make her ill at ease, but surely she was used to attention from the opposite sex. Still, the empathy he felt for her forced him to smile as she approached.

"I'm Blake Sorenson. What can I do for you?"

Harv grunted, and Blake caught enough of the man's smartass retort to grasp what *he'd* like to do for her. The woman winced, her face turning a darker shade of pink, as though she'd gotten the gist of Harv's insolence too. Damned if Blake's hackles didn't rise to her defense. She covered her embarrassment well, though—he had to give her that. The sexiest dimples dusted the corners of her mouth as she threw the switch on a megawatt smile that went clear to her expressive eyes.

"Mr. Sorenson, I'm Tori Michaels." She stretched out a graceful hand, her fingers tipped with drop-dead red nails that matched her lipstick.

Blake clasped her hand. "First, the name's Blake, and second, would you excuse me for one minute?"

"Of course."

He immediately regretted the loss of her warm touch as he released her hand and strode toward Harv. The imbecile straightened and dropped his arms to his sides as soon as Blake pushed into his personal space, looking down on him a good three inches. The man always looked rumpled, as though he'd slept in his clothes and left the house without benefit of comb or razer.

"What the hell, Farrington? In case your mother didn't teach you any manners, let *me* enlighten you. A *lady* just walked down those stairs. That means you don't ogle, you don't make disgusting noises, and you sure as shit don't advertise your lack of good upbringing by embarrassing her. Not to mention, the *lady* is here to see me, which makes her *my* guest…in *my* hangar. Now…I'd be happy to remove your snarky smirk if you can't manage it on your own. *Capisce?*"

For at least ten seconds, anger and humiliation coalesced in Harv's expression with no clear indication of which would win. Maybe Blake would get a chance to hammer his point home after all. Nothing would please him more than putting his new aircraft mechanic in his place. The guy always had something smart-ass to say and was late for work more times than not. Blake wouldn't be sad if Harv decided to quit—except he was a good mechanic, and competent help was hard to find these days.

When Blake had finally agreed to take the job with PTS Security after nearly six months of his friend, Matt Iverson, hounding him, his new bosses had searched long and hard for someone who met Blake's demanding requirements. Bringing his experience as a military pilot and the assets of Sorenson Aviation into the mix, he'd reserved the right to approve the successful candidate. Harv had qualified handily as an aircraft maintenance technician, but Blake still wavered on whether he was a decent human being…or a jackass.

Harv finally gave up the stare-down with a shrug of his shoulders. "You're right. Sorry, Blake. It won't happen again."

Pleasantly surprised, Blake backed off a step. Harv bent to grab the tools he'd used on the aircraft. Straightening, he glanced toward the woman. "I apologize, ma'am." Barely acknowledging her nod, he whirled and strode toward the toolboxes on the back wall of the hangar.

Blake jammed his fingers in his front pockets before turning back to her, hoping like hell he hadn't embarrassed her further. No worries on that score. Anger now flashed in her eyes.

"There was no need to dress him down on my account, Mr. Sorenson. I assure you I can take care of myself." Voice as cold as an Arctic ice cap, her glare withered any manly reaction he'd suffered from her obvious charms.

Well, hell. Back to last-name basis already. Damn shame. His slow appraisal swept over her one more time before he jerked the map from beneath the magnets that held it and spun it through his palms, forming a tight roll. "I'm sure you can. But I didn't do that for you. That was for me. Now, what is it I can help *you* with?"

For an awkward moment, it didn't appear she would answer, obviously struggling with some internal conflict. That was okay with him, because he'd wasted enough time already. He needed to be in the air, en route to a secluded safe house, currently home to one of PTS Security's clients, including the man's wife and two children. Blake hated when the actions of supposed grown-ups created an unsafe situation for kids.

Time to go, regardless of how forlorn Ms. Michaels looked. Forget the desperation suddenly pooling in her eyes or the way her fine ass distracted him from the business at hand. He had a job to do. Besides, women were trouble, fickle to the bone. Hadn't he learned that the hard way when Celine filed for divorce, while he occupied a hospital bed, wondering if the doctors could save his torn and mangled leg?

Grabbing his gear and the map, he nodded toward the apparently mute woman. "Nice meeting you, Tori Michaels. Stop by and chat anytime you're in the area." He eyed her one final time as he pulled the brim of his ball cap down to almost touch the rim of his shades.

As he reached the halfway point to the helicopter, damned if it didn't sound like she stomped her foot, stopping him midstride, and pulling an amused grin from deep within at the image her petulance conjured in his head.

"Blake...wait, please. We got off on the wrong foot." Frustration and apology rang true in her voice, but he could also hear her amusement.

Well, the lady has a sense of humor. And she did call me by my first name. Grinning wider, he turned to face her, peering over the rim of his dark glasses.

"I'm sorry. I'm a little sensitive about needing a man to stand up for me. I shouldn't have snapped at you. Could we start over? Hi. I'm Tori

Michaels." There came those damn dimples again, accompanied by a full-blown smile.

Blake groaned his appreciation of the entire package—feisty though she might be. He'd have to be careful because her sincerity was dangerously appealing, and, apparently, he wasn't immune. "There's nothing I'd like more, but to be honest, I've got about thirty seconds before I need to be in the air. Actually, according to my boss, I'm already late. So, lay it on me in ten words or less. Or maybe you'd rather meet me for a drink sometime?" Just because Blake didn't bet on love-everlasting didn't preclude the occasional hook-up.

"I'd like to interview you for an article in *Everyday Heroes* magazine. It's a special edition for Memorial Day." Obviously ignoring his alternative suggestion, words tumbled from her enticing lips...until she stopped abruptly.

Maybe she'd finished what she'd wanted to say, but more likely, it was the disappointment and outright hostility heating his blood and putting a scowl on his face that'd highjacked her pitch. He'd never been able to disguise his animosity. "Jesus! You're a reporter? Honey, I don't do interviews. You're wasting my time and yours. Damn shame." He gave her a mock salute before he whipped around and continued toward the chopper.

Hell if that isn't a waste. Just my luck. He could swear he felt her eyes drill into his back with every stride he took to reach the waiting aircraft. She'd have to do better than that. He shrugged off his curiosity and forced the hotter-than-hell reporter from his mind.

The forest surrounding his new home on Skyline Ridge, a mere three miles from Cypress Point on the Oregon coast, never failed to soothe his soul, and today was no different. He'd moved from Las Vegas, where the terrain was different, and trees were an afterthought. When Matt Iverson, or MacGyver as he'd been tagged by the other members of his SEAL team, suggested Blake go to work for PTS Security, he'd considered the offer for months before accepting. That the owners, MacGyver, Coop, Luke Harding and Travis Monroe, were all former SEALs was no small thing Blake had in common with them. They were all good guys who possessed some mad skills. Once he'd come to the truth that those men, who'd become his friends as well, would have his back just like he'd have theirs, his decision was made. Still, there was no way in hell he was moving to San Diego, where his prospective employer was headquartered. He wanted mountains and seclusion.

He'd gone nuts over this place, all one hundred and thirty-two acres. Not because of the five thousand-square-foot monstrosity that was now his home. Or the tiled floors throughout. Or the four bedrooms. Or the fireplace in nearly every room. Or even the pretentious stone moat. Rather, it'd been the evergreen trees that he could see from every single window in the circular…or octagonal…or whatever the hell shape the house was. He liked that it was three miles from the nearest small town, a mile and a half of that on a private road. And he liked that all he had to do was take off in his planes or the Bell to have an unparalleled view of the Pacific Ocean.

Blake had started building his hangar and clearing the bare minimum of trees for a runway the day the sale closed.

This morning his world was bathed in sunshine, yet a fog bank hung offshore to the west, not yet burned off. The delivery men had finished loading the supplies and, apparently, taken off in their truck, leaving it blessedly silent, except for the rustling of the wind through the trees. Blake stowed the bag containing his gear in the cargo area, slid the bay door closed and climbed in the front, already going through the checklist permanently etched in his brain.

Check switches: position for start.

Fifteen years as a pilot in the Navy SEALs, thirteen of those as a Special Forces team leader, had burned a lot of things into his memory. Some he'd rather forget. Others, like preparing a craft for takeoff, came more naturally than breathing.

Anti-collision light: on.

It'd been a damn good life, until it wasn't. He'd crash-landed a few choppers in his day, but there'd only been one he hadn't walked away from. Picking up stragglers from another SEAL team about to be overrun, he'd pushed his luck a little too far. He was still haunted by the rocket grenade screaming toward them—the shudder of the aircraft as it clipped them—two of five Navy SEALs who'd narrowly escaped being captured alive, perishing on his watch.

Main rotor: brake off and clear.

Four of them had made it out alive, including Blake. MacGyver had been one of them. His injuries had been minor under the circumstances. The other two men were also injured but ambulatory. Blake's leg had taken some shrapnel as the chopper blades came apart, and it hung mangled and useless below the knee. MacGyver had carried his sorry ass four miles through enemy-held territory to the last take-out point.

Engage starter: check oil pressure.

Blake's leg had looked like ground hamburger when he'd finally gotten a chance to look at it, but it'd healed far better than any in the medical profession had expected. It was only when he was really tired he still walked with a slight limp. The scars would always be with him, on his body and in his head. But hell…he'd been luckier than some.

Main rotor turning: release at fifty-eight percent.

He and MacGyver had formed an unbreakable bond in those four miles. Turned out it was easier to open up to another human being when faced with his own mortality. Blake had helped MacGyver and some of his buddies a few months ago when they needed a hand. Thus, the offer to work for their private security company. It was a part-time gig for him, which was perfect because he also ran his charter service from his home atop Skyline Ridge.

Stabilize at flight idle for one minute.

He'd bought his one hundred thirty-two acres of trees with a VA loan and the equity from his place in Vegas. He earned a good living with the charter business, enough that he'd added a six-passenger Beechcraft Bonanza to his list of assets since the move. Anything he made working for PTS Security he squirrelled away for a rainy day. His needs were simple.

Throttle to seventy percent. Generator on.

Maybe he'd travel for pleasure someday.

Headset on.

One more sweep of the gauges, and he settled his hand on the throttle. His heart dropped into his stomach as the passenger door suddenly swung open and a leggy brunette vaulted into the seat beside him.

Blake didn't like surprises. When he found his voice again, disbelief swirled in an ever-tightening spiral of anger until he couldn't hold it back. "What the hell do you think you're doing?" He whipped off his headset just in time to realize he was shouting.

Tori flinched, but it didn't stop her from continuing to buckle her lap belt before she turned what could only be described as frantic eyes on him. "You don't understand. My job depends on getting this interview. My boss was quite clear. If you could just give me fifteen minutes of your time and a quote or two, I promise I'll never set foot on your property again."

Blake scowled, his first inclination to toss her ass out, but something about her nervous demeanor made him hesitate. What kind of boss put that degree of pressure on a reporter to get a lousy interview? Last he looked, stories like his were all too common and not worth the paper they were printed on. And why send an unseasoned reporter, which he'd bet his right nut she was, to bear the wrath of men like him?

A slightly embarrassed smile started in her eyes and traveled to those holy shit red lips, and she tossed her head, sending thick strands of silken waves over her shoulder. "I really need this job. I'd be so grateful—maybe I could return the favor sometime."

Bingo! I just bet she could. Blake's gaze slid over her again, taking his sweet-ass time, noting the way she blushed and fidgeted, even as she made no move to retreat. Not that she'd used blatant sexuality to get her point across. Based on her aura of sweet innocence, Tori had no clue what lustful response her words had inspired. His Spidey-sense kicked into high gear. He got it. Her asshole boss had sent *her* because she was walking, talking temptation. So…who the hell *was* her boss? And what was his game? Did Tori realize the man had staked her out as bait? Was she a willing conspirator or a sacrificial lamb?

All he had were questions, too damn many to answer now, while MacGyver and Travis waited on him. With no small effort, he tamped down his irritation, managing a nonchalant shrug that, hopefully, hid his curiosity.

Blake reseated his headphones, grabbed another set and handed it to Tori, watching as she positioned it over her ears. "You should be able to hear me now."

Those damn dimples appeared, and she gave him a thumbs-up.

"Like I said, I don't do interviews, so you can ride along, but anything we talk about is strictly off the record. Agreed?"

Her troubled eyes searched his face and held for several seconds, but she finally nodded.

No doubt she was already hatching a plan she thought would get him to change his mind. Given enough incentive, he'd even let her believe it might work. He turned his head away from her as he gripped the throttle and the chopper lifted off.

"Okay, hang on tight, Tori Michaels." This was bound to get interesting.

Chapter 2

White-knuckled, heart-pounding, mind-numbing fear had a choke hold on her throat. Tori *hated* helicopters. She definitely hadn't thought this through when she followed Blake and jumped in with him as he was about to take off. Her brain had misfired at the prospect of losing her job and the trickle-down effect that would have on her life…and the life of her six-year-old son.

Having been a stay-at-home mom since Isaiah was born, proud owner of a journalism degree but no work experience, it'd been unimaginably difficult to land a job. Within weeks of discovering the untenable financial position she'd been left in when her husband died, the bank had foreclosed on her house. Options were a thing of the past. She'd needed a job, even a temporary one. It didn't matter that her new boss had a preset interview list or that he would accept nothing less, because there was a chance, however small, she'd be hired on in a permanent position if she performed in a manner that exceeded her boss's expectations.

If she didn't find a way to change Blake Sorenson's mind, she could kiss that possibility goodbye. Even her temporary position would be in danger, with small likelihood she'd land other employment before she was evicted from her rental house, putting her and Isaiah out on the street. She couldn't let that happen.

The helicopter leveled off, and Tori's stomach finally caught up to the rest of her. She swallowed hard, willing her breakfast to stay down as she focused on the horizon. They were headed east, into the morning sun, and if the miles of dense timber below were any indication, they were somewhere over the Siskiyou National Forest.

Suddenly, the gravity of her situation hit her full force. She had no idea where they were going…or how long they'd be there. The man she was with was a total stranger, and first impressions hadn't exactly won her a place in his heart. What if he'd allowed her to stay onboard only to teach her a lesson? Would he drop her at his first stop, abandoning her to find another way home? Perhaps it was what she deserved, and she wouldn't really blame him, but the realization she was at his mercy put a damper on her determination.

Uncertainty ratcheting her tension, she glanced toward him, only to find him facing her, his jaw set in a hard line. The sunglasses he wore hid whatever he was thinking, except for the serious frown creasing his forehead. Tori caught her bottom lip between her teeth as she swung toward the front again.

Blake's warm chuckle came through her headset. "Are you all right? You're looking a little green. You're not going to puke on me, are you?"

Oh God, I hope not. "I don't think so. I'm sorry. Not a fan."

"Of what? Flying?" This time he issued a full belly laugh. "You could have fooled me." He leaned toward her until she looked at him. "You do remember coming along on this flight was your idea, right?"

"Yeah, that decision might have been just a tiny bit too spontaneous." Tori couldn't help laughing. When she looked toward him again, a grin teased his lips. "I'm sorry. I don't know what I was thinking." Seemed she couldn't stop apologizing either. In fact, since the second she'd laid eyes on the exceptionally attractive Blake Sorenson, her brain had failed to engage before opening her mouth. Resisting the urge to slap her palm to her face, she shrugged. "You could have kicked me out. Why didn't you?"

"Could have, I guess. Too late now, though. This is a round trip—in case you were wondering."

Though she couldn't see his eyes behind his dark glasses, something about his rugged features kept her from looking away. His words, and the sincerity with which he'd uttered them, eased her uncertainty, but she was still curious. "You didn't answer my question. Why'd you let me tag along?"

It sounded like he might have sworn as he returned his attention to the controls. "I make it a rule to get to know *every* woman I come across wearing red stilettos."

A laugh burst from her lips, and she studied him doubtfully. "Really?"

"SOP."

"SOP?"

"Standard operating procedure." Blake pushed the control stick to the right, causing the craft to roll slightly, and Tori grabbed the cushion of her seat to keep from sliding toward the door. "Relax. I've been flying a long time. You're in good hands."

It wasn't his hands she was worried about. Besides, those hands looked incredibly strong. And capable. The idea of being *in* his hands wasn't completely distasteful. His arms and legs were muscled and powerful, and his chest filled out his T-shirt nicely. Not that the observation made her feel any better, but he was undeniably easy on the eyes. And, okay, maybe the confidence and authority that enveloped him like a second skin *did* make it a tiny bit easier to breathe.

"So…red stilettoes, that's what does it for you?" Tori tilted her head and crossed her ankles, immediately drawing his focus to her legs.

Blake gave a mirthless laugh. "Don't even try to play that game. You women know exactly what you do to men when you wear four-inch heels. If they're red, even better. You *want* us to notice and then you act all innocent when we do and follow it up with a come-on. Right? Admit it."

"You might be partially right." Tori flicked her bangs out of her eyes with a swipe of her hand.

"Do tell—which part?" Blake's nostrils flared as his eyes remained hidden behind his shades.

"It's not only women. Most people dress to be noticed. Take *you*, for example."

"*Me?*"

Tori let his skeptical objection go unanswered. "The aviator sunglasses. The tight, Navy SEAL T-shirt stretched just right over those manly pecs, the sleeves barely able to wrap around your massive biceps. Formfitting jeans that hug you in all the right places and highlight your…assets. Are you going to tell me you don't want anyone of the opposite sex to look twice?" Tori stopped, her observations challenged by Blake's steady perusal.

He jerked the sunglasses off and hooked them on the neck of his shirt, squinting from the sun streaming through the windows. "I wear the glasses because I've been too close to too many IED blasts and, as a result, bright light gives me headaches." His grim demeanor seemed to melt away as he locked his chocolate-brown gaze with hers and winked. "But you got me on the rest. Heck yeah, it's hot as hell when a woman appreciates a man. Even hotter when she lets him know. So…my assets…that's what does it for you?" It was obvious his use of the exact words she'd uttered had been intentional.

Tori choked, trying to stifle a laugh, but couldn't hold it in when she glimpsed the humor dancing in his eyes. He laughed with her, and the shared moment seemed to eliminate some of the tension that strained her muscles.

"I'm impressed, Mr. Sorenson. You may be the most honest man I've spoken with in quite some time. Makes me wonder—why aren't you willing to grant an interview? What don't you want to talk about?"

His expression slammed shut as though he'd just remembered she was a reporter. A muscle in his jaw flexed in obvious irritation. Whether the butterflies in her stomach reawakened due to the sudden cold front that loomed between them or her ridiculously inappropriate attraction, fueled by the impenetrable control emanating from him, was a question for another day.

A few seconds later, he sighed and returned the sunglasses to the bridge of his nose. "It has nothing to do with honesty or the lack of it. Everything about my military career that isn't classified has already been written. My successes, my failures and my medical discharge—all out there on the web."

"Then, obviously, you didn't always hate reporters."

He issued a sardonic laugh. "Three years ago, my kid brother attacked a woman in Iraq and got himself shot by a Marine whose job it was to stop him. He was high on drugs and had just seen his best buddy blown to pieces, but there was no excuse for what he did. He lost everything that day. His military career. His self-respect. And the use of his legs."

Tori's heartbeat stuttered at Blake's revelation and the anguish in his voice. Even as her chest ached for his sacrifice...and his brother's... images flashed before her eyes like an old-fashioned slideshow. The day her husband, Ken, came home from the hospital in a wheelchair, both legs gone after his fighter jet had been shot down during a predawn bombing run. Four-year-old Isaiah hiding behind her, terrified of the stranger who'd returned home in his father's shattered body. The dreadful days that followed—she'd never forget. The sounds, the smells were imprinted on her brain.

Her fingers curled around the edges of her seat again. "That must have been devastating for both of you. I'm so sorry."

He didn't seem to hear her. "The press crucified my brother after Christian's court martial was dropped and he was dishonorably discharged. He'd made a bad choice, but he'd also been through hell. When Christian finally left rehab and moved in with me, reporters called every day for weeks or showed up on my doorstep, hoping to get a new picture to splash across the front page. He was a prisoner in my house and in that damn chair. In his mind, there was no reason to go on living. He never said it, but I knew. It was five months before I could leave him by himself and trust he'd still be alive when I got back."

Tori slammed her eyes closed, but tears squeezed from between her lashes. She turned her face away and prayed Blake wouldn't notice the moist tracks down her cheeks. Suddenly, she could see herself, and the entire journalistic profession, through the same lens he was using, and what she saw disgusted her.

"So yeah, I hated those bastards, and I made myself a promise. I don't do interviews." Blake pushed the controls to the left and swung the front end of the craft toward a log cabin nestled within a clearing at the foot of a mountain.

Tori cleared her throat. "How's your brother doing now?"

The way Blake's head jerked toward her, her voice must have given her away. He would no doubt think it was sympathy for him and his brother that made her cry, and that was never good for a man's ego. When he reached gently to dry her tears with his thumb, surprise made her turn her face toward him.

"You're the first reporter who's ever asked how he's doing. Thanks for that." Raw emotions chased shadows across his face, but his voice held tenderness, and the wisp of a smile grabbed her attention. He dropped his hand and turned again to the controls. "No need for tears, sweetheart. Christian is doing well. I've never seen him happier. He's getting married in a few months."

"That's wonderful." Tori's forced cheerfulness sounded pathetic to her ears, but Blake didn't seem to notice.

He set the helicopter down expertly on an asphalt pad inside the tall fence that encircled the small acreage. If not for the cozy-looking log cabin positioned at the base of a tree-covered slope on the western edge of the property, she might have guessed it to be a prison yard. A treeless, scrub-brush-dotted band of flat terrain formed a barren perimeter around a narrow strip of grass, some outbuildings and the two-story cabin that nearly blended into the shadow of the old pines. What was this place?

Just then, a large ATV appeared from one of the sheds and roared across the sandy ground toward them. Two men sat in the front, both broad-shouldered and muscular, even from a distance. The passenger held a military-looking rifle angled across his body.

Uneasiness niggled at her senses. "Um…you did say this was a round trip, right?"

Blake focused on the approaching ATV as he removed his headset and motioned for her to do the same. "Don't worry. They're harmless. As soon as we unload the supplies in the back, we'll be on our way. I'll have you home before lunch."

Tori regarded the two men skeptically as they parked and jumped from the vehicle on Blake's side of the helicopter. "If you say so."

Blake's cocky grin suggested he was about to remind her again she hadn't been invited on this little jaunt. Admittedly, she deserved whatever he was thinking behind those mirrored sunglasses. She brushed the hair back from her face as heat crept up her throat and into her cheeks.

Instead, he tipped the brim of his ball cap toward the men waiting outside. "C'mon. I'll introduce you to my bosses." He reached across her and opened her door. "Later, you can tell me about yours."

God, he smells so good—like rain on a summer day...and essence of man. The instant appreciation of his scent distracted her from his words for a second, but then her current situation rushed back and destroyed the erotic fantasy she'd conjured. Just as well. She had no business thinking of anything beyond how to get the interview she needed.

Tori pushed her door open. "Shall I ditch the heels?"

His chuckle drifted over his shoulder as he climbed out. "Hell no. I want them to get the full picture of why I brought you." She wiped away a smirk as she crawled out and walked around the front of the aircraft.

Blake slid the cargo door open as the two strangers stared at her feet. *Good Lord! Are men really so easily sidetracked?* It certainly seemed to be true. There had to be something in that bit of information she could use to get her story.

She smiled and stuck out her hand toward the driver of the ATV. "Hi. Tori Michaels."

Blake stepped into her space, brushing her shoulder with his arm. "Tori, this is Matt Iverson. You can call him MacGyver. Everyone does."

"It's nice to meet you, MacGyver."

"Same here." Still stoic, the man shook her hand.

"And this is Travis Monroe." Blake's piercing gaze seemed to hold a warning for the dark-skinned man.

Tori extended her hand, and Travis took it between both of his as a smile pulled at his mouth. His examination swept down her length and up slowly. Blake issued a guttural sound to her left. *Did he just growl?* She pulled her hand back and forced a smile. "Sorry to crash your place without an invitation. I didn't know where we were going."

Travis's scrutiny darted to Blake. "What the hell, man? This is supposed to be a *safe house.* A *secret* destination? Who else did you tell?"

Blake waved his words away. "Relax, Travis. We're not taking the nickel tour. As soon as the cargo is unloaded, we're out of here." A frown creased his brow. "Besides, Tori hates to fly, and she couldn't find this place again if her life depended on it."

That made her sound like a complete idiot, but it was true and at least the men were no longer looking at her like they thought they'd have to kill her to keep her quiet. *That's probably a good thing.*

An apology registered in MacGyver's eyes. "Don't pay any attention to either of them, Tori. Welcome to our little oasis. If Blake vouches for you, you can stay as long as you like."

Blake grunted. "Let's get this stuff unloaded. I promised I'd have her back in time for lunch." He didn't look at her as he grabbed an armload of boxes and strode toward the ATV.

Blake Sorenson appeared to be the king of mixed signals. Tori couldn't keep up. At the hangar, he'd regarded her with blatant appreciation, then abruptly dismissed her when he learned she was a reporter. Yet he'd allowed her to ride along with no effort to oust her and was warm, charming and honest-to-a-fault during the flight. Now, he'd flipped again and, apparently, couldn't wait to be rid of her, focusing solely on unloading the supplies and moving them to the cabin.

He wasn't the only mystery afoot, though. His bosses, obviously in better-than-average shape and armed with a lethal-looking rifle, had expressed concern that Blake had shared their location. Travis had called this a safe house, *a secret destination.* After Travis's cryptic comment, Tori had done her best to hide her curiosity, afraid that sounding too interested, on top of being a reporter, would result in the revocation of her welcome card. She only wanted to get back in the air and head toward home so she could beg, bargain and plead with Blake for the story she needed.

Forty-five minutes later, Tori rode standing on the bumper of the ATV next to Blake, holding on to the roll bar, while they made their final trip to the house. When they stopped in front of the enclosed front porch, two Latino children, a girl and a boy, burst through the screen door, laughing and chasing each other. Their obvious joy brought a smile to her face.

Blake dropped to the ground beside her and gripped her waist to help her down. He'd insisted on lifting her onto the bumper too, due to her tight, short skirt. Yeah…she hadn't really dressed for outdoor activities.

As her feet touched down, a woman appeared at the top of the porch steps. "Lucinda, Antonio, come into the house, quickly. Remember what Mr. MacGyver said. We're not to go outside during the day." The petite, black-haired woman fell silent and began to wring her hands when she saw Tori and the three men standing in the yard.

Antonio, whom Tori guessed to be a few months younger than Isaiah, glanced toward the woman long enough to trip and fall, hands first, into the sand, rocks and brush of the xeriscape that rimmed the strip of grass. The boy let out a cry as he landed and came up with a bloody scrape on his forearm from an unyielding bitterbrush plant.

Tori hurried to him, ignoring the gasp from the woman she assumed must be Antonio's mother. She inspected the scratch and smiled at the teary-eyed boy. "I know it hurts, sweetie, but a little water to wash away the dirt and blood, some antibiotic ointment and a Band-Aid…you'll be good as new in no time. I promise."

Antonio sniffled. "Really?"

Blake appeared beside her and examined the boy's arm too. "She's right. Just keep it nice and clean."

"Lucinda, bring your brother and come in…now." Their mother glared at Tori distrustfully.

The girl grabbed Antonio's uninjured arm and dragged him toward the porch.

A man, with black hair and a salt-and-pepper mustache and beard, put his arm around the woman's shoulders in the doorway, leaned to kiss her temple and pushed past her and down the steps. He stopped to give the children a hug and ruffled the boy's hair. The kids disappeared inside the house with their mother, while the man continued toward Travis and MacGyver. He looked strangely familiar. Where had Tori seen him before?

"I agreed to this safe house for the protection of my family, but I will not rob my son and daughter of their childhood. We're hiding from the hate group that wants me dead. If they will find us simply because my children play outside, we might as well return home. *Sí?*"

"No shit," Blake said under his breath.

Tori covered her mouth so the grin trying to break free would go unnoticed. Whoever this man was, she'd heard him speak before. Recently. *Somebody wants him dead?* It was going to drive her crazy until she remembered where she knew him from.

MacGyver and Travis exchanged a glance, and Tori could clearly see the man's first salvo had already won the war.

Travis crossed his arms over his chest and frowned, obviously a pathetic attempt to appear stern. "Your safety, and the safety of your family, is our responsibility, Mr. Perez. It's imperative the rules are strictly enforced." After another glance at MacGyver, Travis relaxed his stance. "However, in this case, I think we can bend the rules a bit. If the kids stay within a twenty-foot radius of the house and check in with one of us when they come and go, we can live with that. But if conditions warrant, we'll revisit the issue."

"One more thing. If we're going to live together for a while, you must call me Rafael."

"Deal," Travis said, and the two shook hands on the new arrangement.

Rafael Perez? There's something familiar about that name. Rafael Perez. Rafael Perez—as though repetition would suddenly reveal the answer. He had a wife and two kids. Somebody wanted him dead—a hate group, he'd said.

Rafael returned to the house. Blake, Travis and MacGyver began unloading the last few boxes from the ATV, carrying the supplies through the open doorway.

Wait! Rafael Perez? Tori regarded the safe house and the family in a whole new light as the details of the news story she'd read filtered through her memory.

"What's wrong?" Blake walked toward her, a frown drawing his brows together.

"Nothing. Um...just tired, I guess." *Lame.* But Tori couldn't imagine he or his friends would be thrilled to know she'd figured out who they were protecting. Or that she was the only one outside their small group who knew where the assistant DA from San Diego was hiding. And not from just any hate group—a militant neo-Nazi brotherhood, members of which Rafael had recently sent to prison.

Holy hell. Did I ever pick the wrong party to crash!

"Ready to go?" Blake was still frowning.

"Yes." Tori smiled her brightest phony smile and let him help her into the back of the ATV, now that the seat was no longer taken up by boxes of food and household supplies. MacGyver drove them to the helicopter and made small talk with her while Blake readied the aircraft for take-off. When he signaled, she ducked down and proceeded to the door, waving goodbye to MacGyver as she climbed inside. As though on autopilot, she buckled her lap belt and positioned the headphones over her ears. They lifted off and soon leveled out, heading northwest, back the way they'd come. The return trip would be no easier for her, but she'd be glad to see the last of the safe house.

"You okay? You're awfully quiet." Blake's deep baritone vibrated in her ears.

"I'm fine." If she begged, would he change his mind about the story? Could she buy him off with a week's worth of home cooked meals? A month's worth? Now that she knew what had happened to turn him sour on reporters, she couldn't blame him. Not when she'd gone through her own hell after Ken's death. Some things just needed to be left alone.

Tori smiled. "Thanks for letting me ride along with you today. I'm sorry the interview didn't work out, but I *do* understand." Better than he would ever know.

"Yeah. About that—what are you going to do?" He seemed genuinely concerned.

Tori shrugged. "I don't know yet, but I'll figure out something." There had to be a way to keep a roof over her son's head.

"Are you going to tell me who your boss is? And why my story is so important to him he's willing to threaten your job?"

Like I haven't asked myself that question a few dozen times already. "I thought maybe you'd know why. I assumed the two of you might be acquainted. David Donovan, my editor, wasn't inclined to elaborate. He's not exactly a man who reacts well to having his motives questioned. Do you know him?"

"No, but I might just look him up."

"Oh no, please don't. Not on my account. It'll be embarrassing enough being fired for incompetence. If he has a black eye or something, I won't be able to keep from laughing, and he'll think I've gone off my rocker." Tori was kidding, of course...but she wasn't. She didn't need anything else to feel guilty about.

Blake chuckled as he retrieved his cell phone from his back pocket. He sobered as he read the text that had apparently just come in. Suddenly, the helicopter banked sharply to the right and started to circle.

Tori reached out to brace herself on the control panel. "What are you doing?"

"We're going back." His curt declaration left no opening for discussion.

Alarm prickled beneath Tori's skin. "What? Why?"

"They're under attack." His voice was so calm, he might have been talking about what he'd had for breakfast.

Attack? Did that mean the neo-Nazis had discovered Rafael's hiding place? *Attack* to Blake probably meant something entirely different than anything she'd ever had to wrap her head around. Would bullets fly? People get hurt? Her breath stalled in her throat as a band of frigid fear squeezed her chest.

Chapter 3

Blake pushed the throttle into the red zone and took everything the old Bell could give him. They were eight minutes out. A lot could happen in eight minutes.

Under attack by air. Could use a hand. The text from MacGyver painted a grim picture. His friend wouldn't have sent that message if he'd thought they could handle the situation on their own.

To the southeast, a thick cloud of black smoke billowed into the sky. *Shit!* Blake glanced at Tori. Eyes wide and unblinking, arms wrapped protectively around her waist, her chest rose and fell rapidly. *Damn it to hell!* This is why he shouldn't have let her come.

She turned her head, and the fear in her eyes cut him to the core. "They're burning the cabin, aren't they?"

"Looks that way." He couldn't lie to her. They would drop over the ridge behind the house in about two minutes, and she'd see for herself. She didn't ask who *they* were, and he was grateful for that. Blake had limited experience with radical white supremacists—just enough to know how dangerous their brand of terrorism could be. Sebastian Wahl, leader of the hate group who'd made it their vendetta to silence Rafael Perez, had recently been emboldened by a couple of wealthy and high-profile donors and had quickly risen to the top of the garbage heap.

Just beyond the next rise, an Apache helicopter lifted from the smoke, hovered for a second and belched two rocket grenades from the tubes protruding from the belly of the chopper. One grenade hit the shed to the right of the house, sending more smoke, flames and debris thirty feet in the air. The other one went wide, burying itself within the mountainside behind the cabin and didn't explode. *A dud—they aren't infallible.*

Tori flinched as though she could feel the heat of the blaze from here. Her breaths became short and erratic. "They're all going to die! We don't stand a chance against weapons like that."

"Don't count us out yet. I've made a few modifications on this old bird." Blake flipped a switch on the control panel. The hydraulics whirred into action, and the turrets under the craft's nose locked into place.

"What was that?" Tori looked from him to the disaster on the ground.

"A little surprise for the occupants of that chopper." Blake jerked his chin toward the Apache that was now strafing the compound.

Damned if a sliver of a smile didn't soften her mouth for a heartbeat. "Well…okay. What can I do? I *need* something to do." The volume of her voice increased as the words tumbled from her lips.

Blake tossed her his cell phone. "Text MacGyver. Tell him to keep his head down. We're coming in hot."

Blake hugged the treetops as he skimmed the ridge. The element of surprise was on his side, and he wanted to keep it that way.

Tori's fingers flew over the screen, tapping out the message to MacGyver. "Done." She dropped the phone in her lap.

A hundred feet behind the gunship, Blake hit the trigger. Fifty caliber shells sliced through the tail section of the unsuspecting target. The Apache banked sharply to the port side and descended in a steep dive before the pilot corrected himself and began to climb. Smoke came from the fuselage, and the craft appeared to maneuver sluggishly.

Blake skimmed over the top and circled, lined up and fired again as the other pilot positioned his weapons to retaliate. "Hold on!" The warning probably wasn't necessary. Tori had a life-and-death grip on her seat cushion.

He didn't let up, continuing to spew lead, until dual puffs of smoke burst from the Apache's weapons system, and two grenades streaked toward the Bell. Blake jammed the throttle forward and scrambled for altitude. The whine of the rockets was all too familiar as they homed in on their target. One whooshed by, low and to starboard.

Blake continued to climb, praying he could get enough velocity to stay on the right side of the power curve. Otherwise, this maneuver would end badly. Considering the alternative—getting blown out of the sky—the risk seemed the better option.

The rocket disappeared beneath the front of the chopper, and he held his breath. *It could still miss us.* The aircraft shuddered as the grenade struck the tail section and spun them around.

Tori's gasp practically created a vacuum in the airtight cabin. He glanced her way and found her gaze locked on him. Fear marred her gorgeous features, and he cursed the strange attraction that had resulted in him allowing her to ride along. She could have been safely on the ground—jobless but alive.

Time slowed. He opened his mouth to tell her to put her head down and brace for impact when an alarm shrieked from somewhere in his array of gauges and jolted his brain from the slow-motion safety net of shock. By rote, he flipped a switch and quieted the alarm. Seconds ticked by. *No blast. The grenade didn't explode.*

Another dud. Somebody should tell these guys to do business with a reputable arms dealer next time. Then again, the world was a safer place if they didn't.

He reached for Tori, sliding his hand possessively around the back of her neck, his thumb gently caressing her cheek where one of her dimples hid. "Smile for me, sweetheart. We're not done yet." Blake almost got an upward movement of her full, red lips and counted that good enough.

Moving his hand back to the controls, he swept the skies around them for the Apache helicopter. The Bell drifted to the left when he asked it to turn. *Damn it.* The tail rotor had evidently been damaged, though how severely, he couldn't be sure. Didn't matter. He'd been a Navy SEAL for fifteen years. *And SEALs. Don't. Quit.*

Using both feet simultaneously on the pedals and two hands on the control lever, not to mention a whole lot of come-on-baby-you-can-do-this mojo, he coaxed the chopper into position.

The crew of the other gunship wasn't having any better luck. Their fuselage was spitting flames and the craft obviously wanted to roll to the left when the pilot tried to pull it around. *Surely, he'll see the error of his ways and give it up.* Blake would be just as happy if the battle ended with the enemy tucking tail and running. He didn't need another notch on the butt of his rifle.

Apparently, a happy ending for all concerned was not to be. The other pilot fought his damaged aircraft in the turn until he was almost lined up to take another shot.

Tori braced her arms against the front of the chopper. "What are you waiting for?"

For him to give up and limp away.

Blake didn't say the words out loud. She wouldn't understand. Only his brothers-in-arms could fully appreciate how tired he was of killing. Maybe he was still in the wrong line of work.

Tori touched his arm, as though she thought he hadn't heard her, and brought him back to the present. The trigger compressed beneath his hand,

and the *rat-tat-tat* of heavy ammunition erupting from both turrets vibrated the chopper. He sprayed the enemy aircraft with shells until one split open the fuel tank. The blast went from the fuselage forward, blowing the tail off. The flaming cockpit, still directed by the spinning of the blades, careened to the left before spiraling into the ground, spreading fuel and fire over at least a hundred yards of parched forest.

"You did it!" Her warm hand fluttered down his bicep and settled on his forearm. Those killer dimples made another appearance. That lives had been taken apparently hadn't sunk in yet. She held out his cell phone, the screen brightly lit. "MacGyver says everyone's all right. You saved their lives!"

Pride shone from her bright-blues eyes, and damned if it didn't heal a bit of his jaded soul. How the hell did she do that—make it okay that they were steadily losing altitude as long as she sat beside him? *Damn fool!* Clearly, he would be in trouble if he didn't put some distance between him and this sexy, dark-haired woman as soon as possible.

She was a breath of fresh air to his glass-damn-near-empty. She had the look of forever about her, and he had a damaged heart and jaundiced spirit where women were concerned. As much as he'd like to explore her softer side in a no-strings-attached, all-night-long sexcapade, she unquestionably struck him as the kind of woman a man took his time with…and then took home to meet his mother. He had no intention of doing either of those things, so he needed to put a cap on the fascination she bred within him.

The Bell shuddered and drifted in a spiral to the right. Blake stopped the spin with small, quick movements of the cyclic control. "Tell MacGyver we took a hit. We're dragging the left skid and we'll be coming down hard." Blake removed his sunglasses. "Then make sure you're buckled in tight and brace yourself."

He was doing his best to guide the crippled aircraft away from the flaming ruins of the log cabin in case his crash landing didn't go as anticipated. He could see figures on the ground near the outbuildings—MacGyver and Travis waving him in. Apparently, the smoke billowing from the fuselage had alerted them to the problem.

MacGyver's next text wasn't as cheery as the first. *Where r u going? Tail rotor damaged. Set it down.*

Nope. That wasn't going to happen. Not here. Blake had seen Mr. and Mrs. Perez, standing between the cabin fire and the fence. The two kids took turns hugging a big black dog held on a leash nearby. Emergency landings of a helicopter tended to be messy, and Blake wouldn't jeopardize the Perez family by trying to land in the compound.

The top rotors still turned at high speed. Without the tail rotor to stabilize the craft, the top blades would begin to spin the rest of the helicopter as soon as he reduced altitude and throttle. To possibly avoid that, the landing had to be steep and fast. Regardless of how much experience a pilot had in the subtle art of crashing, and Blake had plenty, eventually the time would come when there was no choice but to touch down. Sometimes it wasn't pretty, and then sometimes the spinning blades slammed the helicopter into the ground with a force several times normal until there was nothing except small pieces left of it and everything in its path.

Tori groaned as she tested her seatbelt. "Did I mention I hate to fly?" Her voice trembled slightly, and it was obvious she was trying not to fall apart.

"I think I *did* hear that somewhere." He had to give her credit. She was handling this better than the uneventful flight from his hangar. "You do realize flying isn't the problem here, right?"

"Very funny. Do you always crack jokes when you're about to die?"

Blake grinned, then gave his full attention to the task. Control the spin and set her down on the first clear patch of ground. That sounded easy enough. He'd done it a couple dozen times...usually in the dark...under enemy fire. How hard could this be?

In addition to the log cabin and outbuildings burning and kicking up smoke, the fire from the Apache helicopter's explosion and subsequent crash had ignited a blaze quickly spreading east in the thick, dry underbrush. Blake surveyed the expanse of forest to the northwest, but there was nothing but treetops as far as he could see.

"Look for a clearing, road or anything big enough to land on." A low-fuel warning light flashed red in the center of his control panel. The fuel line must have taken a hit. Blake pushed a series of buttons, and the light went out. "Sooner rather than later would be good."

Tori nodded her understanding and leaned closer to the window, peering toward the ground. Apparently, now that she was in the middle of a desperate situation, she'd found her calm resolve.

"There!" She pointed ahead and to the west, where another mountain in the Coast Range jutted into the sky. "I think there's a road down there. Is it wide enough to land on?" Tori swung around, her pleading eyes a sure sign of how badly she needed him to say yes.

Blake searched and found the clearing she'd indicated. The ribbon of dirt was nothing more than a service road, probably built years ago, before the spotted owl controversy nearly shut down the logging industry. At one time, the trees had been clear cut in a strip, ten to fifteen feet wide, on each side of the road. Vegetation had filled in much of where the forest had once been, but there were still areas where nothing grew. Probably due to the lava rock that covered the ground from volcanic activity eons ago. The clearing was within a two-mile radius of the safe house. Providing the landing went well, his friends would find them. It wasn't perfect... but it would have to do.

He gave Tori a thumbs-up, and relief flooded her face. "Listen to me, sweetheart. When we start down, it will feel like we're going way too fast. If I don't keep the speed up until the last second, the helicopter will start to spin. Spin equals out-of-control, and we don't want that, right?"

Some of the relief dissipated from her eyes, replaced by dread. Even so, she nodded.

"When I give the word, I need you to lean forward, tuck yourself into a ball and close your eyes. Stay just like that until we touch down. Then get out and run. There's smoke back there, and we've got a fuel leak...so this baby could blow." Blake looked away from his task of keeping the craft on the correct trajectory long enough to make sure Tori was listening.

Anguish filled her eyes, but she swallowed hard and raised her chin. "What if one or both of us are injured and can't get out?"

"Don't worry about that. If you're able, you go. Don't look back. Understood?"

"And if I can't?"

Damned if it didn't look like a hint of rebellion in the way she held his gaze. Any other time he would have enjoyed that. Encouraged it even. Blake turned toward her so she could see his face. "I will get you out, Tori Michaels." He enunciated each word clearly and forcefully, willing her to believe him.

She stared for what seemed like a long time, clearly analyzing his promise, before she nodded once and pivoted toward the front.

Blake aligned the Bell with the strip of roadway the best he could and kept his eyes on the spot he'd chosen for the landing. "Okay, sweetheart. Lean forward."

She complied instantly, all traces of insurgency gone.

He lowered the collective and began to descend, leaving the throttle alone. The ground raced toward them. His instinct was to throttle back—slow the descent. Sweat poured into his eyes with the effort it took to stay on task. The trees blurred in his peripheral as the aircraft dropped below the treetops. The landing spot he wanted was a hundred feet ahead...eighty... sixty. He pulled the throttle back and brought the nose up to decrease air speed. Twenty feet. Blake lost sight of the X he'd mentally painted on the road. Now he was flying by braille. Raising the collective to slow the descent, he kept the helicopter moving straight ahead.

At the final second, he throttled back, decreasing the speed of the rotors, and the skids hit the ground. Bouncing, the chopper gave in to the spin of the blades. The front end swung to the right, crossways in the road. Something snagged the fuselage as the tail section veered to the left.

Tori's upper body was flung toward the side of the cabin, her head slamming into the glass, leaving a smear of blood as she was tossed the other way. He reached for her, pushing her limp body back into the crash position.

The forward momentum tipped the aircraft. The whirling blades hit and dug into the hard-packed dirt of the road, disintegrating upon impact.

Bits of debris flew everywhere, embedding in tree trunks twenty feet away and shattering the windows of the cockpit. Rocks, dirt and smoke billowed up around them.

The controls that surrounded him useless, Blake threw his upper body over Tori's still form. All he could do was hold on and wait for the careening hunk of metal to come to a standstill. On its side, the crumpled cockpit slammed into a pile of rocks and stopped abruptly. A sharp pain bit his shoulder. Another his cheek. When he swiped at his face, his fingers came away red with blood.

The absence of movement was almost a shock. His body hurt everywhere, and it was a few seconds before he could disentangle himself from the mangled levers. He removed his lap belt and automatically checked for Tori's pulse. She was alive but the blood that matted her hair on the side of her head wasn't a good sign. He didn't have the luxury of not moving her. He'd have to take a chance her injuries weren't critical.

Blake unlatched her belt and gently moved her to his seat before crawling over her to force the door open. Blue sky, bright enough to hurt his eyes, greeted him when he stuck his head out. He had no idea where his sunglasses were. Dirt still hung in the air. The Bell was in pieces, the fuselage spitting flames. Sections of the top rotor big enough to identify stuck from the ground at odd angles.

The forest was eerily silent, confirming the fact he and Tori were alone. How badly she was hurt was yet to be determined, but he'd promised to get her out...and he was a man of his word.

Chapter 4

Tori heard a man's voice as though from a long distance. Opening her eyes would take more fortitude than she currently had available. Her head throbbed, and every time he called her name, a steel hammer slammed into a metal plate in her forehead. As hard as she tried, she couldn't put a name to the man, though his voice was slightly familiar.

The air smelled of smoke, and her throat burned with acrid dryness. Something was wrong. Was she sick? Sleep. She needed sleep.

"Tori? Can you hear me? Wake up, sweetheart." Someone leaned over her, and she flinched.

The sudden movement started a chorus line of tap dancers between her ears, and she groaned. Her hands came up to push at the shadow that hovered over her. Suddenly, her wrists were caught in a strong grip, and she panicked. The harder she fought to free herself, the less movement her captor allowed.

"Tori, it's me…Blake. You're safe. You hit your head during the crash, but you're going to be fine. Open your eyes, Tori. Look at me."

Crash? I was in an accident? Why can't I remember? Tori opened her mouth, and a lungful of smoky air made her throat itch. She coughed spasmodically, and her eyelids flew open.

A man knelt beside her. She'd seen him before, but his name fled before she could grasp the memory. Blood trailed from a nick on his left cheek, and she would have reached out to gently soothe it if he hadn't been immobilizing her wrists. She glanced at his hands, where they captured hers, and he released his grip as though he'd only then realized he still held her.

He raked a hand through his hair, rumpling the thick, dark strands and giving the impression he was harmless. Strangely, Tori wasn't afraid, instinctively trusting the man. Nor was she in any pain, except for the cacophony in her head. *What crash?*

"There you are. Welcome back. You banged your head pretty good. How do you feel?" The man's smooth baritone vibrated through her, tripping her comfort switches with his reassuring manner.

Now...if only I knew his name. I mean, seriously, how often do I wake up to a hot-as-hell, built-to-last muscleman leaning over me?

He tapped her forehead. "Your head? How bad is it?"

"Feels like there's a monster truck rally going on in there." Her words slurred, and she tried to smile, but the effort proved too much for her. "Who are you?"

The man's eyes widened, his gaze darting to hers and holding for a heartbeat too long. Turning to a small black bag beside him, he rifled through it and produced a pencil-shaped flashlight. "My name's Blake Sorenson." He shone the light in first one eye and then the other, nearly blinding her with its brightness, before flicking it off. Concern filled his chocolate-brown eyes. His lips parted slightly, and he released his breath as though he'd been holding it in. Unruly black hair and a scruff of whiskers added to the rugged appeal of his bold features. A scar, white against his tanned skin, zigzagged above his right eyebrow and disappeared into the hair at his temple. Blake Sorenson? She'd heard the name before, but it was as though that memory was buried beneath a rising tide of confusion. "Are you a doctor?" Whoever he was, he was a man of few words, to be certain.

Blake dropped the flashlight back in the bag and offered a thin smile. "More like an EMT. I'm retired military, special ops. Knowing enough to treat broken bones, concussions and minor wounds in the field has come in handy over the years."

"I see." *Ex-military—just like Ken.* Hopefully, Blake had returned with fewer scars than her late husband. "So, will I live?"

"You have a slight concussion. Nothing to worry about. The monster trucks will eventually go away. As soon as help arrives, we'll get you checked out by a real doctor. In the meantime, no foot races or heavy lifting." He winked as he settled on his butt beside her, extending his long legs out in front.

Tori turned her head gingerly and squinted at her surroundings. Rocks, brush, downed logs and lots and lots of trees. Smoke hung in the air. *Okay, this isn't funny anymore.* She jerked her head toward Blake, and her stomach rolled with the quick movement. "Where are we? How did I get here?"

"I carried you...from down there." Blake hooked a thumb toward his left.

Tori scanned the direction he indicated, raising carefully on her elbow when the ground dropped below her line of sight. Sitting straighter, she could just see the smoldering remains of something and a plume of smoke in the canyon below.

"Is…is that a…?"

"Helicopter? It was, before we crash landed it." From the return of his concerned frown, she must have blanched.

Her memory returned in a blinding flash. The job—the interview—the helicopter…

A groan escaped as she tried to hold on to the contents of her stomach. "No. No. Oh God, I'm so stupid." She shook her head as though she could deny what was becoming all too obvious. She'd flouted the one promise she'd made to her son—had insinuated herself into Blake's day for the sake of that stupid story. And almost died. Could be dead right now in the wreckage smoldering in the gully—killed in the same manner as Isaiah's father. At least that was what Isaiah would think, because Tori would *never* tell her son his father's death hadn't been an accident.

She tried to sit up, but Blake pushed her down gently. "I said no foot races, remember? MacGyver and Travis will be here soon. Just take it easy until then." He caught her wrist and laid it carefully on her stomach.

"They're not bringing a helicopter, are they?" Fear brought tears to her eyes, but she fought them back. Undoubtedly, Blake had been privy to her moment of weakness, though.

"I doubt it. More likely they'll bring the ATV and call for an air ambulance if needed."

"Promise me you won't let them put me on another helicopter. Please." Tori reached for his arm to pull him closer.

Confusion swept Blake's countenance. "Only if your medical condition is stable when they arrive. It won't be a picnic traveling out of here by ATV, you know. It'll be rougher than hell."

Tori shook her head vehemently and tried to rise again. Blake leaned over her torso, blocking her attempt.

"You don't understand. I don't *ever* fly in helicopters. Ever!"

"Yeah? You could have fooled me." A frown drew his brows together and his words were almost a growl.

She covered her face with her hands. "I know. I know, damn it. It was stupid of me to jump in yours." Flinging her hands away from her face, she barely missed Blake as he jerked back just in time. "But I didn't think you'd end up in air-to-air combat!"

A pained look that might have been guilt traveled over his face and disappeared just as quickly. "Look, sweetheart, it was your idea to come along on the flight. I didn't invite you, and I sure as hell didn't expect you to invite yourself." Blake dropped his head, and his chest expanded with the deep breath he took. When he looked toward her again, his eyes no longer danced with fire. "What the hell does that even mean—you don't *ever* ride in helicopters?"

The defensive words on the tip of her tongue stalled. The hand of grief, never far away, squeezed her heart until there was nothing left but an ache. She glimpsed flashes of the past: Ken getting ready to go to the airfield, using his prostheses without her nagging him. Isaiah begging his dad to let him come.

"You want to ride in a chopper?" Ken had asked him.

Isaiah had beamed exuberantly.

Then her husband's eyes had sought hers. "You too?" And his smile was the one he'd always worn before his injury.

Suddenly, hope for their relationship—their family—had filled her too. She should have known better.

Tears threatened, but she'd be damned if she'd let them fall. There'd been enough crying. She firmed her jaw and returned Blake's stare. "I told you—I don't like flying."

Something unreadable flashed in Blake's eyes. "I think this goes way beyond fear of flying. You were scared shitless when you strapped yourself into the passenger seat, both times. Yet, while we were under attack, you were right there with me, relatively calm and focused on what needed to be done. Where'd that come from?"

He was right. The realization jolted her, but, a second later, she had the answer. "Those kids—whatever their parents did, the children don't deserve to die. I was thinking about them."

The faintest trace of a smile appeared. "Well, what do you know? We *do* have something in common." Blake stood in one motion but didn't look away from her. "Stay down until help arrives. I'm not your enemy, Tori."

Suddenly, the sharp crack of a rifle startled her. Something warm splashed her face at the same instant Blake dropped to his knees. Horror filled her as blood gushed from the left side of his forehead and streamed down his cheek. He appeared dazed and shook his head, almost losing his balance. As another shot whizzed over them, he threw himself on top of her and rolled them to his right, where a small outcrop of rocks provided meager cover.

Still protecting her with his body, he reached beneath his shirt and, suddenly, there was a gun in his hand. "You'll have to be my eyes, Tori. I can't see well enough."

Tori slid from beneath him and turned on her stomach to survey the area. Fear and shock had frozen her, but now that she had a job to do, she was on it. "Who is it? Did you see anyone?"

"No. The other chopper—I didn't think anyone could survive that crash, but someone must have." Blake's words slurred, and he swore beneath his breath.

The handgun hung loosely in his hand, and Tori's decision was made without debate. She slipped the weapon from his grip and moved out of reach as he made a half-assed grab to get it back. Yeah, he would be no help. "I can shoot. My husband taught me well." The words were more to assure herself than to mollify him.

"Your husband, huh? Shit!" Blake rolled to his back. "Have to tell you…called MacGyver and Travis…should be here soon. Remember… don't…shoot…them."

Tori glanced toward him. His eyes were closed. Blood covered one whole side of his face and neck. His mouth hung open slightly. His expression was peaceful…and that was the last damn thing she needed right now.

She jabbed his side with two fingers. "Blake? Wake up. I can't do this by myself."

Blake rolled over again, landing against her side. Relief rushed through her. She hadn't known this man yesterday, but he was all she had now. Hopefully, she was on the right side of this fight. He'd said they had her concern for the children in common. That and the fact the shooter, hiding in the thick foliage, was trying to kill *them* would have to be enough. And, besides, he made her feel safe and how often did that happen?

"Stay with me, Blake. Okay?"

One eyed, he propped himself on his elbows and glanced at her, a crooked grin making him look half crazy. "I'm not going anywhere, sweetheart."

There was some comfort in his sincerity, and Tori smiled before turning her attention to watching for armed and dangerous vermin who wanted them dead. *Holy crap! If we get out of here alive, Blake has a lot of explaining to do.*

Five minutes ticked slowly by and nothing happened. No one fired a shot. No one snuck up on them. It was like she'd imagined a mysterious killer had pinned them down. But, she could hear Blake's breaths, more labored with each passing second. Head wounds bled a lot, but it couldn't be good that he'd lost so much blood. Was the gunman just waiting for him to lose consciousness?

"I've got an idea." Tori had been turning the plan over in her mind for the past few minutes. They had to get the man pinning them down to show himself...and the only way to do that was to give him another shot. "I'm going to make a run for that tree." She tipped her head toward a large fir about twenty-five feet on the other side of Blake. "When he pokes his head out to shoot, we'll know where he's hiding. I'll be able to work my way around behind him."

Blake was shaking his head before she finished her sentence. "Like hell. That's what he's waiting for—one of us to do something stupid. What if he shoots you before you get to the tree? Hell no. We're staying put until MacGyver and Travis show up or that guy gets impatient and comes for us." Blake's one good eye was starting to glaze over.

Tori fumed at Blake's abrupt dismissal of her plan. How long was he willing to wait for his friends to save their asses? "Is it stupid to want to get you help before you bleed to death?"

"What? This? It's just a scratch. The cavalry will be here any minute."

"How do you think this will end if you pass out on me?"

He started to argue but then stopped without saying a word and hung his head until it rested on his folded arms. Tori waited for him to admit her crazy idea was the best they had. Should she be glad...or more afraid now that he apparently agreed with her?

When Blake lifted his head, the worry in his brown eyes held her captive. "Okay, Tori, we'll do it your way. Make it count." Suddenly, he rolled to his right, gained his feet effortlessly and sprinted for the fir tree.

"Blake! No! Get back here!" He wasn't a hundred percent. He'd never make it. She should be the one to take the risk. If he heard her protests, he ignored her. He was halfway to the tree when the first shot rang out. The bullet kicked up dirt a foot behind Blake. He kept moving, dodging to the right and the left.

Belatedly, Tori searched the terrain in front of her. When she spotted the gunman, she was shocked at how close he was to where she lay on the ground. He must have been on the move the whole time, creeping ever-closer, and she hadn't seen him until now.

He fired again. Though she was terrified for Blake, she forced herself to focus on the shooter, lining up her target in the sights of the semiautomatic pistol. Her hands were shaking so hard, pulling the trigger would be useless. Ken had taught her to shoot so she could protect herself and Isaiah if someone broke into the house while he was deployed. At the time, she'd doubted her ability to pull the trigger on another human being and told him so. Ken had assured her that if her life or her son's was ever in danger, she'd find the courage. The emptiness in his eyes had been proof her husband knew exactly how much courage it took.

Tori forced herself to focus only on the shooter, and a small measure of calm settled over her. When he pulled the trigger again, she squeezed off three rounds in quick succession. The first one went wide, missing him. The second struck him low in the torso. The third slammed into his shoulder, spinning him partway around and down on one knee. The rifle flew from his hands as his gaze locked on hers. The hate in his expression was like a physical blow.

To her right, she saw Blake dive for cover behind the thick tree trunk, and her immense relief was like a weight lifting from her chest. But the gunman didn't stay down, and when he scrambled toward the fallen rifle, panic replaced any courage she might have had.

She pushed to her knees and aimed the gun with both hands. She was shaking, and her lungs hurt for want of oxygen. A smirk appeared on the gunman's face, even as he stumbled to his feet and started toward her. He knew she had nothing left. In desperation, she emptied the clip. Six shells and she managed to hit him once in the leg. It didn't stop him.

From somewhere behind her, the loud clap of a gunshot echoed through the forest. An instant later, the gunman, approaching from the front, stumbled and fell. This time he didn't get up.

She turned to observe Blake's position. He pulled himself up awkwardly to lean against the tree trunk and gave her a thumbs-up. Tori closed her eyes, concentrating on stopping the uncontrolled trembling of her body. Shouts filtered to her ears from behind and above.

Thank God. The cavalry has arrived.

Chapter 5

When the hell had he gotten so old? There wasn't a doc in the Cypress Point ER who looked old enough to have finished med school, let alone have any experience with bullet wounds. Yet, here Blake sat, shirtless, on the edge of an examination table with a monster headache, while Peter-fucking-Pan used fourteen stitches to close the laceration left by the bullet that had grazed the side of his forehead above his eyebrow.

The doctor had also removed a small piece of rotor blade from his shoulder, where it had embedded itself after hopscotching across his cheek. Minor in the scheme of things, but, thanks to the cleaning and disinfecting, both spots burned like hell beneath the sterile bandages the nurse had taped in place.

Yeah, I'm one lucky son-of-a-bitch.

Impatience fueled his frustration, having spent enough time in hospitals for a dozen people. Tori had been wheeled from the ER a little while ago. He'd insisted she be evaluated first, even though he was the one bleeding. The doctor had agreed with his diagnosis of concussion with a mild contusion but had admitted her overnight for observation out of an abundance of caution, and Tori had argued the staying-over part all the way to the elevator. If the kid in front of him, masquerading as a doctor, ever tied the final stitch, Blake was headed to the second floor to see, with his own eyes, she was resting comfortably.

Across the room, near the entrance, MacGyver spoke with the local sheriff. No doubt he was trying to put a good spin on the dead body they'd left in the wilderness and the forest fire they'd inadvertently started. The silver-haired sheriff of Curry County didn't look happy. Thankfully, Rafael Perez, the client whose life they'd saved today, had the ear of someone higher up in the chain of command. The FBI had jurisdiction, probably exactly the reason Sheriff Danner was looking so put out.

"Okay, Mr. Sorenson. I've done all I can. Keep the wounds dry and clean. Take ibuprofen for the pain and swelling. Those stitches can come out in a week to ten days." The doctor eyed Blake's bare chest and arms. "You're obviously not a stranger to wounds like these. You probably know as much as I do about proper care, so I'll leave you to it."

"Thanks, Doc." Blake had to resist the urge to reach out and ruffle the man's hair.

The doctor signaled for an orderly to clean up the station and strode away as Blake pulled his T-shirt over his head and tugged it down.

He stood, testing his balance, before pushing away from the table. He searched the room for the nurse who'd taken Tori upstairs. Just as he lay eyes on her, trying to calm a new trauma patient the EMTs had brought in, he felt MacGyver's large presence behind him. At six feet five, his friend had a good three inches on Blake, and he was all muscle.

Blake turned. "We good with the sheriff? I have to live here, you know."

MacGyver's easy grin flashed. "Perez called the feds. Sheriff Danner isn't thrilled about the FBI tromping around in his national forest, but he realizes the futility of arguing. We got a positive ID on the shooter in the woods. Kevin Bradley—member in good standing with Sebastian Wahl's group of neo-Nazi lowlifes."

"What now?" The safe house had been destroyed. Perez, his wife and his children had been lucky to escape without injury.

"The feds have Perez and his family in protective custody for now, but our assistant DA is already rattling the cage. We've got twenty-four hours to find another safe house. Luke's on his way with the whole team. This just turned into a full-scale security operation." MacGyver lowered his voice. "All we have to do now is plug the leak."

Blake frowned, running the thoughts he'd been pondering through his mind one more time. Someone had indeed given away the location of the safe house, and that someone could be him. "It's too damn coincidental. They show up in an Apache helicopter as soon as I leave? Somehow they had to know I was hauling supplies and for who...and followed me." *Goddammit!* How had he missed spotting them?

Tori Michaels—that's how. The blame for this cluster lay smack in the center of Blake's shit. But how did she know he had any connection to Perez? Only four people, besides his bosses, had been aware he was ferrying supplies—Harv and the three guys who'd hauled them to his house and loaded them in the chopper. Of those four, only one had been privy to the details of his mission. So help him, if he found out it was Harv, he'd feed his nuts through a grinder.

When he glanced at MacGyver, his friend nodded toward the emergency room exit, and Blake followed him outside. As soon as they were far enough away that they no longer had an audience, MacGyver held out a badly damaged cell phone in a plastic bag, the case blackened and charred, the screen melted and twisted out of shape. Not sure what MacGyver was showing him, Blake cocked an eyebrow and waited.

"How well do you know Tori Michaels?" MacGyver rubbed the back of his neck, and a frown caused a divot in his forehead.

Was it Tori's phone? After the crash, the fire hadn't raged out of control, but there'd been plenty of smoke and heat—enough to destroy what was left of the Bell and its contents. Where was MacGyver headed with his show-and-tell?

"We found this in the wreckage, along with pieces of her driver's license, a recorder and what appeared to be her press ID card." MacGyver regarded him with narrowed eyes.

"Yeah? I know she's a reporter, bro. She came to the hangar looking for a story. I turned her down." His brother Christian, MacGyver and MacGyver's girlfriend, Kellie Greyson, understood Blake's aversion to reporters...and why. No surprise MacGyver would think it strange he'd allowed one, even a gorgeous one, to tag along. Still, he had the uneasy feeling he didn't have all the pieces of the puzzle. "Why don't you tell me what I'm looking at?"

MacGyver flipped the bag over in his hand. "Travis did a sweep on what's left of the Bell. This phone contains a GPS chip and fairly sophisticated software. It couldn't have been cheap. It was activated and still busy sending out its signal when we found it. If someone was monitoring Tori's whereabouts, they knew exactly where she was every minute."

Anger flared instantly as Blake crossed his arms over his chest. He'd considered the possibility it was Tori who gave their location away...but then he'd dismissed it as impossible. Mostly because he'd gotten to know her on the flight, he'd liked what he saw, and his instincts had told him she wasn't the type who'd willingly bring about the death of innocent children. Obviously, his reasoning had been flawed. Or perhaps he'd been thinking with something other than his brain. *Jesus!*

Tori was the wild card. He knew nothing about her, other than what she'd told him. Where was she from? If she *never* flew in helicopters as she'd said, why had she decided to hitch a ride in his? Did she really work for a magazine editor who would fire her if she didn't get an interview with him? That bullshit story should have been his first clue. Blake ground his teeth together. Two kids had nearly died because he let his guard down. And she'd acted like she cared about them.

Oh, hell yeah. He'd fallen for the short skirt, the long legs and the four-inch heels. Even now, he wasn't sure if he was furious because she'd conned him, or if he was angry because she wasn't the sweet, innocent woman he wanted her to be.

With thumb and forefinger, Blake rubbed his eyes, taking a minute to rein in his temper before raking a hand through his hair. "I don't know her at all…but I *will* before this is over."

Perhaps he hadn't controlled his anger as well as he'd hoped because MacGyver shook his head. "Lots of people have GPS locaters in their phones. Her set-up might be overkill if all she's doing is getting directions to her next interview, but let's see what she has to say before we jump to conclusions." He returned the bag with the phone to his pocket. "You saw how she was with those kids today. She didn't strike me as a coldhearted bitch."

Blake could agree with that. She hadn't come off smug or superior in any way. She'd blushed, embarrassed, when he'd admired her red heels and what they did to her legs. What kind of a damn Mata Hari could pull that off? Yet, the circumstantial evidence was growing. Had Tori led the would-be assassins to the safe house of her own volition? Or had she been used, unknowingly? Blake would have his answer in a few minutes. He turned and started toward the emergency room door.

MacGyver stopped him with a hand on his shoulder. "Give her a chance before you pass judgment, Blake. Damn it, I liked her. From the way you were acting all jealous and possessive, I thought maybe you and her might hook up."

Blake swung around. "Jealous?"

MacGyver laughed, raising his hands in surrender. It was enough to make Blake crack a grin, but guilt was riding him hard. He scraped both hands down his face, roughened by two days' worth of stubble. "Shit. This isn't how I imagined this playing out."

"You don't know she's guilty yet. Find out. If she is, maybe there are extenuating circumstances."

Blake watched a car pull in and park in the lot before he focused again on MacGyver. "She probably saved my ass out there in the woods. On the other hand, for a reporter, she's a pretty fair shot." For starters, she had some questions to answer. If she was aiding Sebastian Wahl, she'd have her day in court, despite the fact she was the only woman to successfully burrow beneath his defenses in a lot of years.

"I know. If the gunman had overrun your position or if you'd passed out, we could easily have been too late." Seriousness seeped into MacGyver's voice.

Blake shifted his weight, following his friend's meaning. Shit yeah. It could have been ugly if she hadn't stepped up. "I'll find out if she has someone to look after her for a couple days, so she won't be alone. Maybe I can convince her to stay at my place. That should be enough time to find out if she's a snitch for radical neo-Nazis."

A slow smile crept across MacGyver's face. "Keep your friends close and your enemies closer?"

"Yeah, something like that. Do me a favor, though. Keep this conversation on the down-low for now, okay?"

"What conversation?" MacGyver cocked his head like a curious puppy dog. "I'll contact Luke and see what he's come up with for a safe house."

"Hey, I've got plenty of room. Why not make my place your new safe house? It's big, secluded, and we'd have our own air strip. Tori was in the office, so if someone from Sebastian's crew was monitoring her location through her phone, they already know where we are. But they'll need boots on the ground to find the house, and, with the team there, we'll see them coming long before it's a problem. We can set up a barracks in the hangar for the guys."

"Damn. You sure about that, bro?"

"Absolutely." Blake was thinking ahead and, sure as hell, Tori was more likely to agree to stay with him if the house was full of people...especially a certain pair of kids.

"Not a half-bad idea. I'll run it by the rest of the men. Travis and Coop are already there, so the two of them could start things rolling." MacGyver tossed Blake a set of keys. "Harv thought you might need your wheels. I'll give him a ride back to the hangar while you check on Tori."

It was unusually selfless of his aircraft mechanic to go to the trouble of running Blake's vehicle into town, but maybe Harv was trying. Blake should give him the benefit of the doubt. Besides, there were more pressing issues to worry about.

"This is for you too." MacGyver produced a cell phone from his pocket, handing it to Blake. "It's a burner. Yours didn't survive the blaze, either."

The two men parted company, and Blake reentered the ER, stopping at the front desk long enough to ask for Tori's room number, then strode toward the elevator. He hated to admit it, even to himself, but he was worried about her. She'd impacted the side of the helicopter forcefully and lost consciousness, but that wasn't his only concern. Tori had grabbed his gun and proceeded to shoot a man. Hers wasn't the kill shot, but he'd bet she could use someone to talk to just as he had all those years ago when he'd taken aim at an enemy fighter for the first time.

Truth told, he was looking forward to seeing the hot brunette again. It was as though she'd crawled under his skin. He couldn't stop thinking about her. And not in a find-out-if-she's-the-enemy way, but in a scenario that put them in much closer proximity…with way less clothes on.

Shit! She could be colluding with a particularly nasty group of racists. Maybe this *wasn't* the first time she'd shot a man. He should be concentrating on determining whether her actions were voluntary when she led Sebastian Wahl's thugs to the safe house. Not Tori barefoot, as she'd arrived at the hospital, having lost those fucking red stilettoes somewhere along the way. Her clothes had been rumpled and covered with dirt and grime. Her shirt had come untucked and hung askew, the bottom two buttons either missing or she just hadn't given a damn. The silky, brunette hair he'd ached to run his fingers through when he first met her had been ratted and messy with small sticks and dry leaves peeking between the strands. But it was the vacant stare in her nearly transparent blue eyes and the lifeless mask she'd worn that had heightened his protective instincts.

The elevator stopped, and Blake stepped off on the second floor. Being attracted to a woman on the periphery of a mission like this was something he'd never had a problem with before. And he wouldn't this time, either. He was a grown man, a former SEAL. There was nothing he couldn't do if he set his mind to it.

Tori's room was halfway down the hallway on the right. There seemed to be an excessive amount of activity outside her door, and stirrings of unease quickened his pace. Two nurses, apparently having an earnest conversation within a foot of the open doorway, quieted and watched his approach. He sidestepped them and pushed into the room.

The bed was made pristinely, a hospital gown draped across the foot. Otherwise, the room was empty.

"Excuse me, sir. Who are you looking for?" one of the nurses said from behind him.

He turned halfway. "Tori Michaels. Downstairs, they told me this was her room. Where is she?"

"This was her room until she decided she was leaving," the nurse huffed.

"You let her leave?" Blake's gaze darted between the two nurses.

the collar of his leather jacket against the wet fog swirling with the cold ocean breeze. Almost twenty-one hundred hours. Many of the small, one- and two-story houses along the street were dark and apparently vacant. Waiting, no doubt, for peak season when they'd be rented out all summer to families with kites, beach balls, kids and dogs.

Pelican Loop was just that—a street that eased into a semicircle, exiting nearly where it started, and bordering a quiet strip of beach. Blake walked briskly on soundless feet, catching every movement, his ears straining for every noise. Only two of the homes on the beach side of the loop showed any signs of life. Lights brightened the windows of the farthest one away, and a dog stood at the corner of the house, barking. He couldn't tell whether the animal was sounding the alarm because of Blake's approach or if he was simply yapping at the tide rolling in. Two cars were parked in the driveway. A woman stuck her head from the open front door and commanded the dog to be quiet.

Blake located the house numbers of the small home near the center of the loop, confirming it was Tori's address. Twenty feet from her garage, he slowed and stepped into the shadow of a neighbor's hedge. No car sat on the concrete apron. Tori had apparently been so intent on getting home, she'd left her vehicle at his place.

A figure crossed in front of a window toward the back of the house. Sheer kitchen curtains did little to hide Tori's shapely figure as she opened her refrigerator and placed something inside. Through the glass pane of a room closer to the street, Blake watched the flicker of a TV screen, partially visible from where he stood—red, blue, white and then black for a heartbeat before the lightshow started over again.

The kitchen went dark, and Tori, her curves accentuated by tight leggings and a snug-fitting sweater, turned on a lamp in the TV room. Her long, wavy hair, dark against the light-colored top, made his fists clench as the desire to run his fingers through it nearly scuttled his real reasons for being there. Simply walking into the room, Tori was sexier than any woman should be. A large bowl rested in the crook of her elbow, and she carried a cup of something in her right hand. Blake suddenly wanted to know what she drank before bed. Coffee? Tea? Hot toddy?

He forced the obsessive thoughts from his mind as she leaned down with one of her mind-blowing smiles, puckered those red lips and kissed someone just out of his line of sight.

Shit! There was someone in the house with her. Ah, the husband she'd mentioned who'd taught her to shoot—not well, but good enough. Blake had almost forgotten she was married. Had wanted to forget, more likely.

"We can't keep them here if they don't want to stay. Ms. Michaels left against medical advice. I've got her signature right here on the AMA." One of them slapped her pen on the clipboard she carried and strode down the hallway toward the nurses' station.

Blake's mind was whirling. Why would she take a chance like that? And why leave without saying so much as *bite me* to him. The other nurse was still staring. "How long ago did she leave? Do you know where she went?"

His words were terse and guttural, and the remaining nurse backed up a step. "Are you a relative?"

Aw hell, here we go. If he said no, the nurse would refuse to discuss Tori with him. That would do him no good, but he didn't have time or patience to act out a lie. "I'm the guy she was with when she got hurt. I brought her in. Where the hell did she go?" His voice gained volume as he loomed over the nurse.

"She said she needed to go home. Something important that couldn't wait. She called a cab, and it picked her up about twenty minutes ago."

Well, what do you know? Contained anger and raw intimidation. Who knew that would work? He reached for her shoulders and tugged her close for a peck on the cheek. "Thank you. You're a lifesaver."

The prim and proper lady blushed and hurried after the other nurse.

Blake had his cell phone in his hand before the elevator doors closed behind him. He pushed the first-floor button, then dialed MacGyver.

"That was fast. Did you find out what we needed to know already?" There was road noise behind MacGyver's voice.

"Well, maybe. She took off without a word. Signed herself out."

"Oh damn…that makes her look guilty, doesn't it?"

"It sure as shit does. Listen, I need her address off her driver's license." If she thought Blake was going to let this go, she was dreaming.

"I've got that here somewhere," MacGyver said.

It seemed like forever before he came back and read Blake the address. "Hey, bro, keep tabs on your temper, right?"

"Right." Blake ended the call as the elevator door opened. Her address on Pelican Loop put her less than five minutes from the hospital. There were small towns all up and down the southern coast. What were the odds the reporter lived in Cypress Point and he'd never run into her before? Of course, his trips to town were infrequent, shopping at the grocery store once a month followed by a quick stop at the liquor store and ending with a couple beers at the Rusted Lighthouse. *Huh! Maybe I should get out more.*

Four minutes later, he flipped off the car's headlights a block away from Tori's address and pulled to the curb. He stepped out, tipping up

He didn't make plays for other men's wives, so the attraction he couldn't seem to shake had to go. The disappointment he'd felt in the woods was magnified this time. *Holy Christ, get a grip.* He had a job to do.

Blake started to step from the shadows but froze immediately. His gaze caught on a flicker of light behind her house, out where the surf rolled. There and then gone. Still he waited and watched. Minutes ticked by while the hair stood up on his arms and his skin tingled with tension. Had he really seen something? Could it have been a fishing boat, out too late and just now heading for the harbor? Or young lovers walking on the beach? It could have been anything or nothing. His sixth sense was working overtime.

Seeing things now. It'd been a long and stressful day. His body was telling him he needed some shut-eye. The sooner he put this confrontation with Tori behind him, the sooner he could hit the sheets. Blake stepped from the darkness of the hedge and strode toward Tori's front door. Four steps led to an eight-by-twelve covered porch with a swing in one corner. Plastic buckets and children's shovels sat neatly beside the entrance. Blake skirted it all and rang the doorbell.

A few minutes passed, and he was just about to start pounding on the door when he heard footsteps approaching from inside. The sudden glare from a single bulb over his head cast stark shadows around him as he squinted and shielded his eyes.

It was another few seconds before Tori opened the door and peered through. "What can I do for you?" Her voice held no hint of friendliness.

Anger hit Blake like a sack of cement. Was she really trying to pretend they hadn't gotten beyond the acquaintance stage with everything they'd been through? What the hell was she trying to pull? Surely, she'd checked to see who it was before she'd answered the door. She was holding it open about eight inches, her body blocking access—like it would take him even a half second to gain entrance whether she wanted him in or not. And where the hell was her husband? What kind of a man let his woman answer the door alone, after dark, dressed to kill?

The next instant, a hint of a smile flickered across her face, and she stepped back, swinging the door open another foot or so, still standing in the gap.

With a gargantuan effort, Blake swallowed his anger. His plan to convince Tori to stay at his place for a few days while she recuperated had self-destructed as soon as he remembered she was married. Maybe her husband wasn't man enough to do the little things that would keep her safe, but surely he wouldn't allow his wife to stay with another man. So, if

Blake wanted to maintain any contact with this woman while he worked out whether she was a lying snitch, he needed to play it cool.

He smiled and swept a glance over her face, feeling a certain amount of curiosity and satisfaction when she trembled. Suddenly, not sure what to do with his hands, he stepped back and hooked his thumbs in his front pockets. She caught her bottom lip in her teeth and slowly, leisurely scanned him from top to toe. Despite her marital status, desire heated his blood and made him itch to reach for her.

Her beautiful blue eyes widened, and her pupils dilated as her focus settled on his lips. Hell, she was as turned on by him as he was by her. And with her husband just beyond that door. What the hell? Had he misjudged her that badly? Was she a cheat as well as being complicit in attempted murder?

He needed to ask her how she was doing. Maybe offer to stay in touch. And get the hell out of there before he did something he'd regret forever, like lose his moral compass in those eyes and that sexy-as-all-hell mouth. A groan vibrated in his throat as he forced his gaze to meet hers.

His sense of decency made her off limits. Yet, his body's reaction to the raw need in her expression was instant and volatile. Words, intended to put a friendly spin on his appearance at her front door, caught and wrapped around them like a caress.

"Hey, sweetheart. You forgot to say goodbye."

stay with you until I get back. Okay, sweetie? Can you do that for me?" Tori hated that lying to him was the last thing he'd remember about his mother, just as he had his father.

She stole a glance toward her captor. He was still pacing back and forth between the door and the table. A glimpse of something shiny caught her eye beyond the window, and then it was gone. The sound of hurried footsteps, buried beneath the roar of the surf—or was she imagining things? A dark shadow, moving fast. The stranger didn't seem to notice, so maybe it was only wishful thinking.

Suddenly, the memory of Blake standing at her front door brought confusion and then a glimmer of hope. He wouldn't have left just because she walked away from him. The door had been open. He would have followed her. Or could he have gone around back? Another glance at the intruder told her he was getting more nervous with each pass. She was almost out of time.

Tori jerked to her feet and pulled Isaiah with her, shoving him toward the living room. "Go watch TV until we leave, Isaiah. Then call Auntie Jane. Don't worry. Everything will be all right."

As Isaiah started walking on his own, Tori peered at the man and flinched as he beckoned her toward him, a gloating smile showing his teeth through the bottom portion of the ski mask. She forced herself to take one step and then another. The next instant, a furious, dark-haired warrior in a Navy SEAL T-shirt burst through the back door, and her heart nearly stopped.

Tori threw herself sideways, against the cabinets, as Blake kicked the knife from the stranger's hand, grabbed two fistfuls of his black sweatshirt and slammed him against the wall on the opposite side of the room. The man hit the wall hard, and the air whooshed from his lungs, yet it appeared the impact had little effect. Tori tensed when, with a roar of anger, he stomped toward Blake.

In the center of the kitchen, Blake waited. His rage was apparent, yet he held it in check, not moving until the man in black was almost on him. Then he swung his fists in a one-two punch. Bones and cartilage snapped, and blood spurted, and the man who might have made her son an orphan crumbled and lay moaning on the floor. Blake rolled him to his stomach, produced handcuffs from somewhere near his belt and bound the bleeding man. The ski mask came off with a flick of Blake's wrist.

He straightened and glanced toward her. "Do you recognize him?"

Tori was trembling uncontrollably, and no sound came when she tried to answer him, so she shook her head. Pressing against the cupboards to keep herself upright was all she could manage.

Blake punched a number on his cell phone and explained to the 911 dispatcher what had happened and gave her address. He stomped toward her and bent to retrieve the knife he'd kicked from the attacker's hand. Then he regarded her with his piercing eyes, and his countenance softened.

Concern drew his brows into one, and he stepped closer, then stopped and raked a hand through his hair. "You should make sure the boy's okay." He tipped his head in the direction of the living room without looking at her. "Is your husband home?"

"My husband?" Her head was throbbing, and it hurt worse when she frowned, trying to understand what he was talking about.

"If not, you'll probably want to give him a call. The police will have questions for all of us when they get here." Blake remained poker-faced as he dropped the knife on the table, turned away and punched another number into his cell phone. "I have to check in with MacGyver."

"Right. Um…I'll check on Isaiah…and…maybe…make some coffee." If her legs would only hold her up long enough. She pushed away from the counter, putting one foot in front of the other until she reached the relative darkness of the living room. It'd been one hell of a day, and now blessed numbness was stealing over her.

"Isaiah, are you okay?"

The boy sat straight on the couch, his eyes devoid of emotion as he faced the black TV screen. Tori sat beside him, wrapped him in her arms and lifted his small body onto her lap. As soon as he settled against her, he grabbed ahold, clinging to her with arms and legs.

"Mommy? Mommy?" He called to her over and over as he cried softly, his tears falling on her breast.

A six-year-old child should never have to go through what just happened, especially not in the safety of his own home. The intruder's viciousness and the terror her son had experienced could scar him forever. Make his life a living hell. She'd have to get him help—a psychiatrist. How would she manage that if she lost her job?

Shutting out her worries, Tori rocked him. "Shh. Don't cry. It's over. You're such a brave boy. I'm so proud of you. Please don't cry, Isaiah." After several minutes, his body relaxed, and his breaths came easier, interspersed with hiccups. He'd apparently reached the end of his endurance.

Exhausted and adrenaline depleted, her son had fallen asleep in her arms, and she never wanted to let him go. But she'd heard the police arrive, without sirens, a few minutes ago. Their blue and red lights flashed comfortingly through the partially open blinds, creating a kaleidoscope of shapes and shadows on the walls. Men's voices filtered into the room.

Tori placed a pillow beneath Isaiah's head and covered him with a fleece throw, leaving him on the couch, where she'd be able to hear him if he woke, and returned to the kitchen.

Blake stood and pulled out a chair for her beside his at the table. "Is the little man okay?"

"Yes. He finally fell asleep."

The man who'd bled all over her floor was no longer there, apparently having been escorted out by some of Cypress Point's men in blue. Detective Gary Addison, whom she'd met in passing at the school Isaiah attended, stood when she entered the room, taking his seat again after she slid into the chair Blake held for her. Detective Addison's daughter was in Isaiah's class. Would he remember her?

The detective appeared to be in his early forties, with graying temples and strong features. His scrutiny was heavy with empathy. "Tori, may I call you Tori? I was hoping we'd meet again. I'm sorry it's not under better circumstances." The friendliness in his eyes helped to ease her tension.

"Of course, Detective."

"It's Gary, please." The smile he gave her disrupted his rigid façade and made him look younger.

Blake sat forward with a grunt and reached to cover her hand on the table, and she bestowed a small smile on him. What would she have done if he hadn't been there? A violent tremor shot through her, and Blake wrapped her hand in both of his, his warmth radiating to other parts of her body.

"Ask your questions, *Gary*. Ms. Michaels is under doctor's orders to make it an early night." Blake's emphasis on Detective Addison's first name earned a curious glance from her. Had it upset him that the detective had greeted her as a friend?

Gary flipped a page in his notebook and cleared his throat. "Okay, Tori. Tell me what happened."

She started with Blake ringing the front doorbell and her answering. Her mouth went dry when she got to the moment in her story when she saw the masked stranger holding a knife to her son's throat. Blake brought her a glass of water as she recited the part where he appeared and saved her from being kidnapped and murdered…or worse. By the time she finished, her head felt as though it would explode with each beat of her racing heart.

"Did you recognize the man?"

"No."

"Yet you were prepared to leave your house with him?" Detective Addison eyed her over his notebook.

Instant anger enveloped her as she stared back, momentarily shocked. "I didn't want to go with him, if that's what you're implying. I would have done *anything* to keep my son safe." Tori pushed her chair out with the backs of her legs, stood and braced her arms on the edge of the table. "You're a parent, Detective. How is it you don't know that?"

"Okay, Detective. We're done for tonight. If you have any more pertinent questions for Tori or me, give me a call and we'll meet you at the station house." Blake rose beside her.

Two dots of bright red appeared on the detective's cheeks as he continued jotting his notes. When he looked at her again, he was all cop with no pretense of friendliness. "Where is the boy's father, Ms. Michaels? Could he have had anything to do with what happened tonight?"

Tori dropped her head, massaging her temples with her fingertips while she digested the question. She wanted to laugh, but emotions betrayed her, and her eyes rimmed with tears. It was surprising that she had any tears left for Ken. Or maybe she'd become so pathetic, the tears were really for herself.

She felt Blake's tension as his shoulder brushed hers. Suddenly, she needed to sit in the worst way. Backing up until her calves bumped against her chair, she sat on the edge and stared at the detective. "I sincerely doubt that, Gary. Isaiah's father, my husband, died two years ago."

The silence created a vacuum in the room. Apparently, the detective had no more questions.

Blake fished a business card from his wallet and tossed it on the table. "Do I need to show you the door, Addison?" Anger emanated from Blake as he stared down the detective.

Finally, Gary closed his notebook, shoved it in his shirt pocket and pushed to his feet. He had the grace to look embarrassed as he observed her. "I'm truly sorry for your loss, Ms. Michaels. I'll be in touch." He grabbed the card Blake had dropped on the table and hurried from the kitchen. She heard the front door open and close.

Tori heaved a sigh as she rose. "Well, let this be a lesson. I should have stayed in the hospital like the doctor wanted."

Blake chuckled softly. "Yeah. Why didn't you?"

"Because I have a son to take care of." She turned away from him and took a step toward the living room. "I have to get him to bed." Tori stopped and turned back. "I don't know why you came, but thank you, Blake. Thanks for…everything." She left him standing silently beside the table.

She'd thought Blake had probably gone, but, a few minutes later, he came up behind her as she stood, half dazed, staring at her son's tear-stained cheeks. "Tori, can we talk for a minute?"

Exhaustion and stress were keeping her from thinking straight. Today had been one trauma after another. She hadn't even had time to process her own feelings of guilt over the shooting of another human being. How was she supposed to deal with her son's fear and shock? Her head felt as though it might split open, and the pain was making her nauseous. The last thing she needed was more conversation. "I'm so tired, Blake. Can it wait? I really should put him to bed." She stepped toward Isaiah to lift him into her arms.

Blake caught her wrist and tugged her to a vacant spot on the end of the couch where Isaiah was sleeping. He turned on the lamp beside her and sat in front of her on the edge of the coffee table, his knees caging hers in as he leaned toward her. "No. It can't wait, Tori. You can't stay here. It's not safe until we know that thug was acting alone. There could be a dozen more out there just like him, waiting until you and Isaiah are alone again. You need to pack some things for you and the little man and let me take you someplace safe."

As tired as she was, the warning in his words made it through the haze in her mind. Of course. He was right. She didn't know who the man was who'd broken into her house and threatened her son. She didn't know why or what he'd hoped to get from her. The assumption he was working alone and that she'd been a random target made sense. She had no enemies. No ex-boyfriends. No secrets. And she didn't owe anyone money. Yet.

As unlikely as it seemed that she'd been targeted by a loner, the idea there were others preparing to finish the job was also utterly ridiculous.

But what if she was wrong? What if her intruder was somehow related to the people who'd tried to kill Rafael Perez and his family earlier? But she didn't know the assistant DA before this morning. She wasn't even supposed to be with Blake. Was that why he'd shown up at her door? Had he come to warn her she might be in danger?

"Did you know this might happen? Is that why you came?" Rather than feeling grateful, the possibility made her angry.

"No. I was worried about you. Why'd you leave without saying a word?"

"I told you. I had to get home to my son." That was the truth, just not the whole truth.

"I'd have given you a ride, and I'd have appreciated the opportunity to thank you for saving my life." Blake lay his hand over hers, where it rested on her thigh. She was powerless to look away. "Was there some reason you didn't want to see me again?" His confidence unnerved her...almost as much as the trace of a smile that played over his features.

"Well, I didn't think taking another ride from you would be smart after what happened the first time." Tori tried to make her voice light and teasing, hoping to alleviate the seriousness that emanated from him.

Blake laughed. "You got me there. I'm glad I decided to come by and check on you, though." He grew solemn again. "I sent a picture of your intruder to MacGyver, and he sent it to his FBI contact. The man's name is Edward Nox. Do you know him?"

"No. Should I?"

"He's a hitman believed to be working almost exclusively for Sebastian Wahl. Does that name ring any bells?" Blake slid his hand under hers and rubbed his thumb over her knuckles.

"The white supremacist spokesman who'd like to see Rafael Perez dead?" Tori couldn't ignore the warmth of his touch or the safety in his nearness.

Blake's eyebrow shot up, and when his neat row of stitches furrowed, he flinched. "One and the same. And...you knew this how?"

"I listen to the news occasionally." Despite Tori's quick retort, guilt gnawed at her stomach for not telling Blake at the time that she'd figured out who the client was they were hiding. Not that it would have made a difference. She pulled her hand from his and crossed her arms in front of her.

Blake leaned back and raked a hand through his dark hair. "Look, there's a lot I don't understand about what went down this morning, including how you got on Sebastian's radar. But that doesn't change the fact that you are, and you won't be safe here as long as that's the case. Let me take you somewhere."

Tori looked at her son. If there was even a chance Blake was right, she couldn't take the risk, not with Isaiah's life at stake. "I can stay with my sister. She lives a few miles north."

"I'll drive you...if you're sure that's what you want to do."

"What do you mean? I don't have a lot of other choices."

"I'm offering you another choice. You can stay with me. You don't have to worry about bringing trouble to my doorstep like you would with your sister." His words were heavy with meaning. So much so that the danger to her sister almost overshadowed his outrageous offer. *Almost.*

"Besides, you shouldn't be alone for a few days. A concussion is nothing to mess around with. And I feel responsible. Hand to God, there's a whole army of people moving into my house as we speak, including the Perez family. You won't ever be stuck alone with me...unless you want to, of course." His sexy grin caught Tori off guard, and she felt something clench low in her stomach. "Can you think of someplace safer for Isaiah than an official safe house?"

Tori cocked her head and forced herself to look away from his lips. "That's crazy. I've got a little headache. That's all. It'll go away once I forget this day ever happened. Jane is family. She'd be crushed if she found out I was in trouble and didn't go to her."

"Yeah, but is she an *almost* EMT? I might come in handy."

His eyes teased, but she sensed his determination. Was it just her imagination, or was he keeping something from her? He'd proven he was a good man today. He'd saved her life. She trusted him—she just wasn't sure how far.

"Your injury is worse than mine. Why didn't they keep *you* at the hospital?" Tori contemplated his line of stitches as she waited to hear his answer.

"I could state the obvious, but you'd accuse me of being chauvinistic, so let's just say I'm not as polite as you."

"That's probably the first thing we've agreed on all day." Tori groaned and rubbed her temples. "You're not helping, you know."

"I'm trying to." He flashed that damn cocky grin. "I'm trying to do the right thing here. In this case, the right thing happens to be you and the little man staying at my place until it's safe for you to come home."

"You don't think that suggestion is just a tad inappropriate?"

"Why? You said you're not married. Is there a boyfriend I should know about?" He didn't give her a chance to answer. "I'm sorry for your loss. Losing a loved one is a wound that never quite heals. Sorry that asshole, Addison, brought it up that way. I can't imagine how hard it is for you."

For the second time today, Tori admired his honest sincerity. Ken would never have let his emotions be known. He'd kept it all inside, with the pain and anguish, until he couldn't take it anymore.

"Thank you...and no, there's no boyfriend."

"Good. Then there's no reason you can't think about your health and the safety of your son first. I'm sure the doctor explained that concussions can be serious. Maybe you should give her some credit for all those years in med school." The amusement in Blake's eyes was proof he knew he was wearing her down.

"Why? Why do you care?" It'd been a long time since anyone had, and Tori's suspicions wouldn't be laid to rest easily, though his argument was logical, and his concern seemed genuine.

Blake pulled back as though astounded by her question. "Has no one ever offered to help you before? You're a stubborn woman, Tori. Hell bent on taking care of yourself and your son, but you don't have to do it alone. Why? I don't know. I've never needed a reason to care about another human being before." He reached out to smooth the worry from her brow, and his hand dropped to her waist.

For a moment, it seemed he would pull her close…maybe kiss her. For sure, there was a moment when she wanted him to, but then he released her and straightened, stuffing his hands in his pockets as though they had a will of their own and he wasn't about to give in.

Okay, maybe she was a little disappointed. It'd been a while since she'd experienced attraction to a man. Even longer since a man had flirted openly and acted as though he was interested. She liked him…too much, apparently, but military men were still off limits. Trying to handle Ken's PTSD had taken everything she had, including her husband and Isaiah's father. Watching a good man destroyed by forces she couldn't fight had broken her into so many pieces she'd never be whole. PTSD was a silent killer, and it wasn't always possible to tell who was infected. When Ken died, she'd made herself a promise. She would never put herself or Isaiah in that position again. She wasn't falling for a former Navy SEAL, no matter how hot and sexy he was. And that pretty much precluded her moving into his house and staying with him.

"I appreciate your offer and everything you've done, but I can't stay with you." Tori stood, looking into troubled brown eyes—windows to his soul—that called to her on a primal level. She longed to give in and answer that call, but the need to safeguard her son and her own heart from any further pain won out. "I think you should leave now." She brushed by him and strode from the living room toward the front entrance. As she turned the knob and started to pull the door open, his hand covered hers and forced it closed again.

"Why?" Blake stood directly in front of her, so close his breath stirred her hair.

She jerked her hand from his with such force she almost lost her balance and reached out to steady herself. The closest solid surface was his chest and, rather than risk any further physical contact, she tried to back away. At the same time, he caught her elbow and left her no choice but to brace one hand against him.

"Easy. Are you okay?" Concern filled his voice, mirrored on his face.

His masculine scent swirled around her as something sensual flickered in his eyes. Within inches of her, Blake's strength and compassion fueled her desire and a longing for things she shouldn't want. Drawn to the security he offered, she ignored the small voice that warned of heartache to come from this moment of weakness.

Tori focused on her hand as she slowly traced the curve of his bicep upward to his shoulder. Noting the hitch in his breath, she could almost feel his intense perusal. She lifted her gaze to his and slid her hand around the back of his neck as though she'd done it a hundred times.

Glancing back and forth from his eyes to his mouth, she pulled his head down and stretched on her tiptoes. This was so wrong. She'd be sorry. The lecture she'd just given herself was fresh in her mind, yet a force greater than fear argued for one kiss. Just a taste and she'd be satisfied.

Her lips met his softly, gently. He leaned into her, a groan urging her on, but he didn't touch her. Control was hers, almost as though he knew what she needed.

Fire ignited in her belly, and heat exploded through her body. A moan surfaced, muffled by his mouth as he slanted his head and took the kiss deeper. As she sought to get closer, his powerful arms encased her, folding her against him, taking back control. His mouth plundered hers. Lost in a need so great it blocked out all reasonable thought, she swept her tongue inside his mouth, tasting, delving in an intimate dance of discovery.

Blake's hands caressed every curve as they slid down until he palmed her butt cheeks, lifting her, grinding his erection against her. Holding her off the floor with one arm, his other hand worked beneath her sweater, cupping her breast, plucking the hard peak, all the while claiming her mouth with searing kisses. Her panties were wet through and her feminine parts ached for more.

What am I doing? Holy hell, he felt so good, so right, but what happened to her vow—military men are off limits. How long had it been since a man made her feel like a woman? But that was no excuse for throwing herself at him. *He must think I'm an easy conquest.* No wonder he asked her to stay with him. No doubt, in his mind, she was a sure thing. She wiggled from his grip until her feet touched the floor.

Blake backed off immediately but looked decidedly unrepentant. He cleared his throat as she tugged her sweater down.

Tori closed her eyes in hopes she could disappear and not have to face him. But, no, he was still standing in front of her when she opened them. There'd be no vanishing act today. She groaned and whipped around to face the door, unable to stand still under his examination.

"I'm so sorry. God, I don't know what came over me. Do you think we could forget that…that…" She wasn't even sure what label covered pathetic widows with no self-control.

Blake laughed softly. "Not a chance." His voice was thick and gruff. "So, I'm curious. What are you sorry for? That you're a beautiful, sexy woman with needs? Or that it was me you turned to? Because honestly, I'm not sorry for either of those things, except, it'll probably be harder to convince you to go home with me now."

"Oh God." She was a complete idiot. A tease. She could go on and on, but it only made her feel worse.

Blake placed his hands on her shoulders, drawing her back against him despite her efforts to stand straight and maintain a degree of separation. "How about I sweeten the deal?" His breath on her neck tickled her sensitized skin.

Oh great. What proposition did he think she would agree to after that shameful display?

Blake continued without encouragement. "You agree to bring Isaiah and stay, in your own room, with a lock on the door, until Sebastian is no longer a problem." He paused.

Did he expect her to be able to look him in the eye every day too?

He traced a finger down the column of her throat, setting her atremble. "If you'll do that for me, I'll give you the interview you wanted."

Chapter 7

What the hell was I thinking? I should never have kissed her back—never let it get so far out of hand. But he had. Not only that, Blake had enjoyed every second of her in his arms. *Shit.* He couldn't get enough of her. And when she'd come to her senses, she'd left him on fire, needing more and with the worst case of blue balls he'd ever had. Damned if he didn't feel like a horny seventeen-year-old again.

The good news was, she'd taken the bait, agreeing to stay with him in exchange for an interview. It was a carrot he was willing to give. Maybe not right away, in case she decided to cut her end of the bargain short. Besides, judging by the silence that had descended like a layer of ice in the cab of his Tundra after he'd loaded them and their meager luggage, Tori wasn't in the mood for talking at the moment.

That would have to change if he was going to get her explanation for the GPS signal her phone had been transmitting. He glanced her way. "You okay?"

She shrugged, a gesture that made her seem more vulnerable and him feel like an asshole. "A little nervous, I guess."

Blake smiled. "Don't be. The Perezes are good people. You've already met MacGyver, Travis and Coop. They'll bark, but they're on your side. Same with Luke. You'll like him. The other men can be a little rough around the edges, but they mean well, and they won't be in the house much. They came to work, and they take their jobs seriously. In this case, that means keeping Rafael Perez, his family and *you* alive."

A thin smile fled as she glanced in the backseat, where Isaiah was sleeping. The boy had been doing a lot of that since Nox had used him to gain Tori's cooperation. He would likely have some issues to work through, but he had the love and support of a mother who obviously cared. He'd be okay, providing Tori hadn't done anything to get herself thrown in jail.

"Tell me about Isaiah." As much as he despised himself for using him, the boy was the key to learning what was really going on with the mother. And if Tori was a plant for a neo-Nazi hate group, Blake needed to know.

Tori hesitated just long enough to make him wonder. Then she smiled as only a proud mother could. "Isaiah is the best thing that ever happened to me. He's six…going on twenty-six…and a good student—top of his first-grade class." Tori frowned. "I guess I'll have to call his teacher and get him excused for a few days." She was silent for a moment, then seemed to shake it off. "His favorite thing is reading, but he loves riding his bike and playing baseball too. Since his father—Isaiah is painfully shy around men, but we're working on that. And he's got a killer collection of model cars."

Blake didn't miss the sadness in her unfinished sentence about Isaiah's father, nor the pride in her voice when she spoke of her son. "What kind of cars does he like?"

"Anything fast. Camaro, Mustang, Charger—the originals—not the new ones the car manufacturers came out with the past few years. His father got him hooked. Ken was restoring a Dodge Charger, and Isaiah had wanted to help so badly. After Ken—I mean, Ken said he was too young to help on the real thing, so he bought him a model car kit he could work on by himself." Tori abruptly fell silent and turned her head away.

What the hell? Why would a father reject his kid when all he wanted was to spend time with his dad? Tori had obviously chosen her words carefully so as not to badmouth the guy. Maybe there was more to the story that didn't make Ken look like such an ass. Blake tamped down his rising anger. "It's okay to talk about him, you know. Might help with the grieving process."

She didn't respond, and Blake mentally kicked himself.

Okay…none of my business. "We'll have to introduce Isaiah to Travis. He's into the old muscle cars."

"Sure." Tori smiled, but clearly they'd gone backward in his attempt to get her to open up.

Blake turned left onto his private road and wound around the mountainside until his office appeared in the headlights. The hangar was just up the hill, fifty yards or so, the big doors open and light spilling out to illuminate the Mi-17 Russian-made transport helicopter located on the pad his Bell had occupied that morning. He parked beside Tori's Kia, Coop's Explorer and two other unfamiliar vehicles. As soon as he cut the engine, Blake tapped out a text to MacGyver.

He climbed out and strode around to open her door, smiling at her obvious confusion. "The house is a little off the beaten path. It's about two hundred yards north of the office as the crow flies. It's a bit farther on foot…but MacGyver will meet us in a few minutes with the ATV."

Tori stepped from the truck, a hint of interest brightening her eyes for the first time since they left her place. "You're kidding!"

"Afraid not. The old guy I bought this place from was a big-time conspiracy theorist. He was convinced the government was out to get him, so he built his house in a ravine, tucked into the hillside with hundreds of years of old-growth timber overhead. It can't be seen from the air or reached on foot without setting off a series of alarms that lets me know someone's coming before they get within rifle range." Blake opened the rear door and reached across the seat for the sleeping Isaiah. Hefting him onto his shoulder, he grabbed one of the bags and stepped back. "Can you get Isaiah's backpack?"

For a minute, it appeared she would argue with him about carrying the boy, but finally she nodded, reaching for the pack. "Thank you. I'm not sure I would have had the strength tonight."

Blake could only imagine how hard that admission had been for her. Nor could handing off the care of her son to him have been easy. Maybe they were making progress after all. "I don't think either of us is at the top of our game after the day we've had." He started walking, zigzagging through the trees until the path smoothed out and became more distinct. Tori stayed close behind him. A few minutes later, he heard the rumble of the four-wheeler just before it topped the ridge, holding them captive in its headlights. Blake stopped and waited for MacGyver to pull alongside.

"Hey, man." MacGyver searched his face before smiling and addressing Tori. "You've had an eventful day. Let's get you to the house and Kellie can help you get settled in your room."

Tori smiled as though sincerely happy to see him. "Thanks for the lift, MacGyver. I'm dragging a bit tonight."

Blake tossed both bags on the floor behind the driver's seat and settled Tori in the backseat with Isaiah on her lap, then hopped in the front. "Kellie's here?"

"Yeah. She caught a ride with Luke and the team. Sally and Jen may come up on the weekend too." MacGyver exchanged a silent nod with Blake.

Kellie, MacGyver's girlfriend, was an ex-Marine and one of Blake's best friends, mostly because she'd brought Christian out of his angry period. Seemed only fair since she'd been the one who'd shot his little brother in the line of duty, creating the angry period to begin with. Blake still had to shake his head at the strange-as-hell friendship they'd forged. Despite the circumstances that left Christian paralyzed and Kellie questioning her very existence, she'd proven to be a damn fine person.

Blake had been a long time coming to that conclusion, but they were on the same page now, and having her here would make things easier for Tori. If Luke's wife Sally and her daughter Jen joined them, even better.

MacGyver parked the ATV at the edge of what would be Blake's yard if he ever got the time or the enthusiasm to do the necessary landscaping. For now, a gravel path led through the au natural forest setting, toward his front door. He lifted Isaiah onto his shoulder and helped Tori drag the boy's pack from the floorboard before grabbing her bag.

She was quiet on the way to the house, and as he walked her across the stone moat spanning the small creek that meandered by the front, she merely raised an eyebrow in curiosity and kept her thoughts to herself. When they reached the door, he held it open and waited for her to enter first.

Inside, a blond-haired, green-eyed woman gave an excited cry as she ran down the stairs and barreled toward Blake. He managed to drop the bag and catch her with one arm as she hugged his neck. "Shit, Kellie. Give a man a little advance warning, would you?" Damn, it was good to see her.

She stepped back and studied him, clearly taking in the sleeping boy draped over his shoulder with interest. Her amused grin gave way to a satisfied smile, and, thank God, she kept any comments about his lack of parenting skills to herself. She shifted her attention to Tori, standing close by Blake's side.

"Hi. You must be Tori. I'm Kellie. Come on. Let's get you and this sleepy little guy up to your room. Once you're settled, there are leftovers in the refrigerator. I'll hook you up if you're hungry." Kellie grabbed the bag Blake had dropped and snagged the backpack from Tori's hands, then looked back and forth between Tori and Blake, obviously waiting for him to either place the kid in Tori's arms or head upstairs with him. Blake voted for seeing Isaiah and Tori to their room, but she evidently had other plans, holding out her hands and waiting for him to transfer the sleeping boy to her arms.

"Are you sure you can manage him? I could carry him up for you." Blake hated the exhaustion and doubt in her eyes and blamed himself for putting it there.

"I've got him. Thanks for the offer, but I'm an old hand at this." She smiled her gratitude, but uncertainty was evident in the trembling of her hands.

Blake was pretty sure he'd just gotten the answer to his question from earlier. No, nobody ever *had* offered to help her, and damned if it didn't make him want to do something, anything, to convince her there were still good people in the world. Namely him, though why he wanted her to believe that was a question he couldn't answer. *Hell, maybe I hit my head harder than I thought.* He watched until she climbed the stairs behind Kellie, then followed MacGyver into the kitchen.

"Uh oh, bro. You've got that look on your face. What's up?" MacGyver strode to the island in the middle of the kitchen, crossed his arms and leaned his hip against the edge.

Blake continued to the cupboards, rummaged for a cup and poured himself some coffee. He held the carafe out. "You?"

"Might as well. Looks like it'll be an all-nighter." MacGyver grabbed a cup from the dish drainer and Blake filled it to the rim. MacGyver lowered his voice. "What'd you find out?"

The elephant in the room never stood a chance when MacGyver was around, so Blake had expected his first question would be about Tori. Blake glanced toward the doorway and the stairs beyond. There was no sign of her, and, unless Kellie had changed in the weeks since he'd seen her, she'd no doubt keep Tori talking for a while.

"Nothing much." He grimaced, reliving the scene in Tori's kitchen and coming to the same conclusion he had several times already. If he'd been five minutes later, she would have been gone, and he didn't want to reflect on what might have happened to her. "I keep wondering why Sebastian would send someone to take her out if she was knowingly funneling him information. I'm certain she didn't recognize Nox, and I'm also sure he wasn't there to pay her for services rendered. She was scared, not for herself, for her son. Hell, I might be too close to the situation to judge impartially, but I'm having a hard time believing she's in cahoots with Sebastian." Blake scowled and rubbed the back of his neck. "Maybe I better sit this one out."

MacGyver chuckled. "If your gut is telling you she's innocent, maybe you should listen. I happen to agree with you. So, let's assume we're right for a minute. How did she end up at your hangar this morning with a high-tech GPS in her cell phone?"

"She said her boss, some magazine editor by the name of Donovan, sent her to interview me. She wouldn't take no for an answer because that SOB said her job was on the line." Blake wanted to know who the hell Donovan was, and if he was given an opportunity to break the guy's jaw, he wouldn't pass it up.

MacGyver took a swallow of coffee. "That's a good place to start. Let's find out who this guy is and if he's acquainted with any of Sebastian's lowlife friends. I'll get Coop on it first thing in the morning."

"Good idea." Blake would be more than happy to squeeze information from the dirtbag if it would hurry things along. "Let's say he is our guy, and he figured out a way to keep tabs on Tori and lead Sebastian's thugs right to us. How did he know Rafael Perez was in Oregon and that I'd be ferrying supplies to the safe house this morning? Getting that Apache helicopter so close behind me without giving away their presence was no small feat. There's only one explanation. We've got a snitch on the inside." It didn't take a genius to recognize that Tori was the common denominator.

"I know what you're thinking, but consider this: Sebastian's first move, after failing to eliminate Rafael Perez at the safe house, was to send Edward Nox to silence Tori. Why would he do that? It makes no sense if she was working for him. He had nothing to gain. But if Sebastian and this Donovan were using her without her knowledge, they might have been afraid she'd talk to us and blow Donovan's cover." MacGyver frowned. "Maybe Nox went rogue and wanted revenge for her part in shooting the guy in the woods—Carson."

"Except, as far as the public knows, Carson died in the chopper crash and, hopefully, Sheriff Danner will keep the real story to himself since the FBI is calling the shots. Sebastian probably didn't expect Tori to survive, and when he learned she had, he could have decided to tie up loose ends." Blake heard a sound and glanced toward the door.

"The son-of-a-bitch left some big threads hanging when his boys didn't finish *us* off." Travis grinned as he strode into the room, Coop right behind him, and went immediately for coffee.

Luke Harding, the fourth partner in PTS Security, followed a few seconds later, stopping to shake Blake's hand. "Good to see you. Thanks for letting us take over your place. Nice setup you've got here."

"I'm glad to have the company. I've been rattling around in here alone for too long." *Huh?* Why the hell had he said that? Blake usually liked being alone, but tonight something made him crave companionship. *Yeah. Her name's Tori Michaels, and she's upstairs in a bedroom just down the hall from me.*

"Let's hope we don't get any more company, but we're ready for Sebastian if he makes a play." Travis broke into Blake's musings and handed Luke a full coffee cup. One by one, the four men pulled out chairs at the table and sat. Blake joined them.

"Alford, Warner, and Crenshaw laid out a perimeter in a radius of a thousand yards with the house in the center. We've got cameras with auditory capabilities every hundred feet. Monitors are up and running in the office. Alarms are operational but will only sound off in the office tonight. We spotted some elk on the monitors just after dark that might cause a problem if they break a beam." Coop chuckled. "I thought we'd give our guests a night to settle in before we scare the hell out of them."

"Considerate bastard." Travis grinned as he raised his cup in salute to Coop. A dusting of laughter went around the table.

"The men are on four-hour shifts around the clock. A mouse couldn't get through without us knowing. There'll be enough human scent in the woods after tonight the big game should move on and avoid this area." Coop went through his checklist, grinning with pride. He loved the tech end of things, almost as much as he loved blowing things up, and he made sure PTS Security stayed on the cutting edge on both fronts.

Blake had met Crenshaw and Warner when he flew to San Diego to see the operation after accepting the job offer. Ex-military, they both worked and played hard, and Blake had liked them instantly. He trusted them to not only do their jobs well, but to also manage the team members under them. Alford was an unknown, but so far Blake had no reason to doubt his bosses' judgments in the hiring department.

After they'd covered the current situation, shop talk gave way to small talk, reminding Blake how comfortable he was with these men—his brothers-in-arms—all cut from the same Navy SEAL cloth. He'd missed the camaraderie, and, at times like this, he was grateful to MacGyver and Travis for bringing him into the fold. Too much alone time wasn't a good thing.

A door closed somewhere above, and light feet descended the stairs. Kellie strode into the kitchen, a smile on her pretty face, and went to stand beside MacGyver's chair, reaching out to touch him possessively, as though she couldn't help herself. MacGyver glanced toward her with a smile before sliding his arm around her hips and pulling her to his side.

They make the whole soulmate thing look easy. Blake frowned and tamped down the pinprick of envy that threatened to weaken his convictions on the treacherous subject.

"I like her. She's beat, and Isaiah's still sleeping soundly. I assured her she wasn't being rude if she tried to get some shut-eye too." She frowned at Blake. "What the hell were you thinking? Do you know *anything* about women? For damn sure you don't know how to show a girl a good time on a first date."

"Hey! She stowed away in my chopper. That was no date, first or otherwise." Blake's protest was lost in the laughter of everyone at the table, including Kellie who, apparently, had only been baiting him. *Damn her.* He threw his hands in the air and, in the interests of being a good sport, grinned while he took their good-natured ribbing.

The thing was, he couldn't argue with Kellie. Though nothing that happened today had been his fault directly, Tori shouldn't have been in his helicopter. He'd downplayed the crash to her, but that didn't change the fact they'd been damn lucky…and the certainty that things could easily have gone to hell rested squarely on his shoulders with the subtlety of a two-ton boulder.

Blake ran his hands over his whiskered face and stood, carrying his coffee cup to the sink. "Whatever. I'm too tired to defend myself, and you wouldn't believe me anyway, so I'm going to get some sleep. Wake me for a shift later."

"Hell no," Luke said. "We've got it covered for tonight. You need some ibuprofen and some down time."

Blake didn't protest too much. Luke was right. He left them talking in the kitchen and took the stairs two at a time. Slipping inside his room, he leaned into the door and closed his eyes against the pounding in his head. After a couple of minutes, he emptied the contents of his pockets on top of the bedside stand and placed his handgun in the drawer. A quick trip to the adjoining bathroom produced four gel caps, which he swallowed in one gulp. Choosing not to waste time undressing, he dropped to his mattress fully clothed, removing his boots only as an afterthought.

It was one of those nights when his brain refused to shut off, despite his need for sleep. The events of the day paraded through his mind as though by rehashing them he could somehow change the outcome. He couldn't. Remembering the softness of Tori's skin as he'd held her, how she'd tasted, the scent of her hair, calmed his racing thoughts.

He was just drifting off when a high-pitched scream jarred him from what had promised to be a pleasant dream. Automatically jerking the nightstand drawer open, he reached for his weapon as the haze of sleep fell away. He landed on his feet beside the bed just as the scream died. Four long strides and he yanked the door open, stepping into the darkened hallway. The silence was thicker than ever, bringing with it the suspicion he'd imagined the whole thing.

The house was too quiet. Apparently, MacGyver and the others had returned to their duties outside. Not even Kellie stuck her head out to see what was going on. Blake started down the empty hallway, prepared for the worst, even as common sense told him no stranger could have gotten inside without alerting every operative currently on Skyline Ridge.

As he reached the next bedroom, the door opened, and Rafael Perez stepped into the gap. Backlit by lamplight from within the room, he held a baseball bat with both hands. The big black dog at his heels raised his muzzle toward Blake. Man and dog were obviously prepared to defend their family.

"Are the kids okay?" Blake's whisper seemed loud to his ears.

"Yes. They were sleeping, but the noise frightened them. It came from that direction." Rafael pointed toward the last two bedrooms on the floor.

"Okay. I'll check it out. You stay with your family." Blake waited for Rafael to step inside and turn the lock before moving on.

At the next door, Blake listened. Hearing nothing, he turned the knob and stepped inside. Enough moonlight streamed through the open curtains to quickly determine the room was empty.

The last room had to be Tori's. He stepped to the door and pressed his ear to the framework, pausing to listen. At first, he didn't hear anything, but then the soft sounds of a child crying filtered through the crack. Tori's voice was a low murmur in the background, but he couldn't make out her words.

Blake tapped on the door, and Tori stopped talking. Soon he heard someone brushing against the other side. "It's Blake. Is everything all right in there?"

"We're fine. I'm sorry we disturbed you." Exhaustion tinged her words.

Blake slid his weapon into his back waistband. "Do you mind opening the door so I can see for myself you and Isaiah are okay?"

There was a long pause before the lock turned and Tori swung the door open. "Isaiah had a bad dream and waking up in a strange place scared him." She leaned her head against the side of the door. "He didn't mean to cause problems."

"He didn't. May I come in?"

Tori stared at him, her pretty blue eyes filled with concern, before she stepped aside and allowed him to enter. The bedside lamp revealed the pale features of the boy, leaning against the pillows, his tears having turned to sniffles. He watched Blake warily as though the blow to his confidence from earlier warred with a kid's natural curiosity.

Blake continued to the bed and knelt beside it, eye level with Tori's son. "Hey, Isaiah. My name's Blake. Your mom said you had a bad dream."

"A nightmare." Isaiah bobbed his head and looked toward his mother.

Blake heard the door close and Tori's bare feet came closer. He focused on Isaiah. "I get it. I can't tell you how many times I've woke myself up screaming. It's no fun, is it?"

Isaiah's head wagged back and forth emphatically. "No. It's scary... even after I'm awake."

Blake nodded. "You're lucky you have someone who's pretty and smells good, like your mom, to hug you until you're ready to go back to sleep." He caught Tori's eye and winked, managing to wring a partial smile from her.

Isaiah sat up and reached for Tori's hand as she perched on the edge of the mattress. "Is that what you do when you have a nightmare?"

Blake laughed. "It's been a while since there's been anyone matching that description who wanted the job."

"Then what *do* you do?"

"Well...weather permitting, I might go for a run..."

"Outside?" Isaiah's eyes widened, and Tori issued a sound that might have been a squelched chuckle.

Blake was relieved to see her start to loosen up. "If it's the middle of the night, or if there's snow on the ground, I usually go to the gym downstairs in the basement. I punch a bag or press a few pounds. You'd be surprised how fast working up a sweat will take your mind off your troubles."

"You have your own gym? Can I see it sometime?" Isaiah leaned forward, excitement chasing the worry from his small face.

"You bet. If it's okay with your mom, I'll show you tomorrow." Both looked at Tori, Blake working hard to imitate Isaiah's puppy-dog eyes.

Tori's attempt to retain her serious demeanor was doomed to failure in the face of her son's delight. She broke up laughing, and those sexy-as-all-hell dimples rocked Blake's world again. They were lethal, and damned if he didn't want to find a way to keep her amused.

She tousled her son's hair fondly. "Okay, but that's tomorrow. Right now, it's time to sleep."

Isaiah giggled, wrapped his small hand around Blake's fingers, and lay back on the pillows. His eyes closed partway, and he looked as though he was ready for anything *but* snoozing. Laughter shone in Tori's eyes as Blake considered whether to pull his hand back or stay until the boy dropped off to sleep. How long could that take?

After a brief hesitation and a shrug in Tori's direction, he flopped on the bed beside Isaiah. As soon as his back hit the mattress, the kid rolled toward him, threw one small arm across his chest and burrowed into Blake's side.

"Uh oh. What's this?" Blake hugged the boy who yawned and tucked himself even closer. Possessiveness stirred within Blake...and an unfamiliar longing deep in his soul. He studied the boy's face while he tried to get a handle on his emotions. If the guys heard about this, they'd have all kinds of ammunition for razzing him. Maybe he didn't care what his friends had to say. Tori stood on the other side of the bed looking at them, and it made his heart beat a little faster to see her happy for a change. Maybe *that* was what he cared about.

As soon as she looked at him, her cheeks flushed a rosy pink, and she leaned across the bed. "Isaiah, let Blake go, honey. He needs to get some sleep too." She smiled, an apology worrying her eyes. Tori tried to pull Isaiah to her side of the bed, but he'd apparently become dead-weight in a matter of seconds. She pushed back the hair that had fallen in her face and jammed her hands on her hips. "Isaiah, this isn't funny."

It's a little funny. Blake grinned, and the boy smiled up at him. "Tori." To forestall her irritation with her son, Blake raised his arm to distract her. When her gaze narrowed on him, he pointed toward the closet. "It's okay, really. I'll stay until he goes back to sleep. Why don't you grab a blanket from the closet and cover him?" Belatedly, the idea that *she* might want a say in whether he came or went, knocked the grin from his lips. "Uh... unless that's not okay with you."

Strange—staying here with her was what felt most natural to him. Judging by the frown that dragged her brows together, those feelings were not reciprocal. After all, the last time they'd been alone and in close quarters, they'd both gotten a little hot and bothered. A frosty couple of seconds later, she huffed out a breath and turned toward the closet. After disappearing from sight, she lingered there considerably longer than it should have taken her to find the extra bedding. He opened his mouth to ask if there was a problem when she stepped from behind the closet door with the blanket over her arm and a gentle smile curving those full lips.

Chapter 8

Isaiah warming to Blake almost instantly lodged an ache in Tori's chest. Her search for the extra blanket was taking twice as long as it should for fear she'd blubber like a baby in front of Blake. She had no family except her sister. Jane was a terrific aunt, but Isaiah needed a male role model too, as much as Tori hated to admit that. Her son had reached out to Blake, a wonder in itself, but the miracle was that Blake hadn't minded. He'd spoken to Isaiah as though what her six-year-old son had to say might be important, instead of dismissing him as merely a child. She could kiss him for that.

Oh, crap! She'd already done that—flat out lost her mind and threw herself at him. Her cheeks no doubt reddened as the heat of humiliation swept through her. She carried the blanket to the bed and leaned over to tuck it around Isaiah, partially covering Blake in the process. She brushed a kiss on the side of Isaiah's ear, catching Blake staring as she straightened. He aimed his lethal grin at her and his eyes appeared to darken a shade in the dim lamplight.

If she needed any further proof that she'd given him the wrong idea by initiating that kiss, it was there in his smoldering gaze. She'd made a colossal mistake in judgment, and she had to set things straight with Blake, but not while her son could overhear.

Tori had kissed Blake out of gratitude for saving her and Isaiah. That was all it was. Though, there was a possibility she'd been influenced by how close he'd stood and his masculine, outdoorsy scent. That sexy damn grin of his was partly responsible for her temporary insanity too.

She wouldn't lie and tell him the kiss meant nothing to her. There'd been enough sparks flying to ignite a small bonfire. That was the problem. Blake was ex-military—a SEAL, for God's sake. If Ken had come home broken beyond repair, what horrors did Blake see when he closed his eyes at night? No…she wasn't going there again.

"Hey, there's room under this blanket for you too. I'm sure Isaiah would want you to get some rest." Amusement sparkled in Blake's heavy-lidded eyes.

Damn him. "We wouldn't want to give Isaiah the wrong idea."

"He dropped off while you were looking for the blanket. And you probably don't want to know what I want." Blake's voice lowered to a whisper, and he watched her with an intensity that made her shiver.

With an effort, she resisted the urge to cross her arms to hide the hard peaks beneath her thin shirt. She had to get this out before she lost her nerve. "Blake—"

"You and I came damn close to cashing in our chips today, Tori. Are you telling me you were willing to die with me, but you're afraid to lay on the same bed with your son between us?"

Blake was taunting her, and Tori wasn't about to dignify it with an answer. Nor was she willing to have this conversation where Isaiah might wake up and overhear. She turned away and strode toward the door. When she stepped into the hallway, she left the door ajar with a purposeful glance over her shoulder. About a minute later, Blake joined her in the hall, closing the door silently behind him.

"Was it something I said?" he whispered to her back.

Tori turned to face him. "We should talk about what happened earlier." When his perusal dipped to her chest, she gave in and crossed her arms.

With a soft laugh, he grasped her wrist and tugged her down the hall behind him.

"Wait. Where are we going?"

He kept on walking, speaking quietly over his shoulder. "We're not going to discuss this out here in the hall. We're going to my room."

"But, Isaiah—"

Blake reached his door and pushed it open. "Isaiah is sound asleep, Tori. The place is surrounded by security, and we're literally two doors away. He'll be fine." He pulled her inside the room and closed the door. Tori didn't move while he strode toward the bed, turned on a bedside lamp, took something from beneath the tail of his shirt and put it in the drawer of the nightstand.

At the foot of the bed, he stopped and placed his hands on his hips. "Okay. Where were we? Oh, right. You wanted to talk about what happened earlier. Which part? The kiss? Holding you so close I could feel every devastating curve? Or maybe our bodies grinding together in all the right

places? There's really no need. I bet I know what you're going to say."
Blake moved a few steps closer, his attention never wavering, a smirk
giving him the appearance of a panther stalking his prey.

"Really? Please, go on." Tori laid a hand over her heart, willing it to
stop pounding so hard.

"You think initiating that kiss was a mistake. You didn't mean to suggest
you were interested in anything more. You're a single mom and you've got
your hands full raising your son. You're not looking for an involvement
that's not in Isaiah's best interests. So, thanks, but no thanks." Blake raised
an eyebrow as though waiting for her to deny his words.

"Wow." Tori wouldn't, even if she could.

"I get it, but now it's my turn. We shared some deeply intense, personal
moments today, including almost dying. In my mind, holding you...
kissing you...was the only halfway normal activity. I've wanted to kiss
you since the moment you walked down those stairs outside the office in
those damn red stilettoes. I would have eventually, if you hadn't finally
succumbed to my charms." A teasing smile faded, leaving him looking
unsure. Vulnerable.

"Four years ago, when the Navy kicked me loose with a leg I didn't
know if I'd get to keep, my wife walked out on me. *Forever, true love,
soul mate*—those are things you find on a greeting card, not in real life.
I'm not looking for more either, but that doesn't mean I wouldn't enjoy the
hell out of spending some time with you and Isaiah...if you're agreeable.
No promises. No strings."

Tori didn't know what to say for a minute. "I'm sorry about your wife.
That really sucks." The callous woman had obviously ripped his heart out
at a time when he'd needed her the most. As a result, he didn't believe in
true love anymore, and that was okay. She didn't either. Was he offering
all the trappings of a relationship without the commitments of one? She
was tempted to take him up on it.

Only one thing wrong. His military service meant he very well could
be afflicted with the same syndrome that had killed Ken. The risk would
always exist, hiding in the shadows of Blake's mind. If Isaiah's reaction
tonight was any indication, the more time they spent with Blake, the stronger
her son's attachment to him would grow. When the inevitable happened,
her son would be devastated. Again. *Not happening.*

Blake rubbed his eyes with thumb and forefinger. "For the record, I
didn't blab all of that for sympathy. I wanted you to know we have more in
common than you think." He removed his watch, laid it on the nightstand

and stretched out on the bed, one arm thrown over his head and an I-dare-you glint in his eyes.

Tori moved closer to the opposite side of the bed and dropped down on the edge. She sat on something hard and remembering the pager her new boss had signed out to her, she reached in her pocket and set the device on the nightstand. Her cell phone was gone, burned in the wreckage of the helicopter, no doubt. She'd forgotten about the pager she'd shoved into a pocket of her denim skirt this morning, until she undressed at home to take a much-needed shower. Planning to replace her phone first thing, she'd dropped the pager into a pocket of the skinny jeans she'd changed into.

"For the record, everything you say while I'm here is *on the record.* That was the deal, right?" Tori managed to keep a straight face.

"Well, that's not exactly what I had in mind, but I know when I've been out-foxed." Blake smiled and, with his free hand, patted the empty mattress between them.

Tori contemplated his open smile, his dark good looks and his body to die for. When he caught her studying him, she looked away. Her admiring glance wouldn't look much different to him than Isaiah's. The difference was Isaiah needed that connection, but she couldn't give it to him. Why couldn't Blake be a doctor or an accountant? The only man she and Isaiah had been drawn to since Ken's death, and he had to be a former SEAL and moonlight flying helicopters. A wave of sadness engulfed her. "I told you this morning you're the most honest man I've ever met. You deserve the same, so...I have a confession to make." She turned around and stretched out on her side, taking care to maintain sufficient space between them.

Suspicion flashed across his face, and the line of stitches on his forehead made it look as though his brow was permanently raised in doubt. "Okay, I'm listening."

Maybe he thought he already knew what she wanted to tell him, but that was impossible this time. He seemed to withdraw from her without moving an inch, a self-imposed distance growing between them. Still, she had to make him understand. "My husband was an Air Force pilot. Two and a half years ago, his plane was hit by enemy ground fire while he was on a mission, and he ejected at the last minute. He was hurt badly. Doctors couldn't save his legs."

Blake reached to stroke her arm. "Are you sure you want to talk about this?"

Tori nodded once, not at all sure. "Six months later, I brought him home. He'd changed. He was so angry all the time. Isaiah wouldn't go near his father. He was only four. He barely remembered Ken anyway, but now Isaiah was terrified of him.

"Then one day it was like someone flipped a switch, and the man I'd married finally came home. He smiled and laughed, played games with Isaiah and started working with his prostheses. He'd had no interest in learning to walk with them before that. I let myself believe we'd be all right." Tori's voice broke and she cleared her throat, refusing to cry.

Blake caressed the inside of her arm, and that small gesture made her feel protected. "Tori, you don't have to—"

"Yes, I do." A ragged breath escaped. "Ken got a job, part time at a flight school, teaching people to fly. Helicopters were his passion."

Blake's hand stopped abruptly, and tension pulsed from him.

Tori rolled to her back, not wanting to see the sympathy in Blake's expression. "He'd never offered to take Isaiah or me with him when he flew, but that day he did. I'll never forget the joy on Isaiah's face when his father hugged him and asked if he wanted a ride in a helicopter."

"Shit." Blake's profanity was barely a whisper.

"We all went. Ken took his student up first. Isaiah was so excited, he couldn't be still. Then it was our turn, and Ken let Isaiah sit up front with him, all the while pointing out different things on the ground and answering all his son's many questions. It was the best day we'd had in months. When we landed, we all stepped off, planning to stop somewhere on the way home for lunch. But then he got a call on the radio. He said, 'I'll be a few more minutes, babe. There's something I have to do.' He got behind the controls and took off...and flew that helicopter into the side of a mountain." Tori stopped because tears had come from nowhere and were rolling down her face. She swiped them away, angry all over again.

Blake gripped her shoulder, disbelief and regret warring in his expressive eyes. "I'm sorry, Tori."

She laughed, but it sounded strained even to her ears. "Don't be sorry for me. Isaiah saw the whole thing. He was inconsolable. I told him it was an accident. I knew that was a lie because I found the note Ken left on my pillow when we got home. That son-of-a-bitch planned it, right down to Isaiah and me watching him burst into a huge ball of fire on impact. I *hated* him so much, but then I realized I couldn't possibly hate him as much as he must have hated himself."

Blake's touch saved her from the chill that tried to get a foothold in her heart. Then he caressed her cheek, drying her tears with his thumb. "Goddammit, Tori. You've got a right to be mad as hell."

He still doesn't get it. She spit out a harsh laugh, reminded of his words from a minute ago. "I didn't blab all of that so you'd feel sorry for me. I told you so you'd understand why what happened between us earlier can never happen again."

Blake raised up on his elbow and stared at her. "I'm afraid you lost me."

"I made two promises in the weeks following Ken's suicide. The first was to Isaiah. He had such a fear of helicopters, he made me promise never to ride in one. I'm not doing so well on that one after today. Promise me you won't ever tell him."

He held his hand up like he was taking an oath. "Not a word. What was the second promise?"

She reached toward Blake and traced a finger along his rough jawline. "That I'd never put Isaiah in a position like that again. I swore I'd never get involved with anyone who might hurt him, even accidentally. No helicopter pilots, no race car drivers…and no military men. There are a few others on the list, but you get the idea."

Blake leaned away, his eyes wary. "What do you have against military men?"

Now he's starting to catch on. "There are too many men returning from the Middle East with time bombs in their heads just waiting to go off. I didn't know what Ken was suffering from until it was too late. That's one drawback recruiters don't talk about. I can't—I won't put Isaiah through that again."

"Wait a minute. That's insane, Tori. Not every returning vet goes through what your husband did, and some of us simply adjust better. Or surround ourselves with brothers who know what we did and saw over there. We stay connected so if we have a bad day, there's someone to talk it out with. Instead of trying to forget the past, we use it to make a difference—like helping Rafael and his family."

She knew his argument made sense, but…"You don't know what it was like, watching my son come apart a little more every day. Holding him when he screamed at night. Thinking I was going to lose him too. It would destroy him if he lost someone else he cared about."

Blake stared for a long time, a frown marring his sculpted features. Had she misinterpreted his kindness to Isaiah as affection? Maybe his only interest was getting her in the sack for some no-strings-attached sex. He'd spelled it out for her, after all. *No promises. No strings.* Oh God. How had she missed that? And would this humiliating day never end?

"I see." Abruptly, he lay back against the pillows. One hand scraped across his face before he sputtered a dry, humorless laugh as he stared at the ceiling. "Everyone loses people they care about. I guarantee your husband won't be the last death Isaiah grieves. You're not doing him any favors by choosing who he can get close to. Hell, he might lose *you* someday, and if you haven't allowed him to stand on his own two feet, fail and stand up again, you're right, losing you *will* destroy him."

"He's a little boy. It's my job to protect him." Her heart ached, and she tried to keep the tremble out of her voice.

"Do you really think it's fair to take my measure with the same yardstick as your husband?" Suddenly, Blake was angry. Tori could hear the steely precision in his question.

"I'm not judging you, Blake, and I'm sorry if I've upset you. My decision has nothing to do with you, personally."

Another laugh echoed sharply. "I gotta tell you, it feels personal." He glanced toward her, a tender smile easing his frown. "If Isaiah were my child, I'd do everything in my power to keep him from being hurt too, so I get where you're coming from. He's a great kid, and you've done an amazing job raising him." Blake closed his eyes, and his chest expanded with a deep inhale. "But…that's not going to stop me from proving you're way off base on this one. Isaiah already trusts me, so you might as well get onboard."

His words echoed in her head. What had she done by bringing Isaiah to stay at Blake's house? What he'd said was true. Her son had only just met Blake, yet a bond existed. She'd set Isaiah up for more heartbreak. Guilt and dread tore her up inside. Useless tears prickled at the back of her eyelids. She had to do something. Should she pack up her son tonight and leave, tearing him away from the one man who'd formed a connection with him? Or wait until Blake rejected Isaiah and then try to pick up the pieces? There was no winning this time, and it was her fault.

Tori sighed. "Blake, please don't make this harder." For her son, she would plead.

Blake didn't respond.

She raised up to look at him. His eyes were closed as though feigning sleep. The barest hint of a sexy grin, tipping his lips up at the corners, annoyed her. Who the hell did he think he was, lecturing her on raising her son? No interview was worth putting up with his arrogance. No job worth sacrificing her standards. She collapsed on the pillows with an exaggerated groan.

Why does he have to be so damn good looking? And why does what he thinks make one iota of difference to me? One quick perusal of those broad shoulders and the outline of his pecs and abs through his T-shirt was enough to start an ache in her core. Anger roiled within her, as though her lack of self-control was his fault too.

Punching her pillow, Tori rolled to her side to face him in case he dared to look at her again. She studied him, expecting his eyes to open any minute, and he'd flash that damn sexy grin as though he was God's gift. But he didn't. He was so quiet, perhaps he really was sleeping. Tori huffed in disbelief. *How does someone fall asleep so quickly? Even if he hasn't been through the same hellish day as me. Okay, let him have his beauty sleep, but if he thinks this conversation is over, he's mistaken.*

Tori slid her legs off the mattress and got to her feet. Isaiah was just down the hall, and she should get back to him. She chanced one glimpse over her shoulder in case she'd awakened Blake when she moved, and the peaceful expression on his face stopped her. His rugged features and strong, stubborn jaw were relaxed for the first time since she'd met him. The element of danger that seemed to shadow him was gone.

Ken had never looked like that or slept so soundly after returning home. Was it possible Blake had his PTSD under control? Could she take that chance?

The image of Isaiah holding Blake's hand so he couldn't leave, sleeping curled into Blake's side, made her smile. He'd been right about one thing. Her son evidently did trust him. How or why that had happened was a mystery…and a miracle she would always treasure.

Gratitude to the man who lay sleeping brought the threat of tears, and she smiled as she reached to brush a fallen strand of hair from his forehead. Tori stopped just short of touching him, not wanting to wake him, but the anger she'd felt a moment ago dissipated as though it'd never been there.

Damn it! She wasn't supposed to have feelings for him. He was just a story—a way to keep a roof over her son's head. Yet, the tripping of her heart was more than mere gratitude. It might even be more than appreciation for his kindness to her son. If it wasn't, would she still feel his lips on hers—the sense of safety in his arms?

Despite his peaceful façade, Blake Sorenson was a dangerous man. Even now, the events of the day paraded through her memory like some old-time horror flick. She'd almost died. Twice. Worse yet, she'd shot someone. Actually fired a bullet into another human being. Would have killed him if she'd been a better marksman. Every time she closed her eyes, she saw him jerk as the lead tore through his body. She'd had no choice. The man would have killed them both, but did that give her the right to take his life? How was she going to live with that?

Blake had fired on another helicopter until it exploded and crashed. He'd entered her kitchen and taken out her assailant with his bare hands. He'd been a Navy SEAL with all that that entailed. Obviously, he was a man who'd been trained well and prepared to handle days like this one, but whatever else Blake was, she had no doubts Isaiah was safe in his home.

Tori started, pulled from her musings as her pager vibrated to life.

Chapter 9

Blake jerked from a light sleep, the buzzing of a thousand bees or possibly the hum of a spy drone initiating a strong instinct to duck for cover.

Wait a minute. What the hell? Where was he?

Right. He'd been talking to Tori and had evidently fallen asleep. Shit! *Way to impress a woman.*

The sound came again, and his senses went into hyperdrive. The next instant, someone bumped the bed, and from half-closed eyes, he watched Tori reach for something on the nightstand. The buzzing stopped. *Not a drone. A cell phone vibrating on a wooden stand.* Except, Tori's phone had been destroyed in the helicopter crash.

Without moving, he tracked her as she palmed something and raised it closer to her face. A narrow display screen lit up for only a second before it went dark again, and Tori's silhouette moved toward the door to the hallway.

A pager? Haven't seen one of those in years.

Tori opened the door just enough to squeeze through, closing it behind her with a quiet click. *Well, hell. This doesn't look good. Who pages a person in the middle of the night?* She'd apparently left the room in search of a landline, and that she'd gone to great lengths not to wake him was unmistakable. He had a bad feeling about this. Maybe she was merely being courteous, but it was much more likely his suspicions about Tori's association with Sebastian had just been confirmed. *Fuck!*

Blake rolled to his feet, opened the drawer and retrieved his handgun, then waited a few more seconds before following Tori.

The only landline in the place was in his office, with an extension mounted beside the back door in the kitchen, for those infrequent times he needed to take care of business from the house. Tori shuffled through the dark living room and foyer, clearly searching…unsuccessfully…before turning toward the kitchen. When she disappeared inside, Blake descended the stairs, hurried through the house and plastered himself against the wall beside the entrance.

He heard the last few tones as she dialed the phone and then she said, "Do you know what time it is?"

She sounded sleepy and grumpy. Blake allowed himself a smile, relief stealing over him. Maybe she was checking in with the sister she'd mentioned. Maybe he shouldn't be eavesdropping. He leaned his head back against the wall, preparing to leave her in peace, when her one-sided conversation caused his gut to churn.

"No, I didn't get it yet…because he refused and, while I was trying to change his mind, someone nearly killed me—twice."

Okay, probably not her sister.

"I didn't answer my cell phone because I lost it, and my home was broken into…I can't go back there for a while. It's not safe…Yes, I still need the job, Mr. Donovan. I'm trying to get the information you want. I need more time."

Blake grimaced. It was her boss, Donovan. Were they discussing the interview or something more ominous—like the whereabouts of a certain assistant DA?

"I don't think it would be wise to tell you where I'm staying. I'm not sure this line is secure, and someone may still be after me…Don't worry. I'm safe…A couple of days…to Portland? Okay, I'll contact you when I have it." She hung up, muttering under her breath.

At least she hadn't told Donovan where she was staying. That would give Blake time to find out who the hell the man was and where he fit into Sebastian's organization. And then Blake would have to determine if Tori was complicit in the attempt to kill Perez. *Damn it!* He should have kept his distance, but hell no, he'd had to get to know her…and her son, and he'd started to like them. That meant tomorrow was going to be just as fucked up as today had been.

He stepped away from the wall, into the kitchen doorway, and flipped on the overhead lights.

Tori whipped around, her eyes wide. She clasped a hand to her chest. "You scared the crap out of me, Blake!"

He strode toward her. "Did I? I'm sorry, sweetheart. I didn't mean to." Blake stopped mere inches in front of her, trying hard to check his anger. "Who were you talking to?" His forced civility apparently didn't impress her.

Irritation mixed with exhaustion in her body language, and her angry gaze snapped to his. "Excuse me? I didn't realize my coming here with you made you my new keeper. If I had, I wouldn't have come." The trembling of her chin contradicted the heat in her words.

Blake's anger flared at her flippant comment. He had every right to ask. *Or not.*

If his house guest had been talking to anyone other than Sebastian Wahl himself, Blake's demand to know who it was had been out of line. Since he already knew it wasn't Sebastian, he still owed her the benefit of the doubt. He'd practically insisted she come here and stay. If he stripped away her right to privacy, she sure as hell wouldn't stay long.

Just like that, Blake's anger cooled. It was everything he could do not to reach for her and somehow alleviate the distrust that was now staring back at him. Whether he chose not to believe she'd been promising Donovan information that went beyond the scope of an interview with him or he no longer cared that she was selling them out, the result was the same. He had to keep the lines of communication open with this woman.

Despite what he'd told MacGyver earlier, keeping the enemy closer wasn't the entire reason Blake wanted her here anymore. Hell, he was totally fucked. He should call MacGyver and the others and tell them what he'd overheard, because they hadn't been compromised by some ridiculous attraction to a pair of heels. They'd make their decision based on the facts.

But he couldn't—not yet—not while there was any chance she was innocent.

Blake stepped into her personal space and bent his knees so he could look her squarely in the eyes. Her soft, feminine scent floated around him, making it hard to concentrate on anything but her closeness. "Hey, I didn't mean anything by that. You were gone when I woke up, and I wanted to make sure you were okay. When I heard you talking on the phone at o-dark-thirty, I thought you might be calling your sister. She'll be worried about you if she hears what happened at your house earlier so, yeah, you should call her. I'd have waited until morning, but whatever you think." He gave her a teasing smile, disgusted with himself for how easy the lies tripped off his tongue. Not only that, instead of confronting her with what little he'd overheard of her conversation, he'd given her the perfect out. All she had to do was take it.

A wisp of a smile softened Tori's expression. She crossed her arms as though she was cold or perhaps feeling guilty. "I'm sorry. I shouldn't have jumped to conclusions. Just tired, I guess. I'm not usually the house guest from hell."

Blake laughed. "Forget it. I tend to come at people with both barrels loaded sometimes. Sorry if I upset you."

"It wasn't my sister. My boss, David Donovan, paged me. Part of my job is to be available twenty-four/seven, and since you agreed to the interview, and I might actually get to keep my job, I figured it wouldn't hurt to call him back, even if it is the middle of the night. What can I say? The guy's a jerk. If I didn't need this job so badly, I'd tell him what he could do with his pager." Tori gave a one-shouldered shrug and managed to look sexy and apologetic all at the same time.

Her surprising honesty multiplied his guilt for the suspicions he still couldn't seem to shake. For considering the need to check her pager for two-way message capability, which would allow another person to pinpoint her location. The device was practically an antique, from what he could see, and, based on her immediate search for a telephone after Donovan had paged her, Blake probably didn't need to worry about any high-tech options. Pagers operated with radio waves and contained no software. Someone would've had to physically plant a tracking device in the solid-state case and then be within a half mile or so. If they were that close, he'd already know.

Blake dipped his head and rubbed the nape of his neck. "I won't argue that, especially since you're under doctor's orders to take it easy and get lots of rest." He stepped aside and motioned for her to go first. "Come on. I'm taking you back to bed." *Oh, hell.* "Wait, that didn't come out right. I'm not taking you back to bed, more like seeing that you get back to bed." The air between them seemed to crackle with feverish intensity, and Blake stopped long enough to assess her reaction, hoping to slow the pulse that hammered in his temple. "Unless you want me to, that is."

Her beautifully shaped lips curved in a tender smile and one of her dimples appeared. His gut clenched as a surge of desire tightened everything in his groin. He was playing with fire...and damned if he could make himself care.

Suddenly, her smile vanished. "I should make sure Isaiah is all right."

"I'm sure he's fine. He was sound asleep when we left." An image of the boy, snuggled under his arm so peacefully, reawakened the something-missing-blues he'd wrestled with since he carried Tori from the crash site. A rush of possessiveness tugged at his out-of-control emotions, and he had to remind himself he still didn't have enough answers to trust her a hundred percent.

"I better get back. He was feeling much better after talking to you, but he'll be afraid if he wakes up alone." She started to step by him but hesitated, tipped her head and studied him, her vivid-blue eyes troubled. "Are you still worried about something?"

Oh, just a few dozen things. Like keeping Rafael Perez alive, solving the puzzle of Tori Michaels without leaving her son parentless, and since when do I lose my fucking mind over a woman and her kid? He shook his head. "I'm good...as long as *we're* good."

"Okay then." Tori turned her head but remained motionless as though there might be something else she wanted to say.

Blake's glance drifted restlessly over her, admiring her long, graceful legs and well-formed curves that begged to be memorized. Damn, she even rocked sweats and a T-shirt. When he scrolled back to her face, she was watching him.

"Thanks for being so sweet to Isaiah. He doesn't usually warm up to men, not since his father died." Her gaze skittered away again.

"My pleasure. He's a good kid. Easy to be around...like his mother."

Tori's eyes narrowed thoughtfully. "I'm glad you think so, because he's not going to let you forget about taking him to your gym."

"I never forget a promise...even when it involves reporters and interviews." Blake winked, hoping her dimples would come out to play again. He wasn't disappointed.

"About that...will you have time tomorrow to answer some questions... for the interview, I mean?"

"There's no rush, is there? You just got here."

"Actually, there is. In two days, Donovan expects me to deliver a draft of the article to him in Portland, personally, and he'll give me my next assignment." Her voice held a touch of vulnerability.

Grim determination flooded him. He stepped closer, though he hadn't intended to, and combed his fingers through her hair, fisting a handful of the soft, shiny strands. "The hell you are. It's not safe, and it's not happening. I have an office full of computers. You can e-mail it to him, like everyone else in the twenty-first century."

"Blake, I can't stay hidden away here forever and pretend I don't have bills to pay." Tori smiled, but her jaw was set stubbornly. "I appreciate your concern, but I already told you I need the job, and this isn't negotiable."

Her blue eyes widened when his other hand dropped to her waist and pulled her toward him. He inched forward to meet her halfway, and she offered no resistance. A gentle sigh seemed to signal the lowering of her defenses, yet he saw the same conflicted emotions in her eyes that warred within his chest.

"You're sure as hell not going alone...and Isaiah stays here." The overwhelming need to protect them exuded a force that was almost tangible. "I'll take you myself, and that's not negotiable either." A flicker of satisfaction surfaced when she didn't rush to argue. "How do you feel about small planes?" Blake anchored a lock of hair behind her ear, knowing he should step away, unwilling to.

She smiled with a touch of recklessness. "Planes I can do."

Relieved, Blake laughed. He didn't doubt that past circumstances had made her strong enough to do anything. "What? No argument?"

She shook her head. "Are you disappointed?"

"God, no. Surprised maybe."

Her eyes sparkled with humor as she feigned indignation. Damn, he wanted to taste her again, claim her so there was no question she belonged with him, but the memory of their conversation before he fell asleep stopped him. Because of his military background, she wasn't interested in giving this attraction between them a chance to run its course. Although, right now, her soft, vulnerable body, so close to his, gave him every reason to think otherwise. Until she was ready, he wouldn't push her. She'd endured enough pain, and unless he could change her mind, he'd only end up hurting her more. After all, he couldn't give her forever, any more than her dead husband could. He'd learned the hard way there was no forever in matters of the heart.

Blake's phone vibrated in his rear pocket, startling him. The urgent sound shattered the quiet of the night, severing their fragile bond. Tori jumped and backed away as though they'd just been caught by a high school principal, making out in the janitor's closet.

Coop's name was on the caller ID, and it was too late for a social call. "What's wrong?" Blake said as soon as he accepted the call.

"We've got a breach in the east quadrant." Coop wasn't one to waste time getting to the point. "That's where the elk were hanging out earlier. Luke and his crew are checking it out, but if there's anyone awake in the house, they might want to keep their heads down until we determine if it's a credible threat. I'll get back to you as soon as we know something."

"Got it. Keep me posted." Blake was already moving toward Tori who was peering from the windows into the blackness of the forest that surrounded the house on three sides. "Get down." He reached her in two strides, his hands curling around her waist, and pulled her down below the window casings. "Don't move." Ducking low, he shuffled to the back door and the flip of a switch enveloped them in darkness, broken only by the moon's rays filtering through the trees behind the house.

"What is it?" Tori sat on the floor near the wall, eyes wide and arms laced around knees pulled tightly to her chest.

Blake returned to her and leaned against the wall beside her, stretching his long legs out. "The perimeter was breached, though there's a good chance it was only an animal. One of Coop's alarms went off and Luke is investigating. They'll let us know if we should worry. In the meantime, this is only a precaution."

"So...we just sit here?" There was no fear in Tori's voice, only a hint of impatience.

Blake turned his head to study her profile while he tried to ignore the clean, flowery scent of her hair. Her hand rested on her thigh, and, without thinking it through, he reached to cover it with his. "Well, we could talk about what almost happened before Coop interrupted us."

"You mean whatever this is that keeps putting us in awkward positions?"

Blake chuckled. "What you call awkward, I would describe as interesting, even promising. You can't deny an attraction, right?"

"Attraction is too civilized a word. Animal lust is probably more accurate." Laughter filled her voice.

"Okay. I'll accept that. What are we going to do about it?" Blake pulled her hand to his lips and kissed her fingers.

"Obviously, we should ignore it. You don't trust women, remember?"

"And you don't trust military men. Does that mean if I want to kiss you and you want to let me, we couldn't put our distrust aside? For the sake of animal lust, I mean?"

"Well, when you put it that way, it sounds...interesting." The pulse in Tori's wrist kicked up a notch.

Blake's cell phone vibrated, and he swore under his breath as he released Tori's hand to retrieve it, glancing at the caller ID screen. "Hey, Luke. What'd you find?"

"False alarm," Luke said. "We figured we'd have a few bogus hits with all the big game in the area. Coop will work on making the alarm more selective."

Blake stood and pulled Tori to her feet. "A meeting with our guests might be a good idea, sooner rather than later. Just so we're all on the same page the next time an alarm goes off."

"You're right. Let's plan on that after breakfast. Aren't you supposed to be getting some sleep?" Luke ended the call without further comment.

"Is everything okay?" Tori wrapped her arms around herself again, calling attention to the pebbled tips of her breasts beneath her T-shirt.

Blake forced his attention back to her face, and his jeans got a little tighter in places. "Just some elk, like we thought." He rubbed the back of his neck with a frown. "You should go check on Isaiah and try to get some sleep. I'll see you both in the morning."

She hesitated just long enough to make him believe she didn't want to leave alone either. When she took a step toward the doorway, he moved aside to let her pass and enjoyed the view of her retreating form until she strode from sight.

Chapter 10

Tori woke, rolled over, and stretched in languid comfort, all before she missed the warmth of her son's small body curled beside hers. The spot next to her was cold and empty.

"Isaiah?" She jolted upright, searching the room. Sliding from beneath the covers, she hurried to the open bathroom, checking behind the shower curtain, and then glanced in the empty closet. It wasn't like him to wander off, especially in a strange environment.

Don't overreact. He's a curious six-year-old boy. Who was she kidding? All the pep talks in the universe wouldn't keep her from throwing her body in front of a locomotive if it'd save her son one more minute of pain.

Swallowing around the fear in her throat, she rushed to the hallway door, yanked it open and skidded to a stop just short of crashing into the solid wall of Blake's chest.

He stood in the open doorway, his right arm raised as though preparing to knock. As she stumbled backward, he reached to steady her. "Whoa. It's only me, the jerk that keeps sneaking up on you."

Tori had to force her mouth closed. Blake was dressed haphazardly in untied tennis shoes, sweats and his customary T-shirt. A black sweatband, with *US Navy* emblazoned in gold letters, concealed most of his forehead. His jet-black hair was wet and hung in clumped strands over the cloth, partially covering his fresh stitches. A sheen of perspiration glistened on his skin, and when she looked again, the damp stains on the shoulders of his gray T-shirt, and where the fabric pulled tight across his unbelievably brawny pecs, were obviously the result of a strenuous workout. Sweat had never held such appeal before.

Tori stared…from his sinfully ripped body to his mouth, cocked in an engaging grin, over the sexy-as-sin, whisker-covered planes of his face to stop on his chocolate-colored eyes. *Holy hotness! Was he this incredibly gorgeous yesterday? Easy girl—no drooling.*

Red hot heat pooled in her cheeks, and she dragged her gaze from his to somewhere over his left shoulder. "Isaiah is gone. I was just going to look for him."

"No need. He's in the kitchen having breakfast and bringing grown men to their knees with his wisdom." Blake leaned one arm on the doorjamb above her head.

"I'm sorry. I'll have a talk with him."

"Why? He's not bothering anyone, Tori. He's just being a kid. It's not even his fault he's down there. It's mine. I was making too much noise in the hallway early this morning and woke him. And you were right, he didn't let me forget about taking him to the gym." Blake laughed genuinely as though he'd enjoyed being with her son.

Some of Tori's uncertainty lifted, and she smiled. "You took him already?"

"Well, it was more like he took me…and the little man has discovered the climbing wall." Blake pulled up the hem of his T-shirt to wipe the sweat from his face, baring a delicious view of his sculpted abs.

"Climbing wall? Isn't that dangerous?"

"Not if it's done right. It's challenging…and builds confidence. Isaiah could benefit from that, just sayin'." Worry creased his brow. "I wouldn't let anything happen to him, but I guess I should have asked you first. I hope I haven't overstepped."

Tori shook her head, embarrassed, yet touched by his assessment, and she didn't trust her voice. "Uh…no. Not at all. Thank you for taking him. I'm sure he was beyond excited. I almost wish I could have seen him."

"Be careful what you wish for. We're going again in the morning, early, and Isaiah specifically asked if you could come too." Blake laughed when she rolled her eyes. He dropped his arm, straightened, and turned toward his room. "I'm going to jump in the shower. Go grab something to eat if you're hungry. There's always plenty of food when the crew's around. Luke wants to say a few things about the breach last night before we disburse." Amusement sparkled in Blake's eyes as he observed her. "Um…don't get me wrong, you look great, and the guys are gonna stare at a smokin' hot woman anyway, that's just how we roll. But you might want to…" His focus dropped to her chest.

Oh crap! She'd been too concerned about Isaiah to worry about her appearance. One glance confirmed the hard, pebbled peaks of her breasts were standing at attention beneath the semi-sheer fabric of her white camisole. Mortified by her body's obvious betrayal, she wrapped her arms over her chest, squishing her ample bosom into submission.

One corner of Blake's mouth ticked upward. He stepped close enough that their bodies almost touched, and the heat emanating from him singed the frayed edges of her willpower. Rough hands wrapped around her upper arms with tenderness, strangely contradictory for a man of such strength. When he ducked his head until his lips almost caressed hers, she stopped breathing.

"Don't. You should never cover up that beautiful body." His voice was a gravelly murmur, barely audible. Then he tipped his head to the left, grazed a kiss across her cheek, and headed for his room without looking back.

It was a full thirty seconds before Tori closed her mouth.

Well…shitballs! How was she supposed to keep her distance when he came across so sweet and scrumptious—when one brush of his lips sent her heart racing into outer space? Tori shook her head, hoping to recapture the initial reason she'd forbidden her traitorous body to react to his touch. Apparently, his proximity turned her brain to mush and encouraged other parts of her anatomy to engage. Maybe, after his intoxicating scent dissipated and her nerve endings stopped tingling, she'd be able to get back on track.

Tori retreated to her bedroom, grabbed some clean underwear, and headed for the shower. She only had a slight headache this morning, along with a dullness that resembled a migraine hangover, but the hot water through the pulsating showerhead proved to be the best medicine she could have asked for. By the time she towel-dried and dressed for the overcast day outside her window, a smile graced her lips, origin unknown.

That's my story, and I'm stickin' to it. The charming Blake Sorenson had nothing to do with her lighthearted mood.

Thirty minutes later, as she descended the stairs, voices from the kitchen raised in boisterous words of encouragement.

"You've got this!"

"You can do it!"

"Take your time."

When Tori strode through the doorway, Kellie waved from the other side of the room while putting a plate of sausage, eggs, and pancakes into the microwave. The delicious breakfast odors drew a loud grumble from Tori's stomach, but no one seemed to notice.

Isaiah sat at the kitchen table, playing a game on someone's iPad. Blake, MacGyver and Luke surrounded him, looking on and cheering. Tori's heart nearly burst with joy at the smile on her little boy's face as he concentrated on the screen.

Without warning, his spindly arms flew into the air. "Yes! I did it! Did you see?" He tipped his head up, looking into Blake's face as the grown man raised his hand for a high five.

"Did I see? I'll never forget it!" Blake winked at Tori, smiling every bit as proudly as Isaiah.

"Just a bunch of big kids, eh?" Kellie stopped beside her, holding the plate of food she'd warmed and some eating utensils. "Hungry? Come on. I've gotcha covered." She strode to the table and set the dish in a spot across from Isaiah. "Coffee? Juice? Milk?"

Tori waved a hand. "You certainly don't need to wait on me. Just point me in the right direction and I'll get it myself."

Kellie studied her for several seconds before pointing to the dining chair she'd pulled out a few inches. "Not today. Sit. Coffee *and* juice?"

"Just coffee, please. Cream and sugar if you have some on hand." Tori slid into the seat and picked up her fork. She really was hungry, but she couldn't look away from the three men giving Isaiah congratulatory slaps on the back. No matter what quirk of fate had brought them here, her son's happiness made it all worthwhile.

Isaiah literally beamed. "I found the treasure, Mom!"

"Way faster than anyone else." Blake pulled out a chair and sat next to Isaiah. "He's a natural. Right, little man?"

"Right!" Isaiah giggled. "Do you want to play, Mom?"

"How about you show me the ropes a little later? Okay?" Tori's glance flickered over Blake. A white cotton shirt had replaced his typically snug T-shirt, sleeves rolled to just below his elbows, enough buttons left undone at the neckline to reveal a smattering of dark chest hair. He'd shaved, and, though she'd found his rough stubble totally sexy, this new, cleaned-up version was equally appealing.

"Remember what I said, Isaiah? I need to borrow your mom for a while. Maybe it'd be okay with her if you hang out with Kellie this morning." Blake regarded Tori again, a question in his eyes.

Kellie appeared beside Isaiah, ruffling his unruly blond hair. "How about it, Isaiah? Want to try some kickboxing? I'm a pretty good teacher."

Isaiah smiled, excitement lighting up his face. "Yes! Is it okay, Mom?"

If he'd asked if he could scale Mt. Everest, Tori would have found it impossible to deny his request at that moment. How long had it been since she'd seen him so confident and happy? Equally as comforting was the look of expectancy and eagerness Kellie directed toward her, as though Tori's objection was the last thing she expected or wanted.

Tori smiled at her son as she swallowed the "we don't want to be a bother" she was about to utter. "It's okay with me, if..." She glanced toward Kellie just in case she'd changed her mind in the last second or two.

"All right then." Kellie nodded as though she knew how hard the concession had been for Tori. "Isaiah, let's go find some gloves that fit you."

He jumped up, ran around the table and hugged Tori. "Thanks, Mom." Then he ran to catch up with Kellie.

Tori felt Blake's scrutiny burning into the side of her face, but she refused to look at him until the scalding of tears behind her eyelids receded.

Luke cleared his throat and stood. "I already spoke with Rafael and his wife. The alarms weren't set to audible last night when the perimeter was breached, but if it happens again, it'll be loud around here for a while. If you hear them, you and Isaiah should return to your room, or stay if you're already there, unless you hear from Blake, MacGyver or me. That way, we'll know exactly where you are if we need to find you in a hurry."

"It's only a precaution," Blake said. "We don't expect anyone to get close enough to the house to cause a problem."

"Right. Just so we're all on the same page." Luke nodded toward MacGyver.

"That's my cue. We have to get back to work." MacGyver's chair scraped across the floor as he stood and headed for the back door.

"You have everything under control here?" Luke threw the question out there but didn't wait for an answer as he followed MacGyver.

"I'll check in later for my shift," Blake said as they filed out, and silence settled around the two left sitting at the kitchen table.

Tori moved the food around on her plate. "That was really sweet of Kellie. I hope it's no bother." Immediately she clamped her lips shut after the words she'd sworn she wouldn't say had escaped.

A deep sigh came from the opposite end of the table. "Why do you do that, always assume it's a hardship to help out or spend time with Isaiah? He's a great kid, Tori. Anyone you ask around here will tell you the same thing, so stop worrying that you or he might be putting us out. It's simply not the case." Blake leaned his elbows on the table. "I'm glad you're both here."

Tori glanced at him, half afraid he was being sarcastic, but he seemed dead serious. She knew what a special kid Isaiah was, but it was hard to forget how his father had made it his mission to avoid their son…until that final day…and look how that turned out.

"I like having you here, Tori." Blake grinned. "Now, finish your breakfast if you want that damn interview. You might not get another chance." He pushed his chair back and stood. "I'll be out front when you're ready. And dress warm. It looks like rain out there." He started toward the other room.

Tori finally found her voice. "Thank you, Blake."

"You're welcome," he said over his shoulder before he disappeared through the doorway.

Emotions always had a way of destroying her appetite, and today was no different. Tori forced down a couple of bites of sausage before taking her dishes to the sink, discarding the unfinished food and rinsing her plate. She moved the last few dishes that had been soaking in the sink to the dishwasher, rummaged through the cupboard until she found soap and started the cycle. Then she ran upstairs for a raincoat and hiking boots before heading outside.

Tori found Blake gently rocking the porch swing, a book open in his hands.

He set the paperback aside and got to his feet as she approached. "Ready?"

"You bet I am." She took a small notebook and a pen from her pocket. The truth was, butterflies were swirling in her stomach. A lot depended on this interview, but she'd succeeded in changing Blake's mind against all odds. Hell, she shouldn't even be alive today. A little thing like stage fright wasn't going to stop her now. "Where are we going?"

Blake motioned her toward the porch steps. "For a hike. I want you to see for yourself how safe you and Isaiah are here."

A stone path led from the steps to a shallow creek, complete with an arching footbridge, like something right out of the Scottish Highlands, so different from anything she would have expected from this man. Careful not to let her amusement show, Tori stepped aside and waited for him to lead the way. Instead, he placed his hand on the small of her back and guided her toward a break in the trees. "Did you call your sister?"

"Oh, no. I forgot. She's probably at work now." Hopefully, her attempted kidnapping hadn't made the morning news, but Jane would be beside herself with worry if she'd tried to call and couldn't reach her.

Blake pulled a cell phone from his pocket. "Here. This is for you until you can replace yours. It's a burn phone, which means no one can trace you. Why don't you call and leave a message for your sister? I'll give you a few minutes."

Tori took the phone as he strode ahead on an overgrown trail. She dialed her sister's number and got her voice mail. "Hi, Jane. Just wanted you to know I lost my phone, and this will be my number for a while. Isaiah and I will be away from home for a few days. I'm about to get that interview I told you about. Wish me luck. I'll call you later. Love ya, Sis." Tori ended the call and hurried to catch up with Blake.

He stood on the edge of a rocky promontory, looking out over the sloping ground below. As she approached, he turned, his finger to his lips, and held out his hand. When she took it, he pulled her in front of him and, bending slightly, pointed downhill through the trees. An airy breath of delight escaped as a mama deer and two tiny fawns strolled into her line of sight.

"No more than a couple days old," Blake whispered next to her ear.

"Oh...they're so little! Will she be able to protect them?" The doe's ears flicked in her direction, and Tori threw her hand over her mouth, hoping she hadn't scared them away.

Blake chuckled softly. "The first thing she teaches them is to hide and stay hidden until she comes back for them. You could walk right by one in a thicket and never know it's there."

"But predators can smell them, right?"

"Well, there's that." Blake shrugged. "But that doe will defend them to the death. She'll take down a full-size coyote or dog with her front hooves. Might not kill them, but they'll know they screwed up before she's done."

"What about hunters or poachers?"

"If she stays on Skyline Ridge, she'll be fine. No one hunts on my land." Tori glanced over her shoulder. "Not even you?"

"Especially not me. I've seen enough death and dying to last twelve lifetimes. Caused some of it myself, and there were times I tried to prevent it and couldn't. So, as ridiculous as it sounds, I'll buy my meat at the store and pretend it comes that way, all packaged up in plastic." Blake turned away from the doe and her babies. "Let's go this way."

They walked without speaking for the next few minutes, while Tori tried to imagine what kind of violence Blake must have seen. Was he remembering enemies he'd been forced to kill in service to his country? Strangely, his stand on hunting gave her hope that by shooting a man she hadn't turned into a bloodthirsty monster, undeserving of forgiveness. Perhaps someday she'd look back on the incident in the forest without guilt eating her alive. That day couldn't come soon enough, but, for now, she had to stay focused on Isaiah's safety and keeping her job.

Blake stopped next to an old rail fence, partially rotten with age, and pointed. Ahead, the terrain flattened out, forming a meadow with thickets of trees bordering a slowly meandering stream. A hundred yards beyond, the forest picked up again, dark and forbidding. "This is the safety perimeter Coop and his team set up. It runs all the way around the house and hangar. Motion-activated cameras send back video to monitoring stations in the office. Someone watches those screens day and night. Armed men are posted out here in case the cameras miss something. If someone wants to get to Rafael Perez, his family or you, first they'll have to cross an area just like this without being seen." Blake turned his head to look at her. "Trust me when I tell you Isaiah is safe here."

Tori gave a tight nod of her head. She did trust him. In fact, for the first time in two years, she felt as though she could give over control to someone else, knowing the enemy, real, or imaginary, was locked out. But why did his assurances sound like a warning?

Finally, she broke eye contact with him. "How old were you when you joined the Navy?"

He turned to look out over the meadow before he answered her. "Nineteen."

She waited for him to continue, hoping he wasn't going to make her pull his entire story from him, one question at a time.

"My parents were killed in a car accident when I was twelve. Christian was seven. Our uncle, Dad's brother, raised us. He was a retired Marine, never married. Christian and I decided there wasn't a woman alive who'd put up with his crotchety ass." Blake laughed as he bent to pluck a long stem of grass. "Joining up seemed like the right thing to do at the time."

"But you chose the Navy?"

"My one rebellion." Blake's grin popped as he raked a hand through his hair.

"What made you want to be a SEAL?"

He shoved his fingers in his front pockets and hooked his thumbs on his belt. "I wanted to make a difference. That sounds cliché, but so much of the regular military is about politics. That means nine times out of ten someone behind a desk who has no idea what's going on over there is making decisions that affect a boatload of lives. With the SEALs, one of the bureaucrats assigns the mission, but the officer in charge takes it from there. When the rub comes, and it usually always does, we're able to trust that the team leader knows how to stay within the guidelines and still get us home."

"How many missions did you take part in?"

Blake's jaw clenched. "Thousands."

Tori could feel the tension emanating from him. Maybe this trip down memory lane she'd forced on him wasn't such a good idea after all. Ken had never wanted to talk about his military service. After he'd come home, if some of his buddies visited, told stories and reminisced, Ken's state of mind had suffered for days afterward.

Suddenly, she didn't care whether Donovan got his story or not. It was time to wind this up and let Blake off the hot seat. "You were a SEAL for fifteen years. What made you decide to get out when you did?"

His nostrils flared as he turned partway and looked out over the meadow. "It wasn't exactly my decision." He walked a few steps then turned back, his hands flexing into fists at his sides. "Two SEAL teams hit the Taliban, each from opposite sides. Our intelligence was wrong. They had over a hundred fighters holed up a mile away. We had to fall back, but not everyone got out. Some escape routes had been cut off, and people were trapped. When my men and I got to the choppers, I sent them on without me, borrowed a helicopter and went back."

Something close to agony played across Blake's face. "There were five men still under fire. Two of them were seriously wounded. They were running low on ammunition. When they heard the chopper, they hauled ass in my direction. Caught the enemy fighters off guard and bought some time to get them onboard and lift off. We took a few rounds, but the chopper held together long enough to get us a few clicks away before she went down."

Tori couldn't stop her groan, but he didn't seem to hear her.

"The two injured men didn't make it. Hell, they might have been dead before we crashed for all I know. Their wounds were serious enough they didn't stand a chance of surviving without immediate medical attention. MacGyver was one of the men I picked up. He and the other two were beat up pretty good. My leg hadn't fared too well, and it was bleeding like a mother. There was no way I could run, much less walk…so MacGyver carried me over his shoulder—four miles to the last take-out point. That was the day we met." Blake raised tormented eyes to lock gazes with her. "That was also my last mission."

"I'm so sorry, Blake." The ache in Tori's throat made her words nearly unintelligible. She closed the gap between them, compelled to comfort him, regardless of whether he would allow her touch in the midst of his own personal devastation.

His distress was palpable as she pressed close, hugged his waist and leaned her tear-dampened cheek on his solid chest. "I'm sorry. We're done here. Donovan can go straight to hell."

It wasn't clear whether he'd heard her, but his strong arms locked around her, and then he was crooning words of comfort...*to her.* "Shh...it's okay. No tears necessary, sweetheart. I get caught up in memories sometimes, but that part of my life is over and done with. It's all good."

He pressed a kiss to the top of her head, then moved her hair away from her throat and brushed soft lips across her sensitive skin. His hands slipped inside her open jacket to gently surround her waist and hold her in place. She sucked in a breath as his possessive move made her nipples tighten and her thighs clench to quiet the need growing in her core.

The warning bells in her head sounded right on time, but Tori turned a deaf ear, not yet ready to be the adult in the situation. After a minute or two, she turned her face to peer up at him, the words to tell him they should go back ready on her tongue. Instead, the intensity in his eyes stole her voice and kept her from looking away.

With infinite patience, Blake lowered his head, his breath mixing with hers, whispering across her cheek, until his lips barely met hers in a tentative joining.

Tori closed her eyes at the last second, and a moan vibrated in her throat. The gentle pressure of his kiss deepened as though he'd just been given the go-ahead—and maybe he had, because she'd completely lost her ability to reason. She wrapped her fingers in the placket of his shirt and pulled him toward her as she leaned in. Blake didn't seem to mind, pressing the full length of his arousal against her belly. And still she shamelessly needed more.

Suddenly, Blake pushed her away.

Confused, Tori waited breathlessly for him to say something. Horror grew as the silence lengthened. Had she misunderstood his signals and thrown herself at him again? *Oh, God!* She squeezed her eyes closed. "I'm so sorry. I did it again, didn't I? Oh, man. I'm just going back to the house and lock myself in my room for the duration." She tried to squirm out of his grasp, but his strong hands were still clasped around her waist.

"What? No, you didn't do anything. *We* did something, and, frankly, I'd like to do it again." He leaned closer and lowered his voice. "Only with less clothes on." A roguish grin pulled at his lips, which he seemed determined to keep under wraps. "I'd like to finish this right here. Right now." He brushed another kiss on the corner of her mouth. "Except for one thing."

"What's that?" Tori gave him a doubtful smile. Should she be relieved or ashamed? On the one hand, a hot, sexy man, whom she liked and felt safe with, had apparently been as turned on by her as she'd been by him. On the other hand, she'd totally lost her friggin' mind!

Blake leaned toward her ear as though there were any number of people around who might overhear him. "I don't really want to share you with anyone right now, but remember when I told you about the video cameras?"

As though on cue, a wolf whistle pierced the quiet of the meadow, and rowdy male horselaughs followed, seeming to come from everywhere and nowhere at the same time.

"Hey, you two, get a room," someone shouted.

"Big brother is *always* watching, man." A hearty laugh swelled and then faded, blending eerily with the sigh of the wind.

"Oh. My. God." Tori pushed away from him so fast, she stumbled back a few steps. The idea of strangers watching their shared moment, regardless of whether it was a mistake, was humiliating. The fact that Blake had found it amusing was demeaning. "They can see us now? Are we on video too?" *Damn it!* She got her answer when he wouldn't look at her. "You couldn't have told me before we made a public spectacle of ourselves?" Only then did she notice the fury in his tight jaw and blazing eyes.

She started to turn back the way they'd come, but Blake snagged her wrist. "Listen for a minute, Tori. I'll take care of them. Believe me, heads will roll. But none of this changes the fact I'm attracted to you. I'm not ashamed of it, and I don't care who knows."

"You don't get it, do you? Your buddies see us going at it laugh, and say, 'Looks like Blake might get some tonight.' It's different for women. I'll be lucky if someone doesn't post that video on the internet before the day is over…with my name and phone number." Tori shook off his hand, turned and stormed toward the house.

Chapter 11

Blake tapped on Tori's door and took a step back in case she came out swinging. How he'd managed to piss her off so badly without even trying, he had no idea. She had a gift for keeping him off balance.

He was about to knock again when the door swung open. Tori leaned her head against the edge and peered up at him.

"A peace offering." Blake held out the video tape clutched in his hand. Coop apparently had a much better understanding of women than Blake. He hadn't even looked up when Blake burst through the office door, just handed him that damned tape while continuing to watch the monitors.

"Who were they?" The growl had rumbled from Blake's throat.

"Already gave them their walking papers. They won't be back," Coop had said.

Tori studied him for a bit before she focused on the tape. Instead of accepting it, she jerked a hand through her wavy tresses and opened the door a little wider before she turned and strode out of sight.

Blake hesitated for a moment, weighing his options, then stepped into the room. Tori, looking as incredible as ever in tight jeans and a gray off-the-shoulder sweater, climbed on the bed and sat cross-legged with her laptop balanced on her thighs. Beside her, all the luggage she'd brought for herself and Isaiah was open and partially filled with their things. Apprehension wrapped its sticky tendrils around his chest and pulled them tight.

She continued to watch him as he strode closer and tossed the tape on the foot of her bed. Glancing at his offering and then back to him, she shook her head. "Thank you. That was thoughtful of you after…" She cocked her head to the side and a hint of a frown touched her lips. "I'm sorry. I acted atrociously. It wasn't your fault, and you didn't deserve to be treated that way. It seems I'm constantly behaving in a manner that requires an apology. I'm sorry about that too."

A half laugh escaped her. "I have to go before I do or say something that'll make you regret saving my life last night, but I didn't want to leave without saying thank you for being so kind to Isaiah, you and everyone here. It means more than you'll ever know."

Fuck! Too bad Coop sent those idiots packing. It sure would feel good to kick the shit out of them about now.

Blake turned his back and sat on the end of the bed, dragging his hands down his face in aggravation. When he'd spoken with Luke this morning about what information they'd been able to garner about Tori and her boss, Donovan, there'd been good news and bad news. What little he knew about Tori had checked out, including a degree in journalism from Washington State and the death of her husband, one Kenneth Michaels, in a helicopter crash two years ago. It'd been ruled an accident, and the note Tori claimed to have found had never been entered into evidence. Without a doubt, she was protecting Isaiah from that truth.

The bad news was Donovan had no known connection to Sebastian Wahl. Or maybe that was good news. Especially if Blake couldn't change her mind about leaving.

"How's the story coming?" He shifted so he could glimpse her from the corner of his eye.

"Pretty good, I think. I'm almost finished."

"Did you get everything you needed from me? You didn't ask anything about Christian."

"On purpose. The story isn't about your brother. It's about you." Tori spoke softly, and Blake recognized the compassion in her voice.

"I appreciate that. Can I read it when you're finished?" He could tell by her hesitation he was pressing his luck.

"You mean before it comes out in the magazine?" Her soft laugh made him turn his head and glance at her.

He smiled. "Yes, before it's published."

Tori turned the screen of the laptop toward him. "Help yourself."

Blake held her gaze for a minute before drawing the laptop closer, quickly reading through her draft. *Shit!* "You made me sound like a hero."

"Again, on purpose. You *are* a hero to us mere mortals." She took the device from him and repositioned it on her lap.

Blake sure as hell *wasn't* a hero, but that was probably exactly what Donovan's readers wanted to think, so who was he to argue. Anyway, he didn't want to talk about the story. "Where will you go, Tori? You can't take Isaiah back to your house. We already decided it wasn't a good idea to go to your sister's place. Do you have friends or family out-of-state where you could stay for a while?"

The instant she became defensive, he heard it in her voice. "I'll deliver the story to Donovan in Portland. Isaiah and I will stay there for a few days.

Blake stood and turned toward her. "Let Isaiah stay here...please. You know he'll be safe with us. Can you say that with certainty if you take him with you?"

Tori didn't answer, but she also didn't refuse his request immediately. That was a good sign.

"I promised to fly you to Portland myself. Let me make sure you get there and back safely. Your son needs you, Tori. You owe it to him not to take reckless chances." Hell, yeah, he was pushing too hard, but he had to make her understand the danger she might face. Hadn't almost being kidnapped last night taught her anything? And, yes, he was having trouble remembering she might be a snitch—because he'd convinced himself she couldn't possibly be guilty—because she and Isaiah had become important to him.

Talk about being reckless. Maybe he should look at his own reflection in the mirror.

Tori groaned and dropped her head in her hands. A moment later, she looked up, new determination in the set of her jaw. "Okay. I'll let you take me to see Donovan and bring me back...on one condition."

"Which is?"

"No more up close and personal between us—kissing, hugging, flirting, or sexual innuendo. Agreed?"

"No flirting? That's going to be tough. I'm a flirt by nature. You do realize you kissed me first at least once, right?" Blake winked, holding a carefree grin firmly in place.

"Take it or leave it, Sorenson." Tori was obviously struggling to remain straight-faced, but the sparkle in her eyes told him she wasn't as angry as she'd like him to believe.

Blake raised his hands in surrender. "I promise to be on my best behavior. But, should you make the first move, all bets are off, sweetheart."

She pursed her lips and frowned, then waved away his comment as though she thought he was joking. "Deal. When do we leave?"

"Tomorrow morning, six o'clock. Pack an overnight bag in case the weather turns bad."

This time, her eyebrows flew upward, into her bangs.

"Ask Luke or MacGyver." Blake rushed to make his case. "Anyone who flies a small plane will tell you the weather is always a factor. But...if you want to ignore my advice...and don't mind sleeping in your clothes...it's your decision."

* * * *

Blake went over the Beechcraft's recent maintenance report with Harv, keeping an eye on the path Tori would follow from the house, half afraid she'd changed her mind overnight and opted to find another way to deliver her story to Donovan.

"You should be good to go, boss." The mechanic took the clipboard back and hung it on the wall near the aircraft. He'd been on his best behavior since Blake had gotten in his shit for his treatment of Tori the first morning she showed up.

"Good job. Thanks, Harv." Blake forced himself to give the man his due, but it still jacked his jaw just having the guy underfoot. His reservations resulted from his suspicion that Harv coveted more responsibilities within PTS Security. Blake was a firm *no* vote on that one. He didn't need a man with a flash temper and questionable judgment carrying a concealed weapon on Skyline Ridge.

His next glance down the path to the house relieved his most pressing anxiety. Tori strode toward the hangar, Isaiah next to her, toting her overnight bag. Kellie accompanied them. Blake studied Tori's face for telltale warnings of her mood. If anyone had told him he'd care whether a woman was happy or not, after Celine left him high and dry, he'd have told them to jump off. Despite the havoc his ex-wife had wreaked on him, Tori and her son had gotten under his skin.

She laughed at something Kellie said, and the lighthearted exchange made him smile as he circled the front of the plane and started toward them. He stopped abruptly when Harv headed down the path, straight for Isaiah, crouched in front of him, and lifted a hand, inviting an amiable slapping of palms. Isaiah didn't hesitate. The sharp clap was loud in the crisp morning air. Harv said something and reached toward him, and Isaiah happily surrendered his mother's bag.

Blake seethed in barely controlled anger as Harv rose and extended his hand toward Tori. When they shook, and she graced him with a dimpled smile, a dangerous growl erupted from a dark place inside Blake. He spun around, needing to purge the image from his mind and lose the attitude before his overprotectiveness made a fool of him, nearly flattening

MacGyver and Luke in the process. That they'd approached to within two feet of him without setting off his internal sensors was troubling to say the least. His two bosses each took a step back, indicative of the over-the-top hostility Blake was sure they could read in his body language.

MacGyver, who'd known him the longest, recovered first. "Hey, buddy, everything okay?"

Blake lowered his head and raked his fingers through his hair. "Yeah. Just about ready to take off."

MacGyver peered over Blake's shoulder, a skeptical tilt to his head. "I see that."

Thankfully, Luke seemed oblivious to Blake's dark mood. "Just because Coop couldn't find anything in Donovan's past to link him with Sebastian doesn't mean you should let your guard down. Coop's good...but not infallible." Luke's warning mirrored Blake's own conclusion.

"I don't plan to." Whatever Donovan's part in this, Blake didn't trust him and wasn't about to turn his back on the man.

"And you'll keep us in the loop, right?" MacGyver looked more worried than he should.

"I'll check in. You'll know where we are every step of the way." Blake removed his sunglasses from their usual spot on the neck of his T-shirt and slipped them on. "I promised Tori the boy would be safe here. Don't make me out a liar."

"He's in good hands." MacGyver looked beyond Blake again, a contented smile on his face.

Blake snuck a peek at what had grabbed his friend's attention, and a smirk tugged one corner of his mouth upward. Finding Kellie had been good for MacGyver. No doubt he would soon follow Luke and Sally's example and make an honest woman of Kellie. Yeah...both of his friends had found what Blake swore didn't exist, their soul mates.

He turned just as Isaiah bumped into him, the kid's arms twining around Blake's legs. The look in his eyes when he tilted his head to stare at Blake was just a hair over unsure, stopping short of scared. Blake's heart stuttered, and he unwound the boy's arms before kneeling at his eye level.

"Mornin', Isaiah. I knew I could count on you to get your mom here on time. I'm sorry about postponing our trip to the gym this morning, but I'll take you again as soon as your mom and I get back. Now I need you to promise you'll pay attention to everything Kellie says while we're gone. Okay?"

Isaiah hugged Blake's neck. "Okay. You'll take care of my mom, right?"

The question and the tremor in his voice nearly broke Blake, and he nodded solemnly, glancing over the boy's head to where Tori stood, apparently not wanting to get too close. "You bet I will." Blake wrapped his arm around Isaiah and picked him up as he stood. "Kellie has your mom's cell number, and you can call and talk to her anytime if you get worried." As he spoke, he glanced toward Kellie, and she nodded.

He leaned away to look in Isaiah's face. "Guess what? There are some other kids staying here you might enjoy meeting. Antonio is a year younger than you, and his sister, Lucinda, is a couple years older. And they've got a dog. Kellie will make sure you get an introduction because…I'll tell you a little secret—they could use a friend like you."

That seemed to catch his interest, and he squirmed to get down. As soon as his feet touched the ground, he scurried to Kellie and shoved his small hand into hers.

Just then, Harv stepped away from the women to stow Tori's bag behind the rear club seats of the airplane. Then he turned and smiled. "Pleasure meeting you ladies officially…Isaiah." He gave the boy a two-fingered salute before facing Blake. "I've got an appointment this morning, boss. Since we're about to be out of aircraft to work on, I was thinking I'd take the rest of the day off. Okay with you?"

"Sure, Harv. Take as much time as you need." Blake tried to shrug off his unfounded animosity toward the mechanic, hoping Luke and MacGyver hadn't picked up on it, but he was perversely relieved the man was going to take off. It seemed an infinitely better option than him hanging around, sowing discontent among the off-duty men.

Blake tried to catch Tori's eye to see if she was ready to go, but she was staring in the direction Harv had gone. His irritation building, he watched as Harv and one of the newer PTS operatives exchanged greetings on the path between the runway and the hangar. Harv gestured toward the man's sidearm, and he removed it from his holster, slid out the clip and handed it, grip first, to Harv.

Oh, hell no! Before Blake could take a step toward the pair, MacGyver reached them. Blake could tell from MacGyver's stance he was pissed. Blake couldn't hear the words he spoke, but Cole reclaimed his weapon and made a hasty retreat. Judging by MacGyver's scowl, Harv hadn't been able to forgo a smart-ass remark before sauntering toward the office, where his truck was parked.

MacGyver glanced toward Blake, and Blake couldn't resist a grin. *Yeah…welcome to my world.*

When he turned his attention to Tori again, she was tracking Cole's movements, visibly shaken and pale. As Blake watched, her hand went to her throat, only to drop to her side again when she caught him studying her. With obvious effort, she straightened and flashed him a watered-down smile before she started toward him.

What the hell?

* * * *

She fidgeted in the seat beside him as though she was trying to crawl out of her skin, crossing and recrossing her legs, rubbing her arms and refusing to look at him. Her noncommittal one-word answers to Blake's efforts to communicate were starting to get on his nerves. Once he'd reached a cruising altitude of six thousand, five hundred feet, he leveled off and let the plane's autopilot take over. Sliding his headset down around his neck, he noted the beautiful blue-green waters of the Pacific stretching as far as he could see on his left. On the right, the Cascade Range of mountains formed a dark-green backdrop.

"Want to talk about it?" He could only assume anything to take her mind off whatever was yanking her chain right now was better than nothing.

"About what?" Tori whipped toward him, her features etched with caution.

"Whatever is bothering you."

"What makes you think—" A derisive laugh punctuated the abrupt end of her denial. "Jesus," she whispered, jerking her gaze back to the mountains outside her window. "May I ask you a rude question?" She hesitated for a moment before swinging her head around, making it impossible for him to look away.

"Shoot." Whatever was bothering her had those normally crystal clear, blue eyes lined with pain. His stomach knotted in dread.

"Ironic." A miserable groan erupted from between pale lips. "How long before you could look at yourself in the mirror after you...after the first time you shot someone?"

Okay. That explained a lot. It wasn't about Isaiah or wanting to take off by herself while danger still tracked her. Something, maybe Cole drawing his handgun in her vicinity, had served as a catalyst for this moment of self-doubt...bordering on a panic attack.

The paralyzing guilt that came from turning a weapon of death on another human being—he could deal with that. All he had to do was close his eyes to remember his first kill in living color. But far worse had been the handful of men, boys really, he'd had to drag from the battlefield after their first times had left them unable to fire their weapons at another living soul.

It had briefly crossed Blake's mind that Tori might have a problem handling her role in stopping the shooter who tried to kill them after their chopper crashed. Plunged immediately into the situation at her house that night, the possibility had been forgotten…except by her, apparently. Now he owed her the truth, but the last thing someone in her position needed to hear was that he never looked too closely in the mirror.

"I'm not going to lie to you. That's a tough one." Blake forced himself to maintain eye contact when every instinct made him want to hide from her searching gaze. Even now, almost twenty years later, her question stripped him bare. Suddenly, the remorse and confusion he thought he'd dealt with years ago reared their ugly heads, and it took a concerted effort to stuff them back in their boxes.

He cleared his throat and concentrated on words that might help Tori. "Time and distance are your friends. And I don't mean geographical distance. Emotional distance, wrapping the memory in every single reason you pulled the trigger, every justification for what happened." His first had been with a knife so as not to give away his team's position before they located their target. Sometimes the grisly scene still highjacked his nightmares.

"I thought that man in the woods was going to kill us…but what if I was wrong?" Tori rubbed her hands on her thighs.

"You *weren't* wrong. First rule, you don't get to change the events. You grabbed my gun. Why'd you do that?" Blake turned partway in the seat and leaned toward her.

"Because…he shot you. He tried to get close enough to finish us off."

"Right. What else?"

"You were bleeding. I was afraid you'd bleed to death if we didn't do something."

"And you wanted me to live?"

"I didn't want you to die." Her expression said she thought it was a stupid question.

Blake tamped down a grin. "Why?"

"Because, hell, I don't know!" Tori threw her hands in the air.

"Yes, you do. Why?"

"Because…I thought you were one of the good guys. Because…you didn't kill us landing the helicopter and you carried me, unconscious, out of the wreckage. Because…heroes are hard to come by." She turned her head away and gave a bitter laugh. "And because…I like you."

Blake chuckled. "Now we're getting somewhere. If you hadn't bought us enough time for MacGyver and Luke to get there, I'd probably be dead right now. It was a justifiable use of deadly force, Tori. I'm not just saying that because he could have killed me with his first shot. He wouldn't have left any witnesses alive. If you hadn't taken my gun, come up with that ridiculous plan of yours and shot him first chance you got, it's likely you wouldn't have gone home to Isaiah that night. Plain and simple."

She whipped around and stared at him. "I didn't think of that. Holy shit, you're right."

Blake white-knuckled the edge of his seat to keep from threading his fingers through her hair, turning her face toward him and gently kissing those trembling lips. He did his best to wipe those thoughts from his mind as he leaned back. "Can I ask *you* a question?"

Tori pulled herself up straight, and her eyes widened as a weak smile bathed her features. "Of course. Anything."

"Where'd you learn to handle a gun?" The question had plagued him from the moment MacGyver had questioned her motive for showing up at Blake's hangar. He needed the answer, even now, when he was ninety-nine percent sure she was simply a reporter who'd taken the odd assignment because she needed the job and the money to provide for her son.

Tori twisted a lock of hair, wrapping a curl around her finger before tucking it behind her ear. "My husband gave me a few lessons. Ken thought I should be able to defend myself and Isaiah." Dropping her head, she crossed her hands on her lap. "We'd lived in the same middle-class neighborhood since Isaiah was born. I never understood why he was worried…until I found the note he left behind."

She slowly lifted her head, and the agony in her eyes was like a punch to the gut.

"Ken was afraid he would lose it and hurt us. He wanted me to be able to…stop him if that ever happened." A shrug lifted one shoulder. "I guess I wasn't a very good student, because he decided to take matters into his own hands. He took his own life rather than live with the possibility he might forget he was home, instead of over there in that hellish war, and kill his wife and child."

Fuck! Blake closed his eyes for a long heartbeat, hoping when he opened them the pain in her body language wouldn't be so tangible, but he couldn't block out the sounds. Tori's breaths heaving in and out of her lungs. Her choking back a sob. The softly uttered obscenity that mirrored his own.

No wonder she was determined not to bring a veteran into Isaiah's life. She'd seen firsthand what war could do to a man. Her experience had ended in tragedy. Who was he to tell her it didn't have to be that way? He'd had his own issues when he came home, and if he hadn't been Christian's only family, if he hadn't been forced by necessity to man up and take care of him after his paralysis, Blake's story might have ended the same as Tori's husband.

He turned sideways on the seat and reached for her hand, her rules be damned. Tears rolling down her cheeks, she gripped him desperately and leaned toward him to bring his hand to her chest. A growl formed in his throat as he reached to undo the latch on her seatbelt and lifted her onto his lap. Her head fit perfectly beneath his chin, the warmth of her body against his as natural as his next breath.

Blake held her for several minutes while she fought back tears. As far as he was concerned, she'd damn sure earned the right to cry. He remained silent, except for an occasional whispered word to remind her she wasn't alone.

After a while, she quieted and soon she raised her head to look at him. She ran her fingertips down his chest, igniting small fires in her wake. "I'm sorry, Blake. I didn't mean to spill all of that on you."

"We're even then, because I didn't mean to break at least half of your rules less than twenty-four hours after you laid them down."

"I'm pretty sure that was my fault too." She pushed to her feet, and he held her steady until she dropped into her own seat. "Thanks for listening... and for your advice."

"My pleasure." Without thinking, he reached to brush his knuckle down her cheek but caught himself and let his hand drop. She'd set her rules. He'd promised not to initiate anything, and he kept his promises—almost always.

He could only hope it was disappointment that slid across her beautiful face.

Chapter 12

"Mr. Donovan will see you now." The long-legged receptionist stood and preceded them down a lengthy hallway. Tori had a hard time not sneaking a peek at Blake to see if he was ogling the woman's legs, along with her four-inch heels. Not red, at least. Tori dismissed the ridiculous twinge of jealousy that popped up from nowhere.

Finally, the woman stopped, knocked and pushed a door open. Without hesitation, Tori stepped across the threshold. Blake grumbled something she didn't catch as he followed her into David Donovan's office. The receptionist closed them in with a sharp click of the door latch.

Tori's gaze roved the large room. Donovan was lifting a decanter with some amber liquid inside from a glass bar near the windows of his high-rise workplace.

"Tori, so good of you to come." Donovan, looking impeccable in a three-piece suit and tie, sauntered toward her. The very real possibility he'd bathed in expensive cologne seemed to float in the air around him.

Yeah, like I had a choice. She'd been so nervous when she interviewed for the job, she'd barely taken note of how young he was, but now it was clear he was a handful of years younger than her, twenty-five or twenty-six. Dark-brown hair, hazel eyes, and boyish good looks, paired with his position of authority, probably made him attractive to young, ambitious women. Tori might have thought so too if she could have gotten past his insufferable attitude.

"Mr. Donovan, I'd like you to meet Blake Sorenson. Blake, this is my editor, David Donovan."

"You brought our hero? Good job, Tori. Apparently, I underestimated you." Donovan held out his hand, and, for the count of two, Tori waited for Blake to reciprocate.

She wanted to kick him by the time he did.

The smile Blake allowed was nothing more than a showing of teeth. "Donovan. I've wanted to meet you ever since Tori told me you would fire her if she didn't get an interview with me." The piercing gaze he directed at her editor was equivalent to a glove slap in the face.

She *was* going to kick him as soon as she got a chance.

Donovan laughed. "I was about to have a drink. Will the two of you join me? It's Kentucky bourbon, barrel-aged to perfection." He retraced his steps to the bar and set out three glasses before he glanced at them, the question hanging in the air.

Tori shook her head. "No thank you, Mr. Donovan.

His gaze swept to Blake. "Lieutenant Commander?"

"A drink is always welcome...but you can drop the rank. That was a long time ago."

Donovan poured the bourbon in another glass and carried it back to where Tori and Blake still stood. "Please, sit." He swept a hand toward two leather chairs positioned in front of a large mahogany desk and took a seat on the other side, turning his full attention on Blake, leaving Tori feeling like a spectator. "In this business, I can't afford to spend the time and money training a new reporter if she doesn't have what it takes. Tori has an excellent education. She's personable and quite attractive, don't you think? But, unfortunately, she has no experience. So, yes, a new employee with her background has to meet certain criteria." He smiled and took a drink of his whiskey. "I understand from Tori the test was difficult in this case. I hope she wasn't too troublesome."

If Tori didn't get her temper under control, she wouldn't be surprised if smoke started billowing from her ears. She'd gotten the interview Donovan had insisted on, almost been killed in the process, written the story and complied with his demand to deliver it in person. Now, they were talking about her...right in front of her...as though she was invisible. Worse, like she was a side of beef. She'd expected Donovan to be rude and condescending, the arrogant jackass, but Blake, she'd hoped for better from him. She plopped her purse on the edge of Donovan's fancy desk, accidentally knocking over one of his framed pictures. Both men turned their heads to stare at her. Amusement shone in Blake's eyes. *The jerk!*

She searched until she found the thumb drive she'd copied her story to, laid it on the desk and pushed it toward her editor. "Here's your interview, Mr.—"

"Troublesome? No, I wouldn't use that word." Blake had interrupted her without so much as an *excuse me*. "We got off to a bit of a rough start, but once the dust settled and we had a chance to talk, well, I could see how important this job is to her. Right Tori?"

Now he's asking what I think? Through narrowed eyes, she glared at him, his cocky grin making her angrier by the minute. How could he be so sweet and yet so obtuse?

She returned her attention to the man in the three-piece suit. "Thank you for the opportunity, Mr. Donovan, but this job isn't exactly what I had in mind." Tori rose, holding her hand in front of Blake to keep him from standing. "Please, don't get up. I'll find my own way back to the airport."

As she moved to brush by him, he snagged her wrist and shot to his feet.

At the same time, Donovan stood. "I apologize to both of you. That was offensive and presumptuous of me. Tori, I think you have an amazing career as a reporter ahead of you. I have a permanent position opening here. If you want it, it's yours." He held his hands up, palms out. "Don't answer right now. Let me take you and Blake to dinner tonight. No shop talk. Give me a chance to make amends. After dinner, if you decide you like the idea, we'll work out the details over a glass of wine. Sound fair?" He glanced back and forth between Tori and Blake.

Some of Tori's anger evaporated, caught by the offer of a permanent job. It was what she'd worked for—the prize that'd made her jump in the helicopter with Blake against all reason. Would Donovan change? *Probably not.* Was a secure life for Isaiah worth taking a risk? *Yes.*

Blake had wanted to leave for home as soon as she turned in her story. Would he stay? Considering his opinion of Donovan, she wouldn't be surprised if he made an excuse so he could head home without having to sit through dinner with the man. That would be fine with her. She could swing a cheap room and get a commercial flight back in the morning. She was still a little peeved with him, anyway.

"Sounds fair to me. What do you say, Tori?" Blake's deep voice vibrated off her frayed nerves, and she glared at him. Still holding her wrist with a familiar grin riding his lips, he cocked his head. "This could be your dream job. At least hear the man out."

"Are you sure? But you wanted to—"

"Just say the word and I'll get us rooms. We can head back in the morning." Blake's easy manner seemed sincere.

Damn it! How could she continue to be mad at him if he was going to do a one eighty and go all considerate on her again?

Donovan, watching their exchange from a front row seat, clapped his hands together, making Tori jump. "Okay. It's settled." He picked up the handset of his desk phone and dialed a number. "The Kimpton RiverPlace Hotel is only six blocks away. I know the manager there. They have a nice restaurant onsite. I'll take care of this. It's on me." He turned away and spoke into the phone. "Yeah, let me talk to Joe for a minute." Donovan covered the mouthpiece. "Do you have a car, or shall I have them send one?"

"Got transportation covered," Blake replied.

Donovan nodded. "One room or two?"

"Two." Tory and Blake answered at the same time.

When Donovan turned back to his phone call, Blake pushed into her personal space and lowered his voice. "The guy's a creep. You sure you want to work for him?"

What was he doing? Playing devil's advocate? A minute ago, he'd happily joined Donovan, excluding her from their conversation. Then, as soon as Donovan's back was turned, he'd switched gears, concern etched deeply in his furrowed brow.

Suddenly, another possibility occurred to Tori. Had it all been an act? Had Blake only gone along with Donovan's rudeness, talking about her like she wasn't in the room, to highlight it for her—as if she wouldn't have noticed? "Pretty sure I don't, but it's the break I've been hoping for."

"You and Isaiah can stay with me until you find something else."

"That's a nice offer and I appreciate it, but I've imposed on you long enough. It was only supposed to be an interview, you know." Tori's smile earned a wink, along with his sexy grin. The exchange and his closeness caused her stomach to do a little somersault that stole her breath like an upside-down carnival ride. She was almost sorry he didn't argue.

Donovan clattered the phone back in its cradle, giving Blake and Tori time to move apart. "All set. You can get settled and see some of the sights if you want. I'll meet you at the hotel restaurant at seven. Does that work for you?"

"We'll be there," Blake said.

"Good. The reservation will be in my name. Now, if you'll excuse me, I have another appointment." Donovan walked them to the door, his goodbyes graciously phony to Tori's ears.

All the way back to the car, she vacillated. Was she doing the right thing? If she accepted the job, they'd no doubt have to move to Portland. Would Isaiah adjust well? Would she find someone to watch him during the summer and after school that she could trust? Donovan had made it sound like he expected her decision tonight. Would he withdraw the offer if she needed more time?

As they entered the dimly lit parking structure, where they'd left the rental car, Blake moved closer and placed his hand at the small of her back, setting a quicker pace through the expanse of concrete and vehicles. The way he tensed as he scrutinized the rows of cars reminded her of the dangers inherent in large metropolitan areas, and relief that she wasn't alone gave way to worry. If she lived here, there was a good chance she'd be making this trek by herself, or one like it, daily.

Don't be ridiculous! Tori frowned at her own paranoia. Maybe she wasn't a big city girl, but she wasn't a fool either. She'd take a self-defense class—or learn karate. Somehow, she'd make it work...for Isaiah.

Blake had the key in his hand when they reached the rental car, a gray Chrysler 200. Unlocking the passenger side, he stood guard while she scooted in, locking the door before he swung it closed. He strode around the rear of the midsize car, and the driver side door unlocked as he reached for the handle. Sliding behind the wheel, he started the engine, and backed from the parking spot.

Speaking of paranoia! But his attention to their surroundings gave her a sense of safety, which made her like him even more. *Oh God.* She was getting in too deep, depending on him too much. The sooner she got herself and Isaiah out of his house, the better.

Blake paid the attendant and pulled out of the parking structure to the street. She felt his intense inspection turn toward her. "You haven't said two words since we left that asshole's office. Are you okay?"

"Yeah." She shrugged. "Just thinking."

"About taking the job?"

"What else?" Tori laughed to hide her apprehension. "Thanks for going up there with me, Blake."

"I wouldn't have missed it. For the record, the guy's a grade A prick." Blake's frown let her know just how serious he was.

She couldn't argue with him. "I know, but...it's a job. You don't have to sit through dinner with him tonight. I'll tell him you weren't feeling well or something."

His scowl deepened. "Get serious. I'm not letting you go by yourself. I don't trust him."

Tori chafed a little at his presumption he could tell her what to do, but she let it slide. "You realize how absurd that is, right? If I'll be working for him, there'll be times I'll have to be alone with him." At the thought, a shudder crawled up her back, lodging between her shoulder blades.

Apparently, Blake noticed, and a half smirk tilted his lips. "Right. Maybe you should give his offer a little more consideration."

He was right, but Tori refrained from voicing her agreement, turning away and watching the midday traffic zip by on the city street. This wasn't a decision to be made lightly, but it was *hers* to make.

"Hey, you're not still mad at me, are you?"

"I wasn't mad."

"You're a lousy liar. You know that?" Blake laughed. "You were so mad, you were ready to walk out of there." He signaled and turned left on a one-way street before glancing sideways at her. "Frankly, I don't blame you."

Tori frowned at the amusement in his expression, and the anger she'd managed to stifle in Donovan's office boiled anew. "What did you expect? He was a jerk, and *you*...you threw me under the bus. Do men learn that in school, how to be arrogant and superior, or does making women feel insignificant just come naturally for you?" Tori hadn't meant to raise her voice, and, even as the bitter words poured out, she realized the injustice of lumping Blake into the same category as Donovan. Blake's white-knuckled grip on the steering wheel stopped her rant, and she chewed her bottom lip during the ten-second silence that followed.

Blake's dark gaze held a touch of exasperation. "I thought you'd know I was only going along with him to prove a point." Stopping for a red light, he regarded her, a reckless curve to his mouth.

"Which was?"

"Proving what a douchebag Donovan is. I figured I'd give him some rope and let him hang himself." Blake gave a rueful laugh as traffic started moving again. "Didn't count on pulling the noose tight around my own neck."

His self-deprecating humor proved too much for Tori and she laughed.

"Oh, you think that's funny, huh? Nice." But the relief in his deep-brown eyes was priceless. His grin remained in place as he faced front again. "Holy shit! That must be our hotel."

Blake changed lanes and turned into the long driveway. Immaculately landscaped lawns bordered both sides with twin rows of stately elm trees shading the asphalt from the afternoon heat. The huge, four-story, colonial-style hotel loomed straight ahead. The Willamette River sparkled in the setting sun to their left, and a veritable flotilla of boats were berthed in the marina. In stark contrast to the peacefulness of the setting, a maze of bridges, highways and overpasses intertwined just across the river.

A valet met them in front of the lobby door. Blake handed over the keys and an impressive tip and grabbed their bags from the trunk. A doorman stepped outside and ushered them into the lobby. Blake stood aside, and Tori went first. The interior was opulent with slate tile floors, walls of varying brown tones, blue accents, and burnished wood throughout. A massive stone fireplace lined the wall opposite the registration desk, and tasteful crystal chandeliers sparkled from high ceilings.

"May I help you?" An attractive woman smiled from behind the counter.

Blake stepped toward her. "I believe David Donovan made reservations for us. Sorenson and Michaels?"

"Of course, sir. Everything has been arranged." She was all smiles as she handed Blake two key cards. "Your rooms are on the fourth floor, and Mr. Donovan has made dinner reservations for the three of you at seven. I'll call a bellhop to help you with your luggage."

"Not necessary. We're traveling light." Blake passed the keys to Tori and picked up the two small bags.

"Very well. The elevator is around the corner to your right. Enjoy your stay."

Funny how the desk clerk's warm welcome seemed entirely for Blake. Tori bit her lip to keep the amused snicker from erupting. Frankly, she couldn't blame the woman. Blake was, without question, a hot commodity. As she followed him toward the elevator, she admired his smooth gait, the muscles of his back and shoulders flexing with each tread. His amazing ass and muscular thighs, encased in snug denim, begged to be touched, and the sudden, overwhelming desire to do just that sent a tidal wave of warmth clear to her toes. Too bad she wasn't over being mad at him yet.

Blake stopped abruptly, and Tori bumped into him. She backed quickly away, but not before her hands landed somewhere between his powerfully built hips and the pockets on the back of his jeans to stop her forward motion.

Tori crossed her arms as heat blazed a trail straight to her cheeks. "Sorry. I must have been daydreaming." She looked away from the shrewd grin that spread, unchecked, across his face.

Holding both bags with one hand, he pressed the call button for the elevator, and the doors opened as though it'd been sitting there waiting for them. He swept his arm toward the interior, ushering her inside. Once he entered, Tori pushed the fourth-floor button, and the elevator car whirred to life.

She chanced a covert glimpse toward Blake, only to find him chuckling softly. "What's so funny?"

His eyes glowed with mirth as he raised them to meet hers. "Did you grope me on purpose? You did, didn't you?"

Embarrassment wrapped her in a blanket of God-I-wish-I-could-die-right-here insecurity, which finally managed to piss her off. Three days of Blake keeping her off-balance was enough. The person she'd turned into since she asked him for an interview wasn't who she'd worked her ass off to become for the past two years. She wasn't some wallflower, afraid of her own shadow. She was strong and independent, with confidence in spades. Of course, Blake wouldn't know that because meeting him had started her on a path where fear seemed to hover around every corner. It was high time he was the one caught off guard for a change.

She sent him an innocent smile, served with a dash of indifference. "Maybe. Does it matter?" Her soft voice was a murmur, barely audible above the whine of elevator cables. Perhaps he hadn't even heard her.

She didn't have to wonder for long.

The amusement in Blake's expression faded as he studied her, his brown eyes going two shades darker in the time it took to blink. He dropped the bags and, in one stride, pinned her against the side of the car with his hard, immovable body. His massive arms against the wall on each side of her shoulders thwarted any plan she might have had to escape. Silly man, the thought of forfeiting this skirmish hadn't entered her mind.

"What are you doing?" Tori tipped her chin up until she could look in his eyes, her heart beating faster at the intensity in them.

"Does it matter?" He dipped his head until his hot breath moved the hair near her temple with his soft words. "Yes, it *matters*, because you just flirted with me. There might have been some sexual innuendo in there too...and that makes all your rules null and void." One hand brushed her hair back so her throat was exposed, and his lips grazed the bared skin.

Tori couldn't hide a shiver, which vibrated through her body, as he alternately kissed and licked her neck. "You call that flirting?" She'd intended to argue further but, at the last second, closed her mouth before giving voice to her doubt.

A groan rumbled from Blake's chest, and he stepped closer, pressing his thigh between her legs in a way that made his thick arousal hard to miss. "You know damn well it was."

Did she? Admittedly, she'd carefully chosen her words to redirect his attention, to claim her identity in a world that'd gone temporarily insane. If she recanted now, they'd fall back into the same roles they'd been playing. Her the confused, vulnerable damsel in distress. Him the confident, capable and hot Navy SEAL who, apparently, took rescuing said damsel very seriously. Okay, so she didn't totally hate the part he played, and it wasn't like she hadn't needed rescuing, but enough was enough.

Besides, he smelled heavenly of spice and good, clean soap, and his velvety lips, currently teasing her neck, were presenting an argument for letting go of her rules, if only for a little while.

She raised her hands to gently trace the veins that rose in stark relief on the underside of his forearms. "All right. Let's say maybe I *did* touch your perfectly squeezable ass on purpose, though I admit nothing."

Blake exhaled with a surprised laugh.

"And let's say that constitutes some kind of weird flirting or sexual come-on in your book."

Blake's eyes sparkled with amusement. "Hey! Any man will tell you his ass is off limits…unless the woman is willing to reciprocate." His roguish grin contained just a hint of casual intimacy as he slid his arms around her waist and inched them lower.

Tori slapped his chest and narrowed her eyes in warning until his hands stopped wandering. "Let me get this straight. You want to throw out my rules that you agreed to. Rules meant to protect both of us from repeating mistakes we're determined to avoid. Right?"

An air of consternation bred confusion in his expression. "Well… yeah…I guess. I mean…we're both adults. We know where the line is we're not willing to cross."

Suddenly, the elevator came to an abrupt stop, settled, and a *ping* heralded the appearance of a digital four above the doors as they slid apart. Thankfully, the hallway outside was empty. No one waited for access to the lower levels of the hotel. Blake punched a button, and the doors closed again, the elevator in limbo, its electronic brain awaiting its next command.

Tori tilted her head, a smile working free. "I think this is our floor."

"We're not finished yet," Blake growled.

She sobered, searching his eyes. "Where does that leave us, Blake?"

He stared as seconds ticked by before a crooked grin relieved his solemn expression. "Well, it leaves *me* standing here with a substantial hard-on, wanting to get to know you better."

Tori sputtered a laugh and leaned her forehead against his chest.

He took the opportunity to cinch his arms tighter around her. "Tori, look at me."

When she lifted her head, he drew his knuckle down her cheek with the utmost gentleness. Then his mouth claimed hers, devouring her, his tongue crossing the seam of her lips effortlessly to mix with hers. His taste was heady and addictive. His strong arms pulled her closer, his hands caressing her back before dropping lower to palm her butt cheeks and lift her against the rigid outline of the impressive bulge that amplified the snugness of his jeans.

Tori fisted her hands in his hair and held his mouth to hers, feasting on his beautifully shaped male lips. A moan escaped her only to be muffled in the onslaught of his kiss. He must have taken that as a good sign, because he allowed her to slide down his body until her tiptoes reached the floor, his muscled thigh forcing her legs farther apart.

She barely noticed him ducking down, his hands doing a slow skim down her sides, until his long fingers curled around the backs of her thighs, lifted her off the floor and positioned her legs around his hips. His muscular body held her against the wall, creating the perfect opportunity to rock his hips into her, repeatedly. His maleness right where she needed to feel him, her breasts plumped against his chest wall and his mouth doing erotic things to her lips, neck, chin and the bare skin of her cleavage, Tori's breaths heaved shallowly, never allowing quite enough air.

Can a person suffocate and die in the throes of passion? Still, she was reluctant to cut short the irresistible spell he wove.

Suddenly, he broke away from her, letting her slip down his hard body again, and loosened his arms so she could breathe. Tori sank back against the elevator wall, and Blake steadied her.

He was breathing hard as well. When he met her gaze, he grinned and stepped close again, leaning his forehead against hers. "We need a room, right now. Otherwise, I'm going to rip your clothes off in here and dare anyone else to get on until we're done." His voice was low and scratchy.

Tori smiled, still trying to force air into her lungs.

Her silence must have worried him. He gripped her shoulders and squeezed until she looked at him. "Say the word, sweetheart, and we'll stop right here. I'm sure this hotel has cold water in their showers."

Tori shook her head. Stopping was the last thing she wanted.

Without warning, the elevator doors opened, and Tori stared at the surprised faces of a sixty-something couple who were about to step into the car. She tried not to laugh as their horrified perusals swept up and down the breathless, wild-looking length of her and Blake and came to a stop on Blake's obvious arousal. Her laugh sputtered free, echoing around the interior of the car.

"Sorry. It's all yours." Blake grabbed the two bags he'd dropped and Tori's hand, dragging her out of the car into the hallway and didn't stop until they heard the doors slide together behind them.

Tori broke up in laughter again, until Blake pulled her around in front of him and laid an urgent kiss on her lips. "Your room or mine?"

Her body reacted to his harsh rasp, and she couldn't look away from his dark, lust-filled eyes and his perfect lips. She'd shoved the key cards in her pocket while she followed Blake out of the lobby, enjoying the view. Smiling her agreement, she pulled the cards, glancing at the numbers and comparing them to the nearby doors.

"Whichever one is closer." Grabbing his free hand, she hauled him down the aisle behind her, pretty sure he was gawking at her ass.

Chapter 13

Tori stopped in front of room 422 and fumbled the key card, finally sliding it into the slot only to have the light on the door plate remain red. She swiped the card again with the same result. Unable to wait another second, Blake plucked the key from her hand, unlocked the door, and shoved it open. He followed her into the room, dropped the bags just inside and closed the space between them as Tori threw the deadbolt.

Before she could turn, Blake slid his arms around her, pulling her back against him. One hand toyed with the hard bead that formed with the flicking of his thumb across her breast. She threw her head back against his chest and arched into his hand. A groan left him as he lowered his mouth to the wildly beating pulse in her throat and licked a path to her ear. The aroma of magnolias, with a hint of orange blossoms mixed in, assailed his senses. Sucking her lobe between his teeth, he bit down until she gasped. His need was too urgent, banishing any hope of being a gentle or considerate lover.

He lifted his head, hoping to regain a measure of control over himself. "I didn't intend to come at you like a freight train, but you're making me crazy." He whispered in her ear and a shiver ran the length of her body. Everywhere she pressed against him, he was on fire. Another groan flowed out on a sigh as his hands touched the bare skin of her abdomen and continued upward until there was nothing between him and the delicious weight of her breasts but a thin veil of lacy fabric.

Her sweet ass brushed his swollen manhood, and Blake nearly lost it right there. Even as his feverish brain screamed a warning not to rush this, his other hand unbuttoned her jeans and lowered the zipper. Lost in the sensations caused by the friction of their bodies, he slid his hand between her jeans and the small patch of fabric that covered her hot, wet sex, cupping her mound and urging her up on her toes as he pulled her against his aching member.

A feral growl escaped, bringing back some of his awareness. Reluctantly, he released her and turned her to face him with trembling hands. As much as he wanted Tori, he wanted to please her more. The all-consuming desire racing through him had little to do with his own pleasure and everything to do with slowly making love to this woman...and then doing it again... and again.

The knowledge shocked him. When, since Celine, had he ever wanted or needed a repeat performance with any of the women he'd slept with?

Tori eyed him, worry forming a small crease on her forehead. "Are you all right?"

How long had he been standing there, staring into her eyes? Blake brought her close again and lowered his head to meet her lips. Tenderness held his desire at bay as he gently kissed the corners of her mouth. He let her go and carefully lifted the hem of her sweater with a tilt of his head, watching for any hesitation on her part while hoping his checking out for a few seconds hadn't been a deal breaker.

"I'm great, as long as you're here with me, but I find myself needing to know you're still okay with this." God, he must sound like a first-class chump, but when she smiled and encouraged his hands to lift her top up and over her head, that was the answer he'd hoped for.

"Did I do something to make you think I'd changed my mind?" Tori breathed the words as his lips closed over hers.

Blake straightened and captured her gaze again. Not looking away, he unsnapped her bra and slid it down her arms until it dropped at her feet. "No, but some things are just too good to be true."

A smile formed and spread until her dimples appeared. Blake kissed first one, then the other, before settling on her mouth with a burning kiss. Tori slipped her arms around his neck, moaning into his mouth as she pressed her nakedness against him.

Needing to feel her skin against his, he suddenly had too many clothes on. Reaching one hand over his shoulder, he grabbed a fistful of his shirt and peeled it over his head. His dick jerked behind his zipper as he pulled her into his embrace, landing kisses and nips along her bare shoulders and up the column of her throat to her jaw. She still wasn't close enough, so he placed his hands around her waist and lifted her off the floor until her legs wrapped around his hips. Then he turned and carried her toward the bed.

At the edge of the mattress, he stopped and let her down until her feet touched the floor, enjoying every slow, delicious inch of her. "Don't move." With a hand on each side of her waistband, he pulled her jeans down her legs, inside out, nudging her backward until she bounced on the edge of the bed. He finished peeling her pants off and tossed them on the floor somewhere behind him. Pulling her to her feet again, he stepped back to look his fill. Damn, she was beautiful. Her skin glowed with the heat of her blood pulsing through her veins...for him. That was fucking hot, and, though he didn't think it possible, his shaft hardened even more.

As he admired her body, Tori began to squirm, obviously uncomfortable with his exacting scrutiny.

"Don't move." He repeated his command, and her soft-blue eyes raised to his. "You're beautiful, Tori. Let me look at you."

Her cheeks blushed a rosy shade of pink, but she stilled. Then her focus dropped to the bulge in his pants, and she stepped toward him, her hand outstretched. Blake released her and stood still as her seeking fingers undid the button and pulled his zipper down, allowing his manhood to burst forth as far as his briefs would allow.

Her gaze found his again and damned if he didn't want to know what she was thinking. A faint smile hitched one corner of her mouth as she reached to pull his briefs down enough to let his straining member free. When her hand curled around him, his knees almost gave out. His shaft throbbed and jerked as she inched toward the head, her fingers sliding across the tip in sheer fucking torment of the best kind. He'd be done before he even got started if she kept that up.

Blake caught her arms when she would have dropped to her knees in front of him. "Not that I don't appreciate the offer, but not this time. It's been a while for me, and I'd rather not finish early." Blake stepped toward her, forcing her to back into the mattress and drop down on her ass and elbows, a look of surprised amusement filling her eyes. When he pushed her legs apart and knelt between them, Tori tried to climb farther up the bed, away from him, but his arms, wrapped around her thighs, held her in place.

"Wait. If I can't, then you can't either." She pointed a finger at him, a smile teasing her lips.

"Says who? You don't get to make the rules anymore. I'm in charge now." Blake grinned before running one finger across the white fabric that covered her intimate parts. "Do you have more panties in your bag?"

"What? Why? And who put *you* in charge?"

With one tug, the panties tore. Another tug and they were off.

Tori sucked in a breath. "You ripped them? What are you, a caveman?"

The laughter in her accusation assured him they were still in this together, and it was a good thing. He might have whizzed by the point of no return a few minutes ago. "I always *wanted* to be a caveman!"

She huffed a laugh until his wide shoulders nudged her legs farther apart, and he ran his tongue upward through her wet folds, around her swollen womanhood, and back down.

"Holy hell!" The words jumped from her mouth as though she had no control, which she confirmed a heartbeat later when she slapped her hands over her mouth to muffle her cries as she writhed and arched into his mouth.

Her reaction was so damn sexy, Blake couldn't stop himself from taking the same journey with his tongue, this time stopping at the nub of her sex and bathing it with attention. Her muffled cries, her desperate panting, and the death grip she had on the bed covers told him all he needed to know. One more touch of his tongue to her sensitive core and she came with a shudder of surrender and his name on her lips.

When the trembling of her body eased, and she lay relaxed and pliant, he stood and leaned over her, claiming her mouth for a lingering kiss before he straightened and shed the rest of his clothes. From his wallet, he fished out two condoms and then added another one just in case. *A man could always dream.* In five seconds, he had the package open and the condom seated. He crawled to the center of the bed, hauling her up with him.

When he spread his body over hers, there were tears on her cheeks. Dread swirled in his stomach. Did she regret being with him already? He dried them with his thumbs and kissed her tenderly, somehow managing to put his urgency aside. "Hey, sweetheart. What's wrong? Why are you crying? Talk to me, please."

Tori opened her eyes and smiled into his, sweeping her hand down his bristled cheek. "It's nothing. Really. It's just…more emotion than I'm used to."

Blake studied her for any indication she was holding something back. He hated the idea she might lie to him. Nothing in her eyes or expression gave him reason to doubt her, but the exercise made him remember why he'd come to Portland with her. He was supposed to find out if she was conspiring with Sebastian Wahl to harm the Perez family. Did he really want to know? Could he turn her over to the authorities if she was? An ache formed in his gut. The answer was *yes*, but at what cost?

She must have sensed his uncertainty, because she pulled his head down for a heated kiss, sweeping her tongue into his mouth, allowing him to push his doubts aside, at least for now. With a growl from his diaphragm, he claimed her, his desire all-consuming. His tip at her opening, he rocked his hips and, with one thrust, embedded himself balls deep. He gritted his teeth against the nearly overwhelming urge to take her hard and fast. He'd never hesitated before when seeking his gratification with some woman he barely knew and would never see again, but Tori was different. Though he didn't know her as well as he wanted to, the mere thought of not seeing her again opened the vault of loneliness he'd buried long ago.

Tori thrust her hips upward, causing his breath to expel in a hiss. *Damn.* She was hot, wet silk and fit him like a glove. He filled her completely, and her walls, constricting around him, felt amazing. *Jesus! I could get used to this.*

His lips explored the soft skin of her throat to her breasts, where he teased her, flexing his tongue across the pebbled peaks until she moaned her pleasure. Fisting his hands in her hair, as he'd wanted to do from the first moment he'd seen her, he captured her mouth and thrust his tongue deep as he started to move his hips. Out slowly and back in, their bodies driving together with the force of their lust, he maintained a pace that spawned a torturous anticipation in every nerve ending. Soon, though, his thrusts became harder and faster as any semblance of control deserted him, and he pounded into her with each agonizing stroke, his release building to a blinding crescendo.

Tori's chest heaved with uneven breaths. Wrapping her legs around his hips, she opened herself for him to slip deeper, his name rasping from kiss-swollen lips. He was so close, and yet he didn't want to fly without her. He slid one hand between their sweating bodies to where they were joined. A stroke of his thumb across her sensitive center, and she raked her nails down his back, a little whimper escaping.

With dwindling restraint, he rubbed and fondled until every muscle in her body went taut. Her climax hit with enough force to wrench a cry from her throat, and the way she said his name in the heat of their lovemaking was the hottest damn thing he'd ever experienced. Two more fierce pumps of his hips and he gritted his teeth with a groan of sweet agony. Hands under her firm, round ass, he crushed her against him as he pressed deep and splintered into a thousand pieces.

* * * *

Blake wasn't sure how long he lay there, his body covering hers, his weight pressing her into the mattress. After the best sex he'd ever had, it'd taken him a while to recoup his senses. He quickly slid off her. Not that she was complaining. As he pulled her to her side with him, her eyes popped open, and a tiny purring sound preceded a smile, complete with dimples. He brushed back a lock of hair that'd fallen forward over her face, then groaned and leaned in for another kiss. The need to possess and protect raged through him. Two emotions he'd locked down long ago. Not even with Celine had he experienced this gut-level craving for a woman.

Locking his arms around Tori, he rolled to his back, pulling her on top of him. "I could do that about a zillion more times." He continued to rain kisses on her face and throat.

Her lips curled in a smile. "Really?" She tipped her head toward the nightstand, where two more condoms waited. "And here I thought you were being optimistic with three."

A belly laugh burst from Blake, and he slapped one delectable cheek of her ass...hard.

"Ouch! What—?"

"Behave yourself...or I'll show you optimistic." He dropped his hands to her waist and lifted her horizontally up his body until her rosy nipples were positioned just right. Latching on to one with his mouth, he suckled the erotic tip until a whimper sounded in the back of her throat. Then he released that one, licked the other nipple, and drew it deep into his mouth, rolling it between his tongue and teeth until she raked her nails through his hair. His dick twitched and hardened between her thighs.

Tori's eyes widened, having obviously become aware of his reawakening.

Blake grinned and caught her face between his hands, licking her sexy bottom lip until she opened for him and he swept inside.

Her response was immediate and bold, lifting his hands and placing them over his head, leaning her weight on his wrists—as though she could keep him from escaping and turning the tables. But her mouth on his, her hair tickling his face every time she pulled away for a second and those full, sassy breasts teasing the short hairs on his chest convinced him there was no place else he'd rather be.

Blake raised his shoulders a few inches off the bed, bearing her weight and his with his abs, smacked a wet, rough kiss on her tempting lips and rolled her over until he again pinned her beneath him. Another taste of her and he slid from the bed. "I have to get rid of this condom. Don't go anywhere, sweetheart."

Blake strode to the bathroom, tossed the condom and cleaned up a little. Catching his image in the mirror, he stopped. His collar-length black hair could use a trim and was that gray masquerading as highlights? When had that happened? Shit. He looked rode-hard-and-put-up-wet. He was only thirty-five...going on fifty. All those special ops missions he'd undertaken had obviously aged him. The helicopter crash that killed two wounded SEALs and ended his career had taken a few years off his life too. Then Christian had been shot and come home paralyzed, and Blake's mission had become trying to put his brother's life back together. Yeah, he'd earned every one of those gray hairs.

What the hell business did he have thinking he could be anything to a beautiful, passionate woman like Tori? She had to be at least a half dozen years younger than him. Single mother. Way out of his league. *And don't forget, she still might prove to be a criminal—party to a conspiracy to commit murderer.*

Fuck! He didn't want to believe she was capable of such an act. Did that make him a traitor to his brothers-in-arms, the Perezes and everything he held to be good and true? He should have kept his distance. Should never have had sex with her. Hell, he shouldn't even be in this hotel with her, much less the same room.

Grabbing a wash cloth, Blake stomped to the shower, turned on the cold water and stepped under the frigid spray. Once his partial hard-on was a thing of the past, he cranked the hot water, soaped up and rinsed off. Then he stood with his back to the spray nozzle, letting the hot torrent pummel his neck and shoulders.

Donovan was a jackass, and Blake didn't like him, but the guy didn't fit the profile of Sebastian Wahl's group of hard-asses. He would check with Coop later to see if he'd learned anything about the magazine editor that might raise a warning flag. If not, Blake would have to admit David Donovan was unlikely to represent a physical danger to Tori. He'd have to step aside and keep his mouth shut while she accepted the slime ball's job offer. Blake had nothing long-term to offer her or Isaiah. Permanent wasn't in the cards for them.

An avalanche of emptiness rolled over him, leaving an ache in his chest. *What the hell is wrong with me?*

"Everything okay in here?"

Blake's gaze darted to Tori, standing outside the shower, naked, one hand holding the curtain back. Concern and disappointment warred on her expressive face as the silence stretched. Looking all sexy and vulnerable, her hair tousled from their lovemaking, she waited, a sad smile making him feel like an ass.

"Um...I'm sorry. I didn't mean to take so long, but I needed a quick shower. Feels great. It's all yours when I'm done." *Oh yeah...that's*

*believable. Every guy stops on the verge of another round of amazing
sex to take a shower.*

Her smile grew even fainter. "Oh. Okay." She hesitated as though
wondering what to do next. "You know what? I'll just get dressed and go to
my room." The shower curtain dropped back in place as she started to leave.

"Wait." Blake shoved the curtain aside. She'd obviously picked up on his
doubts. For a moment, she hesitated, her shoulders slumped. It killed him
to see the defeat and pain in her eyes and know the blame was his. Tori had
put aside her fears and surrendered to him. This was how he repaid her?

His hand shot out and caught her arm before she turned away. "I'd like
you to stay."

Please stay. Suddenly, what he wanted was so clear—*her.*

With one smile, the woman had turned him inside out, given him
expectations he shouldn't have, scattered his arguments like wheat chaff
in the wind. He wanted her in his life, if only for a little while, and the
realization scared the shit out of him. What did he know about the domestic
scene, relationships, or kids, for that matter? Nevertheless, he'd pitch his
tent firmly on the side of her innocence and prove it to MacGyver and
the others.

"Please, don't go. Join me? I'll wash your back." A wink from him
loosed her dimples. He offered his hand and, when she took it, helped her
step over the side of the tub and pulled her into his arms.

She melted against him as though they'd done this a thousand times.
Curling her hands around his neck, she brought his lips to hers and dotted
him with soft, wispy, butterfly kisses so gentle it drove him wild.

His hardening shaft jerked, coming back to attention with an agenda
Blake was looking forward to exploring. He slid his hands down her
back, splayed them over her spectacular ass, and held her in place while
he rocked against her soft belly.

She glanced at him, a mischievous smile situated on her dimpled face.
An instant later, she reached to wrap her hand around his erection and
dropped to her knees at his feet. His manhood disappeared into her warm,
wet mouth, her tongue wrapping around him as she sucked him deeper.

Blake fisted both hands in her hair when he thought his legs might give
out. Then he lost the ability to think as all the blood rushed from his head.
Squeezing his eyes closed, his teeth ground together as wave after wave
of pleasure built toward a tsunami in his soul.

Oh yeah. Hell, yeah. I'm totally screwed.

Maybe later, after reason returned, he'd care.

Chapter 14

Tori glanced at her watch. Five after seven. Heaving a sigh, she tapped out a text message to Blake. *We're late. I'll meet you downstairs.*

She grabbed her purse and a sweater, in case the dining room was chilly, and exited the room, carefully closing the door behind her. A quick perusal down the hallway confirmed that Blake was, indeed, late. A frown ruffled her composure as she headed for the elevator. Great. Keeping the prospective boss waiting always made for a good impression.

The black slacks and white silk shirt she wore had been packed only as an afterthought. It was supposed to be a quick trip, just long enough to turn in her story. But it had changed into an overnighter.

Tori's stomach twisted nervously as her mind replayed her phone conversation with Isaiah. He'd been disappointed when she told him they wouldn't be home until tomorrow. She could almost see him jutting out his chin, putting a brave face on for this new development, but she'd heard the uneasiness in his voice. The feeling was mutual. Tori was also anxious about leaving her son in the care of people who were literally strangers to her. Blake had assured her he'd be safe, cared for and probably slightly spoiled before they returned.

Blake. She'd gone and done it now, broken her one hard-and-fast rule. An errant smile tugged at her mouth, and she bit her lip to subdue the unsolicited reminder of their mind-blowing afternoon of sex. Her heart rate kicked up a notch as she stepped inside the elevator, pressed the lobby button and tried to ignore the wall Blake had pinned her against only hours ago. If she was lucky, she wouldn't run into the poor couple who'd walked in and caught them groping and grinding. That was definitely a first for her. In fact, there'd been a number of firsts with the hunky SEAL. *Whoa, is it hot in here?*

The elevator doors slid open, and Tori strode across the lobby and down a short hallway where a maître d' stood behind a podium just inside the restaurant entrance.

"May I help you?" The man's British accent flowed pleasingly over her frazzled nerves.

"I'm meeting David Donovan, party of three. Has he arrived yet?"

"Yes, ma'am. Mr. Donovan is in the bar. If you'd like to join him there, I'll let you know as soon as your table is ready." The maître d' tipped his head toward a dimly lit room to her right.

"Thank you." Tori straightened her shoulders, brushed away her sense of dread and marched into the bar. Right away, David Donovan stood and waved to her from a table in the center of the room. She started toward him, forcing a smile.

When she reached him, he greeted her with a warm handshake and pulled out her chair. "Where's our *hero*?" His emphasis on the last word grated on her innate sense of respect for all military men and women.

Tori seated herself, while trying to ignore the annoyance generated by his reference to Blake in such a flippant manner. "He'll be here any moment."

"Excellent." Donovan pushed her chair in and sat next to her. "My friend, the manager, just came by to say they've overbooked a couple seven o'clock time slots, and it might be thirty minutes or so before we get a table." Clearly irritated, he frowned at the cocktail waitress, who stopped at their table and asked if they wanted drinks.

Super! A thirty-minute wait with Donovan and still no sign of Blake. "I'd like a gin and tonic, please."

"Make mine bourbon neat."

After the waitress left with their orders, Donovan's cell phone chirped, and he lifted it from the inside breast pocket of his suit jacket and glanced at the screen. "I had the car brought around. We're going down the street to another place I know where they don't screw up the reservations."

"But...we just ordered a drink and Blake isn't here yet. I don't mind waiting a few minutes for a table." Tori despised impatience, and rudeness to waitstaff was right up there with lying.

"I *do* mind." Donovan scraped his chair as he got to his feet. "I'll send the car back for Sorenson." He held out his hand to help her up.

Tori stared at the man beside her, who was so obviously ready to make a scene because of a restaurant employee's mistake. If she refused, would she only make it worse?

A warm palm touched her back, between her shoulder blades, and Blake leaned close to brush a kiss on her temple. "You left without me, sweetheart. Sorry I'm late." He turned toward Donovan and offered his hand. "I hope you haven't been waiting too long." His deep, rich voice calmed Tori.

After a few beats delay, Donovan shook Blake's hand, then signaled for the cocktail waitress before pulling a smile for Tori, easing the frustration from his face. "No problem. I was just telling Tori there was some confusion with our reservation. She was gracious enough to say she didn't mind waiting. I hope you agree."

"Of course." Blake moved to the other side of Tori and sat, reaching for her hand.

Tori let him enfold her fingers gladly, glancing at Donovan as he resumed his seat. What just happened? Had she missed something? A second before Blake joined them, Donovan had all but insisted they go somewhere else. Blake's arrival had seemed to change Donovan's mind without another word being said.

The waitress brought Tori's and Donovan's drinks. Blake ordered a beer and leaned back, his shoulder brushing Tori's. With him so close, she was able to reevaluate the situation and relax.

The thirty minutes sped by with Blake answering Donovan's questions as the editor delved deeper into Blake's military career than she had. Grudgingly, she had to admit she should have asked many of those questions and that perhaps Donovan was an experienced journalist who could teach her a thing or two. If she wanted to succeed in the business, she would need all the help she could get.

Once they were seated in the dining area, their orders taken, Tori turned to Blake. "How many lives would you say your actions saved over your fifteen-year career as a Navy SEAL?" From the corner of her eye she saw Donovan nodding his approval.

Blake smiled at her, but she didn't miss the brief flash of pain in his eyes. "SEALs work as a team. Anyone I had a hand in saving could be claimed just as legitimately by every member of the team…so, I hope you're not disappointed to learn I didn't keep a running tally."

On the contrary. Each time she learned something new about this man, she admired him more. The guy was too good to be true, if she didn't count the whole military issue that made her avoid his type. That was still just as relevant as it was before they'd had sex all afternoon. Tori felt Blake's gaze on her as a wave of heat enveloped her. Good Lord. All he had to do was look at her, smile or wink and she was a goner. He wasn't playing fair, and she had to get a handle on her runaway emotions before Isaiah suffered any adverse effects.

"What about deaths you couldn't prevent? Aside from the enemy you targeted, I mean. Did you run a tally on them?" Donovan voiced the question in all seriousness, and his narrowed eyes stared into Blake's.

Silence reigned for a few seconds as Blake studied the other man. "Most were due to team fails…but there are a few I take sole responsibility for."

"And what does that mean exactly—taking responsibility for them?" The mood at the table changed as Donovan pressed Blake further.

A shadow crossed Blake's visage. "Those are the ones I carry with me every day of my life. The ones I dream about when I wake up screaming… wishing the result could be different, but it never changes. Two years of anger management classes twice a week didn't come close to helping me live with myself, knowing I failed them."

Blake swept a cautious glance toward Tori, and she recognized the guilt that seemed to possess him, and something else, shame, maybe. His meaning was clear in that brief glimpse into his soul. She'd been right not to trust him completely. He *did* suffer from the same malady that killed her husband. Sure, he'd adjusted better to civilian life. He had his friends, his trees and his aircraft. But the need to forget lurked just beneath the surface.

I don't want him to be right.

Donovan held up his hands. "Sorry. It wasn't my intention to strike a nerve. Your selfless service to our country is enough. Let's just leave it at that. Can I get anyone another drink?" He signaled for the waitress before anyone answered and made a circular motion with his finger.

Two minutes later, another round of drinks sat in front of them. Tori drank hers quickly, hoping the burn of alcohol would somehow erase the regret stamped on Blake's forehead.

Donovan prattled on, oblivious to the cloud that had fallen over Blake's side of the table. Tori would have given anything to go back and not ask the question that had started them down that road. It was almost as though his pain was hers as well. Her throat ached from holding back tears that no one would understand. She was relieved when Donovan moved the conversation to the magazine publishing business and spoke animatedly about the upcoming special edition which would include Blake's interview.

Tori was able to ask the right questions to keep him talking and was impressed by Donovan's passion and attention to detail that seemed to pervade every aspect of the business he'd started as a twenty-one-year-old college graduate. That achievement alone spoke of his intelligence and determination.

Blake seemed to shake off his dark mood gradually, rejoining the conversation as smoothly as he'd left. When they were finished eating, he rested his hand on her thigh under cover of the tablecloth. His touch set off a maelstrom of reactions in her body, all of them good but highly inappropriate for dinner with her new boss. She rotated her head to study Blake, and relief brought out her smile at the twinkle of mischief in his eyes.

The waitress removed their empty plates and brought the ticket for Donovan to sign. "Hey, darlin', we're going to retire to the bar, so be a good girl and bring us another round in there, okay?" He handed her a hundred-dollar tip.

Blake held up his hand and shook his head. "You and Tori have business to discuss, and I don't need to be involved. I'm going to bail…if Tori's okay with that." He turned his head to look at her.

No. She still hadn't decided what she would tell Donovan. Two drinks in quick succession had relaxed her…but also relegated her brain to about half a step behind her tongue. She needed more time. She needed to broach the subject of moving to Isaiah. And she desperately needed Blake's opinion.

Giving voice to that would make her look like a foolish child in front of the man she might be working for. The three hundred dollars and some change she had in her checking account blinked through her memory like a neon bar light. She needed the job. Besides, Blake had done enough for her, and he had plenty to juggle without being her security blanket too.

She smiled. "Of course. We'll be talking work hours and 401(k)s. You'd be bored stiff." Tori immediately regretted her choice of words when his eyes caught a humorous sparkle.

He leaned toward her and placed a soft kiss on her cheek. "Check in later," he whispered.

* * * *

Apparently, David Donovan could be a charmer when he tried. He'd beguiled Tori into thinking the job he offered was almost the best thing that'd ever happened to her. The pay was phenomenal, the benefits, like health insurance and vacation, were extremely generous, and a flexible work schedule was a dream come true for a single mom. There was no way she could turn it down.

Yet doubts lingered. Not about the job…but the man. There was something about him that made her draw back if he got in her space, shrink away when he touched her accidentally. She couldn't pinpoint a reason for her reactions. Donovan was attentive to her questions and concerns. She didn't get any weird vibes from him to indicate he might use his power and position to gain sexual favors. He seemed genuinely nice. And he was easy on the eyes. So, what was her problem?

Donovan signaled the server and ordered yet another round of drinks. "I'm going to convince you *Everyday Heroes* magazine is the place for you if we have to sit here drinking all night."

Tori laughed, already feeling the slowed thinking process and weakness in her extremities from the first three drinks. "I think I've had enough, Mr. Donovan. I better stick to water."

"Oh, no." Donovan wagged his finger at her as their server placed the new order on the table and hurried away. "I'm not going to be the only one drinking." With a grin, he lifted his glass. "To new beginnings, Tori."

It was the fourth…or maybe fifth toast he'd made in an effort to influence her decision. Reluctantly, Tori clinked glasses and swallowed a sip of her gin and tonic.

He frowned. "How many times have I asked you not to call me Mr. Donovan? I'm not nearly old enough for that distinction. Call me David. Please."

"All right, David. It's getting late. We should call it a night. I'd like to sleep on your offer." Maybe tomorrow, when she was sober, she could figure out why her gut was telling her not to jump into this. "Just give me twenty-four hours and I'll have an answer for you."

"Oh, hell, Tori." He issued an exasperated sigh. "There's nothing I hate worse than waiting for the phone to ring. At least let me call you. Wait—you said you lost your phone. Have you replaced it yet?"

"I haven't had time, but Blake loaned me one temporarily."

"Great. What's the number?" Donovan grabbed a cocktail napkin. "Got a pen?"

Tori shuffled through her purse, strangely hesitant to give the man her new information, considering the reservations she was having after spending the evening with him. "I'm sorry. I don't seem to have one."

"That's okay." He smirked as he seized his phone from the pocket of his jacket. "This'll work better, anyway. Your number?" His fingers were poised to dial.

Tori groaned. All of her senses were screaming *no,* yet if she took the job, he'd need to be able to reach her. Why the reluctance?

Because I need time to think, and I need to take back some control in this life gone crazy. That's why.

Maybe her mind was simply too sluggish, but she couldn't come up with a single way to refuse him without offending him and almost certainly losing out on the job offer altogether.

As soon as he punched in her number, her phone buzzed. She snatched it from the side pocket of her purse and declined the call, forcing a smile. "It won't do any good to call me, David. Do you really think there's anything you haven't already said to convince me to accept your offer?"

Donovan studied her for a moment as though considering her words. "Maybe there's nothing I haven't said, but there *is* something I haven't done." He downed his bourbon, pulled out his wallet and threw some money on the table. "Let's go. I'm going to show you your new office. If that doesn't make you decide to say *yes*, nothing will."

"Tonight?" Tori forced a laugh. Hell no, she wasn't going anywhere with him tonight. The idea of being stuck in a high-rise building with him, alone, creeped her out. She took another drink to keep those very words from blurting out.

"I'm not taking *no* for an answer. Come on. Finish your drink. Let's go." He was standing behind his chair now, impatiently waiting for her to comply, and he didn't appear to be joking.

The tiniest hint of fear permeated her dulled senses. She took another drink to give her hands something to do.

Tori pushed her chair back and stood as Donovan ambled around the table toward her, a speculative gleam in his eyes. She swayed unsteadily, reaching out to grab the edge of the table until her equilibrium returned.

"I've got you." Donovan latched on to her elbow and threw his other arm around her shoulders. "Ready to go?"

"No." He was in her space again, and Tori hated being manhandled. She tried to keep the alarm from her voice but wasn't entirely sure she succeeded. "I mean…I need to use the ladies' room before we go." Why was he suddenly in such a hurry?

"I'll help you—"

"No." She shrugged his arm off. "I don't need help finding the bathroom, David. I've been doing it on my own for a long time."

A doubtful smile curved his mouth, but he stepped back, hands raised in surrender. Was it only her imagination, or did something sinister flash in his eyes?

Tori grabbed her purse but left her sweater hanging over the chair next to hers. Turning, she strode toward the bathrooms. It took all her concentration to put one foot in front of the other and walk a straight line. Even then, she was sure everyone was watching her stagger across the room, and, for sure, she could feel Donovan's eyes following her progress. *Damn it! Why'd I drink so much?* She was a lightweight when it came to alcohol, yet she'd consumed three cocktails and nursed a fourth. Now, when she needed to be alert and cautious, she felt like a wrecking ball, swinging out of control.

Reaching the alcove where the bathrooms were tucked away, Tori ventured a glance over her shoulder. Luck was with her so far. Donovan had turned his back with his phone to his ear. Gathering her courage, she veered away from the ladies' room door and charged into the next closest avenue of escape—the kitchen.

Without slowing down, she wound through the cooks, waitresses and dishwashers, many of whom apparently spoke only Spanish and thought her appearance in their refuge was humorous. *"Con permiso."* She plastered a smile on her face as she hurried by, repeating one of the half dozen Spanish phrases she remembered from high school.

To her relief, no one tried to stop her or deter her from her goal, the back door, propped open, no doubt, to combat the sweltering heat of the kitchen. Just before she crossed the threshold, Tori peeked over her shoulder. Donovan was nowhere to be seen. No one had followed her or seemed the least bit interested in her movements.

Had she overreacted? Her judgment had been impaired by alcohol. What was she thinking? Just because Donovan ordered them didn't mean she had to drink them. Nerves and excitement had contributed to her lack of self-control, but she was an adult, and wanting to make a good impression was no excuse for abandoning her usually strict rules.

In the darkness of the alley, she paused to take stock of her surroundings. The smells of discarded food from the garbage dumpsters against the building got her moving again. The chill in the air helped clear her head, and she started to second-guess herself. What if she'd made a huge mistake? She had no evidence Donovan had wanted to whisk her away from the hotel with some ulterior motive in mind. He'd been a perfect gentleman, only interested in getting her to accept his job offer. The events of the past couple of days had made her jumpy, understandably so, but perhaps she'd let her overactive imagination run away with her.

Yet, the prickling of the skin at the base of her neck persisted.

She left the alley and found a side entrance into the hotel. *Locked!* It took her a few seconds to remember the key card she'd placed in her purse, and a few minutes after that, she finally located it, jammed it in the slot and turned the handle.

The warmth and silence enveloped her, but she wasn't home free yet. Whatever sixth sense told her to get out of the restaurant before Donovan hauled her away to his office building now prompted her to make good her escape before the persistent man realized she was gone and started looking for her. She rejected the elevator in favor of the stairs. Pushing past the heavy door, she halted for a moment, studying the zigzagging flights of stairs that seemed to stretch upward as far as she could see. A whole lot of gin still coursed through her veins, turning her brain to mush and her legs to Jell-O.

Two flights up, her cell phone vibrated inside her purse, and Tori stopped to retrieve the device. The screen alerted her to a new text message from Donovan.

Are you okay? Do I need to come and get you?

He seemed concerned and was obviously tired of waiting for her to return from the bathroom. She resumed her climb, while debating whether to answer. He wouldn't understand why she left. In retrospect, the reason for the pinprick of fear that caused her to run wasn't clear to her, either. Yeah, there was a good chance her fuzzy cognitive function had led her to overreact. *Oh God! He's going to think I'm a nutcase.*

Reaching the third-floor landing, she stopped again, holding the phone with both hands while she typed. *My apologies, David. Shouldn't have drank so much. Stomach not good. I didn't want to embarrass us both, so I left rather quickly. Hope you will forgive me.* It was an embellishment of the truth and left out the part where he scared her. A sucker for emoticons, she ended with a frowny face.

Tori waited for the telltale dots to appear, indicating he was replying. When nothing happened, she started up the stairs again. Just as she reached the top and pushed into the fourth-floor hallway, her phone vibrated again.

No problem. You've got your 24 hours. Feel better soon.

She stared at the message. *Well, hell!* He wasn't upset with her. Which most likely meant there was nothing nefarious behind his desire to show her the office where she'd be working. She'd dramatized the situation and could have easily destroyed her chances for her dream job. Odd that she felt worse about abandoning him without an explanation than about losing the opportunity.

In front of her room, she leaned her back against the door, staring at the key card in her hand. Across the hall and two doors down, Blake occupied a room. The last thing he'd said was for her to check in. The temptation was great, and it scared her to death. Getting attached to this ex-SEAL wasn't an option. Hell, it might already be too late. He wasn't far from her thoughts at any given time.

Her failsafe was that Blake wasn't looking to hook up permanently, either. He had baggage too. If she were to go for the short-term pleasure he and his super-sexy body offered, they'd glow brightly for a while and eventually fizzle out. He'd get bored with her. They'd move on. There might be some pain, but it would only prove she missed his company. From experience, there was no doubt she'd heal, but what about Isaiah? Could she protect him from the inevitable? Would it be such a bad thing if he had a father figure in his life...even for a season?

Tori shoved her key in her purse, dug deep for her confidence and strutted down the hallway. She was about to knock on Blake's door when he jerked it open and stopped just short of running her over.

Chapter 15

"Where the hell were you?" Blake's pent-up concern discharged with more anger behind it than he'd intended.

Hurt flooded her ice-blue eyes. "In the bar. Talking to Donovan." Her tone said he was treading on thin ice. She tilted her head accusingly as her hands dropped to her hips. "You knew that."

"Donovan just called the room and said you'd run out on him without a word. Is that going to be your modus operandi from now on?" Blake crossed his arms.

A smile flitted over her face and then disappeared. "Maybe. What's it to you?"

What's it to me? He snagged her around the waist and hauled her flush with his body. His mouth settled over hers, swallowing her little squeak of surprise. One hand cupped her ass and molded her to his growing erection, the contact blowing the hell out of his self-control. His other hand gripped the back of her head, holding her in place as he slanted his lips over hers and drove his tongue into the velvet heat of her mouth.

Tori melted against him, her hands sliding up his chest to caress the back of his neck, driving him crazy with her touch. The sexiest whimper escaped her, and she hooked her right leg around his hips. The move placed the warmth of her womanhood in line with his aching arousal.

And just how in the hell does she do that? Take me from zero to sixty in two-point-four seconds?

"Are you gonna invite me in?" Her low murmur hissed in his ear.

Her run-together speech, combined with the alcohol on her breath, made him lean back and search her eyes. *Shit!* "Are you drunk?" If the slight glaze in her baby blues was any indication, he already had his answer.

She laughed a little too long, holding her left hand in front of her with thumb and forefinger a quarter of an inch apart. "I might've had a lil' bit to drink."

Hell! Blake backed through the doorway, dragging her with him. He kissed the corners of her mouth before stepping away and closing the door.

"What'sa matter?"

"Oh, nothing much. Just that when I told you to be careful and stay alert, I had it in my head you'd also stay sober."

"Oh, come on. Don't be mad." With a teasing smile, Tori closed the space between them and slapped his chest. "I'm home, safe and sound. And I *didn't* leave with Donovan when he wanted to show me my new office." Leaning into him, she kissed his neck. "Actually, that kinda creeped me out. So, I came right back here to you." She jabbed her finger into his chest. "Please don't be mad."

Blake caught her hands and held her away from him. Her soft lips on his throat was quickly eroding his better judgment. "I'm not mad. You scared the shit out of me, Tori. When Donovan said you'd disappeared, I didn't know if it was intentional on your part or if someone grabbed you." He stopped, and the erratic pounding of his own heart thudded in his ears. *Get a grip, man.* The trained warrior in him that could stay emotionally detached, even in the face of devastating loss, had apparently abandoned ship in Tori's case. Dipping his head, he counted to ten before looking at her again.

"I'm glad you didn't leave with Donovan, although I think the guy is exactly who he says he is, the editor of a magazine who wants to give you a job. I still don't want him hitting on you, though."

Her adorable dimples appeared. "Why not?"

"Because that's *my* job." He pulled her closer and leaned in to roll her lower lip between his teeth, biting down and then taking her mouth in a searing kiss, with all the stored-up passion he'd hoped to release tonight. With a groan, he took a step back. "Let's get you ready for bed."

She laughed low and sexy. "Whatever you say."

Damned if that wasn't what every man wanted to hear from a beautiful woman, but she'd had too much to drink. He took her hand and led her toward the bed. "Get undressed."

Tori gave him a mock salute. "Yes, sir."

Blake turned away with a roll of his eyes. He was pretty sure she wouldn't be happy with herself in the morning, and he wasn't about to exacerbate that by having sex with her when she wasn't in any shape to knowingly consent.

Grabbing his bag from the floor at the foot of the bed, he tossed her the first T-shirt he found. "You can borrow one of mine for tonight." He groped in the bottom until he located the bottle of ibuprofen he'd packed, shook out two gelcaps and poured water from the tap into a glass. Striding to bring her the water and capsules, he nearly stumbled over his own feet when he glanced up.

Tori had completed the first part of his instructions. She was posed seductively on the edge of the bed, totally naked, his T-shirt untouched where it'd landed. A come-and-get-me grin rode her full lips. His arousal increased tenfold, his dick sure to bear the impressions of zipper teeth for hours to come.

At the side of the bed, he handed her the capsules and forced the water glass into her other hand. "Swallow these and drink all of the water." When she did as he said and handed the empty glass back, he set it on the nightstand. Then he shook out the T-shirt he'd provided and summarily jerked it over her head.

A frown marred her brow as he threaded her arms through the sleeves and pulled the shirt down to cover her damned enticing bosom.

"What are you doin'? I thought..."

Yeah, he'd asked himself that same question. He crouched in front of her, looking up slightly to see her eyes. "I'm insuring we'll still be friends in the morning."

She cocked her head as though he was speaking in a strange language, her lips turning down at the corners.

Blake placed his hands on her upper arms, stroking downward to her elbows. "You need sleep more than anything else. In the morning, you'll thank me."

Tori looked doubtful but dutifully kneed her way up the length of the mattress and managed to pull the blankets loose and slip underneath. She pummeled her pillow, then turned it over and did the same to the other side. "Are you sleeping with me?"

"Just sleep. Do you want me to?" He hadn't intended to be anywhere near her in his present state of arousal. That would only make things more difficult for him. But the thread of sadness in her words caught him off guard.

"Yes. I'd like you to hold me. If it's not too much trouble."

Hell, it was likely to be all kinds of trouble, but he couldn't refuse her. He removed his shoulder holster, checked his weapon and laid it on the nightstand beside Tori's glass. While she watched, he stripped off his clothes, down to the charcoal-gray briefs that did nothing to conceal his erection. After checking to make sure the door was securely locked and turning off all the lights, he slid in beside her.

Beads of sweat broke out on his forehead, and he clenched his teeth against the ache in his groin. "Roll on your side so we can spoon." Blake hugged her against his front, dropping a kiss below her ear. "Good night, sweetheart."

His fingers, apparently with an agenda all their own, grazed her pebbled nipple. He groaned, trying to find another spot for his hand that didn't tempt him. She grabbed it, placing it back on her breast.

It's going to be a long night.

"G'night, Blake. Thanks for cuddling with me." She already sounded sleepy.

Cuddling, huh? Ohh-kay! He could do this. He just needed something else to think about. Soon enough, she'd fall into the deep sleep of the innocently sloshed, and he'd slip away for a cold shower. If being this close to her didn't kill him first.

* * * *

Blake awoke to another damn hard-on and sounds of movement in the room. Someone opened the drapes and the early morning sunrays brightened his surroundings as though an IED had exploded in front of him, without the noise...or the pain.

He peeked through mostly closed lids to see Tori's silhouette in front of the window. "Hey, why are you up so early?"

She turned toward him, a tentative smile not quite making up for the way she hugged herself as she faced him. "I promised Isaiah I'd call him first thing."

"Shit. I slept through that?"

"I didn't want to wake you, so I went into the bathroom." Tori looked at her feet.

Blake grunted. Something was wrong. What did she think happened last night? "Come here."

She looked up and took a sideways step. "I'm just going to...um...take a shower."

"Not yet." Blake raised up on one elbow and crooked his finger. "Don't make me come and get you."

Tori looked away toward the bathroom, and a pretty blush cast spots of color on her cheek. "Look, Blake. I know I came on to you last night, but I don't remember a thing after we went to bed. I'm sorry if I...I want you to know that's not who I am. I've never gotten drunk and ended up in a man's bed...until last night."

Damned if it didn't look like she was blinking back tears. Blake pushed himself to the side of the bed and got his feet underneath him. He stalked toward her. "There's a good reason you don't remember anything." Reaching for her hand, he pulled her into his arms and pressed a kiss to her forehead. "We cuddled last night until you went to sleep. I slept too, but it took me longer." His chuckle moved the hair at the edge of her face.

"You drank too much and got a little shitfaced, but you did the right thing not leaving the premises with Donovan." Blake held her upper arms and pushed her back a step. "Now, as for ending up in bed with *this* man, you'll always be safe with me, sweetheart, no matter what. Okay?"

One of those tears she'd been trying to hold back broke free and rolled down her cheek. He caught it with his thumb and then kissed the spot on her face. The wonder in her eyes slayed him.

What the hell was he doing? He was getting in too deep. It was *her*. She made him want things he shouldn't. Hell, half the time when he conjured Celine's face to remind him why he guarded his heart, all he saw was Tori. Smiling. Lost in the throes of passion. Standing in her kitchen, willing to give her life to save her child. Son-of-a-bitch! He was falling for her.

Tori's face brightened with one of her gorgeous smiles, and she nodded. "Okay. As long as we're good. I was hoping I didn't lead you on or something. I mean, we both still have our boundaries. I don't date military men, and you don't invest your heart in any relationship. That's our agreement, right?" She waited expectantly.

Blake had to kiss her just to shut her up, because he'd already crossed the line, but he couldn't tell her that. He brushed her soft hair back from her face. "Right." His voice rasped and rightly so, since his fucking heart was lodged in his throat. He pulled her into his arms again and planted his lips on hers, licking her sensitive, beautifully shaped mouth until she opened to allow him access. Taking everything he needed, he plundered her mouth, imprinting the taste of her on his tongue. Parting her legs with his thigh, he ground his rigid length against the softness of her belly. When it still wasn't enough, he growled his frustration, scooped her up, and carried her to the bed.

Covering her with his body, he felt the strangest sensation, as though he'd come home. With trembling fingers, he brushed a knuckle over her cheek, then kissed her chin and claimed her lips again.

Tori traced the line of stitches on his forehead, her touch light. "Does it hurt?"

He hurt for sure, but the ache was in his balls and only one thing would help that. "No, it's fine." He caught her hand and ran the tip of his tongue across her palm.

She inhaled sharply, jerking her hand away as a tremor quaked her body. His throbbing shaft twitched, and he watched her eyes darken as she smiled. *Jesus!* He wanted to bury himself in her velvet softness again. He craved her like no other woman he'd ever known, but he needed more. He needed her to want him just as much.

Blake kissed her lips hungrily. His blood started a slow boil when she moaned her pleasure. With a last kiss, he scooted down her body until his face rested between her luscious breasts and his erection, straining to escape the restriction of his briefs, pressed against the warm wetness between her legs. With both hands, he pushed the T-shirt he'd loaned her up her torso and over her head until she lay completely naked beneath him.

He kneaded the soft flesh of her breasts, rubbing, tormenting the swollen nubs with his rough palms. With each pass, she writhed and pressed into his hands. When desire glazed her eyes, he took the nipple of one breast in his mouth, scraped his teeth across it and sucked until his mouth was full of her. She uttered a strangled protest when he released one and latched on to the other, giving it the same attention, until she fisted her hands in the rumpled sheets and held on.

"Please…" Her quavering voice came in short pants.

Blake lifted his head and looked in her stormy eyes. "Tell me. What do you want, Tori?"

"You. I want you…inside me. Now." She tugged on his head, but he wasn't finished yet.

He slid farther down her body. "Do you have any idea how hard you made me last night?"

"Last night? You told me to go to sleep."

"Right. Because I didn't think it would be wise to have sex with a woman who wasn't likely to remember in the morning." He kept moving down, over her belly and the cradle of her hips, until his shoulders nudged her legs farther apart.

She opened them wider. "You did that for me? That's so sweet."

A grin formed as he renewed eye contact with her.

"What's so funny?" Playful wariness filtered through her voice.

"Nothing at all. I thought I'd return the favor." His tongue darted out, swiping through her slick folds. As she bucked upward, he scraped his teeth across her sweet spot and settled his mouth there, working her swollen bead with his tongue.

"Blake! I can't—oh God!" Tori reared up off the bed, and he had to cinch his arms around her thighs to hold her in place.

She was so close her whole body trembled. The rapture on her face was almost enough to send him over the edge prematurely. He found her opening with his finger and thrust inside. Her muscles flexed around him, and he inserted a second finger, finding a rhythm that had his dick wanting to join the party.

"Harder. I need—I'm going to..." Tori thrashed beneath him, lifting her hips into his hand as he powered into her.

"We're going to come together, Tori." Blake removed his fingers, and she whimpered. "You wait for me." He rose to his knees and lunged for the nightstand drawer where he'd stocked a supply of condoms the previous evening. He'd had big plans last night, but nothing he'd imagined could beat the reality of her naked beneath him, her eyes imploring him to take her.

Three seconds was a new record for him, ripping into the foil package, seating the condom the length of his rock-hard shaft. *Shit! The way she watches me blows my mind.* He fused his lips to hers as the ache in his balls mushroomed. "Roll over on your stomach, sweetheart. I want you from behind."

She didn't hesitate, flipping over with her bitable ass up. He kneed between her legs until he was close enough to caress the smooth, silken skin she presented to him. *Christ!* At this rate, his heart was going to explode.

Blake lifted her hips slightly and aligned his tip at her opening, letting the anticipation tingle through him for a heartbeat. "Oh shit, babe. I want you so bad. Hold on." He pushed an inch or so inside her and threw his head back as the agony of stopping tightened every muscle in his body. When he started shaking with the effort, he rocked forward, pulling her toward him and onto his shaft at the same time he filled her. His balls slapped against the insides of her thighs and the heat of her womanhood. Again, he stopped, holding her tight against him, allowing her time to get used to him before inching even deeper.

Tori fisted the blankets beside her while she rolled her head from side to side. "Oh God. Blake, that's so good. Need more..."

He pulled out all the way and slid back in slowly, grinding their bodies together. His name whispered from her lips the next time they came together and each time after that, until he picked up the pace. Soon, he was driving into her, holding her hips in place, needing to be closer—deeper. Her velvet clasp on his length and her soft mews urged him on. Lost in her sounds, her scent, and the heady nirvana overtaking him, he dropped down, stretching, covering her fully. With a growl, he wrapped her in his arms while keeping up the grueling pace. Pressure built in his groin and lower abdomen, clamoring for release.

His hands beneath her, he found her hard peaks and plucked them with his thumb and forefinger. Each time he pinched, she treated him to a delicious gyration of her hips that encouraged him to repeat the process.

"I'm so close," he whispered in her ear. One of his hands slid down to her center and toyed with her. "I'm not coming until you're ready to go with me."

"I can't—"

"You can." He slowed his thrusts, pausing deep inside her at the end of each stroke. His fingers dipped into the wetness of her folds and spread the slickness to the peak of her womanhood. Resuming a frenzied pace of thrust and withdraw, he kept time with his fingers as he brought her to the brink with him. "That's it. Let go, baby. Fly with me."

She cried his name, pushing her face into the mattress to muffle the noise. Plunging into her again and again, he rode her as she shook and shuddered beneath him in the throes of precious release. Only then did Blake let himself go deep and stay while his orgasm crashed over him in waves of blessed torment.

Chapter 16

Tori sat in the front passenger seat of Blake's plane with a smile, listening to the methodical man behind the controls hum a tune through the headphones. Wearing a new pair of aviator sunglasses, he held a clipboard and periodically checked off an item before moving on to the next. Just looking at his long fingers and large hands sent a shiver racing clear to her toes. His rugged masculinity and smoldering sex appeal, not to mention his spicy male scent, made her juices flow freely, dampening the crotch of her panties yet again.

He'd been insatiable this morning, though clearly more concerned with her pleasure than his own. Tori flushed with heat at the memory of three full-throttle sessions of holy-shit sex where he brought her to orgasm at least five times. She'd been so blissfully sated afterward, all she could do was stand in the shower while he washed her from head to toe.

Blake curled his hand around her forearm, drew her toward him and planted a hungry kiss on her lips. Removing the headset, he hung it around his neck. "Daydreaming?"

"Uh…maybe!"

"About us? This morning?" His low murmur tickled her chin as he hovered close.

"There is no *us*, Sorenson. It's all about *me*." She laughed against his lips, and he captured her mouth again.

Blake sat straight and regarded her, his eyes dark with lust. "That's the difference between men and women, sweetheart. Women tend to think about sex—play it over and over in their heads—pinpoint everything they should or shouldn't have done, until all the life is sucked out."

"Oh, really?" Tori cocked a brow.

"Damn straight. Now me?" He leaned toward her again. "I plan to relive sex with you just as soon as I get you alone again. If I can wait that long." He grinned as he turned back to his checklist. "Sucking may or may not be involved."

Tori laughed. "You are *so* bad."

"No, I'm so *good*." He pointed to his earphones before setting them on his head again. Evidently, the control tower was finally getting back to him with their departure information.

He was right, damn him. How was it fair that one man could be nice, attractive, and a phenomenal lover? Tori's emotions waffled between happiness and regret. She liked Blake, and the things he did to her body were incredible, but she couldn't have him, not long term, anyway. And he didn't want her for the long haul either. The truth of the matter was Isaiah was waiting for her at Blake's house, and it would be a long time before she and Blake were alone again. As soon as the police caught the person who'd ordered the attempt on her life, she'd take Isaiah and go home, and that would be the end. Going their separate ways would be the best thing for them both.

So, why do I feel lost and empty already?

Blake nosed the aircraft toward the runway and soon they were airborne. Once they'd leveled off, he removed his headphones. "Are you okay?" Concern radiated from him.

Tori forced a cheerful smile. "Fine. Just anxious to see Isaiah."

Blake frowned. "What about Donovan? Have you decided to accept his job offer?"

No. That was the last thing she wanted to think about. "It would be a great job, but I want to talk to Isaiah about moving first."

"You really think he'll be upset?"

"Yes. Isaiah doesn't respond to everyone the way he did to you. He used to be an outgoing boy, filled with questions and enthusiasm. Getting in trouble like little boys are apt to do."

Blake's warm laughter seemed to caress her.

"He's been different since his father died. And then I moved him to Cypress Point, thinking small-town life would give us both a chance to heal. My sister, Jane, lives close by, and Isaiah has made a couple of friends in the neighborhood. He spends most of his time playing with the model cars his dad bought for him." Tori bit down on her bottom lip to stop the flow of words. Why was she burdening him with her concerns? It wasn't his problem.

Blake skimmed his knuckle along her arm. "Have you gotten him counseling?"

Tori bobbed her head. "For eight months. Then one day he broke down and asked me if he could stop going. He said he was starting to forget what his dad looked like when he was happy, and Isaiah never wanted that to happen." Tori blinked back scalding tears and dug deep for a watery smile. "And then you came along, and, for the first time in almost two years, my baby reached out for someone. So, tell me, Blake, what's your secret?"

He gave her a sad smile as he shrugged. "Maybe I'm just a kid at heart myself. Or maybe something in his broken spirit sensed something similar in mine. Then again, it might be as simple as the fact that I think kids are great. It doesn't really matter why, does it? What's important is that you give him a chance to reach as high and as far as he's willing."

Tori stared at Blake. He was right. She couldn't take Donovan's job and move Isaiah away from Cypress Point. Not now, anyway. Not when Blake might hold the key to stripping away the pain that blanketed Isaiah's heart.

Relief flooded her at the decision made, and not only because of her son. Apparently, Isaiah wasn't the only one who needed to stay. Uneasiness tugged at her memory. Blake Sorenson had the power to turn her world upside down and make her forget why military men weren't relationship material. She'd made her choice to keep Isaiah from ever being hurt again. Was she worrying for nothing? Blake had also vowed he'd never lose his heart to another woman. Just one thing wrong with this scenario. If Tori couldn't keep her emotions under control, Blake would rip out her heart when he was finished with her.

* * * *

The sun was shining through intermittent clouds in southern Oregon, and the rays, colliding with the breaking waves on the coast, were spectacular. They were almost home—home, in this case, being wherever Isaiah was. The flight had been smooth and went by quickly as she and Blake chatted amiably.

Tori had opted to keep her decision about the job offer to herself until after she broke the news to Donovan. She wasn't sure why, but it seemed prudent. "Thanks for going with me, Blake, and for flying us to Portland."

"I wouldn't have had it any other way." Distracted, Blake tapped on one of the gauges, a frown creasing his brow.

"Everything okay?" Tori focused on the gauge in question. The needle pegged out at *full*.

"Must have a bad gauge. We sure as hell shouldn't have a full load of fuel at this point." He rapped his knuckles on the glass front again. The needle vibrated and started dropping.

Tori watched curiously as the needle hit the halfway mark, then a quarter tank, and still it plummeted. Curiosity turned to dread as it came to rest at the bottom of the gauge, and, immediately, a red light on the dash began to flash, accompanied with what sounded like the ping of an elevator arriving at the correct floor. Except this alarm kept pinging until Blake flipped a switch next to the flashing red light.

"Um…what just happened?" Tori glanced sideways at Blake, hoping to see his grin and an assurance everything was all right. She didn't.

Instead, the plane's engine cut out for a second, caught again, and purred for the count of three before it cut out again and everything inside the cockpit went deathly still. Blake flipped channels on the radio and swiveled his mic in front of his mouth. "Mayday, mayday. Aw…fuck!" He flicked another switch and suddenly Tori could hear the radio static. "Coop, you got your ears on, buddy?"

Tori's heart dove into her stomach, and she grabbed her seat cushion with both hands. "Oh God, not again."

Blake dropped his hand on her knee and *now* he flashed the grin she'd wanted seconds ago. "Don't panic, sweetheart. Make sure your belt's tight."

"I gotcha, Sorenson. What's the problem?" Coop's voice rose over the static."

"You're gonna want to clear the runway. I'll be making an emergency landing momentarily."

"Copy that, Blake. What kind of an emergency?"

"We're a little light on fuel."

There was a slight hesitation before Coop's voice came back. "How light?"

"Engine's gone." Blake might have been communicating with a traffic controller, lining up for a normal landing. There wasn't an ounce of anxiety apparent in his voice.

That was good, because Tori was terrified enough for them both. Still, she forced air into her lungs and tried for calmly nervous.

"Shit! Are you close enough?" Coop's query hung for a moment, unanswered.

"We have to be. It's the only option." Blake reached for her hand, prying it from the seat cushion, and threaded his fingers with hers. "Do us a favor, would ya', Coop? Make sure Isaiah doesn't witness anything that'll give him nightmares."

"Done. We're standing by with fire retardant. Don't dirty up my runway, Sorenson."

Blake turned his mic off. "You're never going to fly with me again, are you?"

Despite her fear, Tori laughed. "If you can get us out of this alive, I'd do just about anything with you."

This time Blake chuckled. "Tori Michaels, I'm going to hold you to that." He brought her fingers to his mouth for a kiss before setting her hand on his thigh and holding it there. "Do you believe I can land this thing in one piece?"

His eyes were hidden behind the dark glasses, but Tori sensed his seriousness. The only sound was a soft *whoosh* as the craft glided through the air, steadily losing altitude even as Blake worked to keep the nose up. She could see the runway, the hangar and the office in front of them... and a long way down... like miniature game pieces. She was only slightly surprised to see that Blake had already lined up the airplane for landing.

"Yes, I do." In that moment, she believed he could do anything he set his mind to.

He nodded. "Good. Don't move your hand unless you stop believing." Moving back to the controls, he gave the crippled airplane his full attention.

It seemed to take forever for the plane to clear the trees, but all too soon, they were skimming the runway. The wheels hit the pavement with jarring force, throwing Tori forward until her lap belt brought her up short. She was pretty sure she had a white-knuckled hold on Blake's leg at the point of impact, but she was determined not to let go—as though her belief in his abilities would make all the difference.

As soon as they touched down, Blake applied the brakes. Simultaneously, he pressed buttons and flipped switches that changed the configuration of the wings, causing some drag, but they still approached the end of the runway and the trees beyond at far too great a speed.

"Brace for impact," Blake said.

When she didn't move, continuing to stare straight ahead, he threw his arm in front of her as the aircraft bounced over the barrier meant to designate the end of the runway, flopped forward on its nose and slid to a sideways stop just short of the timber.

Tori, her eyes scrunched shut, clung to Blake's arm with one hand and his leg with the other. When their wild ride abruptly stopped, he opened the side door, grabbed the fire extinguisher and her hand, still gripping his leg, and hauled her from the craft. A truck with a large tank and several men riding in the back raced toward them.

"Get back, away from the plane." Blake pushed her toward the side of the runway, and the fear of a fiery explosion finally got her feet moving. The truck, Fire Retardant marked in large white letters on the side of the tank, sped to the end of the runway and skidded to a stop. Coop, Travis, and four men she didn't know piled out with extinguishers and two hoses that appeared to be connected to the tank.

It wasn't until she reached a safe distance and turned back that she realized Blake hadn't followed her. He stood beside the wreckage with the other men who'd surrounded the plane, obviously watching for any indication of fire. There didn't appear to be any danger. In fact, if the plane wasn't tilted on its nose with the tail end in the air, Tori might have doubted they'd just crash landed...again.

More concerning was the blood that streamed down Blake's face. She couldn't tell if it was a new injury, or if he'd broken open the stitches that still trailed along his brow. Either way, she knew him well enough by now to realize he would do what needed to be done before he stopped to take care of himself.

When several minutes passed and no fire resulted, the men visibly relaxed. Needing something to do, Tori returned to the aircraft, intent on retrieving their luggage. Blake and the men were inspecting the left side of the airplane. As she opened the door to grab the bags, voices drifted to her ears.

"Well, I'll be damned," Coop said. "Sorenson, you're a lucky son-of-a-bitch for sure. Come on. Let's get you back to the hangar and see if you need more stitches."

"This had nothing to do with luck, good or bad. This was sabotage." Blake's voice was low, as though he didn't want everyone to know, but when Tori heard the word *sabotage*, she stilled to listen.

"Fuck! What the hell happened?" Travis's voice joined the subdued conversation.

"The plane was supposedly refueled in Hillsboro. The maintenance crew always takes care of us. Harv made the arrangements." Blake went silent as a voice Tori didn't recognize asked a question from the front of the plane. Coop answered, moving off toward the man who stood by the propeller.

"This time the refueling obviously didn't happen, but the fuel gauge and warning light have been tampered with, so it looked like the tank was full, and the warning light never came on until I started tapping on the gauge." Blake stopped again as someone muttered a curse.

"Are you sure about this?" Coop rejoined the group.

"I know it as sure as I'm standing here, and I'm going to prove it. Don't let Harv near the plane until I check it out." Blake sounded angry.

"Harv? You suspect Harv had something to do with this?" Travis jumped in, clearly disbelieving.

"I'm not saying it was him. It could have been Donovan. That's a long shot, but he was the only person who knew we were coming. Hell, it could have been Sebastian Wahl. He seems to have long arms these days. But I want a chance to check out that gauge before Harv starts working on the plane."

Tori tugged the bags from behind the front seats. She didn't know Harv well enough to suspect him. Sebastian Wahl was a ruthless activist who'd apparently tried to silence Blake and her three days ago. Nothing could be put past him. Tori stepped back, preparing to close the door.

Someone cleared his throat, and then Travis lowered his voice. "What about Tori? Is she still on your list of possibles?"

What's he talking about? Blake suspects me? Of what?

Blake laughed. "For this? Travis, the girl hates to fly."

So...what then? Since he knows I wouldn't cause an airplane crash if I was going to be on it, what else is there? The attack on Perez? I had no idea he was even there in that forest cabin. Besides, Blake couldn't possibly think I'd be involved in harming children. Could he?

More laughter and the sounds of movement broke into Tori's shocked deliberations. Quickly she closed the door and carried the bags to the edge of the runway. She dropped to her knees in the soft dirt and unzipped her bag, thrusting her hand inside as though she was searching for something.

Tori looked up as Blake, Coop, and Travis appeared around the rear of the plane. *No wonder he was so adamant about Isaiah and me staying here. He's keeping an eye on me because he doesn't trust me. Sleeping with me was just part of the ruse. It meant nothing to him.*

Blake cast a worried glance and a curious smile toward her, one that she now knew was only an act.

Chapter 17

"Where's Tori? Is she all right?" MacGyver asked the same question Blake had on his mind.

MacGyver snipped the row of four-day-old stitches and pulled them out one by one. Apparently, at some point during the landing, Blake had whacked his half-healed forehead on the instrument panel and torn out enough of his stitches that MacGyver had opted to remove the rest. There'd been more than a few jokes about his hard head from the men who looked on while his friend worked on him.

"She went upstairs as soon as we got here." It wasn't the *where* that Blake was questioning, but the *why*. She hadn't been hurt in the crash landing, not physically anyway, but there'd clearly been something wrong when she stomped up the stairs the minute they'd entered the house. Scared and even traumatized he could understand, but she'd brushed off his concern like a piece of lint. Something more than the crash was bothering her, and Blake had to endure MacGyver's attention before he could follow her and find out what was up.

"Then maybe you can answer my question now," Travis said. "Have you ruled her out as a suspect in helping Sebastian get to Perez?"

MacGyver put Blake's brow back together with some butterfly bandages and started cleaning up. That gave Blake a few minutes before he had to answer Travis's question, but damned if he knew what to say.

His gut told him Tori was innocent, but he didn't have one fact or shred of evidence to back up his hunch. And there was always the possibility he'd let himself get too close to judge impartially. He got to his feet and turned toward Travis. The truth was always the best bet.

"Not exactly." He raised his hands to ward off Travis's frustrated response. "She hasn't given me a single reason to suspect her, except maybe that she was in the wrong place at the wrong time. Frankly, I can't see her working for a scumbag like Sebastian. Isaiah is her whole world. She'd never do anything to put him in danger. I think she's innocent." Blake glanced at each man in turn. "Coop, have you turned up anything that makes me wrong?"

"Not a damn thing. She's squeaky clean." Coop assumed a suggestive grin. "Are you going to tell us about your overnight stay in the city?"

Good-natured chortles met his question.

"Yeah, sure. To borrow one of MacGyver's favorite expressions—as soon as elephants sprout fucking fairy wings and fly."

"That might be a lot safer way for you to travel." Coop didn't miss a beat, hooting a laugh as he started for the back door. "Speaking of that, I'm going to haul the wreckage of your last flight into the hangar."

Blake flipped him off as Coop glanced over his shoulder with a mischievous grin, causing another round of friendly sniggers. Travis followed him out.

When they were gone, Blake eyed MacGyver and Luke, still sitting at the table. The silence was getting under his skin. "If either of you think I'm endangering this mission, I'll make myself scarce until it's over."

Luke and MacGyver looked at each other, and then Luke pushed to his feet. "If you trust her, I've got no problem with that." He checked his watch. "It's about time for shift change, so I'll catch you later."

MacGyver waited until Luke was gone before he turned his scrutiny on Blake. "You were the man back in the day, Blake. You had the best instincts of any SEAL I ever met. As far as I know, nothing has changed... so, why the self-doubt?"

Blake dropped into a chair across from MacGyver and threaded his fingers together on the top of his head. It was a fair question. Too bad he didn't have a good answer. "Hell if I know, bro." Goddamn, he hated to admit it. "I let her get to me, and it's personal now. What if I'm seeing only what I want to see? What if I'm compromised and I get someone killed?"

A half smile curled the corner of MacGyver's mouth. "Well, bro, that's why me, Luke, Travis, and Coop have your back. As Luke would say 'Failure is not an option. We're a team—no man left behind,' and all that shit. Right? Bottom line is *you* trust her. That makes her okay in my book. Same for the others. If it turns out your trust was misplaced somewhere along the line, we're still going to have your back."

Maybe so, but this was one time he needed to be right. "Thanks, MacGyver."

"No problem." He pushed back his chair and stood. "Unless I miss my guess, something was bothering her when we got back to the house. Can't imagine what, after falling out of the sky twice in the past four days. If she wasn't a little moody, I'd be surprised, but she disappeared damn fast."

"I noticed. I'll talk to her before I start work on the plane. Is someone keeping an eye on Harv?"

"He went into town this morning before you arrived. Said he had something to take care of." Another partial smile indicated MacGyver found that strange too. He started for the door. "You and Tori should probably take it easy for a couple of days. Once the adrenaline leaves your system, you'll know you've acquired a few new bruises." The door fell closed behind him.

As Blake started up the stairs, he had to admit MacGyver might be right. His bad leg was more painful than usual, and his back and shoulder muscles were tight and sore to the touch. Hell, maybe that was why Tori had retreated to her room.

Halfway up, he met Rafael Perez descending with his two kids, Antonio and Lucinda. Blake smiled at the children as he stopped on the same step as Rafael.

"Thank you for offering your home to us, Mr. Sorenson."

"It's my pleasure, but please, it's Blake. Are you and your family comfortable? I hope you're making yourselves at home. *Mi casa es su casa.*"

"*Gracias*, Blake. Everyone has been very kind to me and my family. We were on our way down to the kitchen to see if we can be of help. I understand you're cooking for an army of sorts." Rafael chuckled.

"The men take turns fixing meals usually. They're fairly self-sufficient, but I doubt they'd ever turn away help." Blake knelt in front of Antonio, who wasn't looking entirely happy about being volunteered for kitchen duty. "Hey, Antonio, *como estás?*"

"Good," the five-year-old said with a downcast face.

"Did you happen to meet Isaiah yesterday or today? About your size, blond hair, blue eyes?"

"*Sí.*" The boy giggled.

"He's nice." Lucinda spoke up. "We've been playing hide and seek outside."

"You have?" Blake shot a glance toward Lucinda's father.

"They've been staying very close to the house." Rafael hurried to assure Blake. "A few of the off-duty men have been keeping an eye on them while they're outside. It's okay—*sí*?"

Blake straightened to his full height. "Yeah, that should be all right." He addressed the kids again. "Just make sure you don't wander too far."

"We won't," they both chorused together right before they thundered down the rest of the stairs.

Blake laughed as he continued up the staircase. The house seemed quiet, even for as big as it was. He passed his room and the Perezes', where he could barely hear the drone of voices from a TV or some talk radio show. Mrs. Perez, no doubt. She apparently wasn't adjusting as well as her family to their forced seclusion.

Stopping outside Tori's room, he tapped on the door. A few seconds later, Isaiah answered, looking solemn and not at all the happy kid Blake had said goodbye to yesterday. "Hey, buddy, how's it going?"

"All right, I guess." He looked a lot like a kid, kicking rocks, who'd just been told he couldn't do something he had his heart set on.

Blake couldn't help his grin, but it quickly faded after recalling that Tori had planned to discuss the move to Portland with her son. If that was the case, Blake couldn't blame the kid. "Yeah? I saw Antonio and Lucinda a minute ago. They said you'd been having a lot of fun together."

Isaiah brightened somewhat. "They're nice. Antonio is teaching me Spanish."

"That's cool. Listen, Isaiah, is your mom around?"

"Yeah." He searched Blake's eyes and stepped closer. "She's crying, but she said not to tell anyone."

Blake knelt by him. "Well, that sucks. Do you know why she's crying?"

"I think it's because we're moving. I don't know why we have to move if it makes her so sad." Isaiah's blue eyes filled with tears.

Blake's heart wrenched for the boy. "How about if I talk to her. Do you think that would help?"

"Maybe if you tell her not to move, she'll stay here."

Sounded like a damn good idea, though doomed to fail. "Well, buddy, you just can't tell people, especially moms, that they can't do something. And sometimes, moms don't have a choice. They have to do things that make them sad. Do you understand?"

Blake sensed Tori watching him from the doorway and glanced up. "Hi. You got a minute to talk?"

Big blue eyes, surrounded by wet lashes, stared silently.

"Uh...Isaiah, Antonio, Lucinda, and Mr. Perez are in the kitchen. You want to run down and see if they can find you something to do for a few minutes while your mom and I visit?"

The boy turned to look at his mother. "Is that okay, Mom?"

A faint smile turned her lips up at the corners. "Pay attention to what Mr. Perez tells you, okay?"

"Okay." He skipped down the hall toward the stairs, his previous sadness miraculously swept away.

Tori disappeared inside the room, leaving the door partially open. Something definitely had her out of sorts. Blake pushed the door inward and stepped over the threshold, rummaging through his memories from before he'd discovered they were out of fuel. All he could come up with was pleasant conversation and a growing sense of rightness with her by his side. It was true that running out of fuel could have been deadly, if not for the proximity of a place to land. As it was, the small plane had soared like a champ until he was able to set it down.

Blake closed the door and saw her standing by the window, her arms wrapped around her stomach. "What's wrong, Tori?" He moved up behind her, sliding his arms around her torso, and nuzzled her neck.

"Don't touch me." Her reaction was forceful as she slapped his hands away and jerked from his grasp.

"Okay." He held his hands up. "I won't if you don't want me to, but you're going to have to tell me why."

Tori moved to the opposite side of the bed and faced him. "Am I a prisoner in your house?"

"What? No. Why would you ask that?"

"Because I overheard you talking with Travis and Coop out by the plane."

Confused, Blake stared as he took a mental inventory. *The emergency landing. The real reason they'd flown home with an empty fuel reservoir.* He'd touched on several topics with his friends, but the reason for her about-face was still a mystery.

"You brought me here so you could keep an eye on me until you decide if I conspired with a group of neo-Nazis. Do you really think I set those animals loose on Rafael's children? On you?"

His heart plummeted. She'd overheard them talking about her. "Tori, it wasn't like that. I just—"

"Really? What was it like, Blake?" She straightened, and her trembling chin gave away her raw emotions. "It must have been a little like sleeping with the enemy this morning. Right? Did you think I'd confess my darkest secrets in the throes of passion?" She turned away as though the sight of him made her sick.

Yeah. He had to agree with her, he was a douchebag. And it was way past time he leveled with her. "Tori, let me explain. Protecting the Perez family was my priority. I had to be sure about you. Showing up at the hangar the way you did...inviting yourself along on my flight. Your cell phone was equipped with a GPS chip that was transmitting your location the whole time we were together. Christ, Tori, a helicopter gunship showed up the minute we left and could easily have wiped out everyone at the safe house. I couldn't take a chance it would happen again."

"What? My phone...? You thought *I* led that helicopter to the safe house? And you never once thought to ask me?"

"I would have if you hadn't slipped out of the hospital as soon as my back was turned." Frustration sharpened his tone and he instantly regretted his words. He was pissed at himself and taking it out on her.

Tori groaned as she covered her ears with the heels of her hands and pivoted. Her shoulders slumped as though all the fight had gone out of her. "It wasn't me."

"I know, Tori." *Shit!* He should have started with that.

"Are you sure about me now, Blake?" She faced him again, and the emptiness in her eyes ripped a hole in his chest. "Or do you need to fuck me one more time before you decide?"

He flinched, the coarseness of the question from her sweet lips a testament to his betrayal and proof he deserved her anger and contempt. He dropped his hands on his hips, ashamed and heartsick...and terrified he'd just blown the best thing to happen to him in a long, long time. "Tori, please don't make this about us. Don't destroy what—"

"*Us? There is no us!*" For the first time, she raised her voice. Right away, she collected herself, running a hand across her forehead before she focused on him. "If what you say is true and I'm not a prisoner, then Isaiah and I will be leaving first thing tomorrow."

If she'd sliced him with a knife, it wouldn't have hurt as much. He couldn't let her go. "It's not safe yet."

"You didn't bring me here to make sure I was safe."

Blake started to call *bullshit* but only part of his reason had been for her safety. The other part had been to keep her close in case she was the enemy. As much as he hated to, he bit his tongue and let it go. "Don't stay at your house, Tori. It's too dangerous."

She waved her hand in the air, apparently to sweep away his concern. "I'll stop by to collect some of my things and then go to Jane's until I find a place to live in Portland."

"You decided to take the job?"

Tori barely nodded.

"Let me make sure you get there." Blake had no reason to hope she'd accept his help, but he had to try one more time.

She met his gaze with disappointment in her eyes. "That won't be necessary."

Blake fumbled for another argument, anything to keep her talking until he could figure out a way to make her not hate him. But, in the end, there was no way to defend what he'd done.

She whipped around him, padded to the door, and yanked it open. He strode toward her and brushed by the woman who'd come to mean so much to him over the past few days. It took every bit of his strength to drag his heavy heart out into the hallway and down the stairs.

It was his fault. He'd let her in despite knowing better. Celine had broken his young, foolish heart. It felt much the same this time, but he couldn't be in love with Tori, not really. If he was, he wouldn't have suspected her of a deliberate crime, and he certainly wouldn't have kept that fact from her. And sleeping with her? That had been the biggest fucking mistake of his life.

Three of PTS Security's men were taking charge of dinner in the kitchen. They'd put Rafael and the three kids to work. Blake forced a smile and bumped fists with Isaiah.

Kneeling in front of the boy, he looked around to make sure their conversation would be private. "I couldn't talk her out of moving. I'm sorry, Isaiah."

"Is she still crying?" Isaiah's lower lip quivered.

"She wasn't when I left, but it seemed like she might need some time alone. Maybe you could let her be until dinner is ready. Okay?" Blake shoved some wayward strands of hair from Isaiah's eyes.

"Okay."

"Are you good here, or do you want to go with me to the hangar?"

At that moment, Lucinda dropped a pan, and it clattered on the tiled floor. Isaiah looked at Blake with a partial grin. "I think they need me here."

Blake chuckled. "You might be right."

Isaiah trotted across the kitchen to resume his chores while Blake left through the back door, trying hard to ignore the feeling of loss that settled in his chest.

* * * *

It was after midnight. Blake had practically climbed under the dashboard of the Beechcraft, but his efforts had been rewarded. An amazingly simple job of jerry-rigging the gauge's needle had kept it from registering correctly until Blake's rap on the front had knocked it loose. Unfortunately, the evidence hadn't pointed conclusively to the saboteur. In the morning, he and Luke would question Harv Farrington.

Blake had worked right through dinner—not because he wasn't hungry, but because he didn't want to make Tori uncomfortable if she went down to eat. The Perezes' big black dog had joined him a couple of hours ago, plodding softly into the hangar and curling up next to one of the plane's tires. Blake was glad for the company and appreciated the silence.

He finished picking up the tools he'd thought he might need to achieve his goal, put them away and washed up. There was a small refrigerator in the office and a cot he'd slept on many times rather than return to the house alone. It would be fine for him tonight too.

Truth be told, he wasn't looking forward to watching Tori and Isaiah leave tomorrow. Maybe he'd work in the office until they were gone. *Because, shit, yeah, that would make it so much easier to go back to the house.* Hell, he was screwed either way.

He left the hangar and walked to the office, the dog on his heels, just as the shift changed on the perimeter. The men who'd been sitting around a small bonfire, telling stories, grabbed their gear and headed into the dark trees. A few minutes later, the sentries who'd been relieved returned, stowed their gear and walked toward the house, probably for an early breakfast.

Blake climbed toward his private office on the second floor, passing the monitoring equipment at the top of the stairs. MacGyver was just relieving Coop, and the three of them opened some beers, sat and visited for a few minutes. Blake would have been hard pressed to recall the conversation and excused himself before long.

Not bothering to turn on a light in his office, he'd barely closed the door before sinking down on the cot. MacGyver had been right—he was damn sore. Was Tori too?

Shit! So much for getting her out of my head.

Sleep proved elusive. Blake was still wide awake, staring at the ceiling, when the perimeter alarm shrieked its warning.

Chapter 18

Tori sat straight up in bed. The alarm blaring in the hallway seemed to originate from every direction. At once, the sounds of footsteps running outside her door made her slip her feet toward the floor. "If the alarm goes off again, stay put until someone you trust comes to get you," Blake had said after the last incident, which had turned out to be a false alarm. Maybe it would this time too.

She reached out to touch her son in the bed beside her, only mildly surprised he hadn't woken up. Her baby could sleep through almost anything, except his nightmares. When her hand met only cold sheets, she lunged for the nightstand lamp. His side of the bed was empty.

"Isaiah?" Her voice only a strangled whisper, she vaulted from the bed and whirled around, searching in the dim corners of the room. Darting to the bathroom, she flung the door open to reveal more emptiness. The closet door stood open, and she rushed to flip on the overhead light, only to find vacant shelves and unused clothes hangers. She spun around as a chill wrapped her in a layer of goose bumps. Her son was gone.

Somebody finally turned off the alarm. The ensuing silence echoed in her head. Quickly, she donned her robe and slippers. With Isaiah missing, she couldn't wait. If Sebastian Wahl's men had breached the perimeter, intent on finding Rafael Perez, they wouldn't care that Isaiah was only a child.

Tori hurried to the door and yanked it open. Stifling a cry, she fell back a step, a hand flying to her throat. A man stood just outside in the hallway, one hand raised as though preparing to knock.

"Oh, hell. I didn't mean to startle you. Blake sent me." The man lowered his arm and stepped into the room. The light shone on his face enough for Tori to recognize him.

Relief flooded through her, until she remembered the suspicions Blake had shared with his friends after their plane had run out of fuel. Had Blake really sent him? That question would have to wait. "Harv? Isaiah is gone. I have to find him."

"Relax. I saw him downstairs a few minutes ago, having a bite to eat with a couple of the PTS guys. After the alarm went off, they probably took him to the same place we're going. If not, I'll help you look for him." Harv glanced cautiously into the hallway then opened the door and ushered her through.

Something wasn't right. Isaiah never wandered off, and he didn't go somewhere with anyone unless he had her permission. *Well, hell, that wasn't exactly true anymore.* He'd been almost obsessive about staying close to her since Ken died...until Blake had burst on the scene. Still, why would he leave their bedroom in the middle of the night without waking her? He'd clearly been upset by their conversation that afternoon, but the move to Portland must be bothering him more than she'd anticipated.

Two armed men entered through the back door as she and Harv rushed into the kitchen. "Everything okay out there?" Harv motioned for Tori to continue toward the pantry.

"Not sure what set the alarm off yet. We're going up to lock down Perez's room," one of the men responded as they traipsed through the kitchen and continued out the other side.

As soon as they were gone, Harv caught up, took her elbow and led her through the pantry to another door. "Where does this go?" And where was Isaiah?

"Basement." Harv tugged her through the doorway. With the door closed behind them, he pulled a chain over his head and a single bulb blinked on to partially light the stairs leading down.

Tori craned her neck to see around Harv as they descended the stairs, hoping to catch a glimpse of Isaiah, safely ensconced down here. Why hadn't Blake simply told her the cellar was a safe place to go? And why was Rafael and his family being guarded upstairs rather than bringing them here as well? The answer came like a knife in her ribs. Blake wanted to separate her from the Perezes because he still didn't trust her. Would he go so far as to keep Isaiah from her?

Reaching the lower level, Tori spun around, searching the gloom for her son. Finding nothing, she stepped back toward the stairs. "Isaiah isn't here. I'm going to find him."

She managed to get two steps up before Harv's arm slid around her waist, drawing her backward against his chest. One hand clamped over her mouth, jerking her head back so hard she was afraid he would break her neck. Still, she clawed and kicked as he dragged her through a maze of old newspapers, shelves lined with paint cans, and stacks and stacks of boxes. In a far corner, he grasped a sliding metal door and shoved it open enough to squeeze through, half carrying her.

Turning, he closed them in and slammed her, face first, into the cold metal barrier, hard enough to knock the wind from her. While Tori fought to breathe, Harv dropped a heavy iron latch from the door to the concrete wall beside it, making it impossible for anyone to open it from the other side. With the flick of a switch, he dropped them into utter darkness.

Harv jerked her arms behind her, cruelly securing her wrists. Then he shoved a strip of fabric that tasted like stale cigarette smoke into her mouth, and tied it behind her head with malicious force before shoving her into the wall again. Leaning against her so she couldn't move, he lit a torch that hung in a bracket a foot from her head.

Ripping the flaming stick from the wall, he spun her to face him. A smile split his lips. "I don't have anything against you, honey. In fact, I think you're real pretty. But I've got my orders, so here's what's going to happen. We're going to walk down this tunnel until we get to the end. It's nice the old guy that sold this place to Sorenson was sure the government was out to get him. He made it easy for me."

Tori's heart was hammering so hard she felt faint. Willing herself not to pass out while she was at Harv's mercy, she glared her hatred. Was he following Blake's orders? Even though Blake's betrayal had hurt her badly, Tori didn't want to believe he'd turn one of his men loose on her.

"When we get to the end, we're going to climb up to the surface…and you're not going to make a sound. Do you know why?"

It wasn't like she could answer him with the gag so tight, but she tried to wiggle away from him.

Harv snickered. "Because I have the boy."

Tori went still, afraid to move in the face of his unspoken threat.

"Oh, he's safe…for now. But if you do anything to get us caught by Sorenson's men, and something happens to me so I can't get back to turn the kid loose, he's not going to survive. No one will ever find him. Get it?"

Tori grasped on to the fact he was worried about being caught by Sorenson. She should have known Blake wasn't behind Harv's cruelty. She stared into his hard, compassionless eyes until she couldn't stop her own tears from welling. She dropped her head and, with a nod, indicated she understood.

Harv jerked her in front of him. "Start walking, honey."

Tori refused to let any tears fall in front of this monster, but her vision blurred anyway. Every time she tripped on the uneven floor and slowed to keep from falling, Harv gave her another shove. Her wrists and shoulders ached from the tight bindings, but worse was the despair that seeped into every cell in her body. Isaiah was alone and in God only knew what kind of danger. He'd be terrified. There was nothing she could do to help him except make sure Harv made it wherever he was taking her, on the slim chance he would really come back and set her son free.

She concentrated on putting one foot in front of the other. Seconds became minutes and strung together into an unbearable void. There was no way of knowing how much time had passed when Harv finally grabbed her arm and stopped her endless shuffling. Tori lifted her head. The stifling air in the passage seemed cooler, and she could smell pine trees and fresh dirt. Ahead of them, wooden rungs of a ladder were bolted to the cement wall, leading upward to a metal grate. She almost smiled when the moon's soft glow painted shadows on the tunnel wall.

Harv made her go first, without benefit of hands to pull herself up. He climbed so close behind her, his arms caging her on both sides, rubbing his body against her with too much enthusiasm to be accidental. Revulsion threatened a gag reflex she barely managed to tamp down.

He moved the metal covering and stuck his head out first. Apparently satisfied with what he found, he closed the grate and pressed against her again, his mouth close to her ear. "Remember what I said about the kid. Make one sound and he suffers for it, and it won't be pretty."

Like I can forget, you piece of shit.

Tori didn't dare move or even breathe when he ground the hard ridge beneath his pants into her backside while he jammed one hand under her robe and stroked her side. "Too bad I'm being paid extra not to touch you." His hot breath tickled her neck.

Abruptly, he started climbing again, grabbing the back collar of her robe and yanking her up and out of the tunnel at the same time. He hissed a warning for silence as he pushed her to the ground. A minute or two passed before he moved out, dragging her through the thick underbrush on a downhill course.

Tori couldn't tell where she was. There were no houses or outbuildings, nothing but trees and uneven ground. Blake's house was probably behind them, but were they beyond the perimeter his men guarded? With every step she took, she prayed they'd set off an alarm and alert someone to their presence.

Harv didn't seem worried, though, stomping through the brush, rocks and fallen timber at a breakneck pace. Tori stumbled as he dragged her along. Her slippers wouldn't have been her first choice of footwear for an early morning hike through the woods. They did little to protect her from the harsh underbrush. When she was sure she couldn't go another step, suddenly Harv halted.

Ahead, through the trees, a light flashed. Hope flared within her but quickly dissipated as Harv started toward the spot. Far too soon, he hauled her to an overgrown dirt road. A dark sedan waited silently a few feet away. She jumped as the trunk lid popped open.

"Hurry up. Put her inside." A deep male voice startled Tori and she pulled back, but Harv jerked her against his side.

"Do you have my money?" Harv frowned, apparently having trust issues.

"You haven't fucking earned it yet. Put her in the trunk." Whoever sat in the dark interior of the car with the front window partway down was clearly short on patience.

Panic rolled over Tori in waves. Who was it? Why did he want her? Instinctively, she dragged her feet as Harv started toward the car again. When he yanked her hard, Tori whimpered.

Instantly, he held a knife to her throat. "What'd I say, huh? Not. A. Sound."

No! No way. I'm not going in that trunk without a fight!

When Tori clamped her mouth shut and nodded, he hurried toward the rear of the car, pushing her ahead of him. He released one arm to raise the lid all the way, and Tori rammed into him, pushing him off balance, but she hadn't gone two steps before he caught her and slammed his fist into her jaw. As darkness threatened to engulf her, he pushed her. She fell backward into the trunk. Despite her kicking and squirming, Harv wrestled the rest of her inside and slammed the lid.

Tori moaned, the dull ache in her head making it hard to think clearly. She forced her eyes open, determined not to give in to the grayness at the edges of her mind. *No! I have to stay awake. I need to know where they're taking me and be ready if, no, when I get a chance to escape. Isaiah needs me.*

The trunk was empty, except for some crinkly plastic beneath her and something long and thin that she'd landed on, like a shovel. *Oh damn! Not good. Are they going to kill me and bury me out here in the woods?*

Strangely, the possibility brought a measure of calm. Mostly because she had nothing left to lose. She no longer had any faith that Harv would return to Blake's house and produce Isaiah. That was, no doubt, something he'd said to keep her quiet. Well, she was done being a model captive. Angry voices broke into her thoughts.

"Now I'm done. Give me my money so I can get the hell out of here before they discover she's missing."

The car door opened and closed, and Tori started at the smack of flesh on flesh.

"What the fuck?" Harv roared and then something slammed into the top of the compartment where Tori was trapped.

The sounds of scuffling continued for a few seconds and abruptly went silent. Tori held her breath, waiting for whatever would happen next. Something brushing against the trunk made her jerk back just before the lid lifted. A dark form in a short-sleeved T-shirt and a baseball cap stood silhouetted against the dark sky. He held a piece of rope in his hand.

"Can't have you kicking out the taillights, now can we?" He leaned down to grab her legs.

Tori drew back her foot and kicked, hitting dead center on the man's face. Bones cracked with a nauseating crunch, and he grabbed for his nose, going down on his knees. She flopped over the rim of the trunk, landing with a *whomp* on the ground, inches from Harv's face. His eyes wide and terrified, he tried to speak as blood seeped around the edges of a knife embedded in his stomach. Tori stared, unable to look away from the ghastly sight, until she heard the other man's muffled curse. With one last look at Harv, she rolled to her knees, gained her feet and ran.

Tori didn't stop until she dropped from exhaustion. Her lungs aching and heart drumming, she crawled under a downed log and tried to find a comfortable position—impossible with her arms stretched behind her. Where was she? Which way should she go? Blake's house had to be up the hill, but the chances of stumbling on it weren't promising. Better to head downhill, where it was more populated, and find help. If she could only get her hands free.

She tugged and wrestled with the ropes but soon gave up. Lacking the strength to slip from her bindings, she was only making herself more miserable. The gag was another matter, however. It had to go. Carefully catching the top of the fabric strip on a broken stub of a branch, she pulled until the sharp edge of the wood sliced into her cheek. Groaning, she tried again...and again. On the third try, the gag slid down over her chin. Her cheek stung like hell, and it was hard to tell how much dirt she'd packed in the cut, but it was worth it to be free of the gag.

Tori rested a few more minutes before rolling out of her hiding place. As she was about to stand, a sound made her hesitate. An animal hunting in the dark? A pine cone dropping from a tree? Or had someone stepped on a branch? The forest went silent as she waited and listened. Several minutes passed as she crouched by the log. Tori was ready to admit she was hearing things that weren't there. Her heart lighter, she rose slowly to her feet. Immediately, the sound came again, closer this time.

The last of her courage took flight. She ran, without looking back, with no idea where she was going. Through loose rocks, brush, and over treacherous terrain, she didn't slow, heading ever downhill. Without her hands free to keep her balanced, she fell often, picking herself up again, ignoring the scrapes and cuts on her arms. The moon disappeared below the trees, making it harder to find a safe path.

Staying in the shadows, she topped a small rise and started down the other side. Suddenly, the ground dropped away beneath her. Tree branches tore at her clothing as she tumbled. Rocks broke her fall with bone-crushing force. She cried out as her arms wrenched beneath her, and her right wrist popped. Pain radiated through her bones. Her head cracked against something hard, and lights exploded in front of her eyes. Darkness encroached, promising oblivion, and she surrendered.

Chapter 19

The coffeemaker sizzled as it spewed the last of the hot, black brew into the glass carafe. After the all-nighter the men had worked, they'd need that and more. Blake removed his sunglasses and hung them on the neck of his T-shirt, then grabbed the coffee and started to fill the cups of the men who leaned against the counter. Mrs. Perez elbowed into his path and plucked it from his hands with a clucking noise, shooing him away.

"Go. Sit. You need rest." Mrs. Perez turned her back and continued down the line of PTS Security personnel who'd gathered in Blake's kitchen to debrief.

Blake scratched his head and shuffled to the refrigerator, where he pulled out three dozen eggs, five pounds of sausage and half a dozen rolls of biscuit dough. He appreciated Mrs. Perez's concern, though he was a little surprised, given her former reclusiveness.

There was no arguing he was beat. But, if he quit now, he'd only start thinking about the shitty way he'd treated Tori. It was smarter to keep busy.

He stacked the breakfast makings on the counter and reached for a couple of his big skillets and a baking pan, but Mrs. Perez laid her hand on his as he turned on the oven.

"*Está bien.* I cook. Go." A smile softened her features, and then she scurried away to unwrap the sausage and mold it into patties.

Well...hell, maybe she needs busywork too. Blake moved to the table and pulled out one of the chairs. The owners of PTS, joined by Rafael Perez, were going over incident reports with a handful of crew members, while waiting for coffee and breakfast, in that order.

"At one fifteen, the perimeter was breached." Coop read from the report he'd written sometime early this morning. "Thermographic cameras picked up seven targets inside the cordon. They advanced to within two hundred yards of HQ before our guys made contact. Then they simply disappeared from the cameras and melted away, slick as can be. Sebastian's crew has some serious skills. I'd guess ex-military."

Rafael swore, and his brow furrowed. "It's as though they're telling us they can go wherever they want, and we can't stop them."

"That's where you're wrong." Luke held out his cup as Mrs. Perez made a pass with a new pot of freshly brewed coffee. "Just because we *didn't* stop them last night doesn't mean we *couldn't*. We learned a lot about the enemy in just a few hours."

"For example, they came by chopper, which returned to a private helicopter pad four miles north of here, as the crow flies. The helipad is owned by Vincent Cavanaugh, one of Sebastian's wealthiest donors." MacGyver stood, took the carafe from Mrs. Perez and continued to pour coffee for the waiting men. When it was empty, he handed it back to her. *"Gracias, Señora."*

"We knew they were there before they got close enough to set off the alarm. They got as far as they did because we let them." Travis crossed his ankle over his knee and a satisfied smile brightened his rough visage. "Those guys were the grunt team, out for the same thing we were, information. If we'd taken them down, Sebastian would be out hiring more men as we speak."

"We need to get Sebastian and bastards like Cavanaugh, who make his militia possible. And guess who was on his phone last night, giving step-by-step instructions to his people?" Blake grinned. He was proud of the PTS team, proud to be one of them. "Your FBI pal, Special Agent Roberts, got a digital recording that puts Sebastian in charge of last night's foray."

MacGyver lifted his hand and smacked Blake's palm. "We're going to nail his ass. He won't be able to resist coming back since our guys were slow to respond and gave the bare minimum of pushback. Right now, Sebastian is thinking PTS Security operatives are incompetent and that you're a fool for hiring us. And that's just what we want him to think."

The spicy scent of sausage cooking made Blake's stomach growl, and he rose to set out plates and flatware, stopping to hook his arm around the shoulders of the diminutive woman who bustled about cooking for them. When he dropped a peck on her cheek, she turned a vibrant shade of red even as a mischievous grin curved her lips. Blake chuckled. Mrs. Perez was finally starting to lighten up.

He caught the tail end of Luke's plan as he approached the table. "...the alarm system won't be set. Something that shouldn't surprise them since they already think we're careless. The cameras will be operational, and, in addition to our guys, Special Agent Roberts has an FBI team ready to drop in at a moment's notice. I suspect Sebastian won't be far away." Luke peered directly at Rafael. "He'll want *you* to see his face and know he's won."

Coop slapped a hand on Rafael's shoulder. "We'll be ready for him, and with multiple counts of attempted murder on his slate, he'll be an old man if he ever sees the world outside of prison again."

Rafael ducked his head and rubbed the back of his neck. "I can't thank you enough." His voice was thick with emotion.

"Don't thank us yet," Luke said. "Even the best plans go awry, so stay alert, everybody."

A few minutes later, Mrs. Perez pulled the last baking sheet from the oven and transferred hot biscuits to a towel-lined bowl. She turned to the group with a tentative smile. "Breakfast is ready."

The men didn't wait for a second invitation, grabbing plates and filing by the island laden with scrambled eggs, sausage, pancakes and biscuits. Some of them took their plates out in the backyard and gobbled their food while standing. Others pulled up chairs and got comfortable at the table. A loud hum of conversation with laughter interspersed was the mark of a successful mission.

Blake poured another cup of coffee and stood back to enjoy their camaraderie. There was nothing like the connection between men who'd faced danger together. That same connection was what made Blake decide to move across the country and start a new job. His SEAL buddies, new and old, kept him sane. Strange that he could maintain a deep bond with MacGyver and the others, but when it came to a woman, one he liked a lot, he was too damn cowardly to let down his guard.

His appetite sufficiently squashed, he dumped the rest of his coffee and headed for the back door. The alarm had sounded last night before he'd managed to get any shut-eye, but he was too wound up to sleep now. No sense standing around here when he could be giving the Beechcraft another going over to make sure there weren't any other surprises. That was a better use of his time. If he hung out here until Tori and Isaiah came downstairs, he'd probably do something stupid...like try to talk her into staying. He'd barely been able to keep himself from checking on her this morning after all the excitement had died down.

"Blake?"

Hand on the doorknob, he stopped. *Shit! Isaiah. Will the kid be upset if I don't say goodbye?*

The others in the room went silent as Blake turned, forcing a smile to his face. Isaiah stood in the kitchen doorway, his eyes swollen and puffy from crying. Kellie, worry scrunching her forehead, towered over the small boy, her hands gripping his shoulders.

Dark foreboding launched Blake toward the boy as his stomach convulsed with the absolute certainty something was seriously wrong. "Isaiah, what's going on?"

Tears rimmed over and ran down Isaiah's cheeks. "Do you know where my mom is?"

The cold words fell like chips of ice during a thaw. Blake knelt in front of the boy and reached for him, drawing him close. "I thought she was in your room, but it's okay, bud. She probably just went for a walk. We'll find her." Blake nearly choked, forcing words not even he believed around the lump in his throat. Tori wouldn't have left her son by choice.

Kellie shook her head. "I found him outside his room a few minutes ago. He said he was looking for his mom. Tori wasn't in her room, so I suggested we find you."

Blake set Isaiah back a step. "Was your mom there when you went to bed?"

"Yes, but I couldn't sleep. I didn't want to wake her because she was so sad, so I played under the bed. Sometimes I like to do that." Isaiah sniffled.

"Is that right? I bet it makes you feel safe, doesn't it?" Blake wiped the tear tracks from the boy's face.

"Sometimes, but last night I fell asleep. A really loud noise scared me."

"An alarm sounded, but we took care of everything."

"A man came to the door and said you'd sent him…and then he took my mom someplace and she never came back."

Blake exchanged a glance with MacGyver, who'd moved closer and now stood beside Kellie. Blake hadn't sent anyone, so what the hell? "Did you see the man, Isaiah?"

"Uh-uh. Just his legs. He had on cowboy boots with big gold stars."

Son-of-a-bitch! Blake managed to clench his teeth and stop the stream of cursing that begged for release. He pulled Isaiah to his chest and straightened to his full height as the boy hooked his arms around Blake's neck. Fighting to keep his anger in check, he turned to face the men at the table. "Where's Harv?"

"Haven't seen him this morning," Travis said, and the refrain was echoed by several other men in the group.

"Warner and I ran into him when we came through here last night on our way to Mr. Perez's room." Bob Crenshaw stepped forward. "Ms.

Michaels was with him. I thought it was strange the kid wasn't with her, but I didn't get the impression she was under duress."

"Did they say anything?" Blake had emphasized to Tori the importance of staying put if an alarm sounded and especially not standing in front of a window. Hell, the kitchen was practically wall-to-wall windows.

"Now that you mention it, she didn't say anything, which was kind of odd too, because she's always real polite to all the men. Harv asked what was going on outside. We were in and out of here pretty quick and only exchanged a few words."

Blake scanned the kitchen. "What were they doing in here?"

Crenshaw shrugged. "They weren't really doing anything, just standing over there by the pantry door."

"*Christ!*" Blake swiveled slowly and stared where Crenshaw indicated, memories of the week he'd unpacked his few belongings into his new house playing through his mind. "Kellie, would you keep an eye on Isaiah, please?" He lowered the boy to the floor, and Kellie took his hand.

"What's wrong, Blake?" Worry etched lines in her face as she studied him.

"That damned old man." He rushed toward the pantry and through it until he jerked the basement door open.

Goddammit! He was right. The single bulb burning over his head was enough to verify someone had passed through here recently.

"Blake, talk to us, bro. Where the hell are we going?"

MacGyver and Coop followed him as he started down the stairs. "The old man who sold me this house was a crazy old coot. In addition to building where he couldn't be seen from the air, he also gave himself a few different escape routes. I stumbled on one of them when I was moving in."

Blake reached the bottom of the stairs and led the way through tons of shit the previous owner had collected and then left behind. Blake had intended to clear everything out, but the task hadn't been high on his priority list.

A heavy, metal door barred his way when he finally halted. Coop and MacGyver gathered around him as Blake surveyed the iron hasp that usually secured the entrance, now hanging loose. He yanked on the handle, but the door didn't budge. He hadn't expected it to. There was another iron hasp just like this one on the inside so that, once in the tunnel, a person could pretty much guarantee no one would follow him.

"Tunnel, huh? Where does it come out?" MacGyver kept pace with Blake as he hurried back to the stairs.

"It's an old mine tunnel that goes through the mountain. The old man had it shored up with concrete braces all the way. He spared no expense, and the damn thing will no doubt stand longer than the house." Blake took the stairs two at a time and caught himself before he slammed through the door at the top. If Isaiah and Kellie were still in the kitchen, he didn't want to give the kid any more reason to be scared.

Bob Crenshaw was the only one remaining, and he crossed his arms over his broad chest. "Did you find anything?"

"No. The way was blocked. We'll have to go around." *And then I'm going to have that fucking tunnel filled in.*

"Luke and Travis went to line out the men on the new plan, but they'll be available if you need them." Crenshaw glanced at the other two men before giving his full attention to Blake. "I just wanted to say I'm sorry as hell. I should have been paying more attention. I knew something was up, but I was focused on the job I was given."

"You did exactly what you needed to do. You're not at fault here." Harv was and Blake was going to make him wish he was dead.

"I'd like to aid in the search…if you don't mind." Crenshaw straightened and, clearly, determination made it unlikely he'd take no for an answer. His light-brown eyes were still clouded with undeserved guilt.

Blake knew how it felt to hold himself responsible for something entirely out of his control. No amount of talking would make it any better. He clapped a hand on Crenshaw's shoulder. "Glad to have your help." He dug his keys from his pocket as he pushed through the back door into the bright morning sunlight. Automatically, his hand went to the neck of his T-shirt for the dark glasses riding there, and he slipped them on.

One of the four-wheelers sat close to the house, and Blake veered toward the ATV. "The tunnel exit is beyond the perimeter we set up, which explains why we didn't pick up anything on the monitors last night. There's an old forest service road not far from the tunnel exit. This will be the fastest mode of transportation."

MacGyver, Coop, and Crenshaw piled in and hung on as Blake fired it up, made a U-turn and raced along the narrow path leading to the office building and the private road that ended there. MacGyver's phone buzzed a few minutes later, and he filled in Travis on where they were going and why.

"Tell Luke to stay on Perez. We've got Sebastian where we want him. Let's not waste the opportunity." Blake yelled over the engine noise.

MacGyver nodded. "Did you hear that?" he said into the phone. Apparently, he received an affirmative answer. "Okay, if anything changes on either end, we'll be in touch."

Blake's gut churned as he raced along the gravel road circling the base of the mountain. Why had Harv taken Tori from the house? Was he working for Sebastian? Had it been Harv who gave Sebastian the location of the Perez family at the safe house? Of all the questions, that one angered Blake the most. His suspicion it might have been Tori had driven a wedge between them when he'd wanted— What *had* he wanted, anyway? Despite what he and Tori might have had, fate had intervened to tell him just how undeserving of a happy ending he was.

Blake turned on a forest service road, seldom used and overgrown with grasses and weeds. Even small trees had started and sprung up in the center strip. However, some of those trees showed signs of being bent over, and, looking closely, he made out tire tracks on the hard-packed ground. Just one set as though someone had gone in but not come out.

He proceeded cautiously for a few more minutes and then, rounding a corner, he stopped. MacGyver already had field glasses in front of his face, surveying the scene two hundred yards ahead.

"No movement. No one visible in the car. Trunk is open." He lowered the glasses. "Looks deserted, but let's hoof it from here just in case."

"I was going to suggest the same thing." Blake killed the engine, and they dropped out of the ATV, fading into the trees.

Weapons drawn, they approached slowly. When they were within twenty feet, Blake heard someone groaning. He motioned for the others to remain where they were while he crept closer to investigate. Skirting the front bumper and along the side, he stopped abruptly as a body came into view. The groan came again, and Blake hurried to the rear of the car.

Harv Farrington lay on the ground, a long-handled knife buried in his abdomen. From the looks of it, he'd just about bled out, but the agony of his wound had probably kept him conscious. Blake holstered his weapon and motioned the others forward before crouching beside the wounded man.

"Where is she, Harv?"

Harv's eyes opened a slit, and it was obvious he had trouble focusing on Blake. He eventually figured out who'd found him, judging by the way he flinched away. "I'm…I'm sorry, Blake. I didn't hurt her. I…I swear."

"Just tell me two things, Harv, and I'll get you to a hospital. Where is Tori now, and who hired you?"

The man would never make it long enough to get help, but Blake had meant what he'd said anyway. He sensed his friends watching at his back.

"I don't know…where she is. He…was going to…tie her up in…the trunk. I must…must have passed out. When I…came to…they were both… both gone." Talking was obviously difficult for him, and Harv stopped frequently to gasp a mouthful of air.

"Who is he? Who hired you, Harv?" Blake barely resisted the urge to shake the information from the man.

"Not…him. He's…just a flunky…like…like me. I…I don't know…who the…head guy is. Just…just a voice on…on the phone…and a…paycheck." Coughing ravaged Harv, and he spit up blood.

He wasn't long for this world. Blake palmed his cell phone and dialed 911, gave his name and location and suggested they send a chopper before he hung up.

MacGyver leaned over Harv when his spasms released him. "Was it you who told Sebastian where to find Perez at the safe house?"

"No. It wasn't…didn't have anything to do with Sebastian. The man on the phone…didn't seem to…" Coughing seized him again, but this time, the convulsions were too much. He clenched a fistful of Blake's shirt as the life slowly faded from his panic-filled eyes.

Didn't seem to…what? Blake scraped a hand down his rough face.

"Hey! Over here," Crenshaw said. "I found her tracks."

Blake sprinted to where Bob Crenshaw knelt at the edge of the trees.

He held up a blue, fuzzy slipper. "Found this in the trunk. It has a fairly significant tread pattern, so I started scouting around." He pointed to the ground.

A footprint with the exact same markings stood out on a small patch of damp ground where the last rain still soaked the borrow pit. Just one, but it was enough to point them in the right direction. Unfortunately, fresh boot tracks, showing clearly where someone else had knelt to inspect Tori's prints, meant whoever had knifed Harv knew which way she was headed too.

Five minutes later, Blake and Crenshaw ducked into the shadow of the woods. Blake carried a backpack with a first-aid kit, a blanket, and some bottled water he'd stockpiled in the back of the four-wheeler for just such an instance. Crenshaw packed a long rifle and a length of rope coiled over his shoulder. Coop and MacGyver stayed with Harv's body to direct the evac chopper to the spot when they got close, but they were also keeping an eye on the car in case Harv's killer returned.

Blake and Crenshaw spread out, walking parallel to each other in hopes of keeping more terrain in sight. So far, staying on Tori's trail had been mostly luck, though neither she nor the man who tracked her were taking any pains to hide their progress.

It'd been a while since either of them had spotted Tori's prints, or those of her pursuer. Blake was ready to admit he'd lost the trail, double back, and try to pick it up again when Crenshaw whistled. From fifty feet to

Blake's right, the man held up another blue slipper and pointed north. Blake veered toward him, quickening his pace to catch up.

Tori couldn't have been making very good time with one bare foot. Now, with both slippers gone, maybe he and Crenshaw would have an advantage. Unfortunately, so would the man who killed Harv. *Can't go there.* Blake picked up the pace.

Suddenly, Crenshaw stopped a few feet ahead of Blake and signaled for him to take cover. No sooner had they both hit the ground when shots rang out, kicking up a spray of dirt that stung the skin of Blake's face. He rolled sideways and stopped behind the dubious cover of a lodge pole pine. Peering around one side and then the other, he could barely make out Crenshaw crawling on his elbows, the rifle laying across his arms.

His partner halted on the south side of a low rock outcrop and rested the barrel of the rifle across the top. Blake had trained as a sniper too, and he recognized the cautious preparations Crenshaw made. Lining up his sights. Testing the wind. Getting so wrapped up in the target. Forcing everything from his mind except the shot. Becoming an extension of the weapon in his hands.

Blake surveyed the area Crenshaw was focusing on, but nothing moved in his line of sight. In fact, minutes stretched agonizingly long and *nothing* moved. Not the shooter. Not Crenshaw. Even the wind, whispering through the treetops, seemed to hold its breath.

Crenshaw apparently possessed patience in spades. Blake had very little. Add to that the fact he couldn't see anything from his position. Multiplied exponentially by his concern for Tori. Where was she? Was she hurt? Lost? Suffering hypothermia? Every minute they spent waiting for the shooter to poke his head up was a minute that might be her last. *Jesus!* He couldn't hunker down behind the trees and do nothing.

If Crenshaw needed something in the crosshairs, maybe Blake could make that happen. It'd worked for Tori after the chopper crashed. He shifted into a crouch and scanned the area. Crenshaw glanced toward him, and Blake signaled his intention to make a move. Crenshaw nodded and turned his head back to press against the rifle butt.

Blake lunged upward and broke from cover, already running. He'd taken two strides when the gunfire started. Lead hit the ground all around him. One ricocheted off a rock and damned if he didn't feel it whine past his ear. His goal, two trees close together twenty-five feet to his right and closer to Crenshaw, suddenly seemed like a bad choice.

He dove the last ten feet, and then a high-powered rifle belched one round, and the echo reverberated in the silence that followed. Blake peered between the trees to see Crenshaw eject the empty jacket and crank another shell in the chamber.

He leaned into the scope again and jabbed a thumb in the air before rolling to his back. Raising his head, he grinned at Blake. "You in one piece?"

"Hell, yeah." Other than being coated in dirt from head to toe, Blake was a lot better than he'd been a moment ago. He pushed to his feet, brushed mindlessly at his jeans before giving up on that and strode toward his friend. "Good shot." He offered a hand and pulled the other man off the ground.

"Wouldn't have been nearly as good if you hadn't made a target of yourself. Let's not make a habit of that, okay?" Crenshaw picked up the rifle, slung it across his back and policed his brass.

"I'll go along with that," Blake said.

When they strode up on the man Crenshaw had shot, Blake checked for a pulse, more out of habit than anything. The slug through his heart was clearly evidence of his demise. *Damn it!* He hadn't given them a choice, but Blake would have paid any amount of money to be able to question the man. Plucking the wallet from the dead man's pocket, Blake flipped it open and stared at the driver's license. Ray Bennett didn't ring any bells. Who the hell was he? And why was he after Tori? As close as Blake could figure, she played no role in Sebastian's war. Harv had said it wasn't Sebastian who hired him, but who else could it be?

"Blake. Over here." Crenshaw's raised voice broke through Blake's internal deliberations.

His partner stood on the top of a rise, looking down the other side. As Blake stepped up beside him, the ground fell away to allow a stunning view of Cypress Point with the Pacific in the distance. The early morning fog had retreated but still hung over the ocean, waiting to return. For now, the sun rode the crest of every wave as it rushed toward shore.

Blake followed Crenshaw's gaze straight down, and his heart stuttered before kicking in again, this time helped along by a shot of adrenaline.

The drop was a hundred feet or so, but thirty feet down, a sloping rock promontory had apparently broken Tori's fall. It was covered with moss and lichen, and one spindly cypress tree grew on the edge. Tori, her hands bound behind her back, lay unmoving. At this distance, Blake couldn't tell if she was breathing. What he did know was that the tree was the only thing that had kept her from sliding off the rock and falling the rest of the way. If she was alive and regained consciousness, any movement could steal that advantage in a heartbeat.

Chapter 20

Tori moved, and nausea rolled in her stomach. She groaned, hoping that would be enough to make it stop. It worked for a minute, and she retreated into the darkness that offered relief from the bone-chilling cold tormenting her soul.

The voice in her head was calling her back, but she didn't want to stay with the pain that seared her nerve endings nor the deep, wrenching grief for the son she'd never see again. Though, trying to remember how and why she'd lost him led her into a maze where every turn brought more confusion.

Fear. Pain. Running. Falling. But always fear...

The darkness lifted her, enveloping her as though she was a baby to be swaddled. Inexplicably, wherever the darkness pressed against her, warmth bloomed, and hope grew. Tori burrowed deeper, craving more.

An alarm. Where is Isaiah? I searched and...lost my slippers...can't feel my feet...

Her world tilted, and she woke. The out-of-control sensation had her spreading her arms to steady herself. *How long have I been sleeping? And why are there tiny grains of sand under my eyelids?* Suddenly, pain invaded her consciousness, and a moan escaped.

Wait, my hands are free? Her hands had been bound behind her back, making it impossible to stop her fall, but now the bindings on her wrists were gone. The voice in her head was still with her, though, whispering in her ear. A warm breath teased the hair by her temple and raised goose bumps on her arms. She smiled as the deeply sensual sound wrapped around her and tugged her toward awareness.

The tone and volume changed and took on a new urgency. The words, indistinct and faint, were as compelling as the sense of comfort they wrought. Was it normal for the voice in her head to take on a life of its own?

Manic laughter bubbled inside her. Hearing voices was bad enough, but creating an imaginary friend to keep her company? Perhaps she'd slipped a little too close to crazy. Abruptly, the voice hushed, and Tori stirred from her lethargy, wanting, needing it back.

Pushing against the darkness was useless, and she gave up, slowly sinking into it again. The smell of summer rain tickled her memory, and she froze as she recognized the scent. Blake's scent. Was it his comforting presence that had calmed her fears? His solid chest cradling her as he held her securely in his strong arms? The impossibility of it didn't matter as certainty coursed through her veins like flood waters in a creek bed.

"You're okay. I've got you."

Tori wasn't at all surprised when the voice addressed her. A smile pulled at her cracked and dry lips. "You're here." The words scraped through her parched throat.

He must have heard her, though. For a couple of beats, he went perfectly still, except for the tightening of his arms around her. He buried his face in the crook of her neck. His breathing faltered, and his body shook as though some deeply buried emotion had robbed him of restraint.

A moment passed before he raised his head and spoke. "I'd have been here sooner, but Isaiah didn't report you missing until this morning."

Isaiah. "Is he all right? I couldn't find him last night…and then the alarm went off, and Harv came to get us." The horrible memories tumbled from her lips as though the dam had burst. "Harv said he had Isaiah—that no one would ever find him unless… He forced me to leave with him, and there was another man waiting in the woods. I think he…killed Harv and then…he was chasing me and…I fell—" Tori's eyes popped open, and the scene in front of her made her shrink back from the edge. The little piece of rock where she sat appeared to float like an island in the midst of blue sky that went on forever.

Blake's legs and arms surrounded hers, holding down the edges of a blanket tucked around her. At her back, strong and immovable, he crushed her to him until the fear lost its chokehold on her. "I've got you, sweetheart. I won't let you go. I promise."

Those were the words the voice, his wonderfully deep voice, had been saying each time she'd regained consciousness, though she hadn't recognized them until now. How long had he been sitting there, holding her, repeating them? Long enough, evidently, to burn them into her brain.

"Isaiah is fine, or at least he will be once he sees you're okay. He should be getting a call from Bob Crenshaw any minute to let him know we found you." Blake's voice sounded shaky.

Her disappearance had obviously affected him. Sadness engulfed her. She'd been nothing but trouble since the moment they met.

"We didn't have any cell service. Crenshaw hiked back after I climbed down here. Help should arrive soon. MacGyver and Kellie will bring Isaiah to the hospital."

"Hospital? No, please. Just take me home." Sure, she might feel like she'd fallen off a cliff. Her right leg throbbed, her head hurt, and every muscle and joint in her body cried foul, but she just wanted to be home, with Isaiah and Blake.

"No way. You took one hell of a tumble, and you're going to get checked out before I take you home. You scared the shit out of me." Blake pressed his warm lips to the side of her head. "Your ankle is swollen and could be fractured, and you've got a good-size bump on your head. I want the ER docs to make sure there's no internal bleeding or injuries I missed. I'm not willing to take a chance with your life, so don't argue." His tongue flicked out and caressed her earlobe. "Oh, and…just so we're clear…*home* is with me."

Part of Tori was thrilled at his assertion, but another part was saddened. He'd been quite clear he wasn't looking for a long-term relationship. His words were obviously born of relief that she wasn't seriously injured. He cared about her, but that didn't mean he believed her innocent now, when he hadn't yesterday. And it certainly didn't make it any less foolish for her to get involved with a former SEAL. But hadn't she already crossed that line?

She leaned her head on his chest and closed her eyes. "Do you still think I conspired to get Rafael's family and your team killed?" She might have been asking about the weather, so tightly had she held her emotions in check.

Blake sighed against her hair. "No."

Tori waited for more, some explanation. When the silence continued, she finally understood what he wasn't voicing. Enough had been said on that issue.

"Are you still going to take Donovan's job?" Bitterness rang in his abrupt question.

"No." She considered stopping right there, as he had, but the words kept coming. "The guy's a prick."

Blake chuckled softly, relaxing his arms that held her against him.

"I still need a job, though. Before I met you and was almost killed three times, four if you count falling off a cliff, I actually thought it might be the end of the world that I only had three hundred dollars in my checking account. Choosing between paying half the rent or feeding my son was a no-brainer, but the landlord has probably padlocked the door by now."

Blake laughed again. "I've got some bolt-cutters that'll fix your problem."

"Somehow, I knew you were going to say that." Tori nestled deeper into his arms, a sense of being totally protected insulating her from the reality of her close call. "There aren't a lot of jobs available in Cypress Point, so Isaiah and I will probably have to move somewhere with more opportunities for single mothers. California, maybe. Or Alaska. I've always wanted to see Alaska."

Another big sigh bled into a groan, as Blake seemed to waffle between giving his opinion or minding his own business.

Tori raised her eyes skyward when she heard the first sounds of a helicopter. *Oh shit.* "Please tell me they're not going to rescue us in a flying death machine."

"I'm afraid so…unless you feel up to climbing out of this hole." Why did it sound as though he was amused?

Tori squirmed to look over Blake's shoulder at the rope dangling from thirty feet straight up. *That would be a no.* She swallowed, unable to dislodge the lump in her throat. Silently, she twisted back to watch the helicopter approach.

As the air currents began to whip her hair about her face, Blake bent his head to her ear. "Do you trust me?"

She nodded. What choice did she have?

"I'll be with you all the way. I won't let go of you. You can close your eyes and let me do all the work, okay?" He kissed her again. "Close them now, sweetheart."

Tori was only too willing to slam her eyelids shut. Blocking out the image of the basket being lowered by cable was the only thing that might keep her from throwing up.

"Okay. We're going to stand up now. Ready?" Blake didn't wait for her to answer but braced his back against the rock wall and pulled them both upright. "Keep your eyes closed."

He didn't have to tell her more than once. Prying her fingers loose from his arm, he pressed something into her palm. As her hand closed around it, she identified it as the rope that he'd used to reach her.

"Hang on to the rope and stay back against the wall. I'm going to grab the rescue basket. I'll be right back. Are you doing okay?"

Tori nodded, but there was a possibility she was only telling him what he wanted to hear. As soon as Blake let go, her fear returned with a vengeance and she didn't dare move. Thirty seconds later, she heard the metal frame of the basket scrape along the rock ledge, and then he was back, sliding one arm around her waist. She released the breath she hadn't realized she was holding.

"I've got you. Just one more thing to do before they pull us up. We're going to take a couple small steps away from the wall and then you're going to step into the basket and sit down. As soon as you're in and holding on, I'm going to hop in too. The basket might swing a little because I won't be holding it still anymore, but the chopper will have us up top within seconds. Piece of cake, okay? Ready?" Blake tugged her away from the safety of the wall.

For a moment, Tori panicked and started to lose her balance. Her eyes popped open, and she dialed in on Blake's straight in front of her. His assuring smile grounded her, and she threw her arms around his neck. "I'm so glad you're here." Her lips brushed the corner of his mouth.

He chuckled. "Me too, sweetheart, but now's not the time to distract me." Amusement danced in his eyes. "Grab the side of the basket and swing your leg over."

Tori did as he instructed and soon she was half seated and half kneeling, taking care to tuck her injured ankle to her side.

"Hang on now. This could get a little bumpy with the downdraft from the chopper." Blake looked up and signaled to someone steadying the cable outside the bay door.

Immediately, the basket lifted free of its perch on the rock and started sliding toward the scraggly cypress tree that hung off the edge of the promontory. A cry squeezed from Tori's throat as the movement of the basket appeared to drag Blake closer to the edge. As the basket glanced off the tree, Blake leaped, landing inside the carrier, and dropped down next to her. The cable whisked them upward as the basket swung dizzily over the edge.

Blake slid his hand to the back of her head and lowered his mouth to hers. With everyone in the helicopter probably looking on and grinning, Blake's panty-melting kiss made her nipples harden delightfully and stand at attention through the thin material of her pajamas. He didn't let her up for air until the chopper crew dragged the basket into the bay amid applause and whistles.

He stepped out of the basket and extended a hand toward her. When he helped her out, he pulled her into his arms, chastely kissing her cheek before whispering in her ear. "I can't wait to get you home."

The next instant, Isaiah burst from the cockpit and threw himself into her arms. Blake caught them both as Tori stumbled backward. *Isaiah is here...in the helicopter?* She smiled at Blake while she hugged her son, tears needling at the backs of her eyes. She should be scared, but she wasn't. All she could think about were the words Blake had uttered.

I can't wait to get you home.

Chapter 21

Blake didn't stop worrying until the doctor shoved aside the curtain around Tori's bed and gave him a thumbs-up. His hand on Isaiah's shoulder, he guided the boy toward her, only slightly mollified after being summarily banished while Tori was x-rayed and examined.

Isaiah slipped around the side of Tori's bed and gingerly gave his mother a hug. Blake stood back, watching from the foot of the bed as Tori's love for her son played across her face. Blake had said her home was with him from now on, and he'd meant every word, but Tori had yet to weigh in. Her doubts and fears about him were apparent in the way she avoided his gaze.

Dr. Liz Peltier, according to her hospital ID, made some notes on Tori's chart before smiling. "You're one lucky lady. Your feet are in bad shape, but they'll heal. The right ankle has a mild sprain. Stay off it as much as you can for the next week and you'll see dramatic improvement. As you know, your back, shoulders and arms are sore to the touch, and my guess is you'll have some nasty bruises. Your head took a hit as well, but, except for a headache, any other symptoms are residual from your prior concussion. All in all, Tori, it might be a good day to buy yourself a lottery ticket."

"Can she go home?" Blake shifted his baseball cap from one hand to the other.

"I understand the sheriff is waiting to ask Tori some questions, but as far as the hospital is concerned, she can get the rest she needs at home."

"I'll make sure she stays in bed." Isaiah's head bobbed as though his solemn promise wasn't enough.

The doctor smiled. "I'm sure you will, young man. Your mother is lucky to have you." She jammed her pencil behind her ear and stepped to the next occupied cubicle.

"How do you feel?" Blake mentally kicked himself. The answer was obvious, and he'd just become one of those hospital visitors who couldn't think of anything better to say.

"Like what I imagine I'd feel like if I'd been hit by a bus."

Blake stepped up beside Isaiah and squeezed her hand. "Ready to go home?"

Tori nodded but held on to his hand when he tried to pull it free. Her brow furrowed as she scanned his face, then glanced quickly at Isaiah.

"We're ready. Aren't we, Isaiah?"

"Yeah. It's already dark outside, Mom." Isaiah threw his hands in the air as though he couldn't believe they'd been here since midday.

Blake could relate.

Tori hadn't yet asked about Harv or the reasons leading up to her kidnapping, and she clearly didn't want that conversation to happen in front of her son. Blake was happy to postpone it because he didn't have any answers for her.

Coop and Rafael had been on the phone all afternoon trying to connect Harv Farrington to Sebastian...with no luck. Special Agent Roberts had gotten nothing from his FBI wiretap or other sources in his quest for information on PTS Security's flight mechanic. Apparently, Harv had told Blake the truth when he'd said it wasn't Sebastian who hired him.

Though he'd found no rock-solid evidence Harv had been the one who sabotaged the Beechcraft's fuel gauge and warning system, Blake would have bet money he was the culprit. His lack of action had nearly cost Tori her life, something that would no doubt haunt him for a long time.

He brushed his fingers along her jaw and smiled when she looked at him. "Are we good?" It had hurt her deeply when she'd learned he and his bosses had suspected she was involved with Sebastian's group. He'd made a good start at clearing the air on the side of that cliff but regaining her trust wouldn't happen overnight.

Surprise flashed across her face. "Of course. I owe you for saving my life...again."

Didn't she realize all of the attempts on her life had been *because* of him? It seemed counterproductive to remind her. "Yeah, you do, and I'll be collecting on that, starting now." He winked just to see her pretty cheeks turn red and then stepped away. "I figured you'd probably had enough of helicopters, so I sent Coop and the crew back to the house. Kellie went with them and drove my truck back. She's in the waiting room. I'll give her a heads-up so she can keep you company while I bring the truck around to the emergency entrance. I think she brought your phone...in case you need to call your sister."

"Blake?" Tori's serious tone stopped him in his tracks. She sat up and slid her arm around Isaiah's shoulders, pulling him in close for a hug. Was she going to tell him she didn't need his help, that she wasn't going home with him?

"Yeah?"

"We'll never be able to thank you enough for what you've done for us. I should apologize for jumping in your helicopter that first morning and causing you so much trouble...but...I'm not really sorry."

The fist that had gripped his throat when she started talking suddenly let go, and Blake could breathe again. With Isaiah right there beside her, he leaned over and kissed her cheek. "Me either, sweetheart," he whispered. Threading his fingers through her hair, he tipped her head back and stared into her smiling eyes until Isaiah sighed heavily.

With reluctance, he released her, a grin pulling at his lips. "Um...yeah... the truck...I better..." He gave up on talking and simply pointed to the exit.

Tori laughed, her eyes sparkling with mischief. "Don't be too long. I can't wait to get out of here."

"Back in a flash." Nothing could keep Blake away any longer than necessary.

He was fully aware of how damn lucky he'd been to find her on that piece of rock where she'd fallen. If Crenshaw hadn't spotted her—if she'd died on impact...or slid just a little bit farther—if he hadn't gotten to her in time... So many things could have gone wrong. That she was alive, with no serious injuries, was nothing short of a miracle. That she was willing to give him a second chance, after he'd practically accused her of being Mata Hari, was mind blowing.

Stopping at the admittance desk, he asked if there was any paperwork that needed to be taken care of and requested a wheelchair. He found himself staring at a bouquet of roses on the woman's desk. Too bad he hadn't thought ahead and ordered Tori some flowers.

"Pretty, aren't they?" The woman tipped her chin toward the vase.

Blake smiled. "Special occasion?"

"My husband and I have been married twenty years today." The woman beamed.

"Congratulations! He's a lucky man." Blake started to leave.

"Take one for your girlfriend."

Blake glanced back, not sure he'd heard her right.

The woman blushed. "I saw the two of you when you brought her in. It's obvious you love her very much. Take one. I won't miss it."

Blake gaped at her. She thought he was in *love* with Tori? Was he? Impossible. That ship had sailed years ago. He just…liked having her around…for as long as it lasted. That was all it was.

The woman made a clucking sound, separated one of the long-stemmed roses from the others and handed it to him. "Go on. She'll think it's romantic."

Blake was pretty sure he hadn't been *romantic* a day in his life, but he took the flower she held out. "Thank you. I'm sure she'll love it." He waved to the woman as he walked away.

The waiting room was busy, and Blake had to scan the area twice before finding Kellie. She saw him at the same time, tossed her magazine on the stand beside her and strode toward him. "Aw…is that for me?" She made a grab for the stem.

Blake jerked it out of her reach. "Hell, no. It's for Tori."

Kellie jammed her hands on her hips. "Did you really think I didn't know that? Where's your sense of humor, Sorenson?"

After MacGyver, Kellie was the best friend he had, and, yeah, he should have known she was throwing shade. He grinned, sheepishly. "Sorry. It's been a long damn day."

"You've got that right. How's she doing?"

"Great. The doc said she can go home. I'm going to the parking garage to get the truck and bring it around. Would you push her wheelchair to the exit when she's ready and wait with her and Isaiah?"

"You know I will." Kellie stared at him for a second before a smile broke over her face. "How are *you* doing?"

He could read her take on the situation in the folding of her arms across her chest and…damn it…he'd never been able to lie to her. "I don't really know, but there's a good chance I'm losing my fucking mind." He dragged his hand down his face, feeling the heavy whiskers he hadn't had time to deal with.

Kellie's smile broadened. "Why? Because you care about her and Isaiah? You know, Blake, the love of a good woman isn't the worst thing that could happen."

Love again? What's with these women? Tori wasn't thinking long term. She'd said as much. Blake groaned and raked his fingers through his hair. "Unless she's not on the same page."

"That's what you think? Blake, you don't have a damn thing to worry about. Tori is crazy about you."

"How could you possibly know that?" He threw his hands up, not sure if he wanted her to be right or wrong.

"I just do. Have I ever steered you wrong before? Now go. Get the truck and take us home." She one-armed him aside as she walked by on her way to find Tori.

Blake stared after her. *Women! Always thinking they're one up. She has no more idea than I do. How could she?* He rubbed his chin whiskers with thumb and forefinger as Kellie disappeared inside the ER. On the other hand, Kellie was a smart girl. She could be right, couldn't she? Remarkably, he didn't see a single thing wrong with that. A smile slowly spread and refused to go away.

Well, I'll be damned.

On the elevator ride down to the parking garage, Blake started whistling, the sound unfamiliar at first. How long had it been? Hell, he even had a bounce in his step.

Maybe he'd have a conversation with Tori, get everything out in the open. Could he talk her into staying in Cypress Point long enough to see if there was something between them worth pursuing? More concerning, could he change her mind about military men? If she had feelings for him like he did for her and the boy, surely she'd give them a chance. They just needed to spend some time, get to know each other. He could prove to her that he'd come to terms with his PTSD. He'd never hurt her or Isaiah.

Blake lifted the rose and breathed in its scent. He could learn to be romantic. Kellie would tease the hell out of him, but she'd help him if he asked.

The elevator came to a stop and the doors opened. Blake turned right as Kellie had instructed when she'd told him where she'd parked. The truck should be eleven spaces this way, along the wall.

"Hey, buddy, got a light?"

Blake jerked around, not aware that anyone else was nearby. The man stood beside one of the parked cars, wearing Army fatigues and boots. An unruly beard covered his face. He held an unlit cigarette in his fingers, and his question made more sense.

"No. Sorry. I don't smoke."

"No problem." The man walked on toward the elevator.

Blake turned to watch him. *Damn!* He'd been so caught up in his plans, he hadn't been paying a bit of attention to his surroundings. *Stupid rookie mistake.* The man's sudden appearance had jarred him. He knew better. Had taught young sailors to know better.

He clutched the rose and continued his path until he came to the white Tundra…right where Kellie had said it would be. Shrugging out of his backpack, he held it and the rose in one hand while he unlocked the driver's door with the other.

It was only a small sound amid many others, but this one made the hair stand up on Blake's neck. Familiar—like someone blowing through a water pipe. He froze, concentrating on where it had come from. Turning slowly, he scanned the garage. Nothing moved. Faint voices came from the far end, other people looking for their cars.

He'd swung three quarters of the way around when a sharp pain bit his neck. His hand came up to brush at the irritation and encountered something hard. He yanked it free. *A dart?*

His vision blurred as a fog blanketed his mind. He staggered forward, but his knees wouldn't hold him. *I have to get back to Tori.* Falling, he flung out his hands to catch himself, but not in time. His cheek smacked the concrete floor alongside his backpack. The rose landed an instant later and rolled under his truck.

A car skidding to a stop…urgent voices coming closer…he'd been drugged…or poisoned…

Blackness swirled around him.

Chapter 22

Tori shot out of the wheelchair, frowning at the disapproving nurse who hovered nearby, daring any of the hospital staff who looked on with curious stares to say anything. She limped across the slab of concrete to the edge of the sidewalk and back. To say she was spoiling for a fight would not have been an exaggeration.

Nearly an hour and a half had passed. Any minute, Blake would wheel into the emergency entrance in his white Tundra. He'd flash his sexy grin, the one that made her weak in the knees. And then he'd take her and Isaiah home. That was what she'd told herself every few minutes, anyway. But he hadn't appeared. *Something is terribly wrong.*

Kellie had shared Tori's concern. She'd called MacGyver fifty-five minutes ago. He'd be here soon, with Travis, and anyone else they could spare from the house. They'd find Blake. *They have to.* And while they were at it, they could give Tori something to do before she lost her mind. *What's taking them so long?*

Forty-five minutes ago, hospital security had begun a methodical search of all four floors of the hospital, and two orderlies had accompanied Kellie to the parking garage at the request of the hospital administrator, Dr. Fallon. They'd found nothing unusual.

Maybe Blake had decided to run an errand. Maybe the truck had failed to start, and he'd gone to find jumper cables. Maybe he'd run into a friend and stopped for a beer. These and other ludicrous suppositions had been proposed by Dr. Fallon and swiftly rejected by Tori. Dr. Fallon had shrugged his aging shoulders and reluctantly got behind Kellie's call to the Cypress Point PD.

Of course, Gary Addison would have to be the detective sent to investigate their missing person. The law enforcement officer stood with his back to the admittance desk, hands on hips, towering in Kellie's face with whatever excuse he was currently spouting for not doing his job. *Is it too much to ask for the detective to actually look for clues in Blake's mysterious disappearance?*

Kellie threw her hands in the air and spun around, hurrying toward Tori with a scowl darkening her green eyes. "Holy shit! Your friend is a piece of work. I finally convinced him to send some officers to search the parking garage in case we missed something. He said he'd take a look, but that's all he can do until we file a missing person's report…which he'll then sit on for twenty-four hours before committing any resources."

Tori gave the detective's retreating back the evil eye before folding her arms over her chest. "He's *not* my friend!" They knew each other, kids in the same class. Addison had been an ass that night too.

Kellie reached for her hand, worry creasing her brow. "Should you be standing?"

"Oh, please, not you too! I've been sitting in that chair for a solid hour, feeling helpless, and I can't do it anymore." *Damn it! No.* She would *not* sit there doing nothing while Blake was God only knew where.

"I'm sorry, Tori. If it's any consolation, I know how you feel."

It wasn't. *He said he'd be back in a flash.* It wasn't simply something he'd said and didn't mean. Okay, so you had to be there and witness the way he'd looked at her. The promise in his eyes. Blake would have returned had he been able to. There wasn't a single doubt in Tori's mind. It'd been far too long. *Where is he?*

"Where's Isaiah?" Kellie sounded slightly panicked as she halted beside her.

"One of the nurses offered to take him to the break room and find him an iPad. I'll check on him in a little bit. He doesn't understand what's going on yet, and I'd like to keep it that way for as long as possible." Tori didn't understand either, but her gut instinct was that Blake hadn't returned to the ER because someone had prevented him from doing so. *Paranoid much?* Maybe so, but too many strange things had happened in the past few days. She was afraid for Blake deep in her bones, and there wasn't a damn thing she could do.

Detective Addison, flanked by two police officers, strode out of the ER and directly to where Kellie and Tori stood. He greeted Tori with a grim smile. "A preliminary search turned up nothing of interest. There's no sign of a scuffle. No blood. Nobody down there heard or saw anything. I'm sorry, Tori, but there's absolutely no reason to suspect foul play at this time."

Hopelessness washed over Tori, followed immediately by a splash of like-hell determination. Beside her, Kellie gave a surprised squeak and pointed to something Addison was holding next to his leg. "What's that, Detective?"

Addison held up a single red rose, the bloom drooping for want of water. "We found this under his Tundra. I doubt if Sorenson was much into flowers, so—"

"That's Blake's!" Kellie jabbed her finger into the detective's chest. "He had it when he came to tell me Tori could go home." Her glance swept Tori's face. "He said it was for you." Again, the finger stabbed Addison. "He wouldn't have just dropped it. If Blake Sorenson left that garage under his own power, that rose would have gone with him."

Tori stared at the rose, trying desperately to keep up. *It's for me? He wouldn't have dropped it. If he left under his own power...* The words replayed in her head like an old black-and-white film from the forties. A sob shook her, and she covered her face, but it was too late to stop the deluge now that the floodgates had opened. She spun around to run, but Kellie caught her and held on.

"Do your job, Detective." Kellie hissed the words before helping Tori escape the spotlight she'd suddenly found herself in.

Inside the emergency room waiting area, Liz Peltier, the doctor who'd examined Tori, took pity and showed them to a small room beyond the bustle. It was sparsely but comfortably furnished with a conference table and six chairs. Best of all, it was quiet.

"You can stay here as long as you need to." Dr. Peltier smiled sympathetically. "If you need anything, just ask one of the orderlies to find me."

"Thanks, Dr. Peltier." Tori collapsed on one of the chairs as the doctor softly closed the door behind her. Now that she had some privacy, the wretched tears wouldn't come. She sensed Kellie studying her, probably wondering how long before her meltdown became permanent.

Tori flipped her hands up in frustration. "I'm sorry, Kellie. I don't know what's wrong with me. I'm not usually such a hot mess."

"Are you kidding? You're doing fine. We all have our moments where our men are concerned. Lord knows they give us enough to worry about." Kellie dropped into a chair across from her.

Tori started to shake her head. "It's not like that. Blake and I aren't—"

"Don't even go there, girl. I might have believed you before today, but something changed when Blake found you on that rock this morning. It's written all over your face, and—don't roll your eyes at me—this is a good thing."

"You don't understand. I don't date men with military backgrounds," Tori blurted.

Kellie's brow shot upward. "Well, why the hell not?"

Tori didn't want to get into this with Kellie, but she'd said too much, and the look of consternation on the other woman's face said she was still waiting for an answer. "Because coming back from war and trying to blend into society doesn't always work. When it doesn't, it's usually ugly. I'm not willing to subject my son to a life of fear and walking on eggshells ever again."

Kellie was quiet for a moment, but she studied her so intently Tori had to look away. "What happened to you, Tori?" The question hung in the air like a hot air balloon.

Tori flinched as though she'd been struck. The topic wasn't one she routinely shared, but, strangely, the need to explain to Kellie was strong. She rubbed her clammy palms on her thighs. "My husband was an Air Force fighter pilot. His plane was shot down, and he was injured badly. I'll spare you all the gruesome details but, suffice it to say, he didn't make the transition to civilian life gracefully. He killed himself…in front of me and my son. Isaiah is still traumatized, and I guess I probably am too. I swore I'd never put Isaiah in a situation like that again."

"Hell, Tori. I'm sorry. That definitely sucks." Kellie leaned her forearms on the tabletop. "Did Blake mention I was a Marine… spent some time in Iraq?"

Tori's gaze darted to Kellie's. "No."

"Everything about war is appalling. The things I've seen—hell, the things I've done are horrifying. Life changing. I think the latest statistics say twenty-two veterans commit suicide every day in America. That's mind boggling. The truth is, it's unacceptable for even one of our vets to feel so lost, alone and hopeless that he chooses to end his own life." Kellie paused as though considering her next words.

"The other side of that is: for every single person who chooses that path, countless others don't. Like MacGyver. He figured out a way to transition back, while keeping those horrendous memories in a box. Does he ever get moody? Pissy? Mad as hell? Of course he does, but name one person who doesn't. Same with Travis and Coop. Luke—did you know he was captured and held for six months by a radical terrorist group in Afghanistan?"

Tori inhaled sharply. "Oh my God, no." Soft-spoken Luke? He was so...kind.

"His best friend was tortured and killed in front of him. Luke nearly died in the rescue operation that freed him." Kellie laid her hand on Tori's arm. "All I'm saying is, judge the man by his heart, not by his military career. I'm *so* glad I took a chance on MacGyver."

"So...you think I should give Blake the benefit of the doubt?"

Kellie smiled wistfully. "Blake is my friend. I want him to be happy. In this case, it seems like a win for both of you, but my opinion probably isn't the one that counts."

Kellie's phone chirped. She pulled it free of her back pocket and looked at the screen. "Speak of the devil. It's a text from MacGyver. *Sebastian and group are inside the perimeter. Can't leave yet. Will be there ASAP. You and Tori stay somewhere safe and wait for me.*"

Tori frowned and limped the length of the table.

Kellie, looking equally as frustrated, slid one of the chairs out. "You need to get off that ankle."

Tori ignored her, switching directions. "We've been assuming everything that's happened the past few days was orchestrated by Sebastian Wahl. The attack on Rafael and the safe house, the man who broke into my home, Harv abducting me...and now Blake's disappearance." She stopped, abruptly, and stared at Kellie. "What if it wasn't Sebastian?"

"I see where you're going, but who, besides Sebastian, has anything to gain?" Kellie's furrowed brow indicated she wasn't buying Tori's theory.

"You're missing the point. What does Sebastian have to gain by hurting me?" Tori started pacing again, this time barely feeling the pain in her feet and ankle. "All of you thought I might be working for Sebastian, therefore killing me to keep me from disclosing his plans made sense to you." She stopped again and zeroed in on Kellie. "But I'm *not* working for him...so he achieves nothing by targeting me."

"I never believed you were working for Sebastian."

Tori approached Kellie and touched her arm. "What if whoever did all of this was after Blake the whole time? Maybe someone thought they could hurt Blake by hurting me, or possibly draw him into a trap. Kellie, does Blake have any enemies?"

Kellie's forehead crinkled for a moment, and slowly her eyes widened. "Smartphones are too slow. We need a computer."

"My sister, Jane. She'll have everything we need." She glanced at the scrubs Dr. Peltier had offered after Tori had removed the ripped and filthy pajamas and robe she'd left the house in last night. "Including some clothes, I hope."

"I've still got Blake's extra set of keys to the Tundra." Kellie dug them from her pocket and shook them in front of Tori. "Let's retrieve Isaiah and get out of here."

* * * *

Blake's eyes flickered open, and the cracks in the wooden floor, flowing by at a good clip, made him close them again. He couldn't feel his arms and legs, but he knew exactly where his head was. It was about to split open from the grueling headache that hammered between his ears.

His sense of weightlessness gradually gave way to being carried, no... dragged, his arms spread out to the side. Suddenly, his forward motion ceased, and hands shoved him back against something hard. Arms forced over his head, cold steel wrapped his wrists, and then chains scraped against cement as he was hauled up until his shoulders screamed in pain and his feet barely touched the ground.

A light snapped on, so close he could feel the heat of the bulb warming his face. Low voices murmured close by. Through mere slits, Blake looked around, but the light was too bright to see anything but shadows. Out of nowhere, a fist connected with his jaw, and his head flew back against the concrete wall. His knees gave out, and he sagged until his weight was suspended on his wrists. Immediately, another powerful blow slammed into his gut, driving the air from his lungs.

He'd scarcely gotten his feet under him when someone hit him again, cranking his jaw to the right and exploding a fiery light show in front of his eyes. Faster and harder the blows fell, until it was all he could do to stand and breathe—but that didn't mean he'd quit. *Still alive, can't quit.* Besides, he had two big reasons to survive—Tori and Isaiah.

The next time I see her, I'll lay my cards on the table. I'll tell her I want her and Isaiah in my life for good. Hell, I'll make it official, buy a ring, get down on one knee.

The side of his head impacted the concrete wall and blood spilled down his cheek. Gray haze shimmered around him, but he shook it off. *Don't concentrate on the beating. One blow at a time.*

I'll convince Tori she never has to fear me or worry I'll do something stupid. We'll be a family. Maybe we'll have more kids.

Blake slipped effortlessly into his SEAL training—visualizing the life he wanted until it blocked out the pain and uncertainty of reality. A meadow on a sunny day, Tori laughing and smiling until her sexy dimples made him catch her around the waist and draw her close for a kiss. In the middle of the green expanse, Isaiah threw a ball, and a full-grown yellow lab trotted after it and brought it back. And Blake held the hand of a dark-haired little girl who looked exactly like her mother.

Whispers again, and the punches stopped.

"It's no fun if he isn't with it enough to know what's happening," a man said, his voice vaguely familiar.

Footsteps faded to his left, leaving Blake in silence. Who were they? Why were they doing this? He'd pissed off a few people, working with PTS Security, but no worse than his bosses had. It seemed as though he'd been singled out, and it felt damn personal.

But if the man whose voice he'd heard somewhere before thought they'd break him, he'd be disappointed.

Chapter 23

"Hey, guys! I think I've got something."

Tori looked up from the computer screen as Kellie barreled toward her, pounding another number into the face of the cell phone she carried. "Well, I hope it's good news, because I'm striking out here. If you believe the internet, everybody loves the wounded war hero who recovered from his own injuries just in time to take care of his paralyzed little brother."

"Yeah, well, not everybody. I talked to Christian. He said, after his brother was injured and was medically discharged, he started getting threatening phone calls. It went on for nearly two years." Kellie punched the call button, sending the number she'd dialed into the stratosphere, or whatever sphere was the domain of cell signals. It was clear she believed her bit of unsubstantiated hearsay was the answer to all their questions.

Skepticism and frustration, coupled with the anguish that sloshed around in Tori's stomach, put her right on the edge of losing it. "Man or woman? Does Christian have a name or know what his beef was?"

"Apparently, Blake shrugged off the calls as pranks, but whenever he received one, he'd have nightmares and shut himself away from the world for a while. Total PTSD. Christian suspected the calls had something to do with Blake's time in the military, but it was clear he didn't want to talk." Kellie raised her palm, signaling for quiet, then pointed to the phone as she turned her back and strode toward the front porch. "Colonel Dupree? This is Kellie Greyson. How are you, ma'am?"

The screen door leading to the darkened porch opened and closed behind Kellie, and her voice receded into a jumble of indistinct sounds.

Jane set a steaming mug on the table in front of Tori. "I made you some tea." Still dressed in the pjs and robe she'd been wearing when she'd opened the door to them at ten 'til midnight, Jane appeared unperturbed by their late-night arrival and the flurry of activity they'd brought with them. Her strawberry-blond hair fell around her shoulders with just the right amount of messy appeal, in complete denial of having been anywhere near a pillow. She tipped her chin in the direction Kellie had gone. "Wow! She's intense."

Tori smiled and patted the chair next to her. "Thanks for letting us crash at your place, Janie."

Her sister perched on the edge of the seat, and her light-blue eyes, so much like Tori's, shimmered with tears. "I tried calling you back at least twenty times. God, I was so worried when I couldn't reach you, Tori. Don't ever do that to me again!"

"Aw, hon, I'm so sorry I made you worry." Tori picked up the teacup and took a drink, swallowing the lump that threatened to choke off her words. "Did Isaiah finally go to sleep?"

"He was trying to read a book, but he couldn't stay awake, so I'm sure he's sleeping by now. I'll check on him again in a few minutes." Jane peered over Tori's shoulder to the computer screen on the table. "Any luck?"

"Unfortunately, I don't know exactly what I'm looking for. I keep hoping something will jump out at me." Tori rubbed her eyes and squinted at the four-year-old newspaper article from the *Las Vegas Sun* she'd been skimming.

Lieutenant Commander Blake Sorenson had been a hometown hero when he'd returned, crippled from a helicopter crash, after picking up four Navy SEALs who otherwise would likely have been overrun and killed. During his interview with her, Blake had talked about the two who'd died when the helicopter had been shot down as though he'd held himself responsible for their deaths. Yet, thanks to Blake, two men had survived, including one Matt "MacGyver" Iverson.

If the pictures of Blake's scowling features at his homecoming were any indication, he hadn't considered himself heroic in the least.

"Stay positive, Sis." Jane covered Tori's hand as it scrolled the mouse, squeezing her fingers, while a smile curled her lips. "I'm going to check on the I-man. Can I get you anything else?"

"You've done enough, sweetie. You certainly shouldn't be waiting on me." Tori glanced toward the kitchen windows and the darkness that still shrouded her sister's backyard. What was Blake doing right now? Was he alive? Hurt? It'd been eight hours since he disappeared. Fear pierced her heart, but she purposefully tamped it down and gave her sister a smile. "It's late. Why don't you get some sleep?"

"I could ask you the same question."

Tori grimaced. "I'm exhausted, but there's no way I could sleep. Not until I know Blake is safe."

"He must be quite a guy to have put the life back in your eyes. I wasn't sure you'd ever let yourself reach for happiness again. I wish there was something I could do to help." Jane gave a one-shouldered shrug.

Tori stood and slipped an arm around her sister. "Trust me, you've helped more than any one person should have to. You were there for me and Isaiah when our whole world shattered, and you helped us pick up the pieces and move on."

"Oh, please," Jane said. "Remember when Randy Gilbert stood me up for the homecoming dance? I think we're even now."

Tori laughed. "Now that you mention it, I'm not so sure. You have to admit getting the entire student body to call the star quarterback Rancid Randy in the middle of the pep rally was a stroke of genius."

Jane giggled exactly as they'd done eleven years ago at Randy's expense. Tori loved the way her sister's eyes sparkled with mischief. She gave her a hug and shooed her toward her bedroom. "Go. One of us should get some sleep."

Jane's smile dimmed. "Wake me if you learn anything. Promise?"

"I will."

Tori reclaimed her seat in front of the computer, clicked a link to another article, and rubbed the back of her neck. The screen door banged shut and Tori flinched.

Kellie's hand flew to her throat. "Sorry. Is Isaiah sleeping?"

Tori nodded. "I think so. Don't worry, though. He's a sound sleeper." She leaned back and studied the other woman. "Any news?"

"I spoke to my old commanding officer. Colonel Dupree was a captain back then, and she went above and beyond for me..." Kellie dropped her gaze, leaving her comment unfinished.

Blake had told Tori about the Marine who'd shot his brother while trying to stop his attack on an Iraqi girl. He *hadn't* told her the Marine was Kellie Greyson. Tori had obtained that bit of information from newspaper articles she'd read in the past few hours, along with the fact it had been an accidental shooting after Christian grabbed for Kellie's weapon and a struggle ensued. Obviously, the tragedy still weighed heavily on Kellie's conscience.

"She may be able to help," Kellie said. "If the threats were related to Blake's military service, he might have reported them. If NCIS found them to be credible, they could have initiated an investigation, which means there could be a file somewhere containing the name of the man or men who abducted Blake."

Tori's palms began to sweat. "Your colonel can access the information?" Could it possibly be that easy? How could a man, who'd saved as many lives as Blake had in the service of his country, have made enemies as well?

Tori popped from her chair and started pacing. "How long?"

"I explained our situation. She understands the urgency, and I know she'll do the best she can."

Tori threw her a disbelieving frown. "What do we do now? Sit here and wait? I can't..."

"I know. Waiting is hell, especially when it's a matter of life and death. But it's more than we had an hour ago, Tori."

One look at Kellie confirmed that her stress level was off the charts, rivaling Tori's. Nonetheless, Tori could have gone a lifetime without the life-and-death comment that was now taking up residence in the pit of her stomach. She jumped when Kellie's phone chirped.

"Thank God, it's MacGyver." Kellie accepted the call. "Please tell me you've got some good news." A smile slowly crept across her tired features. "Really? That's great. Is everyone okay?" Kellie jerked her thumb toward the ceiling in a things-are-good gesture.

Her smile soon dimmed. "No, we haven't heard from Blake, and the cops are aware he's missing but they haven't been any help so far. Is Coop around? We could really use some help from the information guru."

Apparently left hanging for a moment, Kellie moved the phone away from her face. "It's over and everyone is safe. The hate group didn't stand a chance against a well-prepared security team. The FBI arrested Sebastian, his men, and a couple of his major donors for conspiracy to commit murder." Pride shone in Kellie's eyes and, for the first time, her features held some clue to the amount of worry she'd concealed over the past few hours.

It was good news for Rafael and his family. Hopefully, they'd be able to fit back into their lives only slightly worse for the events that had transpired. Sadly, the children would probably suffer periods of anxiety for a long time, but counseling and the love of a strong family would help.

Relief surged through Tori like a cool breeze off the ocean. The Perez family's happy resolution also meant the men of PTS Security were free to search for Blake now. She leaned closer to the table as Kellie sank into a chair across from her and hit the speaker button on her phone. Men's voices raised in congratulatory salutations interspersed with the sounds of boots trudging on wooden flooring and then a door closing shut out the ancillary noises.

"Coop and Travis are with me. Are you and Tori on speaker?" MacGyver's voice flowed over the airwaves with composed assertiveness.

"Hi, guys. We're here." Tori tried hard to sound braver than she was.

"Good morning, ladies. MacGyver tells me you need my assistance." Coop's deep tone rumbled confidently in Tori's ears.

Kellie quickly went over her conversation with Blake's friend, explaining Christian's theory that the threatening calls had related somehow to Blake's military history. Before she was finished, Tori could hear the keys clicking under Coop's fingers, and she sent a silent prayer heavenward.

"My old C.O. is looking into any reports or grievances involving Blake that might have been filed through the chain of command, but it's a long shot at best." Kellie's voice broke and she covered her mouth for a couple of seconds. "I'm afraid we're running out of time."

Tori peered at Kellie, her confidence taking a hit as the other woman's uncertainty played across her face. Kellie was his best friend, Blake had said. She'd known him far longer than Tori had and, therefore, had more justification to fear for him. On impulse, Tori reached across the table and threaded her fingers through Kellie's, calling up every ounce of strength in her body to share with Blake's friend, her friend.

"It's going to be all right," she whispered, surprised by the conviction ringing in her declaration.

"The military machine has lists for everything, but if you want the real scoop, you have to know somebody." Coop chuckled as the keys continued to click. "Just so happens, I do. Why don't you girls take a ten-minute power nap? I should have something by the time you wake up."

The call ended so quickly, neither she nor Kellie had time to object.

A smile tugged halfheartedly at Tori's mouth as she squeezed Kellie's hand and let go. "He either has a very high opinion of himself or he's done this before. Either way, I feel better already. How about you?"

Kellie gave a short laugh. "He does have that effect on people at times."

"I'm going to check on Isaiah. Do you want some coffee or something? Are you hungry?" Tori scooted her chair back.

"No thanks. I'm going to sit right here and wait for this damn phone to ring." Kellie leaned her elbows on the table and rested her head in her hands.

Tori stood and shuffled toward her sister's spare bedroom. Opening the door stealthily, she peered through the semidarkness, broken only by a single nightlight. Isaiah slept peacefully, his breaths slow and easy. Jane had evidently covered him and turned on the tiny light.

He'd appeared only slightly nervous when Blake had been delayed. Isaiah seemed to idolize Blake, a first in a very long stretch of indifference where other people were concerned. What would she tell him if Blake never returned? For that matter, if Blake was all right and they were all worrying for nothing, how would she explain that Isaiah couldn't be around him anymore because Tori was afraid he would hurt them both? She was borrowing trouble...and teaching her son to do the same. If they found Blake in time...

Coop's ten-minute estimate was approximately six and a half minutes long. Tori heard the chirp of Kellie's phone, closed the door to Isaiah's room and returned to the table just as she pressed the speaker button.

"That was fast," Tori said. "Please tell me fast is good."

"Fast is good...in *almost* everything." Coop snickered, followed by groans from Travis and MacGyver. "Okay, okay. Everybody's a critic."

"Fill them in already," MacGyver growled.

"As you know, four years ago, Blake flew into a particularly hot situation and picked up our boy MacGyver, along with three other SEALs. That was the last mission Blake ever flew, and it was the end of the line for two of our country's best as well. This *could* be a coincidence, but I'm betting not. One of the deceased sailors was James Donovan. His only living relative was a brother—David."

Tori dropped to her chair. *That bastard used me to get to Blake. This is all my fault.*

* * * *

Blake pulled himself up straight as soon as he heard the door latch turn. As the night dragged by, that sound had proven to announce the start of long sessions of brutal ass-kicking. His ass. And there wasn't a damn thing he could do about it...except take everything they dished out.

Only one set of footsteps approached this time. He peered through eyes that barely opened to track the shadowy figure as it pushed into his space and halted. Maybe he was certifiably blind, or maybe they'd slammed his head against the wall one too many times, but the build and stance of the man in front of him looked familiar.

"Hello, Sorenson. I have to say, you look like shit."

Fuck! David Donovan. Blake would recognize that imperious tone anywhere.

"I thought we should have a talk...before you become incapacitated and can't understand why I'm going to kill you. I've been planning this since the day I buried my little brother. When you left Vegas and moved to Oregon, I couldn't believe my luck. You had come to me. It was a sign that revenge would finally be mine."

What the fuck?

"You don't remember him, do you? He was just another body to you. Wounded. Dying. How much of your time would it have taken to try to stop the bleeding? You could have saved James if you hadn't been playing hero."

James? James Donovan? Shit. Sluggishly, the dots connected. James Donovan and another wet-behind-the-ears kid, Wyatt Tomlinson, hadn't survived the day his helicopter crashed in the desert. They'd been ripped apart by enemy fire in a mission gone bad. By the time Blake had gotten there, it would have taken a miracle for either of them to make it, but none of them had gotten a miracle that day. Instead, his chopper had been hit and he'd only been able to keep it in the air for ten clicks or so. He, MacGyver and one other had made it out. Later that same day, another SEAL team retrieved the bodies so they could be shipped home to their grieving families. Blake had carried the guilt of their deaths every day since. And then the threatening phone calls had started.

"What? Nothing to say?"

What could he say that would make Donovan's loss any easier to bear?

"It was a real coup when Harv Farrington agreed to help me. I almost had that stupid bitch in my hands. I had such plans for Tori. I'm sure you can imagine. Of course, I would have let you say goodbye before I ended her suffering. You cheated me out of that, so now you're going to help me convince her to come here." He lifted a cell phone from his shirt pocket.

Anger heated Blake's blood. "If you think I'm going to help you hurt her, you've lost your fucking mind."

The latch of the door clicked again, and two sets of heavy boots tromped toward them. Blake tensed.

Donovan didn't take his eyes from the phone, continuing to dial a number. "Ah…our friends are here. Maybe they'll be able to coax you into saying a few words to the lovely Tori." He stepped back, out of the way, and one of his thugs took his place.

The first blow smashed into Blake's ribs, stealing his breath. He hunched over, stopped from collapsing by the shackles around his wrists that tethered him to the ceiling. His ribs were already broken. He could hear the crackling in his chest wall when he breathed. All they had to do now was cause enough trauma to puncture a lung and he'd be in trouble.

One of them swept his legs from beneath him, and his full weight jerked his arms up straight, straining wrists and shoulders already injured and sending shards of pain tearing through his torso.

His visualizing techniques had improved through nearly constant discipline. To the world he was building with Tori and Isaiah behind impenetrable walls in his mind he added just five minutes, unchained, alone with these assholes. The image was enough to elicit a smirk just as Tori smiled and beckoned him inside the walls.

Chapter 24

The last several hours had been the most frustrating of Tori's life. They knew who'd abducted Blake and why, but they didn't have one lousy clue where he'd been taken. MacGyver and Travis had descended on Jane's house two hours ago as the sun appeared over the eastern mountains. Coop, Luke and a half dozen volunteers from the PTS crew were ready to lift off from Blake's hangar at a moment's notice, as soon as they settled on a destination.

Jane had asked for a personal day from work and bundled Isaiah off to the aquarium at exactly nine. Coop was nonstop on his computer. MacGyver had contacted a private investigator he knew in Portland and asked him to check out Donovan's home and office. He'd struck out at both places. Kellie ran their theory by Colonel Dupree and, though the officer thought it was a lead worth following, she hadn't been able to give them any additional information. Every stone was being turned over by someone, leaving Tori feeling useless.

She was a reporter. At one time, she'd wanted to be an investigative reporter. Her college professors had captivated her with their accounts of breaking the big stories. A good reporter, they'd said, coaxed every last nuance from a clue. What were they missing?

Suddenly, Tori sat forward, remembering the other half of that lesson. *A great reporter teases the smallest string until it begins to fray, then tugs on it to see where it leads.*

The smallest string? Tori ran her fingers lightly over the keys of Jane's computer. The others were looking for known associates of David Donovan. Following the money to see if he controlled any other companies or owned other property. So far, he appeared to be exactly who he'd said he was, the owner and editor of a start-up magazine. No wife. No kids. No money to speak of. Nothing, really, to account for his arrogance.

Tori tapped the keyboard to wake the computer and called up the Multnomah County Tax Collector's website. A sigh escaped as she read the By Subscription Only tag. Undaunted, she searched through her small pile of torn and dirty clothes for her phone that Kellie had brought to the hospital and dialed the number at the bottom of the page.

"Multnomah County. How can I help you?" The pleasant male voice sounded rehearsed, but Tori wouldn't let that stop her.

"Good morning. My name is Tori Michaels. I'm a reporter, and I was hoping you could help me with a tiny bit of research."

MacGyver and Kellie turned curious looks her way. "We're not too busy right now so…sure. What kind of information are you looking for?"

"I'd like a list of properties owned by James Donovan, the estate of James Donovan or any business name beginning with James Donovan."

"That's a fairly common name. You realize that's going to be an extensive list, right?"

"Yes, I know. Can you e-mail it to me?" Tori rattled off her e-mail address, thanked the guy, and ended the call.

"What?" she said when Kellie cleared her throat loudly.

Travis laughed. "Don't let 'em get to you, Tori. These two just wish they'd thought of that."

Five minutes later, Tori's e-mail pinged with an incoming message. Travis, MacGyver and Kellie gathered around as she scrolled through twenty-four pages of names, addresses and property descriptions.

"So many?" Kellie whispered.

Tori sent all the pages to the printer. "We'll split them up. Start by crossing out any that are jointly owned by a spouse. James wasn't married. Next, Donovan took Blake out of the parking garage rather than kill him there. We have to assume he wanted Blake alive to suffer for a while. To pull that off, without drawing unwanted attention, he'd need someplace relatively secluded, maybe with a basement or outbuildings…or remodeling done in the past few months."

Grabbing the papers from the printer, Tori sorted them and handed them out. "Once we get these whittled down to a manageable number, we'll send them to Coop and see what he can come up with."

Travis raised his eyebrows as he accepted the sheets of paper. "You go, girl."

Tori grinned. *Finally, something she could do.*

When they'd cut the number of pages in half, they exchanged sheets and eliminated a few more locations. Tori's gaze kept going back to one on the first page. One and a half acres south of Portland with an old farmhouse from the seventies. There'd been no improvements to the house, but two years ago a new shop was built on the property. Had Donovan planned his revenge that far in advance? Instead of letting it go when his threatening phone calls stopped, had he moved on to another part of his plan? If so, he was a sick, sick man.

"Tori?"

She jumped and looked up to see everyone staring at her.

"You've been studying that same sheet of paper for a while. If you've got a hunch about one of them, let's hear it." MacGyver braced his arms against the tabletop across from her.

Tori's chest suddenly felt heavy. Could she do that? Pick one property to focus on? What if she was wrong? The question must have been written on her forehead.

"It's okay. Tell me what you think. It doesn't mean we won't check out some of the other places too. Special Agent Roberts owes us a favor. He's standing by with backup to help. The private investigator I called earlier is already on his way to one of the locations. We're going to find him, Tori, but you and Blake...you have a connection, and I'm not going to discount your instincts." MacGyver reached for the paper in her hand, and Tori let it go.

"The fourth one down," she said softly.

He studied it for a moment. "Why?"

"The house is old, yet apparently nothing has been updated or remodeled. But two years ago, the owner built a concrete building. It could be a coincidence, but I think it might be part of a well-thought-out plan."

MacGyver laid the paper on the table and glanced toward Travis with a slight nod. Travis stood and retired to the porch, his phone already in his hand. "Kellie, would you call Luke, please? Tell him we're ready to go and we need to fast-track that."

Kellie grabbed her phone and started dialing.

MacGyver's gaze swept Tori's face. "You made a good call. Travis is on the phone with Special Agent Roberts. We'll ask the FBI to get as close as possible and set up surveillance. If it looks promising, we'll be there in just over an hour."

What have I done? Tori leaned back and closed her eyes. One hand covered her mouth.

"We know what we're doing, Tori. We're still on top of the other locations we identified as possibilities. We want to find Blake as badly as you do. Trust us, okay?" MacGyver reached across the table and covered one of her hands.

Tori opened her eyes and stared into his. Trusting wasn't something that came easily to her, yet she trusted MacGyver and the others Blake called friends. Lest she forget, she'd also *almost* trusted Donovan and doing so had enabled him to spring his trap. Would Blake forgive her? Hopefully he would, because him going missing had highlighted one thing in neon shades of orange—she didn't want to live without him.

She forced her lips to curve upward as she faced MacGyver. "Blake trusts you, and that's good enough for me."

He nodded, drew his hand back and stood. "While we're waiting for the chopper, let's send the information on this location to Coop so he can start working on it."

Tori startled as her phone chirped and vibrated on the wooden table. She glanced at the screen and reached out at the same time, then pulled her hand back reflexively. A gasp nearly choked her as her heart began to pound in her ears. "It's him. It's Donovan."

* * * *

"I'm glad I caught you, Tori. You haven't gotten back to me about the job. I wish you'd decide already. I've got a story developing that you'd be perfect for."

Blake seethed as he listened to Donovan's slick bullshit. Lies. He'd say anything to get Tori here…and Blake had one chance to make sure she didn't come. The two muscle-bound goons standing in front of him and the rag they'd shoved in his mouth and dared him to spit out weren't going to make it pleasant.

"If you're interested, I'd like to give you the details face-to-face." Donovan was laying on the charm. Was Tori falling for it?

"Tomorrow would be great. I have a couple other meetings, but we can get together at the office about noon. I'll buy you lunch and we'll discuss the project."

Not if I can help it. One of the bruisers turned partway, sharing a leer with Donovan. It was now or never.

Blake bounced off the balls of his feet, grabbed the chains that shackled him to the beam above him and pulled himself up. He kicked out, ramming into the belly of one man and the kidneys of the other with all the strength he had left. Both men, caught off guard, staggered back and plowed into Donovan.

Blake spit out the rag. "No! Tori, it's a trap! Don't—"

The closest dirtbag slammed his fist into Blake's jaw, bouncing his head off the wall and effectively putting an end to his warning. When his vision cleared, Donovan was no longer on the phone. Had Tori heard him before the bastard ended the call?

The second man righted himself and stomped toward Blake. Two vicious jabs to the ribs emptied Blake's lungs, and pain shot upward to his chest. Nausea rolled over him in waves. He collapsed, the iron manacles around his wrists cutting into his skin as his weight dropped. His strength was gone. The fight was over. It'd been worth it if Tori had heard him. *If there's a God in heaven, please keep her away from here.* She hadn't had anything to do with the war on terror or the tragedy that took the life of Donovan's brother. She shouldn't have to pay for Blake's mistakes.

The punishing blows fell so hard and fast, Blake couldn't catch his breath. Through mere slits, he tried to focus on Donovan. The asshole looked as though he'd swallowed a hand grenade and it was about to blow his insides out. With his last bit of determination, Blake pasted a grin on his face, knowing it would drive Donovan bat-shit crazy. A small measure of satisfaction consoled him as he gave in and let the blackness take him.

* * * *

Tori jumped to her feet as Blake croaked out the desperate warning. Then the sounds of someone being pummeled mercilessly lodged her heart in her throat. "Blake! No! Stop it!" She reached for the phone where it lay on the table, turned up as loud as it would go so everyone could hear.

Travis beat her to it, snatching the device from her fingers. She started toward him, angry and irrational enough to think she could take him and somehow get the phone back. Donovan's arrogant words stopped her cold.

"Well, that was unfortunate for all concerned. Tomorrow at noon, Tori, or Sorenson dies."

The room went still as if all the air had been sucked out of it, and all eyes were on her. The next instant, she was falling. Someone caught her, and when she opened her eyes, she was lying on Jane's bed with something wet and cold on her face and soft voices murmuring nearby.

Blake.

Tori ripped the washcloth away and threw her legs over the side of the bed. She had to go. Donovan was going to kill Blake if she didn't.

She stood—too fast. The floor came up to meet her. Gentle hands caught her and pushed her back down on the bed. Her stomach churned. Maybe she should stay put for a few minutes.

Someone sat next to her. "Slow down, Tori. That phone call, as upsetting as it was for you, gave us a shitload of information we didn't have before." MacGyver. What was he talking about?

"Like what?" she said without trying to open her eyes or move her head this time.

"Blake is alive, most importantly."

Tori shuddered. *Yeah, but for how long?*

"And you were right about the location."

Tori squinted at him. "How do you know that?"

"Just before Donovan ended the call, we heard a train whistle. Coop was able to take the information we had and confirm there was a freight train within a mile of their location at the exact moment we heard the horn blow. Roberts is on his way now."

Tori pressed her hand to her forehead. "Good Lord. How long was I out?"

"Not long. We're just that good." Travis laughed at his own boasting. "Now…are you coming with us? The chopper will be here any minute. We're going to make a big splash when Crenshaw lands that thing in the street out front, so we don't want to keep them waiting."

Tori raised up carefully on her elbows, and MacGyver stood, ready to help.

Her brow shot up as she grinned at Travis. "Just try to keep me away."

Chapter 25

"I'm going in with you." Tori stood toe-to-toe with MacGyver and Travis, jamming her hands on her hips.

Luke, conferring with Special Agent Roberts across the staging area, looked up, his scowl communicating his thoughts wordlessly. He started toward them. *Great!*

"No! You're not." MacGyver's tone and body language warned her that his temper had about reached critical mass. "It's too dangerous for you and for us, and Blake will separate my head from my shoulders if I let you get hurt. It's *not* happening." He loomed over her with a bearing that had surely intimidated many before her.

Tori crossed her arms and held her ground. "I'm going...with or without you, and I don't need your permission."

"Goddammit!" MacGyver threw his hands in the air and whipped around just as Luke sidled up next to him. "Luke, would you please talk some sense into this hardheaded woman?"

Luke remained thoughtfully quiet. Coop joined Travis and they both stepped back a few feet. Tori eyed them suspiciously, noting their spectator stances and half-assed grins. What the hell was that about? Were they laughing at her?

She was worn out, running on adrenaline and determination. The last thing she wanted was a fight with Luke, but this wasn't negotiable. Blake had been there when she needed him—*every* time she'd needed him over the past few days, and Tori *needed* to be there when they freed him... to see for herself he was alive. As stupid as that sounded in her head, no wonder MacGyver was bent.

Luke raised his hand as she started to speak. "You'll do exactly what I tell you?" It sounded like a question, but the hard planes of his face suggested otherwise.

Did he mean he was okay with her going? Luke's query stunned her, momentarily leaving her unable to articulate a reply, and one look at MacGyver confirmed he felt much the same way.

He rounded on Luke. "What the fuck are you doing?"

"Relax, MacGyver. We're not going to feed her to the lions." Luke was still studying her, no doubt waiting for her to change her mind and opt out.

Tori was encouraged by the bit about the lions. "Yes. I'll do whatever you say. Please. Just let me help."

Luke turned toward Travis. "See if Roberts has some Kevlar that'll fit her."

Travis nodded and strode away, and Tori's heart rate kicked up a notch.

"Based on thermal imaging, Roberts thinks there's at least three bad guys inside with Blake. If they see us coming, they'll either kill him or use him as a shield to effect their escape. We're going in fast and hard, and anyone with a weapon pointed at us will likely end up dead." Luke reached for the bulletproof vest Travis returned with and stepped toward her. "Can you handle that?"

"Yes." She squared her shoulders and returned his perusal.

MacGyver scowled. "What's to keep Donovan from stepping out that door and putting a bullet in her head? Trading Blake's life for hers isn't going to win any friends."

If he's trying to scare me, it just might work. Tori rubbed her sweaty palms on her thighs.

Luke raised the body armor over her head and waited for her to thread her arms through the side openings before settling it carefully on her shoulders. "Don't let MacGyver spook you, Tori. We won't give Donovan a chance to hurt anyone." Luke tightened the shoulder straps and snugged the vest around her torso, glowering pointedly at MacGyver, while still speaking to her. "Our objective is to get in and get out with Blake...and failure is not an option."

"Damn right," Coop said, and Travis slapped the palm Coop held up.

The anger seemed to slide right off MacGyver's back, replaced by the cold calculation of a hardened warrior.

Luke finished adjusting her vest but continued to scrutinize her as though looking for any sign of weakness.

He'd be disappointed. Now that she'd gotten what she'd wanted, Tori was damned if she'd let him see the case of nerves that raced along her spine, leaving chills in its wake.

* * * *

Dusk dropped quickly over the rolling hills, where the old farmhouse nestled in patches of tall grass waving in the breeze. Special Agent Roberts had positioned a surveillance team around the building where they suspected Blake was being held, and no one had come or gone since his men had arrived.

The staging area was on a hill a quarter of a mile from the house, surrounded by deciduous trees and natural rock formations. With field glasses, Tori had been able to see—hell—absolutely nothing to indicate there was anyone around. Not a sound drifted across the grassland. No one stepped outside for a smoke. Not even a vehicle waited in the gathering darkness. If Roberts's men hadn't located two pickups parked in the old barn, barely visible beyond the farmhouse, Tori wouldn't have believed they were at the right location.

MacGyver meandered in her direction, and Tori tensed. Twenty feet away, Kellie intercepted him. Joining hands, the couple continued toward her. Tori understood why MacGyver was upset. Hell, she even appreciated his concern for her safety, but she simply didn't have the patience for another argument.

Kellie smiled as they approached, and, behind her, Luke tossed out the contents of his coffee cup and started gearing up. As though that was the signal, Travis, Coop and a half dozen FBI agents began checking weapons or donning a layer of dark clothing over their body armor. Everyone moved quietly and efficiently. Tori jerked her focus back to MacGyver and Kellie as they stopped directly in front of her.

MacGyver glanced sideways at the woman he so obviously cared for a great deal. "Kellie tells me I owe you an apology...and she's right. I'm sorry, Tori. I still think you should stay here and let us take care of this, but I get why you feel so strongly about going. We care about Blake too, and neither of us would appreciate being kept on the sidelines."

Tori regarded Kellie silently. A long-sleeved black shirt covered her Kevlar vest and a handgun was holstered on her hip. Apparently, MacGyver didn't have a problem with the pretty blonde going with them. Then again, Kellie had been trained as a Marine and was, no doubt, a capable member of the PTS team.

Kellie's brow raised. "He means he'd be mad as hell and heaven help the poor bastard who dares to broach the subject. Right, MacGyver?"

He caught Kellie's elbow as she took aim at his ribs. "Yeah, what *she* said." Amusement sparkled in his eyes when she tugged his head down and kissed his jaw.

Tori laughed, despite the apprehension the past hour of waiting had imprinted in her bones. "Thanks, MacGyver. I'm sorry too...for being such a pain in the ass."

Kellie shoved a small bundle she'd been holding against her stomach into Tori's hands. As soon as the weight of the item registered, Tori glanced between Kellie and MacGyver questioningly. The flat black metal of the gun, nestled securely in a lightweight, clip-on holster, instantly reminded her of Ken and his determination to keep her safe from every danger, which now she knew had included him. For the first time, she was grateful, because if she was forced to defend Blake tonight, she'd be ready.

"MacGyver said you knew how to handle a sidearm, and I thought you should be prepared, like the rest of the team."

"Thanks. That means a lot." Tori searched Kellie's face and then swept her attention to MacGyver. No trace of animosity remained in his blue eyes.

"Don't draw that thing unless it's your last resort." MacGyver's features were stern though he was clearly having trouble keeping his concern for her in check.

Luke strode up behind him. "We're ready." His gaze flicked over her bulletproof vest and the holstered weapon she'd positioned slightly forward on her hip.

MacGyver and Kellie peeled away from the group and jogged to where they'd left their gear.

When they were alone, Luke pointed at her. "You stay on my six. Move when I move unless I tell you otherwise. If I say *get down*, it means face in the dirt. If something happens to me, stick with MacGyver or Kellie." He lowered his index finger and took a step back. A slight smile transformed his grim features. "Try not to shoot me, okay?"

He turned abruptly and strode toward the other men, and Tori hustled to keep up in case her lack of attention would precipitate him changing his mind. A few minutes later, the four men and one woman of PTS Security, Special Agent Roberts, and all but two of his men, and Tori, headed out under cover of darkness to find Blake and bring him back alive.

Now that they were on the move, Tori's anxiety settled into a mere buzz of alarm as she concentrated on staying with Luke. MacGyver and Travis took point. Coop was somewhere behind her at the rear of their detail. A few feet to her left, Kellie kept pace with her. The handful of FBI men veered away from the group and were soon out of sight, although they could still be heard occasionally, eliciting groans of frustration from the Navy SEALs. Was that why Luke had agreed to let her come, because he knew they wouldn't be able to sneak up on Donovan's group anyway? Tori grimaced and tried harder to stay right in Luke's footsteps.

She almost ran into him when he halted abruptly and crouched on one knee. Tori did the same, gaping at the building she'd been examining through field glasses all afternoon, now only thirty feet away.

Coop and Kellie dropped down as they came up behind her, and the four of them stayed silent and motionless while Travis and MacGyver approached the building to within fifteen feet before they also crouched to wait, though what they were waiting for, Tori couldn't say.

Luke took pity on her, after her third sigh, and pointed to the right and then the left side of the building. At first Tori didn't see anything, but after a while she spotted movement at both sides of the structure.

He leaned closer. "Roberts and his men. They'll keep an eye on the back and side exits while we go in the front. As a special favor for helping Rafael out, Roberts is allowing us to call the shots."

MacGyver flashed a hand signal that meant nothing to Tori. He and Travis rose and glided silently from shadow to shadow in a straight line for the front door.

"We're on." Luke glanced over his shoulder and signaled to Coop, who wasted no time in catching up with MacGyver and Travis. Then Luke straightened and led her and Kellie toward the house, setting a pace only slightly less urgent than MacGyver's.

When they reached the building, they spread out and pressed their backs to the walls on either side of the door. Less than thirty seconds ticked by before MacGyver faced the entrance, and, with one kick, splintered the wooden barrier. Travis ripped the pieces out of his way and forged inside. Coop and MacGyver disappeared within as well.

Tori's heart pounded in her throat for the count of ten before Luke signaled her and Kellie to follow and dashed through the gaping door. Just inside, he pulled her with him to the right wall of a wide corridor. Kellie hugged the opposite side. Travis, MacGyver and Coop were twenty feet in front of them, moving quickly along both sides of the corridor. Bare bulbs, hanging from a high ceiling, cast gray light over the equally gray interior.

They slowed as they approached closed doors on the right. Special Agent Roberts's surveillance of the inside with thermal imaging had indicated body heat was concentrated in the center of the building. Two doorways loomed ahead. One of them had to lead to where they were holding Blake. Luke held up again, letting MacGyver and the others scout ahead. They made short work of searching the farthest room from the main hallway. Apparently finding nothing, they backtracked to the other door. It was locked, and Travis kicked it in. As all three darted through, gunfire erupted all around, echoing through the empty space.

"Get down." Luke dashed the twenty feet to the opening where they'd last seen the others.

With Luke's directive ping-ponging around in her head, Tori hit the deck near the wall, covering her ears as gunfire blasted from where Luke and the guys had disappeared.

"Where the fuck are *you* going?" Donovan's angry, muffled voice carried along the walls.

Tori lifted her head so she could hear and glanced around for Kellie. Her friend was nowhere in sight. Evidently, she'd sprinted after Luke while Tori had cowered on the floor. Yes, Tori *had* promised Luke. And she *did* hit the ground when he'd told her to get down. Luckily, he hadn't said how long she had to stay there.

Slowly, so as not to make a sound, Tori pushed herself to knees and hands and crawled along the wall, pausing when she heard Donovan's voice raised in anger again.

"This is what I hired you cowards for. Walk out that door and I'll kill you myself."

Crude curses hung in the air for a moment, and then a door slammed.

"Looks like you've got personnel problems, Donovan." That was MacGyver, unable to resist a dig, as usual. "I wouldn't worry about them. You can bet the FBI agents outside have already placed them under arrest. As soon as you drop your weapon, they can read you your rights, and you won't have to die here today."

Donovan laughed. "Aren't you forgetting something?"

"Blake Sorenson would be the first to say taking a bullet is an acceptable trade-off for stopping a worthless piece of shit like you."

What? Is MacGyver trying to get Blake killed? Tori crawled faster toward the room the voices were coming from. As she pressed herself against the broken doorjamb and peered around the edge, she had to bite back an involuntary cry.

Travis, Luke and Coop formed a line in front of the door, weapons drawn and aimed toward the far end of the room. MacGyver had stopped a few feet farther in, having obviously taken on the role of negotiator, though

Tori was unimpressed so far. Kellie stood tensely at his left hand. Their handguns remained holstered.

"I'm so sick of people treating him like a fucking hero. This man let my brother die so he could save himself." The sneer in Donovan's voice awakened the dread in Tori's stomach.

She moved slightly to peer around Coop's legs. Against the far wall, Donovan held a gun to Blake's head, a maniacal glint in his eyes attesting to his mental condition. But it was Blake who commanded her attention. *Is he even alive?* Ostensibly held up by the wall behind him and the iron cuffs that shackled his wrists above his head, Blake gave no indication of consciousness. What Tori could see of his face was a mass of swollen bruises and bleeding wounds. Blood smeared his forearms, where it had seeped from the ghastly cuts beneath the manacles. The front of his T-shirt was ripped and hung open, exposing deep purple bruises covering his ribs and chest.

Tears fell, unabated, from Tori's eyes, and the only thing that kept her horrified gasp from giving her presence away was MacGyver's sarcastic snigger at exactly the right second.

"This man saved more military personnel than you can count, including me. I was there the day your brother died, and you've got it all wrong. I know, because I picked him up and put him in the helo. He was barely breathing, and the left side of his skull was gone. That man you want to kill so damn bad wouldn't give up on him, but I'm telling you it was a gift your brother died without waking up."

"Shut the fuck up! All lies—all of it! And he's going to pay." Donovan jammed the barrel of his gun into the side of Blake's head.

Blake's groan was his first sign of life. Barely breathing herself, Tori drew her weapon.

"All right." MacGyver's voice hardened. "Let's talk about you. Are you willing to fry for an act of revenge that won't bring your brother back? James Donovan died a hero and was awarded the Medal of Honor for actions above and beyond the call of duty. Are you really going to sully his name, along with yours?"

Donovan wiped the sweat from his brow with his shirt sleeve and appeared to consider that, but never moved the barrel of his gun from Blake's head.

What are they waiting for? Why don't they shoot him? But Tori knew why. His brother had been a SEAL. He'd died a hero. *No man left behind.* They were trying to give him a chance, for his brother's sake. Tori respected that...to a point.

"What's it going to be, Donovan? Life in prison is the least you're looking at if you go through with this. Frankly, I can't guarantee you'll leave this room alive."

"Shut up! Just…just let me think." Donovan was becoming visibly more agitated, mumbling to himself.

A hiss close at hand made Tori glance up. Luke's left hand gestured behind his back. Tori hadn't understood any of his earlier signals, but there was no mistaking this one. He wanted her to stand. Since that action would definitely be noticed by the lunatic with the gun at Blake's head, she could only assume Luke wanted her to create a distraction.

That I can do!

"Mr. Donovan." Tori scrambled to her feet, quickly returning her weapon to the holster on her hip, before stepping through the line of men comprised of Luke, Travis and Coop. "James must have been one hell of a SEAL. No wonder you're proud of him."

Donovan's eyes widened, and his malevolent smile bordered on crazy. "Tori, I didn't expect you until tomorrow. No matter. Now we can proceed to the main event. When I hired you for the story, I had no idea you'd be the perfect person to help me make Sorenson suffer. Someone he loves… dying in front of him. It's poetic justice, don't you think?"

He swung his gun until it pointed at her and drew a vicious-looking knife from his belt. Donovan pressed the blade to Blake's ribs and beckoned her closer with the barrel of the gun. Tori took another step toward him… and then everyone moved at once.

MacGyver advanced, drawing his handgun, aimed at Donovan's head. "Drop your weapon. Now!"

Luke surged to his right, sliding his arm around Tori, and dragged her to the floor with him. Kellie fell in beside Travis and Coop as they closed in to back up MacGyver. Donovan's eyes widened and filled with confusion for a few seconds. Then he swore, jerked forward a step and turned his weapon on MacGyver.

In a heartbeat, Blake opened his eyes and roared. A kick of his leg to the side took out Donovan's knee. The sound of breaking bones and Donovan's scream of pain was all Tori heard before Travis slammed him to the floor.

As soon as Luke let her go, Tori clambered to her feet and rushed toward Blake. He seemed to have fallen back into his partially unconscious state, but he whispered her name and winced when she threw her arms around him.

"Keys!" Tori flung the word over her shoulder as she struggled to hold Blake upright. Almost immediately, Kellie was beside her, reaching up to unlock one wrist and then the other, taking some of Blake's weight from Tori so he wouldn't crush her on his way to the floor.

Tori cradled Blake's head in her lap as tears blinded her. Luke crouched beside her and checked Blake's wounds. He squeezed her shoulder briefly, a gesture that somehow said *welcome to the team*. Special Agent Roberts took custody of Donovan and handcuffed him, where he writhed and cried on the floor, his knee turned at an unnatural angle.

Tori heard a helicopter above the din in the room, and the steady beat of the rotors grew gradually louder. Time seemed to stand still as she concentrated on keeping Blake from slipping too deep into himself. When the time came, she hopped in the belly of the chopper beside him, without fear or hesitation, and clung to his hand.

Chapter 26

Blake came awake slowly, the dull ache in his ribcage superseding everything else going on around him…until he squinted through the slits that remained where his eyes used to be.

Someone had opened the blinds since the last time he'd woken, and sunshine splayed across the otherwise drab hospital wall directly in front of him. Sun was good. He hadn't been entirely sure he'd ever see it again.

The curtain around his bed was drawn halfway closed, blocking his view of the door, but he could hear voices out in the hallway and the clank of metal on plates. The kitchen staff was no doubt serving breakfast…or lunch. He'd lost track of the time. Hell, he wasn't even sure what day it was.

A soft rustle of movement grabbed his attention, and he rolled his head to the left. He almost choked on his tongue when he caught sight of a pair of red stilettoes. Someone had one foot crossed over the other and resting on the edge of his bed.

The slight catch of his breath hurt like hell, and he concentrated on not moving as he followed perfect ankles up sleek calves to a healthy display of creamy thigh, until the hem of a short denim skirt blocked his view. An instant tightening below the waist gave evidence that at least part of his anatomy still functioned.

It had to be Tori sitting there, a magazine open and held in front of her. She'd lost her red heels the day his helicopter crashed. That she'd bought a new pair…for him…put an instant smile on his face. He'd know those sexy ankles anywhere, but if she'd heard him moving, she wasn't letting on. "That is *so* not fair." The words grated through his throat like sandpaper on wood.

Without lowering the magazine, she uncrossed and recrossed her ankles. "Somebody mentioned you were a leg man, Sorenson." Tori's voice oozed amusement, but she still didn't show her face.

Kellie had been sitting beside his bed the few other times he'd opened his eyes, and, though he appreciated his friend's vigilance, this was *so* much better. The last time he'd seen Tori, he'd just been released from his shackles, and she'd held him against her warm body while silent tears cascaded down her cheeks. He'd wanted to dry those tears, but he couldn't feel his arms.

A little of the fear and anger he'd experienced when he'd thought she would turn herself over to Donovan robbed him of his contentment at seeing her. "You scared the shit out of me, ya know." He rolled his head back and stared at the ceiling. "What the hell were you doing there? MacGyver and Luke should have known better."

The magazine slapped against her lap, and her heels disappeared below the edge of the bed. From the corner of his eye, he watched a parade of emotions traipse across her face, not the least of which was some anger of her own. She leaned forward, and, for a minute, he was afraid she might leave, but then her anger disappeared, leaving nothing but vulnerability in her expressive eyes.

"Luke and MacGyver didn't want me there either. I told them I'd go… with or without them. For the record, MacGyver is still sure you're going to do him bodily harm." Her wistful smile disappeared as quickly as it'd come. "Don't you get it? I had to go. I had to see you—know you were still alive." Tears rimmed her beautiful blues and a tremor rocked her. "I…I love you."

Her final words were so quiet, Blake was sure he'd imagined them. What he thought he'd heard stole all the moisture from his mouth and left him scrambling for the right thing to say.

"I know I'm not supposed to, we both said no strings. It wasn't intentional, believe me. It just happened." She finally stopped to take a breath.

He crooked his finger at her. "Come here."

"It's okay. I mean, I'm a big girl, and I'm not going to make this uncomfortable for you."

"Tori, come here."

She slapped her forehead. "Oh, God. I wasn't even going to tell you. I've made such a mess of this." Tori jumped to her feet, grabbed her sweater from the back of the chair and caught the magazine before it hit the floor. She looked at him then, though not at his face. "I'm glad you're going to be all right."

"Tori Michaels, don't make me come and get you."

"What?" A frown drew her brows together.

A growl formed in his throat as he pushed through the pain to sit straight, reach out and snag her arm. The growl became a roar as he hauled her on the bed with him.

"What are you doing? You'll hurt yourself. Are you crazy?"

Blake clamped his arm around her, holding her to his side, while he closed his eyes and let the waves of pain roll over him until they lessened. When he dared to move his head, he dropped a kiss on her forehead.

"Yes, I am. Crazy about you, that is."

When her head jerked up, confusion on her features, he caught her lips and snaked his fingers into her silky hair, so he could sample and taste at his leisure. Honey and orange blossoms. He'd never get his fill of this woman.

Finally, he lifted his head and she tried to push away from him. "Blake, I'm hurting you."

He held her fast. "You'll only hurt me if you leave."

Tori stopped and a gorgeous smile, complete with those killer dimples, radiated from her like summer sun. "I'd never do that."

He brought her fingers to his lips. "I know you wouldn't."

"How? How do you know?"

"The same way I know I'd never do anything to bring you or Isaiah sorrow. You were meant for me…and I'm incomplete without you. I love you, Tori. Please believe that."

Tori squealed and covered his face with kisses. Then she found his mouth and brushed it softly with hers before settling in for a long, sensuous kiss that transformed his burgeoning arousal to a raging hard-on.

"Hey, why don't you find me some clothes so we can get out of here? I can't wait to get you home." He was so damn hard, he'd forgotten all about the ache in his ribs.

"Uh…no. The last thing I want is for you to put on clothes." Mischief shone from her eyes and her hand brushed the front of his hospital gown, clearly on purpose.

He sucked in his breath and nipped her throat. "Okay, but unless that door locks from the inside, we're about to make a spectacle of ourselves." Blake could feel every one of his multiple cracked ribs, and the weakness that lingered in his arms and shoulders was worrisome. But his dick was definitely up to the task, so, who was he to argue?

Tori laughed. "Go for it. This is on my bucket list."

He groaned and brought her hand back to his rigid manhood. "Oh yeah? What else is on that list?"

Tori moaned as his lips nuzzled the edge of her shirt aside and kissed the swell of her breasts peeking out of her lacy bra.

Suddenly, someone cleared his throat loudly from the doorway. Tori hopped off the bed, trying to stifle her laughter, grabbed one of Blake's pillows from beneath his head, and tossed it over his obvious erection. Straightening her hair, she turned to face the door, holding her sweater to her chest where her shirt hung askew.

"Well, look who's awake!" Travis yanked the curtain back and strode to the bed. Coop, Luke and MacGyver trailed behind.

Tori stepped back as Blake's four friends surrounded the bed, but Luke draped his arm over her shoulders and tugged her up beside him. "Come on, Tori. I'm not taking this ass-chewing alone." He eyed Blake warily. "Although, if you feel you need to have your say, I'm your man. It was my decision to let her come with us."

Hell, yeah. Blake had had plenty to say on the subject…right up until Tori had blown his mind with her admission. *She loves me.* Even more surprising was the sudden sense of everything being right in his world. Making a commitment to her didn't scare him like it should have, based on previous experience. In fact, there wasn't anything he wanted more.

Blake considered Luke's words for a minute before glancing at each of his buddies in turn. He owed them…big time…for crashing Donovan's party and dragging his ass out of there. *No, that's not entirely true. I owe my brothers for a hell of a lot more than that.*

He swallowed the lump that had somehow formed in his throat. "I don't think I'll be complaining today. We're good." Blake threw Tori a wink. "Besides, I know how stubborn she can be."

"Hey! I'm right here."

The dimples he loved popped on her cheeks and sent warmth into parts of his soul that hadn't seen the light of day for far too long. How could he possibly be upset with her? Or Luke, for that matter?

Kellie had filled him in on the events leading up to Tori showing herself to Donovan, knowing it would be the diversion they needed to regain control of the situation. Apparently, no one had guessed that Blake, hovering on the fringes of consciousness, would be so enraged by the threat of Donovan laying a hand on Tori he'd take matters into his own hands.

The room grew quiet as though each person took a moment to honor the whole, his friends, this band of brothers that kept him sane and always… *always* had his back. And now Tori, his woman, and Isaiah. Maybe he'd even get to be a father to Isaiah, or at least a friend.

Coop, Travis, MacGyver and Luke lined both sides of his bed with perceptive grins all around. Evidently, no one had been fooled by the strategically placed pillow, and, judging by Tori's pink cheeks, she was only too aware of the undercurrent of inappropriate male humor. No doubt, they could use a diversion of their own about now.

"Kellie said you got Sebastian. Is he talking?"

"Hell no," Coop huffed. "He lawyered up first thing. But the judge denied bail at his arraignment, and Rafael says they have a strong case against him."

"Only thing remaining to be seen is how long due process will take." MacGyver dropped into the chair Tori had vacated before they arrived, and a mental image of her feet in red stilettoes, resting on the edge of his bed, threatened to undo Blake's control.

He scraped a hand down his face, hoping to wipe away his persistent grin. "What's his connection to Donovan?"

Travis chortled. "None whatsoever. At least, Roberts hasn't found one. Donovan isn't admitting one either, and he's talking his head off to anyone who'll listen."

"No way." Blake couldn't wrap his head around the idea that Donovan and Sebastian had operated independently of each other. True coincidences were rare.

"Donovan says he planned his revenge for nearly three years. The only help he had was a black-market gun dealer, who sold him a cache of weapons, and the two ball-busters that did a number on you. Roberts has them in custody too." MacGyver slouched in the chair and stuck his long legs toward the hospital bed.

"Donovan hired Tori to find you on the pretext of wanting an interview for his magazine, and he was going to take it from there." Luke removed his arm from Tori's shoulders and hooked his thumbs in his belt loops. "It wasn't until he saw the two of you together he realized he could cause you pain by hurting her. He got to Harv on one of your mechanic's many trips into town. Apparently Harv had a gambling problem that Donovan was going to help him solve if he'd get Tori away from your place. He used Sebastian's breach as cover to sneak her out of the basement."

"By the way, the old guy who built your house is a genius." Travis glanced toward his partners. "We should talk to him about our new safe house."

Everyone groaned.

"What?" Travis grinned as he looked around the group.

"We know Tori didn't lead Sebastian to the safe house, and if Donovan wasn't working for him, how'd Sebastian find the cabin? And why did his man, Nox, try to abduct Tori from her house later that night?" Blake laced his fingers behind his head but quickly dropped them to the bed when the position increased pressure on his ribs, restricting his ability to breathe. He didn't miss the grimaces on the faces of the men, who'd no doubt all suffered similar injuries at least once.

"All good questions, and finding the answers is Roberts's number one priority. He thinks the FBI has a mole who directed Sebastian to the safe house and that they went after Tori to find out what she knew and whether they could use her. I have no doubt Roberts will get to the bottom of the garbage pile." MacGyver jerked his thumb across his throat in a familiar gesture. "Wouldn't want to be that mole when Roberts figures out who it is."

Blake considered that for a moment and had to agree with MacGyver's assessment. It was unfortunate there would always be men like Harv who could be bought by the highest bidder. The PTS team had learned a valuable lesson and dodged a costly bullet.

Dr. Peltier, the same ER doc who'd treated Tori after her fall, strode into the room, glanced at his chart, and frowned. "Mr. Sorenson, are you feeling up to all this testosterone in the room?"

Tori slipped a hand over her mouth, but Blake saw the grin she was trying to hide.

Coop laughed and leaned toward the attractive blond-haired woman in blue scrubs. "Now, Liz, may I call you Liz? We're here supporting our friend. And, for the record, *all this testosterone* hauled your patient's ass out of a bad situation last night. You should be thanking us for making your job easier."

Everyone laughed, including Dr. Peltier, and she laid her palm against Coop's pecs, to his obvious delight. "I am grateful...and feel safer just knowing you boys are in the neighborhood."

Blake groaned. "Ah hell, Doc. Don't encourage him."

"You're free to go home whenever you like, Blake. Just take it easy for a couple of weeks. I'd rather not see you back in here for a while."

"That's for damn sure," MacGyver said. "Enough hospitals for both of you." He included Tori with a jab of his finger.

"I agree." Tori's eyes sparkled with the smile she turned on Blake.

Luke cleared his throat. "That's our cue. Time to head out. Tori, can you get this guy home on your own?"

"I think I can manage."

"Kellie is fixing your favorite dinner to celebrate tonight." MacGyver bumped fists with Blake. "We'll pick up Isaiah and invite Jane if she'd like to come."

"That's sweet. Thanks, MacGyver," Tori said.

"How about it, Doc. Want to join us for dinner?" Coop gave her a hopeful grin.

To Blake's surprise, Dr. Peltier leaned toward Coop as she walked by on her way out. "I have to get back to my rounds, but I get off at six."

"Hot damn. I'll be here to pick you up." Coop flipped a mock salute at Blake and headed out the door, a new bounce in his step.

Travis followed him, shaking his head, and Luke and MacGyver were the last to leave.

Tori went to a cupboard along the wall and returned with the clean clothes she'd brought to the hospital for Blake. "Need any help?"

He shook his head as he studied her face. "No, I've got it."

Damned if she didn't look disappointed but grabbed her sweater and started for the door.

"I changed my mind." Blake was reminded of the words he'd told himself when he'd first experienced the powerful attraction she held for him. He'd been sure even then she was the kind of woman a man took his time with and then took home to meet his family. He'd tried to convince himself he wanted no part of that. He'd been lying to himself.

She glanced back. "What?"

"I don't want just a quick fling with you. I want to take my time and get to know everything about you, every square inch of your body. And then I want to take you to meet my brother." Christian was the only family he had.

Tori hurried to his side and leaned in to kiss him as the shine of tears touched her eyes.

"Are you going to be okay with an ex-military man around the house? Because I don't ever see me letting you go."

"When I thought I might have lost you, I realized how cowardly it was not to give us a chance. Never once did I think of you as ex-military…or a helicopter pilot. It doesn't matter what you were—only who you are now. I want *you*…through good times and bad."

"You've got me, baby. Just try to get rid of me." Blake captured her mouth, stroking the seam of her lips with his tongue until she opened for him, and he tasted every hidden corner. She was his, just as he was hers, and he couldn't imagine a time when he wouldn't want her right beside him. And if she wore those damn red stilettoes…even better.

If you enjoyed *For the Love of a SEAL*, be sure not to miss the first book in Dixie Lee Brown's Hearts of Valor series,

They're brothers-in-arms, Navy SEALS risking their lives for their country... and the women they love.

This is Luke Harding's story.

Six months in a desert hellhole taught Navy SEAL Luke Harding things he never wanted to learn about life and death. Only tender memories of the beautiful brunette he met a few weeks before his deployment helped get him through the torturous days and nights. Back in the States after a perilous rescue, physically and emotionally damaged, Luke's about to plunge into a new kind of war. In a seemingly bucolic Idaho town, Sally Duncan faces real—and unpredictable—danger.

All Sally ever wanted was a safe place to raise her nine-year-old daughter. Her identity hidden behind a façade of secrets and lies, can she trust Luke—a man she barely knows—with the truth? Even as they give in to long-denied passion, a killer with a personal vendetta is setting an ambush that will leave them praying for a miracle and fighting for the future they may not live to see.

Keep reading for a special excerpt.

A Lyrical e-book on sale now!

Chapter One

Heart pounding, Luke bolted upright, wide awake, as though a dose of adrenaline had shot directly into his bloodstream. The sound—no, more a feeling than a sound—came again, pulling him back from the edge of his nightmare—the same damn one he'd had last night and the night before that. The pain in his shoulders and arms was bad, intensified by his sudden movement. Yesterday's interrogation had been more brutal than usual. *Don't think about it. It's only going to get worse. Focus.* Something had jolted him from what passed for sleep these days. After nearly six months in this filthy, godforsaken POW camp, not much surprised him. Yet the strange vibrations that still pulsed in his nerve endings were somehow different.

Hell. What did he know? It wasn't exactly unusual to wake battling a gut-wrenching, hard-to-get-enough-air sensation that sapped his strength and made him want to scream to the God he was slowly beginning to doubt existed. With the dream fresh in his mind, how the hell was he supposed to distinguish reality from the warped images taking up residence in his fucked-up brain?

He lowered himself to his sleeping pallet and strained to catch the sound one more time. His gaze raked the shadows beyond the wire fence that segregated his two hundred square feet of Afghan sand and scrub brush from the rest of the compound. Within its confines, he was allowed to move around as much as he wanted. That was his one freedom, but his harsh captors provided little else. A frayed and rat-eaten tarp to keep out the rain and provide shade from the desert sun. Still, he could be grateful for the times he *was* allowed to stay inside his prison…away from this ruthless and unpredictable terrorist group. Militant jihadists who'd spun off al-Qaeda after Osama bin Laden was killed, they now claimed ties to ISIS and made his life a living hell on a daily basis.

It was unnaturally quiet in the compound, yet something lingered on the stillness of the night air. A sound so familiar it was as though, without it, he hadn't been complete. Shit. He was finally going crazy. Luckily, crazy was preferable to his other options.

A lone spotlight perched atop the locked gate at the north end of his stockade, interrupting the darkness. The moon, a mere sliver, was barely visible behind a thin veil of mist that would leave the ground wet with its touch before morning. The nights were getting colder. Late September or better. Fall already, with winter on the way. The seasons were the same as they were back home, except more extreme. Would his captors give him a blanket to fend off the freezing temperatures of winter? Would he survive long enough to worry about the weather?

Every nerve told him something waited in the dark just outside the fence. The skin on the back of his neck did that creepy-crawling thing he hated, assuring him he was being watched. Instinct screamed for him to stand and fight his unseen enemy, or at least defend himself. But fools perished quickly in this hellhole, and he wasn't fool enough to start a war he couldn't win. Attracting attention was never a good idea. For now, he would lie still on his worn sleeping mat, tucked beneath a shabby canvas lean-to in the darkest corner. His time would come soon enough.

Luke waited on high alert while minutes ticked slowly by. Nothing. No unusual sounds. No indication the fighters were any more vigilant than normal. Damn. It was probably the dream that had him imagining things. He'd have laughed at his paranoia, but his sense of humor had been the latest casualty of his months in captivity.

With an effort, he resisted looking toward the empty mat in the opposite corner of the lean-to. Before his buddy, Ian, had died, Luke at least had had hope. Since the chopper crash that killed three members of their team and stranded them deep within land held by the terrorists, they'd kept their spirits up by planning how they were going to escape. Admitting they'd probably die in the attempt, they'd agreed it would be worth it…as long as they took a shitload of terrorists to hell with them. Yeah, revenge was sweet.

Now, every time he closed his damn eyes, he saw the sword fall again, heard Ian's scream turn to a gurgle as his body jerked and twitched in agony. Each time the death scene played out in his mind, Luke struggled against unseen bonds, to free himself and help his friend and fellow SEAL…to no avail. It'd been nearly two weeks since Ian's death. And Luke was on deck. He knew that…but he wasn't going out without a fight.

Slowly, moving only his arm, he reached beneath the edge of his sleeping mat and pulled a picture free. The meager light was barely enough to make out the image. Sally Duncan and her eight-year-old daughter, Jen. With his thumb, Luke gently stroked Sally's cheek in the worn photograph.

The smoking-hot brunette had captivated him, and the kid, Jen, had flat-out won his heart. They'd met three weeks before he deployed, and he'd instinctively known some bad shit had gone down in Sally's life at some point. Whatever had happened had made her skittish, especially with men, and he didn't have to be told he wouldn't last ten minutes if he moved too fast. He'd played it cool. Didn't rush her. Many a night he'd ended the evening alone in a cold shower because of the petite, sexy woman whose

Mona Lisa smile always made him think she had a secret. And damned if he didn't want to know what it was. The night before he flew out, he'd kissed her—really kissed her for the first time—and asked for a picture.

Jesus! The guys in his unit would have laughed him out of the platoon if they'd ever found out what a wuss he'd been.

But that kiss and this picture had kept him sane through countless days of pain, depravation and intense hatred. She wouldn't let him give up. He had one purpose: to stay alive to see her again. To hold her and feel the warmth of her body against his, see the sparkle in her deep blue eyes as she laughed at one of his dumb jokes. Marvel at her appreciative smile when he did something nice for her. What he wouldn't give to sit with them again in their living room, Sally on one side, Jen on the other, while he held a huge bowl of popcorn on his lap and pretended to groan through some chick flick they'd picked to watch.

The faintest swish of something moving in his peripheral vision jerked his attention to the guard's platform towering over the desert floor a hundred yards to the east. And then he heard it again—the sound that had woken him. The *whop, whop, whop* of a Blackhawk, coming in low and fast. He sprang to a crouch, his heart thumping fast and loud.

The guards on the platform rushed to the far side, pointing and yelling. Then one of them hit the alarm, and its screech drowned out everything else. An instant later, a missile launched from the helo and streaked toward the camp barracks across the compound. The detonation knocked Luke on his ass and lit up the night sky. When the .50 caliber machine guns mounted in the bay of the Blackhawk opened fire on the guard tower and the few unfortunates who escaped the barracks, he decided it was best to stay down.

What the hell were they doing? They had to be Americans, but this was no high-value target. They didn't know he was here. They were just as likely to take him out, along with the dirty bastards who ran the place. It wasn't like he could take cover inside his open-air accommodations. What was he waiting for? There'd never be a better time to make his escape.

He scrambled to his feet, tucked Sally's picture in his pocket and ran for the gate. The barracks were all on fire. A few enemy fighters still fled the burning buildings, screaming and slapping at the flames that hungrily devoured their clothing, while trying to outrun the merciless onslaught of bullets from the chopper. The smell of smoke, gunpowder and burning flesh turned Luke's stomach and propelled him on. He had no sympathy for them, any more than they'd had a gnat's compassion for Ian as he died. *Let them all burn in hell.*

One of the hostiles ran by the outside of Luke's enclosure with a rocket launcher on his shoulder, dropped to one knee twenty feet away and aimed the weapon at the Blackhawk that was still picking off ground forces.

"Hell no!" Luke veered toward the corner of his yard, the closest point to the chopper, and waved his arms wildly over his head. "Get the hell out of here! Go!" A direct hit at such close range would drop the aircraft like a rock. It didn't matter why they were here. He had to warn them.

Not a chance they heard him—he could barely hear himself. It was even less likely that they saw him…but somehow, they knew. The chopper lifted up and away at a steep angle, just as the rocket fired. Even then it only missed the underbelly of the craft by a matter of inches. The Blackhawk continued to move away, circled the blaze they'd created and disappeared behind some hills to the west.

Fucking A! They're safe. Now it was his turn. He swung toward the gate…and halted abruptly. Abdul Omari, commander of this little resort, had apparently managed to hide his sorry ass and survive. He stood a few feet inside the wire, brandishing a pistol, flanked by two of his most depraved underlings with semiautomatic rifles. The only good news was the gate stood open behind them…but Luke would need a miracle to reach it alive.

"Where do you think you are going?" Omari's sneer made his heavy accent even more pronounced.

Luke studied the three. He had no personal knowledge of the man on Omari's right, but he knew the other man too damn well. Ahmed Kazi returned Luke's stare. Blond-haired, blue-eyed, American born and raised, the turncoat was now an interrogator and assassin for the terrorist network. He obviously held a deep-seated hatred for his former countrymen and had brought that to bear with a vengeance on Ian and Luke.

He'd been one cold son of a bitch when the sword he'd raised over his head had ended Ian's life with a hollow thud. Luke would never forget Ian's murderer. How could he? The man's fucking face appeared in his dreams every night. Rage, as black as the pits of hell, burned just beneath the artificial composure he presented to them. His fingers itched to be around the bastard's throat, squeezing the life from him.

Omari spoke a few words in one of the regional dialects. As one, his men raised the barrels of their weapons and pointed them at Luke.

Well, hell. Apparently, there wouldn't be time to come up with Plan B. Out in the open with no cover, his only option was to fight. Seriously outgunned, his odds weren't good. All he had in his arsenal was the training provided by the Navy SEALs—which was considerable—but he'd have to get much closer if it was going to help him against three armed men.

Then, if the planets aligned just right, maybe he'd have a chance. Still, going down fighting was better than dying where he stood.

Luke straightened to his full height and raised his arms, threading his fingers together on top of his head. He dropped his gaze in mock submission as he walked slowly toward his enemies. "Commander, you have many injured men outside. I've trained as a medic. Let me help them."

"You would have me believe you care about my men?"

"Hell no, but I wouldn't allow even an animal to suffer if I could help it." Luke lifted his gaze to take in the commander's skeptical expression. *That's right. Don't believe me, you bastard. Just let me get close enough.*

A handful of men rushed by the gate with weapons drawn, heading toward the west, the direction the helo had disappeared. Ahmed and the other guard returned to the gate, stepping outside to question the leader of the small group.

Omari turned his head for only a few seconds, but that was all Luke needed. He launched himself across the few feet that separated them, grabbed him from behind and applied just enough pressure to snap the bones in his neck before the commander could make a sound. When Luke let him go, his lifeless body slid to the ground. Seizing the Russian Makarov pistol the dead man had dropped, Luke opened fire on the two guards, while the group of men scurried for cover.

The heavily guarded gate was his only way out. Luke was as good as dead if he stayed where he was, so he might as well get in the game. Bending low, he raced a zigzag path toward the opening, ignoring the pain in his extremities from the cruel tortures he'd endured. He was counting on the notoriously poor marksmanship of the local recruits with the Russian-made AK-47. Three men outside the gate went down under his offensive, including Ahmed, before the pistol Luke continuously fired ran out of ammunition. He shrugged off a twinge of regret that Ian's murderer had gone down so easily. A slow, painful death would have been Luke's first choice.

The men crowding around the outside of the gate fired wildly in his direction, but Luke kept moving forward. An instant later, something slammed into his chest, stealing his breath and stopping him in midstride. Unable to move or even breathe, he hung there for a split second, while time stood still. His gaze locked on his goal, a mere half-dozen feet ahead, and he staggered backward, his efforts to stay on his feet ineffectual, until he sprawled in the dirt of his prison yard.

Damn! Get up! Pull it together! He tried to position his legs to stand, but his body wouldn't cooperate. Then the first wave of pain seared his nerve endings. He couldn't catch his breath. He'd been hit. *Those lousy desert rats got in a lucky shot!* The taste of blood filled his mouth. Panic seized him, but he refused to give it more than a few seconds. *New objective—stay alive. Failure is not an option.* The SEAL mantra had been drilled into him again and again during his training until it automatically followed *fuck this* in his vocabulary. One corner of his mouth curved upward in a half-assed grin, and he managed to draw a partial breath.

His gaze focused on the light at the top of the gate, he moved his hand upward toward the source of the pain, stopping when he felt the warm, sticky liquid that coated his shirt. He squeezed his eyes shut and struggled until another breath temporarily took away the ache in his lungs. *Failure is not an option.*

It sounded like a full-fledged war was being waged just outside his containment area. Every bit of his training demanded he get up and fight, but he needed a little more time to rest.

"Stay down!" someone yelled from not too far away in a pretty good imitation of English.

Who are they talking to? Does somebody need help? In a minute, I'll be strong enough to get back in the fight. Failure is not an option.

A sound close by forced Luke's eyes open, and he looked in to the gloating face of the remaining guard. Blood seeped from at least two wounds in his torso, but still he aimed his rifle at Luke. When the sound of the shot reverberated across the open desert, Luke's body jumped in anticipation of the slug tearing through his flesh. Instead, blood ran down the officer's chin, and he did a face-plant in the sand beside Luke.

Then there were people all around him, everyone talking at the same time—in *English*!

"Damn fine shot, Davis! Now, let's get our friends and get the hell out of here before reinforcements roll in." An American soldier, dressed in full battle gear, stood over Luke and talked into a small radio.

More unfamiliar faces appeared behind the first man, each yapping about something that seemed insignificant from Luke's position. He wanted to shout at them to shut up, but apparently there was no longer a connection between his brain and his mouth. *Not that there ever was much of one. Oh, great—now I get my sense of humor back.*

"Are you Petty Officer Second Class Luke Harding?" The man in battle gear knelt beside him.

As hard as he tried, Luke couldn't make a sound—or even nod his head. All he could do was stare until his eyes misted, and he squeezed his eyelids shut so he wouldn't fucking humiliate himself.

They know my name. Somebody knows who I am. Gratitude washed over him even as sorrow intruded into his momentary peace. Except for two short weeks, he could have celebrated with Ian.

The warrior reached for Luke's hand, gripping it firmly. "It's okay, son. You stay with me. You hear me, sailor? That's an order." He leaned over Luke, and there was understanding in his eyes. "We're here to get you home alive, and failure is not an option. You copy that?"

Luke would have smiled if he could have. Did the guy know the phrase he uttered so effortlessly was the only thing holding Luke together?

"Medic!" the man yelled over his shoulder, and two seconds later, another warrior stuck his head into Luke's space.

It was getting harder to breathe. His rasping and gurgling grew louder and filled his ears.

"Chest wound." The second man applied pressure, none too gently, to the hole in Luke's torso.

Jesus, you stupid SOB! Luke would have given anything for the strength to shove him away, while using every four-letter word he knew, but the most he could manage was a pained groan.

"Hang in there." The first man pulled Luke's attention from the medic. "I know you're in pain. The chopper will land any second, and we'll get you onboard. Next stop—a nice, clean hospital and then…Stateside. We're going to give you the good shit so you can sleep through this next part. You're going to make it, sailor, so start planning your homecoming."

Sally. The image of the sweet brunette flashed in Luke's mind. He barely felt the prick of the needle before his eyes fluttered closed on his last memory.

* * * *

This was definitely going down in history as one of the worst ideas she'd ever had. Sally pulled the door handle of Emmett's Chevy Tahoe and jumped out before he'd even come to a full stop in front of her house.

Dating her new boss—had she gone completely mad? Now that he'd proved to be a total dickhead, telling her exactly what he expected of his new office manager…outside of the office…she'd had no choice but to suggest he drop dead, using the f-word, which hadn't crossed her lips since Jen was born. Of course, that meant she'd be pounding the pavement tomorrow, looking for a new job. *Really?* How could she have been so foolish? She needed that job too, especially after her old Explorer had finally died and she'd had to go into debt to get the needed repairs. If only she could have a do-over for...oh, say, the last year of her life.

"We're not done yet, Sally." The SUV's door slammed shut and hurried footsteps followed her up the path toward the lights that glowed from the windows of her rented home.

Sally kept on walking. Her head throbbed as though someone had taken an electric drill to her temples. *Please, God, don't make me listen to anymore.* She shivered and drew the lightweight pashmina tighter around her shoulders. *What the hell was I thinking...wearing a short dress with no sleeves and strappy heels—at night in the middle of April—in the mountains—in Idaho?* Strong fingers circled her arm and bit down as he tightened his grip, jerking her around, making her forget the chill in the air, and bringing her face-to-face with one irate man.

She tried to shrug off his grasp, but he only pinched tighter. Sally swallowed an outraged cry, not willing to let him know he was hurting her. With composure she wasn't exactly feeling, she met his angry gaze. "Look, you made me an offer—I refused. I have a daughter and she comes first. Even if I wanted to become your...slut...I'd never set that kind of example for Jen. Surely you can understand that." Wary of the temper he'd exhibited on the way home, Sally refrained from telling him what a jackass she thought he was for pretending to be nice and normal until she agreed to go out with him. Then he'd hit her with a proposition that would have made a hooker blush.

Emmett yanked her closer, sliding his arms around her waist. "Well, *slut*'s a little harsh, darlin', but whatever you think. This has nothing to do with your kid. I'll find someone to watch her twenty-four/seven because that's how much of your time I'll need."

Anger sparked at his callous disrespect for Jen. Who the hell did he think he was? Of course, she already knew the answer. He was Emmett Purnell, owner of the biggest logging operation in Idaho. He was loaded and charismatic when he wanted to be and didn't like taking no for an answer. He'd smiled, turned on the charm and played the part of a gentleman until he'd managed to break through her barriers and she'd finally agreed to go out with him. *Idiot, idiot, idiot!*

Sally shook her head firmly. "Not interested."

Emmett's hands slid down to cup her bottom and pull her against him roughly. His intentions quickly became apparent as the hard ridge of his erection pressed into her stomach. Shock gave way to fury. She drew her arm back and swung, and her fist met his jaw with a resounding wallop.

Clearly taken by surprise, his head snapped back, but he recovered quickly. His lips thinned to the point of nearly disappearing, and his eyes darkened to glittering black orbs. "I like it rough, baby." He backhanded her so fast and hard, Sally hit the ground before she'd even registered the blow. The ringing in her ears made it impossible to hear...or think. A thousand needles pricked her cheek as the pain and taste of blood sent her to her knees, tying her stomach in knots.

She scrambled to stand, but dizziness and the pain in her still-fisted hand hindered her efforts. She refused to scream—that was sure to bring Jen and her babysitter, Tiffany, out of the house. Sally couldn't take the chance they might get hurt. Besides, screaming wasn't really her style. The best she could do at the moment was crawl out of the reach of the enraged lunatic and hope he came to his senses.

"Go ahead. Touch her again and see what happens, you fucking coward." The suggestion, coming from the darkness behind Emmett's vehicle and delivered with steel-edged composure, took her completely by surprise.

Sally swung toward the new player, forgetting Emmett for the moment. The voice was all too familiar, stirring unwelcome memories. Eyes watering from the blow, she squinted to see the man standing in the darkness just beyond her yard.

"Luke?" Sally staggered to her feet, clenching her teeth against the sick feeling that swirled in her stomach.

It couldn't be *him*. Not the man she'd fallen hard for before he deployed with his SEAL unit over a year ago. Not the man who'd refused to see her when she hurried to the hospital in Bethesda after hearing he'd been rescued from a terrorist prison. Rushing to his side because she'd thought they meant something to each other, she'd quickly learned the truth of the matter. His disregard had let her know, in no uncertain terms, that the feelings had been one-sided. *That* man had no reason—or right—to show up at her door.

Sally searched the shadows near the street, where the voice had originated. When she finally made out his silhouette, her breath caught in her throat.

Luke didn't spare her a glance.

"Who the hell are you?" Emmett turned to face him.

"Does it matter?" Luke's words contained a dangerous warning that Sally had never heard before.

As he stepped from the shadow of the SUV, his military fatigues and the duffel he carried reminded her of the homeless people who'd camped on Elk Creek last fall. A knife in a leather sheath hung at his side. His face was etched with lines of exhaustion, and he might have carried himself stiffly, but otherwise he was the same man she remembered. Light brown hair, longer and a bit more disheveled than the last time she'd seen him, always tempted her to run her fingers through it…even now.

"I'll need your name to give to the undertaker," Emmett sneered.

A humorless smile bared Luke's teeth as he let the duffel drop to the ground. He shrugged out of his jacket and tossed it over the bag. A black Navy T-shirt stretched across his obscenely well-muscled torso, just the way Sally remembered. Dog tags rested against the contour of his chest. His thick arms hung relaxed at his sides, his nonchalance chilling by itself.

"Okay, hotshot, you've got about a second to get the hell out of here if you want to avoid the beating I've got for you." Emmett started toward him at a brisk walk.

Despite the pain that had long since festered into bitterness, she couldn't stand by and let Luke get hurt. He'd been wounded, seriously. He looked strong enough, but what if he wasn't fully recovered? She glanced around for something to use as a weapon, but Jen had cleaned the yard last weekend and put all the garden tools away. Sally backed toward the house, unable to take her eyes off the disaster unfolding in her yard.

Luke's expression didn't change. He remained motionless as Emmett approached.

Her boss took a swing as soon as he was within arm's length. Luke ducked, evading the blow effortlessly, then shoved Emmett against the front of his Tahoe. He held him there in some kind of a headlock until Emmett's legs folded and he slid to the ground, apparently out cold. Luke opened the SUV's door, yanked Emmett off the ground, as though the man who'd towered over her weighed nothing, and stuffed him into the front seat before slamming the door shut.

Luke didn't look at her until he'd retrieved his jacket. As he threaded his arms into the sleeves, he turned to run his gaze over her, his expression dark and brooding.

"What are you doing here, Luke?" Sally's leftover concern gave her voice a trace of impatience.

"It's good to see you too, sunshine." He bent to retrieve his duffel before walking toward her. "Let's go in the house. He'll be out for a few minutes. I'm staying until he wakes up and takes off without causing any more trouble." A gentle hand stroked her cheek, where Emmet's blow had landed, and Luke's piercing gaze dared her to argue. He turned her toward the house and fell in beside her, pressing his hand to the small of her back. "What the hell are you doing, hanging out with a guy like that anyway?"

It wasn't like she didn't already know she'd screwed up. She didn't need a lecture from this man, who'd picked today to show up on her doorstep after he'd cast her away like so much trash. Sally's annoyance grew to irrational irritation. The nerve of him, even if he did rescue her from an uncomfortable, possibly dangerous situation. He had no right to judge her, despite his scent of freshly mown hay with a touch of cinnamon that teased her senses. She didn't have to defend her actions to him…and yet she couldn't keep from doing just that.

"Not that it's any of your business, but he seemed like a decent-enough guy until he'd had a couple of drinks. This is Huntington—not LA or New York. The dating pool here includes anyone single, employed and under fifty." Besides, who would have thought she couldn't trust her boss—a respected local businessman? *Well, he's not my boss anymore. Did one have to give notice in situations like this?*

Luke stopped and turned to face her, his brow shooting upward toward the hair that cascaded over his forehead. Rich brown eyes held her gaze, and she was powerless to turn away. Finally, a smile broke free that reminded her of the man she'd known before he'd gone through hell. "Well…it's good I'm here, then." He winked before opening the door and pushing inside, leaving her standing on the steps with her mouth open.

An instant later, the sound of Jen squealing and shouting Luke's name was followed by small feet running across the room. The wonderfully deep and warm male laughter that spilled through the doorway brought Sally images of Luke catching her daughter in his arms and twirling her around, exactly as he'd done a year ago. Jen had gotten attached to Luke too, and it'd taken her a long time to accept the fact he wasn't coming back. Now, her childish giggles, mixing with his masculine voice, meant trouble and heartache.

Damned if I'll let him hurt my daughter again.

Hands shaking slightly, she covered her face and tried to get her head back in the game. Part of her struggled to understand the toll Luke's ordeal as a POW had taken on him, and she wanted to weep for the man he'd been. Another part wanted nothing more than to hold him and let him know it didn't matter—not to her. But the sting and humiliation of his rejection when he'd refused her entry to his hospital room hadn't yet faded. Maybe she could have forgiven him if it had only affected her. Fortunately, Jen had remained in Huntington with friends, thereby spared the debacle at the hospital, but Luke's actions had hurt her too. Neither of them were up for a repeat performance.

Straightening her spine and squaring her shoulders, she took a moment to compose her expression. The coming confrontation would likely make her extremely unpopular with all parties concerned...but it couldn't be helped. The sooner Luke left, the better for all of them.

About the Author

Photo Credit: Stalnakers Photo Shop

Dixie Lee Brown lives and writes in Central Oregon, inspired by gorgeous scenery and three hundred sunny days a year. Having moved from South Dakota as a child to Washington, Montana and then to Oregon, she feels at home in the west. She resides with two dogs and a cat, who are currently all the responsibility she can handle. Dixie works fulltime as a bookkeeper. When she's not writing or working, she loves to read, enjoys movies, and if it were possible, she'd spend all of her time at the beach. She is also the author of the Trust No One romantic suspense series, published by Avon Impulse. Please visit her online at www.dixiebrown.com.

Navy SEALS are trained to take on all enemies in extreme situations—but there's nothing more dangerous than matters of the heart...

This is Matt Iverson's story.

Working for a security company with his brothers-in-arms has given former SEAL Matt "MacGyver" Iverson a reason to get up every morning. But keeping a runaway bride from harm isn't in his job description...

Former Marine Kellie Greyson is in over her head. A coldhearted ultimatum leaves her no choice but to wed mob boss Tony Palazzi. But when she overhears his deadly plans for her after she says "I do," Kellie flees his casino, only to wind up in a seedy Vegas bar. The next thing she knows, she's waking up beside a protective powerhouse of a man...

Though Kellie's body kickstarts his into high gear, MacGyver is all business trying to convince her that they need each other. Both are looking for missing people—and all roads lead to Palazzi. MacGyver will have to lay all his cards on the table to get Kellie to trust him in a game they might not survive...

Printed in the United States
by Baker & Taylor Publisher Services